l

Utopia
and
Counterutopia
in the
"Quixote"

Utopia
and
Counterutopia
in the
"Quixote"

José Antonio Maravall

Translated by Robert W. Felkel

Wayne State University Press   Detroit

Library of Congress Cataloging-in-Publication Data

Maravall, José Antonio.
   [Utopía y contrautopía en el "Quijote". English]
   Utopia and counterutopia in the "Quixote" / José Antonia Maravall ;
translated by Robert W. Felkel.
      p. cm.
   Translation of: Utopía y contrautopía en el "Quijote", which is "a
revised and considerably enlarged version of the author's El
humanismo de las armas en "Don Quijote", published in 1948"—Introd.
   Includes bibliographical references and index.
   ISBN 0-8143-2294-8 (alk. paper)
   1. Cervantes Saavedra, Miguel de, 1547–1616. Don Quixote. 2. War
and literature. 3. Utopias in literature. 4. Literature and
society—Spain. I. Maravall, José Antonio. Humanismo de las armas
en "Don Quijote". II. Title.
PQ6353.M35513 1991
863'.3—dc20   90-20768

Designer: Mary Krzewinski

Originally published as *Utopía y contrautopía en el "Quijote"* (Santiago de
Compostela, Spain: Editorial Pico Sacro, 1976).

Contents

Translator's Introduction   7

Prologue   17

1   Introduction   20
*Tradition and modernity. Utopia and counter-
utopia. A global interpretation.*

2   Critique of the Present Situation   36
*Traditional economy and monetary economy.
Government by the nobility or by the educated
classes. The double experience of the life of arms.*

3   The Reform of Man and Society   68
*Inner man. The role of love in his renewal.
Adversity and virtue. His social mission. The
forge of a new republic.*

4   The Humanism of Arms   88
*Factors in the reform of the knight. The role of
old-fashioned armor in inner renewal. The
baptismal significance of chivalric rites and Don
Quixote's name.*

5   The Transmutation of Reality   116
         Sorcery and enchantments. Will as a power to
         transform reality. The external world as pretext.

6   The Utopia of Natural Reason   131
         The myth of the Golden Age. The paradigm of
         nature. The image of agro-pastoral society and
         the role of the knight. Government by natural
         man. The negation of this system of beliefs in
         the work of Cervantes.

7   The Novel of Chivalry as
         Utopian Method   178

Notes   195

Works Cited   227

Index   243

Translator's Introduction

The Author

The death of José Antonio Maravall on December 18, 1986, has deprived Spanish historiography of one of its most respected practitioners. Although he was seventy-five years old when he died and had not been in good health for some time, he was an indefatigable scholar who clearly had taken to heart the advice of his mentor Ramón Carande. When Carande retired from the university he told his protégé: "Listen, Maravall, some day your turn to retire will come, and I'm going to give you a piece of advice that will help you stay in shape: always have a new project in the works."[1] When I arrived at Maravall's house in the summer of 1986 to discuss a few final details of the translation of his classic *Utopía y contrautopía en el "Quijote,"* I found him seated at an enormous desk that was virtually invisible underneath a mountain of scholarship and professional correspondence, hard at work on a book on the social context of picaresque literature. The fruits of this constant dedication to his intellectual vocation were present in Professor Maravall's study in a tangible way: one of the long bookshelves behind his desk was lined with a collection of fine, leather-bound volumes, which turned out to be his own works. I counted more than thirty titles. It is sobering to think of the time it would take one even to read such an opus, much less research and write it. And, of course, it is not the quantity but the quality of what Maravall has written that is most astonishing. A very partial list of the books I saw on that shelf reveals a number of works that are universally regarded as classics, some in more than one field (Maravall was the quintessential interdisciplinarian): *El concepto de España en la Edad Media*; *Carlos V y el pensamiento político del Renacimiento*; *Utopía y reformismo en la España de los Austrias; Las Comunidades de Castilla: Una primera revolución moderna; Antiguos y modernos: La idea del progreso en el desarrollo inicial de una sociedad; El mundo social de La Celestina; La cultura del barroco: Análisis de una estructura histórica* (recently published in English translation by the University of Minnesota Press); and, of course, the present study of the social context of Cervantes's masterpiece. A brief consideration of Maravall's philosophical premises will enable us to understand his approach to history and the genesis and significance of *Utopia and Counterutopia in the "Quixote."*

José Antonio Maravall held a chair in the Department of Political Science and Sociology in the Universidad Complutense of Madrid, but his academic affiliation does not sufficiently convey the scope of his research and writing. He was an exponent of what is now commonly referred to as the "history of mentalities," an approach to history which obliged him to make more than occasional (and never superficial) forays into other disciplines such as economics, social psychology, philosophy, and literature.[2] A few years ago Maravall gave a concise statement of his view of history: "History, conceived as events experienced by a society, cannot be understood by isolating components of thought or mentality from the whole. . . . And, needless to say, neither can these components of thought be fully understood if they are removed from the context of the society that produced and conditioned them."[3] Maravall's challenge to the historian is to avoid all over-simplification, neither succumbing to the temptation to reduce historical process to one and only one essential component, nor to the equally dangerous tendency to treat the vast and complex material of history as homogenous, thereby nullifying its diversity. While the analogy is not perfect, readers unfamiliar with José Antonio Maravall might get some idea of his approach by thinking of the works of Fernand Braudel and Lucien Febvre, both of whom he cites frequently and with approbation. Like them, he favored a "universal" or "global" type of historiography. Fortunately, he also shared another characteristic with Braudel and Febvre: he had the intellectual and scholarly equipment necessary to accomplish his goal. This will be apparent to even the most casual reader of *Utopia and Counterutopia in the "Quixote."*

Genesis and Significance of the Book

Utopia and Counterutopia in the "Quixote" is a revised and considerably enlarged version of the author's *El humanismo de las armas en "Don Quijote,"* published in 1948 as part of the quadricentennial celebration of Cervantes's birth. The earlier book set forth the thesis that the meaning of the *Quixote* is largely political, that the novel is a literary version of the political utopianism characteristic of Spain in the first half of the sixteenth century during the reign of Charles V. After the publication of the 1948 version, Maravall continued to study the question of the political and social significance of Cervantes's masterpiece, and he gradually came to the conclusion that he would need to revise the book, not just in order to buttress his argument with references to additional and more current scholarship, but mainly to alter the thesis in a significant way. His opportunity to do so came in 1975 when a friend founded the Editorial Pico Sacro and approached him with a request for a manuscript. Maravall was more than ready, at least intellectually, to take on the task of revising his earlier study of the *Quixote*, but personal circumstances caused him to hesitate: he had recently suffered a serious heart attack and was confined to his home by his doctor's orders, thus making it impossible for him to visit libraries. However, he had already accumulated a vast file of notes over the years and was simply waiting for them to jell. Thanks to that system of work, and thanks also to his prodigious memory, he was able to write *Utopía y contrautopía en el "Quijote,"* now an established classic in Cervantine studies,[4] without ever leaving his home. In the revised version, Maravall seized the opportunity to make an important change in the thesis of the original. While he had previously tended to identify the pseudoutopianism of the main character with the views of the author, he later came to realize that Don Quixote is not Cervantes (a point on which the great Cervantes scholar Helmut Hatzfeld always insisted).[5] Thus, in *Utopía y contrautopía en el "Quijote"* Maravall's brilliantly defended thesis is that Cervantes presents, in his hero, a utopian philosophy which he later demolishes, showing it to be an irrational position which can only lead precisely to the kinds of failures Don Quixote repeatedly experiences. The new title is a logical consequence of Maravall's changed outlook, and it expresses perfectly the thrust of the revised version of the study.

When the work was published in 1976, it was accorded a warm reception by Cervantes scholars. The prominent place given it by Bjornson in his recent MLA volume is evidence of the respect Maravall's study commands. Reviewing the book for *Hispanic Review* in 1980, James A. Parr wrote: "The farther I progressed in Maravall's erudite commentary, the more convinced I became of the essential rightness of both his thesis concerning utopian evasionism and his method of dealing with this particular literary artifact."[6] Parr then went on to say: "If the *Quijote* is first and foremost a satire, as I have suggested more than once, and if it is characteristic of satires that they not be self-referential but point rather at someone or something outside the text, then it is essential that we acquaint ourselves with the possible targets in the real world."[7] Of course, one need not accept the classification of the *Quijote* as satire *sensu stricto* in order to see the validity, even the necessity, of Maravall's historical approach to the text. In his justifiably renowned biography of Thomas Aquinas, Fr. James A. Weisheipl, O.P., warns us that unless we first comprehend the significance of Aquinas's doctrine for the thirteenth century, we will run the risk of rendering it irrelevant to our own age.[8] This is the spirit that pervades Maravall's study: unless the *Quixote* is clearly and correctly grasped in the context of the historical period that produced it, errors of anachronism—the tendency to see false analogies with the present—will hinder our appreciation of the work. Similarly, the better we understand the *Quixote* the more clearly we will grasp the nature of the transition from the sixteenth to the seventeenth century in Spain. Maravall has succeeded in his historical exegesis of Cervantes's text to a degree that few others, perhaps none, could have hoped to attain, thanks to his unparalleled expertise in sixteenth- and seventeenth-century Spanish society.

This is perhaps the place to define more precisely the words "utopia" and "pseudoutopia," which have been used somewhat loosely up to now in a way that might suggest that they are synonyms. For Maravall they are not synonyms at all, as I hope to make clear from the following brief summation of the main ideas in *Utopia and Counterutopia in the "Quixote."* It is hoped that this summary will help the reader to keep Maravall's thesis in sight at all times, for the author sets forth the position of escapist utopianism so cogently that one may be inclined to think (mistakenly) that he is attributing those views to Cervantes.

A utopia, strictly speaking, is a rational social program formulated for the purpose of producing concrete changes in the existing order. It is never exclusively visionary or theoretical. Maravall believes that such genuine utopian philosophy was present in sixteenth-century Spain, in part because of the experience of the conquest and colonization of the American continent. The discovery of America gave such thinkers as Bartolomé de las Casas the perfect opportunity to transcend mere theory and actually construct utopian societies in the New World. He calls this genuine utopia a "utopia of reconstruction." But the word "utopia" in the title of his book does not refer to a utopia of reconstruction but to a utopia of evasion which lacked the most essential element: the will to implement. This is what Maravall finds in the *Quixote:* a pseudoutopia of sheer escapism. And, it must be noted, he finds it not in Cervantes but in the hero Don Quixote, a man whom the author presents as a paradigm of the unrealistic and false utopianism characteristic of the lower nobility at that time. Thus, "counterutopia" in Maravall's title refers to Cervantes's attack, by means of the entire novelistic construct of *Don Quixote,* not against utopias properly understood—utopias, that is, of reconstruction—but against the irrational pseudoutopianism of his hero. Cervantes's insistence that he is not Don Quixote's father but rather his stepfather is due in part to the fact that he intends to disassociate himself from the knight's ideas and even to punish his errant stepson for his reactionary views. According to Maravall, the *Quixote* thus represents a kind of palinode for Cervantes, for he states on a number of occasions that the author probably felt in his earlier years some degree of attraction to this pseudoutopianism, which was frequently couched in terms of chivalric-pastoral mythology, and that under the influence of this mentality the first part of the *Galatea* had been written. Although Cervantes promised a continuation of his pastoral novel and continued to allude to it until his dying days, he never wrote the sequel, for he had come to see that the utopianism of his earlier novel was false and could lead only to evasion of reality. Instead he wrote the *Quixote*, which is thus not only a counterutopia but a counter-*Galatea* as well in which the author's earlier pseudoutopianism is incarnated in his hero Don Quixote. In reading Maravall's analysis, this distinction between author and character must be kept clear at all times.

In chapter 2 Maravall argues that Don Quixote, along with the entire lower nobility of which he is a caricature, is a reactionary who rejects the three key features of the modern state: (1) a standing army with its concomitant emphasis on new methods of warfare; (2) a monetary economy; and (3) bureaucracy, that is, administration by experts. Maravall takes care to explain that the position of Cervantes regarding the vocation of arms is situated between two extremes. On the one hand, Cervantes rejects the position of his main character, seeing it as an example of chivalric decadence, and, on the other, he is not blind to the corruption occasioned by methods of warfare in the modern state.

The next two chapters outline the means by which Don Quixote hopes effectively to combat modern decadence. "The Reform of Man and Society" shows how Renaissance humanism revived the Catholic doctrine of individual merit through faith and works, pushing the idea to limits that at times went beyond Tridentine orthodoxy. For Don Quixote (and here his author would surely agree), we are all what we make of ourselves, using our talents in accord with the divine gift of free choice. Cervantes's knight has chosen to use his talents by assuming a mission which involves the perfecting of mankind, and this mission will be achieved, as Maravall explains in chapter four, principally by means of an inner purification through the use of arms. Maravall explains in detail the economic and social forces at the end of the sixteenth century and the beginning of the seventeenth which caused this archaic mentality (which Cervantes ridicules) to take hold in Spain, forces essentially involving changes in the structure of the nobility and the extension of the profession of arms to individuals who were not nobles by birth. The important thing to Don Quixote is not that he win battles but that he defeat his inclination to evil and win a victory over himself. This is why he must not use modern weapons, for although they are unquestionably more efficacious in destroying opponents, they are highly mechanized and can therefore be manipulated by anybody, regardless of personal courage or lack thereof. They are therefore utterly useless for effecting the inner *renovatio* that Don Quixote seeks. Maravall is at his best here, for his vast knowledge of sixteenth-century political and military theory enables him to relate Don Quixote's rejection of modern methods of warfare to real controversies that were seething in the country at the time. From this chapter the reader will learn that Don Quixote was by no means an isolated eccentric in the panorama of sixteenth-century Spain: people like him were so numerous that Cervantes, according to Maravall's thesis, felt compelled to expose the irrationality of their enterprise by means of the satire of *Don Quixote*.

At this point it could be asked how Don Quixote proposed to put into action a plan for moral reform based on archaic components while at the same time living in the modern world. Since modernity, in Don Quixote's view, had eliminated all possibilities for heroism, he had no alternative but to annul existing reality and turn it into something else. The difference between Cervantes and Don Quixote is patent here: the latter is an extreme voluntaristic idealist who "creates" his own reality by projecting it onto the world, while the former is a philosophical realist who apprehends objects through his external senses and who takes his protagonist to task for not doing likewise.

The chapter "The Utopia of Natural Reason" studies the myth of the Golden Age and the ancillary myths of agro-pastoral society and natural man. These concepts were no mere literary recourse but part of a system of beliefs held by certain regressive social sectors in Cervantes's time, and they were also a common feature of the pseudoutopia of evasion under attack in *Don Quixote*. Maravall shows that there were two dimensions to utopianism, the pastoral and the chivalric, both of which Cervantes portrays ironically in his novel. In this chapter the emphasis is on the former, as Maravall documents that from the late Middle Ages on, Saint Jerome's praise of *sancta rusticitas* came to be held in high esteem and rural life was considered a locus of admirable moral and physical qualities, unlike courts and cities with their attendant vice and corruption. Much of the chapter is given over to demonstrating that this appeal to nature as a model for individual and social life ultimately has the sort of political consequences that are analogized in one of the most clearly utopian sections of the *Quixote*, Sancho's government of the island of Barataria. According to Maravall, the author turns this utopian material in the Barataria episode into a counterutopian statement, for Cervantes had come to realize that the ideal of natural government under the leadership of a "good shepherd" was absurd.

In his brief conclusion, "The Novel of Chivalry as Utopian Method," Maravall explains why the novel is an ideal literary genre with which to portray a utopia. Utopianism is concerned with the actual ebb and flow of human existence, not with rational perfection of a purely logical order (as in mathematics), and so makes use of reason as an instrument rather than as a model for human society. Utopias are products of history (Maravall of course takes the term in its broadest sense), even though they essentially criticize and attempt to restructure some aspect of existing historical and social reality. Thus the novel, being a literary mode between poetry (the ideal) and history (the real), is a perfect vehicle with which to render a utopian vision. In Cervantes's hands the book of chivalry is a means for expressing a whole range of utopian thinking. His attitude toward this material is complex: on the one hand, he shares its negative view of certain aspects of modern society (the venality engendered by modern methods of waging war is a good example), but on the other he rejects the effort to deal with these problems simply by evading reality (as in his hero's insistence on using only medieval weapons) rather than by confronting it and reforming it, which is what a genuine utopia always attempts to do.

Professor Parr called Maravall's study "a basic book, one that belongs in every Cervantine scholar's personal library."[9] Cervantes experts can, of course, read this book in Spanish; but the *Quixote*'s status as the world's first modern novel and its tremendous influence on British and American fiction have made it one of the classics most frequently read in translation. The novel is widely taught in English in American universities, either in abridged form as part of a Great Books course or unabridged in a monographic course. Sooner or later, anyone who would understand the development of the modern novel must deal with the *Quixote*. This translation of Maravall's classic historical-sociological analysis is offered to students and teachers who, though unable to read Spanish, wish to acquire a more thorough understanding of the genesis of Cervantes's masterpiece. To use an oenological metaphor, it is common knowledge that the nature of a wine is determined in part (only in part, it must be remembered) by the nature of the soil that nourished the vines. The soil out of which *Don Quixote* grew may be seen in this partial list of Spanish thinkers whose work Maravall analyzes: Sancho de Londoño, Marcos de Isaba, Martín González de Cellorigo, Pedro de Navarra, Diego Núñez Alba, Juan López de Palacios Rubios, Fray Juan de Santa María, Diego de Valera, and Alfonso de la Torre.[10] For all his respect for history, Maravall is no historicist, and he knows that the

Quixote is greater, far greater, than the soil which nourished it. Historical context cannot sufficiently explain a masterpiece, but it will always be one component, and a crucial one, of a full understanding of this or any other work of art.

About the Translation

In rendering Maravall's exuberant, Baroque style into readable American English, I have attempted to be guided by two noted theorists of translation: first, Saint Jerome, the patron saint of translators, who expressed the essence of "dynamic equivalency" sixteen centuries before the term became fashionable: "non verbum e verbo, sed sensum exprimere de sensu" ("to render meaning for meaning, not word for word");[11] second, Don Quixote himself, who says that the ideal translation will leave one doubting which is the original and which the translation (II:62). I wanted my translation first of all to represent accurately Maravall's thinking both in substance and implication. Secondly, I wanted it to sound natural and in keeping with American English, avoiding idiomatic lapses of any kind. Whether I have succeeded completely in achieving these goals only others can decide. In cases where I feel that the reader should have access to the word or phrase I am translating, I include it in brackets.

I have put references into a currently accepted American form. To make it easy for readers to check quoted passages, whenever possible I have used the English originals of works that Maravall read in translation, and I have searched out English translations of Spanish, French, and other foreign-language works cited. I have added, when possible, notes for quotations that were undocumented in the original (Maravall occasionally alludes in a rather casual way to relatively obscure works). I have corrected a few errors I found in the endnotes, some of which apparently occurred in the process of revising and enlarging *El humanismo de las armas en "Don Quijote."* I have also occasionally added publication data or page or volume numbers to notes where they were lacking. The only abbreviation in the notes with which the average American reader will be unfamiliar is BAE, which refers to the Biblioteca de Autores Españoles, a critical text collection published in Madrid from 1846 to 1880 under the direction of Manuel Rivadeneyra. When Maravall quotes from works of Cervantes other than *Don Quixote*, I use a published English translation if there is a good, fairly recent one available. In such cases I refer to the title in English (e.g., *The Dogs' Colloquy*, translated by Walter Starkie). I use Samuel Putnam's translation for quotes from the *Quixote* except in rare instances (noted in the text) where another translation dovetails better with Maravall's language.[12] All translations are mine unless otherwise noted. I hope to have improved the usefulness of the book for scholarly purposes by the addition of two features not found in the original, a list of works cited by Maravall and an index.

Maravall's study assumes on the part of the reader a degree of familiarity with certain periods of Spanish history, especially the sixteenth century. The text contains frequent allusions to Charles V, Philip II, the battle of Lepanto, the Schmalkaldic League, etc. Readers unfamiliar with such references would be advised to consult a general history of Habsburg Spain; a number of fine works have been done in English. A classic, still widely read, is *The Golden Century of Spain: 1501–1621*, by R. Trevor Davies (New York: Harper and Row, 1965), although in some ways it has been superseded by John Lynch's two-volume *Spain under the Habsburgs*, 2nd edition (New York: New York University Press, 1984). For the reign of Philip II see Geoffrey Parker's fine biography *Philip II* (Boston: Little, Brown and Company, 1978). Also recommended is J. H. Elliott's *Imperial Spain: 1469–1716* (London: Pelican, 1970).

I had asked Professor Maravall if he would be willing to write a new preface for this translation, a request he graciously and eagerly accepted. I was looking forward to hearing his latest thinking on the notion of the *Quixote* as a reflection and criticism of decadent utopianism, and I deeply regret that his death has deprived his new American and English readership of his latest insights.

I should like to express my thanks to Western Michigan University for awarding me a sabbatical leave, without which I could never have completed this project. I also owe a debt of gratitude to a number of friends whose assistance was invaluable. A very special thanks is due Diana Scholberg, whose careful reading of my manuscript has given new meaning to the word "painstaking." Her hundreds of suggestions have contributed in no small degree to the readability of the text. My colleague Jorge Febles spent countless hours helping me to clarify the meaning of a number of difficult passsages in the original. I also received considerable help from Kenneth Scholberg, who checked my translations from Catalan and cleared up more than an occasional difficulty. Finally, I am indebted to my wife Barbara for her tactful suggestions on ways I could improve my renditions of sixteenth-century Latin. I am grateful to all of them.

Prologue

When the centenary of the Emperor Charles V was celebrated some years ago, the University of Granada published a large volume of studies dedicated to him and his world. Included was an article of my own, dealing with certain manifestations of utopian thought in Charles's closest Spanish collaborators. One of the persons necessarily to be considered in that line of sociopolitical thought was, in my opinion, Antonio de Guevara. The Granada volume appeared in 1958, the year of the centenary;[1] I then continued to work on the ideological background of the reign of Charles V and published my book *Carlos V y el pensamiento político del Renacimiento* in 1960. Between 1958 and 1960 I had been reconsidering the work of Guevara as a "utopian vision of the Empire," interpreting it as an expression of "the topics of humanism as imperial program," and I came to realize that Guevara's thinking was related to and yet different from the sociopolitical constructs underlying the *Quixote*. For that reason, when I inserted my study published by the University of Granada into the book as one of its chapters (which is the way it had been conceived from the beginning), I added these lines to the end of the section on the political thought of the bishop of Mondoñedo:

> Formulated not rationally and systematically (it is really incapable of precise conceptual expression) but rather as a group of diffuse hopes and common beliefs of his day, Guevara's thought continued to influence sixteenth-century Spain. Las Casas is a typical representative of such an ideology.[2] This thinking accounts for the utopian content in *Don Quixote*, as I pointed out years ago in an effort to provide a complete interpretation of the novel's political meaning. I am now convinced that the *Quixote* is not a utopia strictly speaking but that its author makes use of the idea of a utopia throughout the narrative in order to discredit those who cling to such a concept. Thus, the *Quixote*,

a genuine anti-Guevara treatise, not only rejects, on a literary level, the Guevarist "elegances" which a López de Ubeda praised, but is in fact a powerful antidote to the extensive and intellect-stifling utopianism in sixteenth century Spain. With good reason did Vossler state that "the eccentricities caused by utopian literature in political, military and economic attitudes in Spain deserve a special study." It was precisely against those excentricities that Cervantes offered his quixotic pseudoutopia.[3]

Now I should like to be even more precise: he presented his work as a counterutopia written to contradict the falsification of the utopian ideal that Don Quixote himself represents.

I refer in the preceding paragraphs to another book I published considerably earlier, *El humanismo de las armas en "Don Quijote"*, in which I offered a political interpretation of the *Quixote* based on the totality of the novel rather than on isolated episodes.[4] In that book Bishop Guevara was cited repeatedly in relation to Cervantes's views. Although I occasionally alluded to the ironic distance Cervantes adopts relative to the social world of his literary creature, I came to believe shortly after my book appeared that it was necessary to emphasize the manner in which Cervantes constructed the *Quixote*: after presenting the reader with the general lines of a utopian vision he turned the whole thing inside out in order to show its impracticability and ineffectiveness. Commenting on my book as well as on two other studies of the *Quixote* published on the occasion of that commemoration [Maravall is referring to the quadricentennial of Cervantes's birth, in 1947], Marcel Bataillon noted that my explanation integrated the two planes of utopianism: the quixotic utopia of the old ideal of chivalry, opposed to the modern state with its disciplined armies and its firearms, and the utopia of right reason in the exercise of power, symbolized by Sancho Panza. Bataillon did add, however, that this was perhaps too simplistic a formula to summarize my work.[5] In reality, such was the substance of my study, and I should only like to emphasize that both planes were articulated to show that the object of the first enterprise was to make possible the passage to the second.

I still believe that the entire development of the first great modern novel is based on this interplay of a double utopian construction, and this is the thesis maintained in the following pages. I have even added much new information which reinforces this aspect of my interpretation. But I now also believe that in the first version of this book I tended excessively to attribute the quixotic mentality of the hero to the thought of the author himself, an occasional reference to the contrary notwithstanding. I am now convinced that one must not only distinguish between the two but even emphasize the distance between them. Thus, I claim in this new, revised edition that Cervantes wrote in order to halt the threatening spread of a type of thought that had lost the spirit of reform proper to it and had come to be nothing more than an escapist refuge toward which a whole sector of Spanish society was moving.

The first edition of this book had a prologue by the great master Ramón Menéndez Pidal. It is well known that Menéndez Pidal always defended the notion of Cervantes's fidelity to the world of the Romancero. And although my interpretation went in other directions, it was not completely incompatible with this thesis and even approached it at several points. In this edition I have eliminated Menéndez Pidal's prologue because, unfortunately, it is not possible for me to open under his aegis a book which purports to prove that Cervantes intended to reject as unreasonable that spirit of the Romancero.

Finally, I wish to mention my reasons for changing the title, for in reediting my own works my usual practice is to let the original title stand. I continue to believe that the formula "humanism of arms" correctly expresses an essential aspect of my interpretation, that which refers to the transformation of the knight. Faced with a certain amount of ridiculous misinterpretation of those words, I should like to recall the fact that my respected and most knowledgable friend Professor Bataillon, speaking of Don Quixote as a "preacher of peace" (an idea to which I subscribe totally and which is amply developed in chapter 5 of the first edition of my book), included the following lines in the Spanish translation of his *Erasmo y España:* "Such pacifism is not incompatible with what José Antonio Maravall calls *Humanismo de las armas en Don Quijote* (Madrid, 1948), a felicitous title to characterize a trend of the Spanish sixteenth century in which Cervantes participated."[6] Later, Professor Ulrich Ricken of the University of Halle, in his address to the Cervantes Colloquium of 1966, organized in East Berlin by Professor W. Krauss, considered my formula "humanism of arms" to be perfectly acceptable applied to the *Quixote*.[7] Nevertheless, I retain that expression only as the title of chapter 4, which deals with the figure of the knight. Since I believe that that is only one part of the work, although it may be an essential element of the overall plan, I have changed the title of the book to bring it closer to the comprehensive interpretation which I have tried to set forth and also to make it more appropriate for the current intellectual climate.

I should like to thank Editorial Pico Sacro for its willingness to publish this book, which, if not totally recast, has been thoroughly reworked, revised, and amplified in order to make it more current and to better support my thesis.

Introduction

Tradition and modernity. Utopia and counterutopia. A global inter-
pretation.

In the heroic poem which sings of the origins of Castille, when the
count Fernán González and his band of warriors come to the Ebro river,
the noble river is called, with powerful, primitive feeling, "a very strong
and very angry water."[1] When centuries later a soul no less inflamed
(albeit anachronistically) by medieval heroism approaches the same body
of water, the impression he receives is quite different, and different also
is the strong emotional response it arouses in him: "Don Quixote and
Sancho reached the River Ebro, the sight of which afforded the knight
great pleasure as he beheld the charms of its banks and gazed upon its
clear and abundant, gently flowing waters, which had the appearance of
liquid crystal. It was a sight that brought back a thousand fond memo-
ries" (II:29).[2] The Castillian count of the poem and the character of
Cervantes's novel are literary creations, despite any reference they may
have to specific individuals. Both of them represent aspects of the
centuries-old enterprise which we call Spain, and they are nourished by
the reality of its history, to which they themselves have contributed.
(This is not intended to raise questions of Hispanic "authenticity," an
undertaking I have always eschewed.) The heroic resonance of the two
characters cannot be more intense, but in the case of Don Quixote his
inner world has been enriched by the remarkable experience of a spiritual movement unknown to his medieval predecessor, namely, sixteenth-
century humanism.

A new vision of the natural world had taken root in the sixteenth
century. Diego de Salazar, who wrote on the art of warfare and was
translator and commentator of Machiavelli, admired the gardens and

20

groves which the Duke of Nájera had planted in his estate.[3] The doctor
Miguel Sabuco praised the therapeutic effects of a pleasant view of the
countryside.[4] A public administrator, Luis Ortiz, suggested that public
roads be improved by planting different kinds of trees, for they would
be a profitable business, give shade to travellers in the summer, and provide a delightful view for passersby.[5] Cervantes was capable of feeling a
sense of renewal and peace in the presence of a landscape: "For this purpose alleys of trees are planted, fountains are sought out, slopes are lev-
eled, and gardens are diligently cultivated."[6] As was the case with
Cervantes himself and with his most cultured contemporaries, the appreciation of nature, the enjoyment of beauty, and the power of love penetrate the soul of his hero and intensify the hero's combative spirit. The
medieval knight was only concerned with leaving behind some testimony of his "good deeds and knightly qualities." But no matter how
intense the passion for war may be in a hero of the humanist period, he
will want his future historian to include in the narration of his courageous life not only the accomplishments of his doughty arm in the affairs of war but also his thoughts and, what is really characteristic, his
tears and sighs. This passage which we invoke in the *Quixote* proceeds
directly from the pastoral genre and is another indication of the connection between the latter and the world of knight-errantry, a connection
upon which we shall later insist, basing on it our interpretation of one
of the two dimensions of Cervantes's work.[7]

Necessarily much more complicated is any possible interpretation of
that hero through whose veins the blood of humanism flows and in
whose spirit, for that very reason, the martial endeavor, platonic love,
the beauty of the countryside, the dignity of letters, and the inner life all
have resonance. The enrichment provided by that new life, whose waters
modern man first tasted at the fountain of Petrarch, makes our comprehension of the extravagant feat of the knight Don Quixote difficult and,
at the same time, more interesting.

Not infrequently an author begins his book with a particular meaning in mind and finds that as he progresses the book begins to acquire
its own sense which winds up imposing itself on the one he had planned
at the outset. The greater the importance a literary work acquires
throughout history, the more noticeable this phenomenon is. The purpose which moved the creators of those masterpieces to take pen in hand
normally remains very inferior to what they have finally achieved. Generally the intention differs from the result. For that reason, psychological
interpretation, which is closely linked to what the author claims to have
accomplished, is insufficient and usually cannot explain what it is that
generation after generation has seen and admired in the work. Therefore
there is no alternative but to call on historical interpretation to reveal to

us in its inspired pages the resonance of the human drama experienced by every period and every people. As a rule, the very protagonists themselves do not have (nor are they capable of having) clear and full consciousness of their own drama. Those who come afterwards are able to witness the acts or episodes of such a passionate performance and follow its complete plot line. They are the ones, therefore, in a position to assign to the various parts their value and meaning; that is, they are able to construe or interpret the historical whole in which those fragments have their logical place. Nor can what an author says he intended to do in his work serve as anything more than one among many factors to keep in mind, and the same must also be said of what his contemporaries claim to see in it. Neither testimony can be valid as a sufficient and decisive criterion for understanding what the author has done, because all of our activities, and not least of all literary creation, are realized by means of a continual unfolding of connections with what has happened before, with what will occur afterwards, and, between these two poles of past and future, with what the author's own epoch does with reference to the circumstances of the world as it perceives it. We must insist, however, that this is an activity which does not reveal its full meaning to those who perform it, and its comprehension will belong to those who live in each subsequent period.

The successive interpretations of the *Quixote* have been studied by Bonilla, Real de la Riva, and various others. They range from that of Tirso de Molina, who limits himself to seeing the novel as the one that accomplished the expulsion of chivalric adventures,[8] to that of Jerónimo de Alcalá Yáñez y Ribera, who apparently considers it merely a work of humor,[9] to that of Francisco Santos, who takes it as an example of slothful, untimely knight errantry, contrary to a life of work in the modern sense of the word (which he supports),[10] to Salas Barbadillo who, as we shall see, suggests an interpretation largely in agreement with our own, according to which Don Quixote appears as a restorer of a natural society based on rural life.[11]

As is well known, Cervantes himself on different occasions has identified two purposes as the motivating forces behind his *Quixote*. In the *Viaje del Parnaso* he states: "In Don Quixote I have supplied / entertainment for the sad and melancholy."[12]

Also famous is the passage in which he claims to have written solely to ridicule and destroy once and for all the taste, absolutely pernicious in his time, for novels of knight-errantry. The things which amuse and entertain us have evolved and changed to such an extent, however, that those of Cervantes's time cannot be adduced to explain the lively and widespread interest which the *Quixote* has continued to elicit. To understand this, it should suffice to recall how the humor of Spanish sixteenth- and seventeenth-century comic theater, for example, is largely lost on modern audiences. Also, the novels of knight-errantry could not really have been a problem at the beginning of the seventeenth century, for the new outlook would be more than enough to exclude them from the literary scene altogether. It is quite impossible to attribute such a significant development to the effect of one single book, no matter how much Cervantes may claim that that was his purpose in writing.[13] Toward the end of the sixteenth century these works had for the most part disappeared in Spain, and only a few titles were published in the seventeenth. At about this same time, or perhaps just a few years later, they also disappeared in Portugal. Historians of literature have amply documented this statement and have explained why this literature no longer satisfied the tastes of the new period. Don Pascual Gayangos noted the "remarkable rapidity" with which knightly literature died out at this time. Evidence of this decline is the almost total absence of editions of these works in the years immediately prior to the publication of *Don Quixote*.[14] In any case, even were it true that "the annihilation of the novels of knight-errantry with a single blow was reserved for the immortal Cervantes," as Gayangos affirmed[15] (contradicting to some degree his own data), there is no doubt that so definitive an achievement must have been due not just to the merits of the book but also to the receptivity of his own period to the ideas it expressed. Indeed, the reiterated protests and condemnations of chivalric literature are, for the most part, prior to the *Quixote,* with the exception of an occasional isolated instance which seems a mere echo of what had been said repeatedly long before.

This is not just a question for literary history; it bears necessarily on every attempt to interpret the *Quixote,* for it relates to the question of what its first readers saw in the novel. What if the profound impact of the *Quixote* and the ready comprehension of its complex world by seventeenth-century Spaniards were due precisely to its relationship with books of chivalry and not to those aspects in which it satirizes them? It is certainly true that for the Spanish mentality of the late sixteenth century, as the immediate precursor of the Baroque spirit and the equally direct heir of Renaissance culture (from which it received its deep attachment to the concrete, real, imperfect, and fluctuating individuality of things and persons), the banal literary idealism of the books of chivalry was unacceptable. This is what was to be rejected from then on through an abandonment of its false and conventional formulism. But the traditional heroic spirit (that is, the type found in seignorial society, for types of heroism change with history) had not died without leaving a trace. This very spirit may have stimulated, albeit anachronistically, some readers' enthusiasm for chivalrous adventures. Alborg cites examples of this type,[16] but the very sources which include them do so with unmistakable irony, mockingly highlighting their character as rare echoes and exceptions to the rule which were destined to die out within a few decades; it is even possible that in certain social strata they had already disappeared.

It was believed by some that the course of the society of that period would abandon the path of heroism, formerly esteemed as lasting and brilliant. (Heroism is the word we use in this book to identify the morals of traditional society.) Among people of this mind such a perception produced a bittersweet melancholy which accompanied their acceptance of the unavoidable failure of the heroic ideal. The *Quixote* was born out of this feeling: breaking with the archaic style of books of chivalry and even anticipating the literary form of the modern novel, it portrays the bitter and serene lamentation of an obsolescent social sector over a new epoch which denies the hero his place in it. It does this in order to relegate this lamentation to the past, although admittedly not without a certain emotion tinged with irony. Menéndez Pidal felt that in order to understand the *Quixote* one must consider Cervantes's proximity to the heroic spirit of the old Romancero.[17] My only comment is that it seems necessary to ask whether the *Quixote* arises out of that proximity or out of the author's perception of that proximity as anachronistic. It is the latter which Cervantes accepts, thus distancing himself from his character. Witness the fact that in spite of all the passages from the old *romances* which Cervantes recalls, none of the protagonists of his novels, plays, and (obviously) *entremeses* responds positively to the figures and ideals of the Romancero, even though at that time Juan de la Cueva and Lope de Vega in his early period had frequently used types and themes from the Spanish ballad tradition.[18] [The closest English equivalent to *romance* is ballad. An *entremés* is a short theatrical interlude presented between the acts of a full-length play.]

In 1529 Fray Antonio de Guevara, like other typical moralists of the time, railed against "the days and nights which many people waste on reading useless books: Amadís, Primaleón, Duarte, Lucenda, Calixto."[19] In popular favor we see a mixture of typical books of chivalry and others of a very different nature: Garci Rodríguez de Montalvo along with Diego de San Pedro, and both of them with Fernando de Rojas. And, were we to pause a moment here, this would oblige us to explain the following difficulty: for what reason did a period which read *La Celestina* or even the novels of Diego de San Pedro also read such astonishing fantasies? And, along these same lines, what meaning can *Don Quixote* have, coming some years later? Gayangos insightfully connected Charles V's arrival in Spain with the boom in novels of chivalry there. Chronologically that is clear; naturally, the phenomenon could have occurred in any case, for it was closely tied to the social mentality of the period, as was the circumstance of the Caroline imperial phase. What the numerous readers of that type of book accomplished in those years during the military campaigns of the Emperor Charles is well known. In other nonmilitary spheres of human activity those readers accomplished the work of Saint Teresa or that of the other equally enthusiastic consumer of such books, Juan de Valdés. But at the end of the sixteenth century another reader of fantastic novels of chivalry, after being at Lepanto, after suffering years of captivity, wrote the *Quixote*.[20]

What change took place between 1529, the year of the reign of Charles V in which Guevara testified to the popularity of novels of chivalry, even though he considered it useless reading, and 1605, when the first part of the *Quixote* was published, when Felipe III had been presiding for seven years over the still extensive Spanish dominions, once more reunited, which he had inherited?[21]

Between these two dates imperial dignity and the Spanish monarchy had once again been separated. With this separation, naturally, we see the disappearance of the ideal of making Spain the cornerstone of an empire under which it could hope to complete the internal reform of Christendom from top to bottom, an ideal arising in the late Middle Ages and fully supported by the collaborators of Charles V. The traditional institution of the Empire, which had a religious and moral mission dating from its distant Carolingian origins, wished to be used by the Spanish people, along with the Church, under the government of the titular head of the Holy Empire in the work of perfection and purification of Christian life. The union with the Empire and with it the hopes for a Spanish leadership role in the highest temporal jurisdiction of Christianity came to an end quickly. But this does not mean that in all groups the deepest beliefs which supported that extraordinary aspiration, a goal clearly in conflict with the situation at the time, were uprooted totally. Perhaps in the different social ambience of *La Galatea,* had he been writing such adventures at that time, Cervantes could have made use of his protagonist Don Quixote to fight heroically—with the heroism of the quill, of course—for the preservation or the restoration of the Carolingian ideal. But for the same reason that he was never to write the second part of *La Galatea* (although he would not rule it out completely), Cervantes, having barely begun the *Quixote,* turned it around in the most ingeniously imperceptible way, in order to arrive at the irony of presenting us with the defeat of that ideal along with the defeat of his protagonist.

Cervantes was aware of the crisis beginning to overtake Spanish society. After all, did he himself not suffer from its effects? Sufficient evidence of his attitude is the *Epístola a Mateo Vázquez,*[22] as well as

numerous references to jail and the captivity suffered by so many victims—a fact he denounces repeatedly in his writings—and to the threats
which hung over the country. He knew well the painful situation of contemporary Spanish society: the critical remarks in his *Novelas ejemplares*,
in some of his plays, and in several of his *entremeses* leave no doubt in
this regard. Cervantes included and systematized this social malaise in the
Quixote but he concluded each episode in a way that forces us to realize
the failure awaiting all the utopians who had suddenly sprung forth in
the Hispanic world of the sixteenth century and who, whether in the
Indies or in Spain, dreamed to an irrational degree of the myth of the
Golden Age. In my own opinion, Cervantes's alleged acceptance of
Spanish society of his time, or, better put, of the social regimen of the
so-called Catholic monarchy, has been frequently distorted. I believe that
he simply sought a solution based on prudent accommodation in order
to be able to continue along the paths of reform. In this solution Cervantes calls attention to the painful results of utopian dreams while
aligning himself with the goals of his friends, whom we could call reasonable reformers.

A grasp of the fundamental beliefs which underlay much of the society in which the *Quixote* was written will reveal a clear connection
between hopes and disappointments, beliefs and doubts, likes and dis-
likes, all existing in a state of profound tension among the generations
just previous to the book. Together with many Spaniards, Cervantes sen-
sibly realized that in the midst of the crisis it was absurd to raise the
utopian image of a "traditional" society in the face of the inescapable
modern world which was imposing itself on all sides; he understood
that the inability to comprehend this world was leading the country and
its controlling groups headlong into a series of disasters each more irreparable than the last. Equally unsatisfactory are the incompetent and
oppressive official State and the utopia of chivalric traditionalism which,
as an answer to the former, only generated confusion; a studied and prudent adaptation to the modern world would be a third alternative, and
there are data in Cervantes's works suggesting that this was his approach. This is the spiritual perspective from which the *Quixote* was
written, and if we see the novel as an exposition of the contrast between
humanistic utopianism and an acceptance of the modern world, while
always searching for ways in which this world might be improved, then
it will acquire a transparent and total meaning.

Thus the attitude of Cervantes toward his Don Quixote becomes
clear: he is moved by a melancholy sympathy with the hyperreformist
ideal connected with the great spiritual movements of preceding generations, as well as by a recognition of the impossibility of realizing this
ideal. Among those movements Spanish Erasmism had extraordinary

power, as is well known. Today there is a need for a reevaluation of the significance attributed to Erasmism, both in its Spanish version and in its original source in Erasmus himself. In general, this reconsideration— which has to some degree already occurred—derives from a fuller and more refined understanding of the whole process of the Renaissance, which cannot be satisfactorily understood as a break with the tradition of the Middle Ages. To consider every survival in the Renaissance of earlier beliefs and attitudes as hypocrisy is untenable. Still working from such a premise, Castro tried to reconstruct Cervantes's lines of thought. Cervantes and Erasmus were interpreted exclusively in light of the picture of the Renaissance drawn by Burkhardt, and everything which did not fit this model and was a vestige of earlier ideals was portrayed as a hypocritical concession.[23] After the work of Cassirer, Gilson, Olschi, H. Baron, Gilmore, and many others, all culminating in the brilliant synthesis of Delumeau, the relationship between the Middle Ages and the Renaissance is tighter and more complex. And from this new perspective we must reformulate the question of Cervantes's thought and what we can and must continue to call his reformism.[24] For example, note how the concepts of *nature* and *experience* in Cervantes are viewed as an anticipation of the world of ideas on which the physics of Galileo will rest, as though this implied a break with the medieval and scholastic world. The truth is that those concepts, not only in Cervantes but in all the literature of the period (including that of thinkers considered founders of a new scientific method), possess a meaning that was more traditional than progressive and new: nature is the order in which things established by God the creator have their cause; experience is the record of isolated facts unconnected with causal principles, the opposite of science. Words also have their history and do not mean the same thing in every period,[25] but in the Renaissance they were still closer to the Middle Ages than to the post-Newtonian age.

Beliefs and ideals closely linked to the spiritual currents of the previous centuries and belonging to the medieval legacy were operative for Cervantes. One encounters tendencies that must be understood in terms of innovative aspirations which sprang from diverse heretical or orthodox sources in the fifteenth century. The influence of these tendencies on Cervantes as well as on the humanism preceding him (Erasmus included) cannot be understood unless one realizes that these apparent innovations came from the reservoir of tradition, whatever transformations they may have undergone. In this line of thought we encounter the reform of man, society, and the Republic, a desire which motivated so many people in the passage from one age to the next; out of this hope, now abandoned but not forgotten, the figure of Don Quixote arose. Bataillon considers that in Cervantes the pastoral idea, classicism, criticism of chivalry, or even his occasionally virulent anticlericalism[26] are Erasmist elements. But these tendencies can only be ascribed to Erasmus to the extent that he represents a compendium of the European cultural tradition of the low Middle Ages, a tradition tinged with reformist tendencies that had taken hold even in the circles closest and most obedient to Rome and which an ever increasing group of writers had tried to connect with the idea of the Empire. When this latter political idea spread throughout Spain due to the presence of the Emperor Charles, it carried with it a strong spiritualist and reformist influence already present in Spain at the time of its entry. The relation of this political concept with circumstances and aspirations surrounding it (recall its strong influence on so many Spanish clergy and laity in the Indies) is the reason why the staunchest supporters of the imperial ideal in sixteenth-century Spain chose the path of Erasmism, although we should not overlook the presence of other forms of spirituality as well. Out of this whole spiritual ensemble came the intellectual situation characterizing the end of the sixteenth century; it was from this perspective that Cervantes raised the human and social problem which is at the heart of the *Quixote*.

Many contemporaries of Cervantes and many who lived later certainly did not see him as anything other than what we would call today a complete man of letters; what they praised were his "imagination and unusual inventiveness" [*el ingenio y la rara invención*], words which in the language of that period designate, as Bonilla has shown, strictly literary values.[27] But it is equally true that in the *Quixote*, a faithful image of life to which "nothing that is human is foreign," it is possible to track down ideas and information about a wide range of subjects. Its pages enable us to speak of Cervantes in relation to medicine, philosophy, law, economics, theology, geography, nautical science, and other fields. In attempting to study the *Quixote* in relation to the principal political problems of the society in which it appeared, it is not our intention to add one more erudite diversion to the list just enunciated (nor to deny these areas of study their importance). The task of interpreting the *Quixote* from a sociopolitical point of view entails much broader and more decisive consequences for the complete comprehension of the work. Obviously one cannot justify an inquiry into the political ideas of any author merely because one's professional and personal inclinations lead to the study of social history and political thought. Anyone who does historical research must confront, first of all, the issue of significance. An author who is important in art or literature, for example, may lack any interest (although this is probably somewhat rare) in the area of political thought. Clearly, in such a case there can be no justification for subjecting the polished beauty of a literary work to the torture of extracting some minuscule political idea without value or consequence.

On more than one occasion the clear political significance of specific episodes of the *Quixote* has been pointed out. Paul Hazard, a writer gifted with fine historical intuition, saw perfectly that "the tremendous buffoonery of the island of Barataria enables Cervantes to have his readers hear, between two outbursts of laughter, the strong, healthy voice of reason attempting to discern the laws of good government."[28] This episode, however, is for us but one single piece which is articulated within a historical-social interpretation of the *Quixote* in its totality.

After many had attempted a strictly literary interpretation, Hatzfeld pointed out that it was absolutely necessary to take into consideration the social side of the personality and behavior of Cervantes's knight, who rides, after all, in the service of society. "It is no mere accident," he states, "that the extreme idealism of Don Quixote, in a disillusioned epoch, seeks to attain those old ideals of a social mission which the Church had entrusted to knighthood, when his motives become twisted and he engages in pagan battle rather than in Christian action in the world." With these words Hatzfeld makes his own, as he admits, the thesis of Menéndez Pelayo according to which the basic content of the *Quixote* is none other than "the high ideal which places the armed warrior at the service of justice and the moral order."[29] These opinions are interesting insofar as they have helped us to see in Cervantes's novel much more than a literary creation; however, they also involve two rather ingenuous suppositions: first, to accept that in fact there ever was a time when knighthood acted on behalf of justice for all men (in spite of its more or less debatable subordination to the Church, it is obvious that the chivalric moral code, and perhaps that of the Church as well, was based on standards very different from those of the Gospel); second, to believe that the creation which Don Quixote represents in Cervantes's social plan ends with the figure of the knight, who thus really becomes separated from his society. I believe that it is necessary to approach the interpretation of the *Quixote* not strictly from the point of view of the knight alone, but of the knight and the world surrounding him. The knight sallies forth into the countryside so that that very world may exist, and without keeping that world in mind it is quite impossible to understand the knight.

What we have just said forces us to do everything possible to keep our view of Cervantes in concrete historical perspective. Consequently, we may ask: Beyond the general connection which every work has with its time, whence comes the potential interest of the *Quixote* as a total construct for Spanish intellectual history in those critical decades in which it was written and published? There are specific aspects which reinforce that interest.

We have called attention to two decisive elements in the mental world of Cervantes. On the one hand, Cervantes, like every thinker up to the seventeenth century, rests on the still-firm ground of medieval tradition.[30] From this tradition come the obvious chivalric elements in the *Quixote,* although much more altered than one might think at first glance. Certainly the problem of the conception of its protagonist as knight is strongly conditioned by the crisis of chivalry and by its drift away from its authentic center during the fifteenth century throughout western Europe. Of course this same crisis, about which we shall speak in greater detail in the last chapter, is also part of the medieval heritage. Both Cervantes, a Spaniard and a European living in the waning phase of the Renaissance, and his creature Don Quixote, born to give witness to one of the greatest dangers to reason threatening Spanish society, were immersed in a world in which medieval vestiges survived, just as were Leonardo, Erasmus, Rabelais, Tasso, and Shakespeare, or, in the world of fiction, Pantagruel and Doctor Faustus.

On the other hand, Cervantes and his character are impregnated with views, ideas, and aspirations which they have received from the spiritual movements of the sixteenth century and which in turn proceed from the crisis of the late Middle Ages and thus herald the arrival of modernity. The preoccupation with his own self-molding (a manifestation of Erasmism or a similar philosophy), a concern which Cervantes transmits to his creature, responds to that zeal to remake man and society which the mentality of the sixteenth century (and its antecedents in the fifteenth) brought forth and grafted onto everything it inherited.

The sixteenth century carried with it a very substantial cargo of utopianism. We have already spoken on other occasions of the manifestations of this phenomenon and of the reasons for it. I should simply like to recall that when I published *El humanismo de las armas en "Don Quijote"* in 1948 as an effort to comprehend the novel by seeing in it the utopian construction which was the culmination of that aspect of sixteenth-century ideology, I also called attention to other currents of utopian thought, currents which I have continued to investigate. Without doubt, in Spain as in all Europe, the century of the full Renaissance presents cases of prophecy, millennialism, and eschatological aspirations; but principally it contains a repertory of utopian programs to be realized within a given set of historical circumstances. (Unlike other types of social thought, the utopia contains a program which claims to be drawn up rationally and seeks to inspire positive reforms through human effort.) I believe that Spanish society was in an especially apt position for utopian aspirations to acquire unprecedented force. This had certainly been in the process of developing ever since the fifteenth century, when the changes in Castillian society gave it the dynamism that carried it into the following century; it seems certain, though, that it was above all the discovery and colonization of the American continent which opened the doors of Utopia among certain groups in Castillian society. To my knowledge, in the second quarter of the sixteenth century there were no other groups in Europe which found themselves so strongly impelled toward such undertakings. (Perhaps this is the reason that they attempted to create them in reality, from Mexico to Paraguay, rather than write them on paper—although there is no lack of noteworthy examples of utopian literature.)

But Charles V, forcing Castillians to employ all their energy as a secondary instrument in a policy foreign to their interests, imposed a change of direction in government which paralyzed the country and quickly provoked signs of economic and social crisis, thus extinguishing those expansive and reformist sentiments which had inspired Renaissance Castille. Let us keep in mind the absurd growth of unproductive public expenditure, the disproportionate increase of credit, the torrential but economically useless arrival of precious metals, the obstacles to investment dictated by the administration's fiscal policy, the consequences of an abnormal horizontal mobility creating the first demographic problems, and various other similar causes which we could add to this list. In addition, we must not forget the repercussions which such occurrences had on the outlook of a large part of the population; anomalous and largely out of step with the epoch, these sectors had already been criticized by the accountant Luis Ortiz in 1558. Criticisms of this nature were expressed with particular urgency among writers on economics who were Cervantes's contemporaries. Remember that individuals such as González de Cellorigo, Pedro de Valencia, Sancho de Moncada, Pérez del Barrio, Pérez Herrera, and many others agreed with Cervantes. They had already pointed out abuses and errors that perverted and degraded the reformist impulse, potentially utopian in its implications, which had come about with such vigor in the Peninsula.

Thirty years before the appearance of the first part of the *Quixote*, some manifestations of the crisis were clearly visible in the country. Even more serious, the values of the controlling forces in Spain were in fact imposed on the society by all means possible, from the repressive techniques of the Inquisition to what we might call the "infiltration" of a Counter Reformation mentality; they truncated or disfigured reformist tendencies and instead allowed escapist dreams to be cultivated. These dreams preserved many elements which came from utopian theories, but the key utopian element they lacked was the will to efficient praxis. They took an escapist attitude with regard to the pressure of reality, leaving the field open to be dominated by the power of an absolutist monarchy which imposed itself oblivious to popular interests. In few places as in Castillian society at the end of the sixteenth century does one see the passage from so-called utopias of reconstruction to utopias of evasion, in the terminology of L. Mumford.[31] What the former possessed in terms of strength of will to transform and construct a new society (think of Alfonso de Valdés, Luis Vives, Las Casas, Zumárraga, Vasco de Quiroga) deteriorated in the face of adverse circumstances which sapped this willpower and forced it to seek escape in dreams of evasion, albeit dreams formed out of utopian elements. This unreal course upon which certain social groups embarked is the one which Cervantes (and others such as González de Cellorigo and Sancho de Moncada) tried to arrest.

Unlike nonconformist, rebellious movements of earlier periods whose echoes can still be heard today (millenialism, Messianism, prophecy), Renaissance utopia, a modern phenomenon, makes its appearance as a historic phase connected to the specific characteristics of the modern mentality. Thus, A. L. Morton, leaving aside antique and classical antecedents, finds the first manifestation of utopian thought in the fifteenth century with the poem "The Land of Cocaigne" (a well-known theme in France and Spain as well as in England).[32] And Mannheim, for his part, sees the movement beginning with Münzer, which strikes us as an indefensible confusion between millenialism and utopia; nonetheless, it is clear that he does associate the phenomenon with the beginning of modernity.[33] That there was in Spain a mentality strongly linked to the characteristics of modernity is quite obvious; hence the construction of America—O'Gordmann has called it the "creation"—and the efforts by some of the leaders we have mentioned to bring utopia into reality. But the force and urgency with which the new political and economic developments pressured the country (hindering their gradual and productive assimilation), together with the adverse circumstances we have pointed out, gave rise to the formation of a stagnant social sector—it would be incorrect to call it marginal—which received echoes of utopian thought, although decisively garbled. In this sector one can observe aspects of the utopian attitude (such was the weight and force of those reformist statements) but not their successful utilization in a sustained and effective utopian program. And thus, toward the end of the sixteenth century we see the phenomenon of the utopia of evasion, which at bottom is merely a pseudoutopia.

Cervantes, because of his familiarity with these very social groups, was led to renounce some of the hopes and aspirations of his youth, hopes which he perhaps later recalled with a certain sadness. He saw men, whose attitudes González de Cellorigo denounced, apparently resigned to take consolation outside the natural order, sadly seeking their refuge outside the walls of reality. Around the middle of the eighteenth century when José del Campillo was composing his curious "debits and credits of Spain," arranged in alphabetical order, he would write for the letter R: "on the debit side, reality."[34] In other words, for a century and a half, Spaniards, or at least certain groups of Spaniards (those who perhaps would have had a more active role to play in a sanely structured society), had been reduced to seeking compensation by living in the sphere of unreality.[35] In his own time Cervantes noticed this tendency to replace utopia, which seeks real and effective social reform, with sterile evasionism. And although he once appeared attracted to this line of thought and under its influence had written the first part of *La Galatea*, in the face of contemporary escapism he abandoned the sequel, even though he always kept it in mind and remembered it until his dying days. In its place, however, he wrote the *Quixote*, which makes clear that when the model of humanist, chivalric-pastoral utopia has lost its force and efficacy, it can simply become an unrealistic evasion of reality and lead to a fundamental failure of the lives of those who follow that route. Thus, the utopia of primitive agrarian life, so popular in the Spanish and European sixteenth century, was inverted and turned into the image of a counterutopia.[36]

Some Spaniards seemed to find shelter in the image of the society Don Quixote sought to restore. In the face of the upsets, difficulties, and crises they encountered in modern society—under the regimen of the State, of money, of bureaucratic administration, of large, organized armies—they tried to take refuge in a society that was as utopian as it was atemporal but which, if implemented, would be purely and simply unreal: a traditional, rural agrarian society without social or economic mobility, one accepting a low level of productivity in the belief that this is preferable to abandoning "natural" or primitive means (for it was widely suspected that "artificial" means—especially money—were the cause of social evils). This is also found in the genuine utopias of the Renaissance—More's *Utopia*, Campanella's *City of the Sun*—but in conjunction with modern factors from which their novelty and efficacy derive.

The society of the villager and that of the knight (it must not be forgotten that knighthood was an institution of the rural world) together made up a formula which came from earlier times and which constituted the final blueprint of the chivalresque world, from Ramón Lull to Cervantes. Thanks to the influence of their classical readings, humanists saw in it the ideal version of the natural order and made use of its utopian possibilities. We find this scheme outlined from the fifteenth century and into the sixteenth, whether with vague intuitions such as those offered by Díez de Games's *El Victorial* or better developed and utilized to support other aspects of their work, as in Alfonso de Valdés or Antonio de Guevara. Cervantes picked up the theme when it was suffering its final deterioration and had been reduced to a mere formula of evasion. From that position he constructed the original lines of a utopia only to show later, with the harshness of his conviction of its failure and with all the resources of comedy and sadness—so highly valued in Renaissance literature—the degree to which people, in seeking such a utopia, abandon all recourse to reason in their behavior and wind up completely outside real, historical space and time.

Is this more than, less than, or perhaps something very different from what many still suppose the *Quixote* to be, a novel of humor and melancholy, laced to greater or lesser degree with moral observations in accordance with the emerging baroque taste? Let us bear in mind that a mere fifty years ago many thought that there was nothing in Rabelais other than satire and parody, and there are those today who still hold that opinion. Nevertheless, by 1880 H. Ligier had written an entire volume on *La politique de Rabelais* that clearly revealed Rabelais's reformist zeal which, impelled by his good sense and love of humanity, led him to a clearly utopian level in the episode of the Abbey of Thélème;[37] later, G. Adler studied him in connection with the theme of the ideal state, placing him between More and Campanella during the Renaissance,[38] while E. de Pompery connected the Rabelaisian Thelemites with the harmonists of Fourier,[39] research which has continued.[40] Work has also been done on the author whose *Aminta* contributed so much to the diffusion of the pastoral myth, Torcuato Tasso, a writer much admired by Cervantes and more given to Counter-Reformation orthodoxy than the author of the *Novelas ejemplares.* This research has highlighted his assertion of freedom as opposed to civilization and of nature as opposed to conventional society; his severe condemnation of the power of wealth; and, finally, the presence of a utopian element fully describable as such in Tasso.[41] I sincerely believe that in the Cervantes of the *Quixote,* rather than in the author of the novellas, plays, and *entremeses,* the problem of the utopian mentality is set forth more clearly than in the other authors we have cited. And if it can be said that in the seventeenth century there is no social novel in the nineteenth-century sense of the word, as J. Casalduero argues,[42] it is no less certain that the seventeenth-century novel is frequently pregnant with social purpose like its sixteenth-century predecessor and can only be fully understood if we determine with precision—as in the case of the *Quixote*—the author's desire to produce a strong critical or reformative impact on the society out of which his work emerges.

Having said this much, I must confess that the *Quixote* is studied here not primarily to understand its place in the sphere of literary history and even less to understand its place in the relatively atemporal field of literary criticism. Rather, the intention is to achieve, through one of the aspects of this work, an approach to the age that made it possible. I do not know whether or not in some other period the *Quixote* could have been written, but without the relation of the work to its particular epoch it would have been something entirely different. From this it follows that in order to understand the *Quixote*, at least in certain of its aspects, we must see it in connection with its period and that our comprehension of it increases in direct proportion to our knowledge of that period.

In order to understand Cervantes's vision of the epoch we shall attempt to grasp the figure of the knight and his surroundings by focusing on that side of him which is oriented toward his society. Of course Cervantes wished to make a point, and I believe, in agreement with Cadalso, who clearly intuited this in one of his *Cartas marruecas* (LXI),[43] that he tried to say something much more profound and serious than many have supposed, but he had to say it in Spain and during the first years of the seventeenth century. This necessarily created a connection between the *Quixote* and the society that saw its publication and quickly elevated its protagonist to the status of myth. Methods of analysis which to one degree or another depart from the one here proposed are certainly possible. However, it is also possible to leave other problems aside and disregard questions of sources, style, structure, etc., and focus on those elements in which the work shows itself to be a social document of the transition from the sixteenth to the seventeenth century. It is our purpose better to understand Spanish society at that historical turning point between two centuries, and we are certain that a study of the *Quixote* from this perspective is a valid means to such an end.[44] Equally and simultaneously, we wish to improve our understanding, or, more precisely, broaden our vision, of the *Quixote*, and in order to do this we must grasp the historical situation of the society which was its contemporary.

It would of course be impossible to take into consideration all the variables operative at the time. Consequently we shall make use of those of a socio-ideological nature relating to the concept of itself that Cervantes's society held, a concept revealed in a series of facts concurrent with the *Quixote*. Obviously some scholars, using a different focus, directing their attention to other areas, and using other research techniques have come (as will others) to different conclusions from ours, though it is to be hoped that these various insights into Spain's most illustrious literary creation of the last four centuries will not be incompatible. Our vision takes in the totality of the *Quixote*, but focused from a particular angle. Needless to say, it cannot claim to be exhaustive.

2

Critique of the Present Situation

Traditional economy and monetary economy. Government by the nobility or by the educated classes. The double experience of the life of arms.

Cervantes lived and wrote when Europe was rapidly organizing itself in accord with the modern political forms that the new, Renaissance individual had brought to Spain. With the Catholic Sovereigns, innovation in Spanish national politics had evolved beyond the level of most other European countries, and the effectiveness of that method of understanding and exercising power had undoubtedly been a decisive factor in the success of their foreign and domestic undertakings. The arrival of Charles V, however, had created among some conservative, privileged sectors of society other very different hopes for which the new forms of national politics provided an inadequate outlet.[1] Yet this modern technique of power had continued to develop along lines foreign to the traditional beliefs of privileged social sectors, which necessarily felt disinclined to submit to the political tendencies of the times. This situation obtained in France with considerable force and was to lead to the armed rebellions among the nobility in the following century. In other parts of Europe its intensity was uneven. But in Spain the political affairs of the Empire, conspicuous by their absence during the Middle Ages, created a more complex state of affairs. The politics of Charles V and the adherence to his program by some Spanish groups—never by the people as a whole—caused irreparable alterations in the life of the peninsular kingdoms and produced disruptions which would last for centuries in the political evolution that had led to an early appearance of the modern State. The latter became perverted and confused with political formulations as different from it as those which proceeded from the

36

Imperial mythology of the European Middle Ages and the Burgundian circle.[2] In any case, Imperial hopes quickly disappeared for the Spaniards, but what did remain in certain sectors was an unquestionable lack of adjustment to the state system.

That position had much in common with that of the humanists. Unlike what we find among engineers, new military experts, merchants, bankers, and others during the Renaissance, the humanists supported traditional ideals, but ideals served by a humane position that was clearly modern in some ways. This is the case which Cervantes will be speaking about and into which he will project his protagonist. For in the *Quixote* it is not one particular episode or an isolated phrase that has political interest; the author intended to communicate an entire, unified enterprise through the whole adventure of Don Quixote. And because in every undertaking it is necessary to consider historical circumstances, we shall begin by seeing what stance the author has our belated knight take in the face of the social realities of his epoch.

The new political form of modernity, the State, rests on three fundamental pillars, each containing secondary lines: a standing army, a monetary economy, and administration by experts,[3] that is, bureaucracy. (We use the word "modernity" here to designate a historical concept, not a chronological one. We call modern not what happens to be near us in time and is connected to us, but rather the new period in which Europe began to live from the Renaissance on, starting approximately in the second half of the fifteenth century.)

Merely by the enunciation of these three pillars of modern politics we can see at once how distant from this ideal is the mentality of a certain sector of society which Cervantes renders artistically in *Don Quixote*. But it will be worthwhile to consider what Cervantes says about these themes, or, better yet, to consider the posture he has Don Quixote assume regarding them.[4]

According to Don Quixote's point of view, there is something ominous in the epoch in which he lives, something which attacks all virtue: the obsession with money. The *aurea fames* was to be the great passion of the Renaissance, according to Ehrenberg[5] and so many other historians of the modern capitalist spirit incubating at that time. That passion for lucre was manifested in the eagerness to accumulate money, and therein lies its greatest novelty. The attack on precapitalist attitudes moved by an unrestrained profit motive is well known; it was implicit in Thomas More's *Utopia* and is present in Vives's treatise *De subventione pauperum*. With words recalling the severe Luis Vives, it is Sancho who informs Don Quixote about this evil: "And today, Señor Don Quixote, people are more interested in having than in knowing. An ass covered with gold makes a better impression than a horse with a packsaddle"

(II:20). To such an extent was this so, that even those (such as government officials) who had grave moral obligations and important duties to God approached these duties with the desire to make money. This behavior was denounced in its time not only by the thundering Bartolomé de las Casas, but by Pedro Simón Abril[6] as well. And the clever protagonist of *The Little Gypsy* presents it as a habitual procedure when she boldly says to a representative of the law: "Bribe, Mr. Lieutenant, bribe, and your worship will have money, but do not introduce newfangled ways, or your worship will die of hunger."[7] Sancho dares to reveal that he is subject to a similar impulse: "In a few days from now I will be setting out for my government, where I go with a great desire to make money, which they tell me is the case with all new governors" (II:36). There are even many moments when the criticism involves a concrete reference to the customs of the Spanish Court, and we find this in the very text of the *Quixote* when Antonio refers to the efficacy of favors and bribes in the capital (II:65).

In the new social situation money had come to be the necessary basis for the success of any enterprise, occupying a role formerly reserved to other values or goods, principally heroic valor and individual virtue. Reduced to a minimum in the Middle Ages, the economy of personal wealth acquired a new and increasingly important place in society. Conspicuously, money in the form of precious metals or in other nonminted forms (credit, notes of exchange, etc.)—indeed, money in general—came to represent wealth by antonomasia, gradually displacing land in this function: "Upon a good foundation you can raise a good building, and the best foundation in the world is cash" (II:20). These words, like all statements to the same effect, belong to Sancho, who always clings to the new notion of economic reality in his time: money is not simply small coins for daily expenses but rather becomes the instrument of exchange in distant marketplaces, the best method to accumulate wealth, and a source of decisive economic and social power in war and peace.

Thomas More, who abhorred the new monetary usage, condemned gold and silver to vile functions which would make them abominable in the eyes of the people. Campanella, mentioning the very scant mercantile activity in *The City of the Sun,* noted that the Solarians only used money to pay for their food when they traveled to foreign countries. The connection between these views and the traditional ones Don Quixote expresses is perfectly clear.

People now go to war with no more altruistic desire than to attain positions in government. Alfonso X in his Partida II recognized that knights were motivated by gain, but that was understood then in terms of kingdoms, land, or treasures, never money. This represents a qualitative change and it is necessary to understand it as such in order to grasp one of the traditional elements of resistance in the period. From the moment money intervenes, the ethics of the combatant, that is, the knight, have changed. Pérez de Guzmán had already denounced this as one of the most deeply rooted evils in Castille in his time.[8] People flocked to modern levies for the army as a means of getting rich by illicit methods, even abandoning the main goal of winning the battle in order to pursue instead the more lucrative one of obtaining money and stealing whatever possible. In the lively narration, attributed to Diego Hurtado de Mendoza, of the war against the Moriscos, we find more than one sad case of a fight that began auspiciously and ended with the defeat and even death of those who thought they had won, simply because they gave themselves over to seeking gain and profit, leaving their arms prematurely abandoned. For such a refined knight as Hurtado de Mendoza this is one of the main causes of the inferiority of the anonymous army of municipal troops to the troops of the nobility.[9] And Diego Núñez de Alba, returning to Spain profoundly disillusioned about the way in which the German campaigns against the Lutherans had been fought, condemned the fact that "at this time some people began to come to war not to live or attain honor in it but to get some money with which to return to their homes. They began to impoverish the countryside because they were living according to their intentions, and as self-interest is so covetous, they found many others to follow their example."[10] García de Paredes requires in a good soldier "that he not be avaricious nor covetous, because the one who is a slave of money can hardly be lord of anybody else."[11] Note that covetousness refers only to riches in the form of money. It is not that Don Quixote rejects booty licitly acquired in combat, but getting it is not the incentive which drives him to do battle throughout the countryside: thus on several occasions he generously leaves it in the hands of his squire and cannot conceive of its value in monetary terms.

Innumerable works of the period attest to and censure the profit motive of the monetary economy and its previously unheard-of mobility of wealth. "Money is idolatry whenever it leads one to disdain other values, such as piety and virtue," according to the denunciation of Luis Vives.[12] Writers directed frequent invectives against the passion for money (but rarely against other material wealth, whether agrarian goods or real estate in general) and they denounced the esteem accorded to people who had money. "I confess," says Pedro de Navarra, "that in this age of ours riches are esteemed more than virtue and that the base and immoral rich man will be better received in many places than the distinguished man who is virtuous and poor."[13] Utilized by humanists (including Navarra, in the last of his *Diálogos*) as a manifestation of the

Golden Age, the pastoral myth involved considerable distrust of gold, the symbol of censurable wealth, but no corresponding distrust of extensive land. In *La Galatea* Cervantes includes this topic of the condemnation of the power of gold. Contrarily, the equating of power and riches is accepted when the latter proceed from inheritance and do not involve huge masses of money, especially in the case of agrarian property. Agriculture, says Gutiérrez de los Ríos, is a liberal art "because of the nobility of its yield, that is, the honorable and licit nature of its profits."[14] These are the earnings possessed by the rich who inhabit small towns in the *Quixote*.

Phrases like "powerful in possessions" [*poderoso en hacienda*], expressing, in an inversion of tradition, the newly established relation between wealth and power, are frequent and imply a favorable judgment. In these cases so much emphasis is placed on wealth, rather than on the strength and valor of the warrior, that a woman is referred to as "powerful" simply because she is very rich.[15] We might recall the satires of Quevedo in this regard and also point out that a study of the picaresque novel in relation to the rapidly advancing precapitalist spirit has yet to be done. All other social evils pale in comparison with those which the new profit motive engendered in the early modern period. Such an *aurea fames* will be sufficient, as we shall later see, to overcome the virtues of the knight, whose restoration as an instrument for creating an ideal society is the anachronistic enterprise in which Don Quixote engages. There are those who believe that the origin of the moral misfortune currently obtaining is in this covetousness. "Gold," maintains Ferrer de Valdecebro, "is the poison of republics . . . for if the passion for this noble metal were tempered in men, the world would require no further reform."[16]

Now, either to give in to the spirit of speculation and profit or to fight against its wicked influence on the soul are both definitely modern positions, born of a recognition of a new fact, new at least in its dimensions. Neither posture will be that of Don Quixote, who keeps aloof from this new situation. Money is for him a secondary matter and the affairs of life need not be expressed in economic forms. Even though Don Quixote accepts, after his second sally, the advice of the innkeeper he took for a castellan and takes care to carry necessary monetary provisions, he does not thereby consider himself obliged to accept that his relations with others should be established in economic terms. Don Juan Manuel, upon laying the bases for the estate of knighthood, had noted: "For you know very well that a man cannot live without eating and drinking and without money,"[17] yet it is necessary to be very careful in the use one makes of these things because they can cause considerable harm both to body and soul. In the world of Don Quixote's relations money has a very short radius. He tells the goatherds it is by natural right that others take him in and give him what he needs. Neither in castles nor in inns is there any reason for a knight to pay his lodging, nor is he subject to any tributary duties. "When did such a knight ever pay poll tax, excise, queen's pattens, king's levies, toll or ferry? What tailor ever took payment for the clothes he made for him? What castellan who received him in his castle ever made him pay his score?" (I:45). (We should point out that this posture constitutes a genuine case of deviate behavior, to which we shall return later, examining it from a slightly different perspective.)

On the one hand, Don Quixote is moving here within the old concept of estates which distinguishes three parts in every organically established society: those who pray, those who fight, and those who work. Upon the latter falls the obligation to produce the necessary goods, not only for their own upkeep but also for that of those others whose vigilance and dangers protect the workers and their possessions and keep their lives tranquil and secure. Elucidating that feudal concept, Don Juan Manuel said that in republics today there are three estates: prayers, defenders, laborers; defenders use the strength of their arm in battle for the protection of those who must apply themselves to the cultivation of the land. Because of this the former were free of any economic burden: "for knights are for defense and they defend others who therefore must support and maintain them."[18] Thus, when Don Quixote claims to be exempt from the obligations which only fall on the third estate, the common people, he bases himself on a traditional understanding of nobility. This view was not only traditional but also in force to a large degree at the time, when being included in the estate of the hidalgo [*fijodalgo*] meant exemption from taxation. [A *fijodalgo*, which is the old form of *hidalgo*, was an individual who did not possess a title of nobility, but nevertheless was distinguished from the third estate by the fact that he lived not from his labor but from his property.] It is true, of course, that in reformers, armchair politicians, political experts and economists, and other people of the period we note the tendency toward the reduction of the economic privilege of the hidalgos, if not its complete suppression. This tendency was motivated in some cases by a rejection of the inequality which such a privilege represented and in others by a desire to eliminate the dead weight which the leisure of that class implied for the successful economic development of a country in a period in which the hidalgos had definitely lost their monopoly on defense. Therefore this is one of the first things against which Sancho intends to guard: "In this island, I imagine, there must be more 'Dons' than there are stones. But enough of that; God knows what I mean. It may be, if my government lasts four days, I'll weed them all out; for there are so many of them they must be as troublesome as gnats" (II:45).

But Don Quixote has another basis on which to validate his exemption: in the form of life which he generously tries to revive, everybody helps everybody else, nobody claims as his own any more than what he needs, and everyone is disposed to share what he possesses with his neighbor. This voluntary limitation to what is "necessary" was a presupposition of such utopian formulations from the sixteenth to the ninetenth century. For this reason the goatherds nourish him without asking him for anything, and the rustics who live isolated among the crags of the Sierra Morena help the needy, and countryfolk generously welcome the knight and squire into their homes and their festivities, whether or not they themselves are hidalgos. They are all people close to the condition of the Golden Age (more on this later), in which they are able to avoid the odious monetary economy by living happily in the bosom of nature.

Barahona de Soto declares this explicitly:

> How well they spent the glorious life,
> those ancient ages with simplicity blessed,
> where money was unknown![19]

Therefore, the knight must not dedicate himself to activities whose objective is to pile up money or to have it as an end, while at the same time he is not denied the right to have an economic interest (indeed, how could he be, belonging as he does to the class which, in principle, was the greatest accumulator of riches!). Whence it follows that, if he may not perform mechanical labor, neither may he practice any profession involving monetary traffic. On the other hand, if it occurs that a knight needs to improve his state, Diego de Valera says, he has three options: serve a lord, work inherited lands, or raise livestock, "for he cannot live indecently who follows the example of our first parents."[20] Antonio de Guevara says that hidalgos living in villages near their vineyards "take great pleasure in seeing them planted, hoed, protected, fenced in, irrigated, manured, pruned, and especially in seeing them harvested," and they participate in many other operations, always simply attired. "Seeing to their country estate and surveying their livestock" are their proper economic activities.[21] Thus, shepherding and agriculture are the only licit sources of wealth. More and Campanella also have the inhabitants of their ideal cities concur in this point.

We have here a doctrine formed by the sublimation of a traditional agrarian society with a predominantly rural base. It is the society which Don Quixote always assumes as a given. In it the system of production is not only archaic and relatively undeveloped, but its very level of productivity is necessarily quite low. The scheme of values of such a society, valid until the eve of the industrial revolution, derives from these conditions. Frugality, simplicity, the lack of interest in increasing natural goods as a proper end; all these are virtues derived from the circumstances of a low-consumption society. "Nature is content with so little," warns Alfonso de la Torre.[22] This ideal underlies the entire construction of Cervantes and will remain alive until the eighteenth-century philosophes. It was an ideal of Christian stoic derivation expressed in the desirable formula of *mediocritas*, which corresponded with the available means of production. Thus, for Cervantes, as for all humanism, the perfect measure of possessions is in "some average quantity" whose lack causes grave calamities but whose excess creates even more painful concerns.[23]

And yet, in the middle of this system is the knight, who is usually rich, given the economy of traditional privileges. According to the doctrinal bases of chivalrous society, those riches are a pillar of valor and virtue to the degree that they maintain the knight in the profession of arms (weapons and horses are expensive, and if he must use his time for battle, keeping himself in readiness, he can hardly be concerned with earning a living). The role of wealth in the hands of the privileged is in part, at least theoretically, to be distributed in the form of donations, gifts, and alms, but above all to support the social figure of the rich and powerful knight. This means that this wealth, as a generator and sustainer of virtue, is itself a virtue by definition. And it is so, according to the established opinion, and cannot cease being so, as long as it proceeds from nature. For the only riches which a knight may keep or have at his disposal are natural ones, not those which are artificial or conventionally created by men. This distinction, which comes from the late Middle Ages, is found in García de Castrojeriz,[24] is repeated in Sánchez de Arévalo in the fifteenth century,[25] and in the seventeenth it is an archaic concept (like all of those which make up the quixotic mentality), but a concept whose vestiges are still detectable even in more advanced economists.[26] Thus this natural wealth is of the kind which can and ought to be desired as long as it is within a legitimate order. To renounce the improvement of one's state which natural wealth makes possible is in fact censurable, according to an early codifier of the estate of knighthood, the Infante Don Juan Manuel.[27] Since, however, the amount of natural wealth in a static, traditional society obeys fixed patterns and is more or less invariable, it cannot be obtained licitly (for what one acquires another necessarily loses) except through one means: the use of legitimate force (i.e., in warfare) as understood in the world of chivalry. Knights, thus, being properly and formally dedicated to the exercise of arms, are the only ones who can and ought to grow rich, precisely as a demonstration of their virtue. The virtues of the knight are thus part of the system.

Because of all this it cannot strictly be said that Don Quixote disdains wealth. Remember how he bitterly laments the poverty of hidalgos alone in his room at the duke's palace the first night that Sancho is away governing his island. But beyond that, the very profession of arms which Don Quixote has made his own is in fact a means for obtaining riches and figures prominently as such in the captive's tale. And Don Quixote himself says to his niece and housekeeper: "There are two paths, my daughters, by which men may succeed in becoming rich and honored. One is that of letters, the other that of arms" (II:6). This does not mean that Don Quixote forgets that there are other means, but only that these do not count for the knight. As medieval man believed and, along with him, the Spanish hidalgo and the nobility of all Europe in the sixteenth and seventeenth centuries, those other means, involving individual labor, are proper to artisans, merchants, and townspeople. Therefore, Don Quixote himself recommends to one of them, the poor Basilio, that he apply himself to an honorable and productive trade. He asks "Señor Basilio to give up the practice of his accomplishments, since even though they brought him fame they would bring in no money, and to devote his attention instead to the acquisition of a fortune by legitimate means and his own industry; for those who are prudent and persevering always find a way" (II:22). Of course that fortune must not exceed certain set limits proper to his social class. Manual labor will never be able to bring in (nor should it) the great wealth which Don Quixote says the knight may hope to acquire. We discover the reason for this in Bartolomé Felippe: republics diminish and fall into ruin "if the common people who live in them are rich, for it is natural for commoners who are rich to be negligent and lazy and they would never work if necessity did not oblige them to do so."[28] Repeating this opinion as a cliché, Thomas More tells us that there are those who hold that it is important to a king and to his security "that his people should have neither riches nor liberty. For wealth and freedom make men less submissive to a cruel and unjust rule, whereas poverty dulls them, makes them patient, and bears down and breaks that spirit which might otherwise dispose them to rebel."[29] Without this limitation of wealth, it is clear that a tremendous upheaval in the order of the three estates would threaten society. Nevertheless, economists of Cervantes's time knew that "a rich kingdom enriches its king and lord," as Pérez de Herrera writes; but in the privileged sectors the static preventionism of the contrary opinion was the view that prevailed.[30]

This society based on estates is essentially static, although clearly it is never perfectly immobile. Its general model, idealized by the pattern of consumption indicated above, is that of a sober sufficiency. Guevara defines it in terms which could well be applied to the mode of life of hidalgos such as Don Quixote:

> Oh how blessed in this respect is the villager, whose needs are supplied by a plain table, a broad bench, . . . a few wooden carving boards, a cork saltcellar, some home-made tablecloths, a frame bed, a warm room, a bedspread from Brittany, a few serge coverlets, some matting from Murcia, a sheepskin jacket worth two ducats, a silver cup, a lance behind the door, a nag in the stable, a buckler in his room, a purse at his bedhead, a cloak on the bed and a maid to prepare his stew. With these furnishings an hidalgo lives as honorably in a village as a king with all his possessions.

It is a fixed economy based on self-sufficiency and oriented not toward production and the sale of surplus goods but rather toward the necessities of life. On this level the superiority of country life is manifest: "It is a privilege of villages that those who dwell in them have flour to sift, a bowl for kneading, and an oven for their baking," and that they have firewood, wine, and so many other things which in cities have to be purchased.[31] It is understood, however, that these limits are not to be exceeded except in special cases, as exceptions due to extraordinary merit.

And so there are ways to attain higher levels, but they are difficult, only open to the personal effort of the most daring and virtuous. The lower the level from which one starts the more restricted is the range of ascent. But it is quite extensive for a knight, who can even conquer a kingdom. If he does so, however, it will not be to satisfy some prince's thirst for conquest, for this would contradict the fundamental pacifism of chivalrous society (see chap. 6), but only as a personal reward for singlehandedly defeating the unjust holder of the kingdom. In exchange for such considerable benefits the knight must endure the maximum rigor, the greatest demands on his virtue, and the harshest difficulties on the road by which only he who accepts the obligations and suffering of knighthood will be able to rise to a higher estate. Within the structure of Guevarian society, while all are subject to the principle of "having what they should," only knights are allowed "to get what they want." Whence Don Quixote can move through the network of a class-based society, which he always respects, and still direct his desire toward very distant limits.

Because he is a knight, arms are the only means that count for Don Quixote. His manner of arriving at wealth will be to attain power, which wealth accompanies. It has been said (by Sombart) that the change of direction from a feudal economy to the capitalist period can be summed up in the following comparison: In modern times it follows that if you are rich, you are powerful, whereas for the medieval world if you are powerful, you are rich. And Don Quixote aspires to be powerful, to attain a kingdom or even an empire, and to enjoy the riches that come with it. These are riches, therefore, which interest him not because of his thirst for profit but because of his desire for power. In the middle of the fifteenth century the humanist Juan de Lucena, committed to the traditional economic concept, believed that "it would be greater wealth to expand kingdoms than to pile up treasures."[32]

Writers who censure people who go to war to acquire money do not necessarily disdain wealth themselves. Juan de Lucena deeply lamented the scant fortune of the knight: "Those who bear arms serve but never grow rich; they continually make their dwelling in huts, bell tents or portable tents, and at times under branches or their own shields"; they suffer from cold and the scorching sun, they die in the field, often without confession, or they remain crippled for the rest of their lives and in spite of all this most of them never escape poverty.[33] Núñez de Alba clearly regrets that wars such as the one he participated in do not improve the condition of good people but enable "the vilest to grow rich." War is, or ought to be, a means for the most valiant and honorable to prosper, although in his war "the best soldiers, the ones who have most scrupulously done their duty, have suffered most and have wound up poor."[34] He reveals the pathetic custom of some valiant soldiers who, on returning home, are forced to hide their penury by pretending to have been robbed. This is also a complaint of Cervantes himself and, sadly, it is what happens to Don Quixote. On the other hand, everything goes to prove that in letters one could really get rich. In the captive's tale we see the son who chose the profession of arms return in poverty while his brother, the judge, grows in possessions and in esteem. Speaking of the new inhabitants of Granada, Hurtado de Mendoza mentions "the arrival of outstanding men of letters whom their profession had made rich."[35] Those who go into arms with high heroic ideals only manage to wind up totally destitute. Such is the sad reality of Cervantes, reflected in his knight whose vain hope causes his downfall.

Yet Don Quixote does not seek to be poor nor does he resign himself to it. Usually he rejects monetary agreements and the new economic forms of money. The reference to the banking practices of the merchants in *La española inglesa*[36] and the mention that the newly rich protagonist of *El celoso extremeño,* in organizing his administration, "put in a bank"[37] part of his fortune prove that Cervantes had some notion of these new forms and even went so far as to make positive use of them in the plots of some of his stories. But in the *Quixote* Cervantes's purpose was not simply to reflect an anachronistic estate-based ideal which prohibited hidalgos from engaging in mercantile activity (as seen in Guevara).[38] He needed to eliminate that new world of money in order to maintain the bipolar meaning of his work and include in it the escapist social utopia some were longing for. While he had perhaps accepted this evasionism in his youth, he now looked upon it with gentle melancholy. To build up his image of Utopia before bringing it to the ground, Cervantes had to wipe away that new world of money. Don Quixote does make use of money on a few occasions, such as when he has Sancho pay the fishermen for the boat sunk in the Ebro; but, as in any medieval city, his use of it is limited both in amount and in the number of times he spends it. It is the position of Antonio de Torquemada, who says that the ancients used gold and silver, but "not to coin money, which was the greatest perdition which could ever come into the world, not because of money per se, for as a guarantor of saleable goods it prevents many evils which would certainly exist without it, but rather because of the covetousness which came into the world along with money."[39] The knight does not seek to accumulate gold calculable in terms of money but rather to conquer extensive and rich dominions which bring with them first an elevation of social rank and later on the riches necessary to maintain it. While the social world surrounding Don Quixote believes that "it is a common thing for the well-to-do to be treated with respect" (I:51), what the knight wants is for riches to come to those who are honorable.

If Núñez Alba had been asked why he went to the war, he would have responded that, although he was already exempt from paying tribute in his native land, he went "in order to elevate my nobility."[40] And his sad lament is due to his not having elevated it more than he did, nor having achieved along with this nobility the material increase, the recompense he expected for his heroic action. Don Quixote, too, expected such recompense for his undertaking, even though material reward was not his principal motivation. He even held that the prize for chivalric action could easily be an entire kingdom. For Don Quixote war requires only an energetic spirit and powerful mettle in the hand which wields the sword; his prize is not monetary gain but nobility and political and patrimonial dominion over both land and people. It was utterly impossible for an anticapitalistic mentality like his to understand the warning of Bartolomé Felippe according to which the prince who goes to war "must know who has more money, whether he or the enemy, how long the war could last and how much it will cost to sustain it. It is necessary to be very vigilant in this matter because money, as is commonly said, is the very nerve of war, for it begins it and ends it."[41] This view of war (already commonplace, according to Felippe) implies the most tremendous clash with the chivalric spirit, as does the new fact that war, an enterprise reserved for the best, had become a business and a source of rich profits for a whole conglomerate of people. They participate in war not fiercely wielding arms but shadily manipulating the huge funds which were necessary to conduct modern campaigns. The devastating testimony of an honorable military man like Marcos de Isaba[42] is sufficient evidence of this state of affairs.

Humanists were opposed to the new capitalist spirit and, moved by a moralizing zeal frequently overlooked by those who have spoken of them, they attempted to establish a utopian collectivist system in which money was looked upon with a most jaundiced eye. Such is the case with More and Campanella. One of the advantages of the village, says Guevara, is that "there is no money to hoard away" (thus the village cannot be a place for the accumulation of wealth), nobody "has to borrow money at interest" (those pernicious banking operations of merchants), and "there are no rates of exchange to lead to usury"[43] (a traditional accusation which pragmatic or lucid Spanish economists had begun to reject around the middle of the sixteenth century).[44] Don Quixote rejects capitalism too, and holds instead to a distant world, temporally undefined, anachronistic and therefore utopian, even though all its specific elements proceed from medieval tradition. We shall soon see the sense in which Cervantes stresses that dose of what we provisionally call medievalism in his character, coincident with the European medievalization of the Baroque. But first let us verify this in its other aspect, namely, Don Quixote's conception of political power.

A modern State, such as the one designed by the Catholic Sovereigns, implies an administration by an organized body of technicians. These are people with knowledge adequate to the exercise of public affairs. They apply judicial ordinances which theoretically extend to the body politic and which they have the authority to enforce (even though strong residual resistance may make this enforcement illusory). The ruler in the modern period has dismounted from the horse on which he spent almost his entire life in the Middle Ages, has doffed his arms, and with pen in hand runs public affairs from a chair in his office.

On the one hand Cervantes undoubtedly did not look kindly on ecclesiastics in government, a point he makes sarcastically when he has a character in one of his *entremeses* direct the following verses to a sacristan who wants to run for mayor:

Is it your job to rule the commonwealth?
Stick to your own affairs; stick to your bells.[45]

Cervantes passes this criterion on to the knight; we only need recall the scene with Don Quixote and the ecclesiastic in the palace of the duke and duchess. Don Quixote, however, lives in a time when we have seen scholars, people with a political education, "ruling and governing the world from a chair," as he says in his famous Discourse on Arms and Letters (I:37). He recognizes that it is necessary to bestow on these men of letters (which in the language of the period means scholars, not just literary men) public jobs, "such posts as must of necessity be allotted to men of their calling" (I:38). A marvellous real figure from the time of Don Quixote, Alonso Enríquez de Guzmán, in spite of his nobility, came to hold that it was not desirable to put a lord who has been occupied for many years in affairs of war into positions of government, for "to be a captain in the field of battle is a very different matter from the governance of people."[46] Don Quixote agrees, up to a point; but what he cannot accept is that the knight should not be free from this system but should have to be subjected to it; that he cannot, like the medieval lord, rise to a position of government by dint of his strength in arms and his martial efforts.

For a public official, for that patrolman of the Holy Brotherhood who attempts to arrest Don Quixote, the knight who wishes to disobey organized public authority and to take justice into his own hands is a highwayman; the violent clash with this point of view brings out the indignation of Don Quixote: "Do you call him a highwayman who gives freedom to those in chains, succors those who are in distress, lifts up the fallen, and brings aid to the needy?" (I:45). (This may be the most impressive example of his abnormal conduct.) There appears to be in these words a Pauline echo which struggles against the juridical formalization aspired to by those who occupy positions in the new style of administration. The State wishes there to be no power other than itself, no law or justice other than its own. It imposes a homogeneity in obedience, even though the form of it may not be the same for everybody (Jean Bodin would call it a geometric harmony). It seeks to eliminate, step by step, privileges and exemptions in an effort to prevent all private activity in the domain of its own functions. In the sixteenth century, in the context of the monarchic absolutism which was gradually being imposed, all vestiges of the medieval doctrine of the right to resistance disappeared from political thought. And this is what Don Quixote simply cannot conceive: "Who, I ask again, is the stupid one who does not know that there are no letters-patent of nobility that confer such privileges and exemptions as those that a knight acquires the day he is dubbed a knight and devotes himself to the rigorous duties of his calling?" (I:45). Well, that "stupid one" to whom Don Quixote refers is the modern State. "Who is so ignorant as not to know," he asks in the same place, "that knights-errant are beyond all jurisdiction, their only law their swords, while their charter is their mettle and their will is their decrees?"

Against this political-juridical individualism of the medieval knight the State imposes its sovereignty, which extends to all and, in principle, to all equally, even though it may be a question of a proportional or geometric equality, using Bodin's phrase. Nobody may oppose himself to it because there is no other justice in temporal society which is above what this sovereignty ordains. Sancho, still acting in accordance with the new mentality of the commoners whose interests are closer to those of the modern political regimen, gives Don Quixote precisely this warning when the knight attempts to exercise his mission of private justice on behalf of the galley slaves condemned by public justice: "Take note your grace," said Sancho, "that justice, that is to say, the king himself, is not using any force upon, or doing any wrong to, people like these, but is merely punishing them for crimes they have committed" (I:22).

Here is why Don Quixote could not help but clash with the Holy Brotherhood. Taking its name from medieval organizations of the time of the Catholic Sovereigns, this organization had changed its character totally and had turned into the repressive police force essential to the new State. Therefore, while Sancho is afraid of it, Don Quixote operates according to a political scheme of privilege and individualism; his sense of traditional nobility causes him to be as outraged as was a real-life lord such as the Marquis of Villena when he rejected the use of arms by commoners against knights. Don Quixote assures Sancho that he will snatch him out of the hands of the Brotherhood, eliminating the adjective "Holy." "The Holy Brotherhood," Sancho warns him on another occasion, "does not observe the customs of chivalry," to which Don Quixote replies by hurling a challenge against it and against "all the brothers and brotherhoods that there are in this world" (I:23).

This ignorance of the generally established norms of behavior in Renaissance society leads in some people to phenomena of disfunction similar, at least at first glance, to cases of anomy, and its end result is abnormal conduct. This arises from an appeal to a system of values and norms perceived to be higher, and although it may appear to be based on personal criteria, at bottom it proceeds, more or less contradictorily, from tradition. In the face of society as it existed in their day, these "mavericks" would claim to be safeguarding social purity. They seem to be cases of what has been called "deviance through excess of social integration."[47] We shall return to this subject.

We shall not take time to demonstrate how the most noteworthy representatives of humanism incorrectly understood the State system or how even their political conceptions revealed an ignorance of the basic presuppositions of that organization. This is evident in the political works, full of moralizing rhetoric, of Vives, Erasmus, More, and others. An analysis of Alfonso de Valdés's *Diálogo de Mercurio y Carón,* in which we still find clearly medieval ideas surviving, would suffice to prove the point. For no matter how much the humanists criticized the lack of culture and the barbarism of the medieval period, their own moral and political ideal was very close to it. Their ideal of the perfection of man and his society arose out of the medieval background, the only difference being that it was upheld with new means and in the context of a new attitude.

In a most interesting dialogue, written by Jiménez de Urrea, two speakers confront each other: one represents the old chivalrous mentality and the other that of the new military discipline typical of the modern state system. The former holds that it is legitimate to attack on one's own initiative an individual considered evil and give him the punishment he deserves. "If the wicked were not punished, the good would not be able to live." "That punishment," the other answers, "is not yours to give." And when the first speaker attempts to defend the validity of his view, at least among those who bear arms ("men of war," he notes, "are different from others"), the second speaker rejects his opinion even with that limitation: "They are different," he replies, "as regards the swiftness of judgment and the severity of punishment, because people who are in the midst of a war cannot be subjected to lengthy trials; nor should their punishments be light but instead heavy and executed with severity in order to control people who enjoy so much liberty." And if quarrels arise, "you will find in captains and judges a better remedy for your honor than in duels."[48] Unable even to comprehend it, the representative of the old chivalric spirit rejects the new political situation in which certain persons and not others are constituted as public functionaries who are alone deemed competent to manage the public welfare. That incomprehension leads him to distrust the new functionaries and to feel irritated if he is told that he must accept them in the affairs of his life, even in such important matters as obtaining justice. "I say that I wish to prove my intention by means of arms, of which only God is judge, and not by the law, because I could run into a Lucifer who is an ignorant, venal, or careless judge, or one who has personal animus against me and will give it to me right between the eyes." His opponent has his answer ready: "On few occasions will you find such judges, and on many will justice be lost through the recourse to arms."[49]

In the chivalric conception the sphere of politics, or, more correctly put, the function of government, theoretically reduced to the simple formula of doing justice and defending the weak, was the responsibility of the knight. "So noble is the office of knighthood that every knight should be a lord and governor of lands" is the opinion of Ramón Lull.[50] This is what had collapsed, not just as a practice which always turned out to be impossible (there are few kingdoms but many knights, Lull added), but also as doctrine. Don Quixote came to accept in principle that government was a matter for experts, although he never stopped hoping that a kingdom would fall into his hands nor did he consider his illiterate squire Sancho unfit for the business of government. And the truth is that Cervantes's presentation of his hero and his correlative world does not involve any contradiction in this detail. As much as the style of public service had changed since the time of the Catholic Sovereigns, as the author of *Guerra de Granada* admits, vestiges of the old mentality were still around at a much later date and to these Cervantes attempted to give expression in a complete social construct. Falling into genuine archaism, some *Cartas anónimas* from the middle of the seventeenth century[51] make the following comment on reporting that the counts of Peñaranda and Castrillo have committed a trivial *faux pas* in taking turns in the viceroyalty of Naples: "The Count of Castrillo held the chair of civil law in Valladolid, and the Count of Peñaranda the same in Salamanca, so that both of them were first lawyers and scholars rather than statesmen and graduates in knowledge of the affairs of knighthood, and thus they undoubtedly erred in their duties, for in court rooms they know little or nothing about government, as experience shows."[52] We see here that a criterion of archaistic purity in defense of what was considered authentic in traditional chivalric society produced a clash with the current political status quo and engendered a divergent attitude. Fully a part of the traditional system, those defenders of the "purity" of bygone times, those deviates (for that is how the public viewed them), were in reality legion, and Cervantes took his inspiration from their behavior.

What is certain is that, these archaistic holdovers aside, the humanists from Vives to Montaigne did not look kindly on a bureaucratic formalization of law, justice, or government. Vives praised natural justice among those who lived in the Golden Age.[53] The Thelemites of Rabelais have only one law: "Do what thou wilt."[54] Campanella observed that in the "City of the Sun" the laws are few, brief, and clear, and they are written on a slab of bronze in sight of all, requiring for their comprehension and application no knowledge of juridical technique. It was the defense of a more natural form of government, spontaneous and in accord with that equity, whose image we shall again encounter when we speak of the Golden Age.[55]

In his construction of the chivalric world on the margin of Renaissance-style politics Cervantes pulled together the threads of that humanist attitude found in Latinists such as Erasmus and Vives or in those, such as Guevara and Montaigne, who wrote in Romance languages. Don Quixote answers to that fundamental rejection of modern political and social organization which, as a representative of the traditional chivalric spirit and of humanistic utopianism, he himself enunciates. In connection with that rejection, and supporting that anachronistic conception at its very base, we find in him as well as in some real individuals who were clinging to the seignorial ideal a shared understanding of the role of arms. This is the area in which Don Quixote most dramatically distances himself from the innovations of his day.

Let us recall Don Quixote on the crest of a hill describing to his squire what he believes to be enemy armies, although they are only two flocks of harmless sheep. Those crack troops which in his imagination are rushing into combat are not organized masses of soldiers who are going to carry out a joint operation under the orders of ranked leaders, thus replacing personal initiative with obedience; according to the quixotic vision, they are two groups of individual warriors accompanied, at most, by their personal entourages, each one of whom will engage in singular combat.

A Tacitist writer who is an expert in the new style of warfare, a contemporary of Cervantes, defends the contrary position. Alamos de Barrientos recognizes that "the energy and valor of armies will be of little avail if they are lacking the obedience and respect due their captains, and wish always to conduct themselves on the basis of energy and resolve."[56] But to renounce that impulsiveness and personal initiative is what Don Quixote will never accept, because for him the decisive quality of his profession is to bring about the triumph of his unique virtues. In order to give a good example to knight-errantry Don Quixote wishes to make himself a mirror of all the virtues, but there is one he never mentions in relation to himself, one whose very existence he fundamentally does not recognize for himself: obedience. Yet the late medieval doctrine of chivalry had been altered by the introduction of a nontraditional point of view in this matter. For example, Pedro IV of Aragón recommended "that [knights] be obedient and submissive to the orders of their superiors" because "obedience is crucial to victory."[57] Sánchez de Arévalo focuses the question of obedience as a purely personal attitude of respect and reverence for the king.[58] Its boundaries, therefore, are very limited and it is viewed as an individual matter. We are dealing with uncertain criteria in a transitional period, and in this matter of obedience we shall soon witness a radical change.

Certainly, there is one moment when Don Quixote does refer to obedience: when he converses with a simple soldier heading for Cartagena to embark and serve the king in an organized modern army, and he gives him the following advice: "The good soldier achieves fame through obedience to his captain and others in command" (II:24). As can easily be seen, this supposition does not apply to his own case. If anything, Don Quixote's recommendation to the soldier highlights the exclusion of obedience from his own ethical system. Diego García del Palacio, on the other hand, mentions it among the principal attributes a captain must have.[59] Obedience will be viewed by a man of the modern period as the most important military virtue of all. It obliges a soldier not only not to attempt to act on his own but even, should it come to that, not to try to understand the reasons for an action. Consider the very great distance between Don Quixote's martial concept and the style of military behavior praised by Alamos: "The decisions and counsels of war are better executed through the obedience of individual soldiers than by their questioning the cause and meaning of them."[60] This obedience characterizes not only the activity of the one who is subject to it, but also that of the superior who is in command and who must count on those who are to carry out his orders. Thus, for both, obedience is the tie which binds an army together and makes possible its unified operation.

But there is a broader and higher concept than that of obedience, namely, the matter of discipline. On no other subject was so much written in the first centuries of the modern age: Marcos de Isaba, Francisco Valdés, Sancho de Londoño, and Mosquera de Figueroa are examples. Everybody concerned with military affairs deals with it.

Here there is a curious difference to be established. Medieval people were full of admiration for the Greeks and the Romans, especially during the autumn of the Middle Ages, which saw the beginnings of humanism. They were also impregnated with the chivalric mentality, which some, at that moment of its maturity in the fifteenth century, were attempting to codify in a system of laws and conventions. It is well known that knighthood had a clear Germanic origin, not only in its rituals, as Marc Bloch has observed,[61] but because it could only have developed in a feudal society. Chivalry, indeed, started in France and later spread throughout western Europe. Nonetheless, Spanish writers from the thirteenth to the fifteenth century frequently refer to the Greeks and Romans (as do the French and others). On the one hand they medievalize them, making them part of the feudal world. Holding them up as masters in the art of chivalry, they cite Alexander and Julius Caesar as examples of knights, and Don Juan Manuel recommends the reading of Vegetius to anyone who wishes to learn that art. On the other hand, they already believe that discipline is the rule in their concept of knighthood—such is the view of Diego Valera.[62] There is, however, a difference: traditionalists praise the moral discipline of the particular individual, the fostering and moral purification of valor in each person. Writers in the line of modernity take a very different approach when they speak of discipline and refer to the precedent of the Romans and their victories; they allude to that discipline operative in ordered armies made up of masses of combatants whose personal morale is of secondary significance because what really matters is the collective behavior of the groups and the order of their movements together. From the dawn of the modern spirit, collective discipline is viewed as the decisive cause of the success of military enterprises. We refer here to the extremely valuable *Tratado de la perfección del triunfo militar* of Alfonso de Palencia (mid-fifteenth century), the great chronicler of Enrique IV. A good Renaissance man, Palencia believed that military victory required two factors above all: discipline and order. The mere exercise of arms, the aspect the medieval knight cultivated exclusively, was insufficient.[63] Not once will Don Quixote praise himself for being disciplined, nor could he do so, for discipline has no meaning in his concept of the art of war. On the other hand, we frequently hear him extol himself referring to "the profession of arms, one that I can never forget" (II:66).

"Skilled" and "daring" are two terms of honor for Don Quixote as a combatant. Both refer to his isolated, individual martial activity, unrelated to that of other people, and both had long been praised in the old chronicles and epic poems exalting the singular action of valiant warriors. Don Juan Manuel recommended that a king threatened by war surround himself with many knights: "the first thing he must do is find many good people and do everything he can so that they will be content with him and serve him willingly."[64] Those many people were actually a handful of heroes known and individually esteemed for their skill in combat. This had to do with the small number of soldiers in a medieval army and, even more, with the fact that very few in those armies had an active role in combat, an aspect studied by Ferdinand Lot.[65] At the end of the sixteenth century it is more generally believed that neither individual boldness nor even "the mass of daring and unsubmissive people is what achieves victories," but rather "a fair number of people armed with virtue, highly obedient and well-trained."[66] When Sancho de Londoño wrote his *Discurso sobre la forma de reducir la disciplina militar a mejor y antiguo estado*,[67] he already had thought out the problem of moving armies of large contingents in an orderly fashion.

"Obedient" and "disciplined" are terms which would earn the disdain of Don Quixote. He leaps into battle when it suits him, decides whom to attack, and goes wherever he chooses; in the general melee and chaos what he looks for is a "one on one" encounter. His is the direct opposite, therefore, of a disciplined action. Nevertheless, discipline is what really moved the armies of his time. Its necessity and importance derive from the invention of the great machine that is the modern army, which has to function with the precision and coordination of a mechanism. There is no way to mobilize those huge masses of individuals in the field so that they do not fall into frightful confusion and become obstacles to each other except to do so in an orderly fashion. It is quite impossible effectively to use weapons as different as mace, harquebus, pike, or artillery unless their placement and operation in the field is carefully organized. With so many participants, the end desired and planned by the higher political authority is unobtainable unless all individuals subordinate their actions to the military authority charged with carrying it out. The medieval knight, contrariwise, acts at best in consort with a very small number of equals. He knows them personally and is aware of their strengths and potential, he uses the same or similar short-range weapons that they do, and he is the author or at least the immediate coauthor of the military ends to be pursued. Spanish writers on the laws of chivalry, far from understanding the new needs of the time—as the Gran Capitán would understand them—emphasize the valor of the individual knight: the author of El Victorial assumes that "it has happened many times that through the effort and disposition of a good knight a battle is won or a great fortress is defended or taken," and, he goes on, "it even happens at times that an entire kingdom is captured."[68] Sánchez de Arévalo, for his part, believes that "in war it is more advantageous to have knights who are great in spirit than great in number,"[69] which implies a way of viewing the role of the combatant in terms of his personal effort and free initiative. Don Quixote is only disposed to fight alone or at most (as in the case of his plan to defeat the army of the Turk) in the company of hardly more than half a dozen other knights-errant; he will use no arms other than those whose offensive efficacy depends solely on his courage, his doughty mettle, and the strength of his arm; and he will only fight in those enterprises which he personally accepts. It is probably unnecessary to mention that More in his Utopia is also opposed to the new methods of warfare.[70]

This concept of the combatant involves a parallel understanding of battles. A battle is an encounter or a series of encounters, few in number, among knights. It is a hand-to-hand combat which is brought about deliberately in the form of a duel or a challenge, even in the middle of a confrontation between two large masses. This is the genuine test of personal valor, the one in which the knight achieves fame and honor. Quite the opposite is the mentality of the military man in touch with the realities of his period. Miguel Sabuco proposed that kings and the pope abolish the laws of dueling, for "it is grievous to behold how many pernicious evils come into the world" because of them.[71] A debate on this theme is the real subject matter of the Diálogo of Jiménez de Urrea referred to above. The character who defends the antiquated point of view admits that he is leaving Castille in order to be free of its "barbarous laws" which have closed the route to military honor "because they prohibit an hidalgo like me from freely going after my honor with sword in

hand." The character whose thinking follows the modern political form
of the State answers that "the law which permitted such a thing would
be considerably more barbarous than the one you say they have in
Castille." The latter considers it an act of treason and rebellion to use
martial actions in personal affairs and not in those ordered by the king,
the only legitimate authority in the rationally structured warfare of the
modern State. With that astonishment born of total incomprehension,
the traditionalist responds: "Treason and rebellion you call it to go into
the field of battle with my enemy and, with the weapons he chooses,
fight him to the death in order to satisfy my honor and conserve my
ancient nobility?"[72]

In the old chronicles and epic poems the challenge is an accepted
means of conducting war, and examples of that mentality survived
among individuals of certain privileged groups until the end of the sixteenth century. (These groups were over the centuries ever more out of
touch with general public criteria.) Leaving aside Charles V's absurd
challenge to Francis I, let us recall another equally inappropriate case,
when the Duke of Alba, in the war against the Schmalkaldic League,
proposed to the Landgrave that they resolve the conflict by means of a
personal encounter.[73] Sandoval relates the case of an hidalgo from the
highlands, Don Martín Alonso, who, despite orders against going into
the open field to do battle, broke through the lines armed with a pike
and killed a corpulent German who had been hurling terrible insults at
the Spaniards from enemy lines. When he returned to his post, the commanding officer ordered him beheaded, and only the insistence of the
Spanish troops could persuade him not to carry out the execution. The
author of this chivalric exploit was obliged, however, to return home
poor and without pay.[74] Fernando de Herrera, in a deeply critical spirit,
says that just before the battle known later as Los Gelves, Count Pedro
Navarro, who already had a number of important victories to his credit,
wished to avoid confronting the enemy in conditions he did not consider favorable; but Don García de Toledo, a young nobleman—and
"young" here means as much as to say "poorly adapted to the newly
established system"—asked permission to attack with the vanguard. He
was obeying an impulse of purely personal, chivalric initiative and devi-
ated from proper behavior due to his grounding in the standards of
chivalry. His inopportune insistence succeeded in breaking down the resistance of the expert count and his impetuosity dragged him and many
of his troops to catastrophe and death.[75]

Nevertheless, in more modern accounts of war or descriptions of
battles, more in line with the new spirit of the times, the nature of warfare has changed. We can verify it in the *Comentario de las guerras de
Alemania* of Don Luis de Avila or in the history of the War of Catalonia

written by Manuel de Melo. And we see the same transformation in the accounts of naval battles, as in Mosquera de Figueroa's description of the victorious campaign of the Azores or in Herrera's *Relación de la Guerra de Cipre y suceso de la batalla naval de Lepanto*. In the latter, for example, the writer tells of the distress of those who were under siege, worn down by artillery and attacks; he also writes of the destruction of strongholds with mines, of bastions for artillery and trenches for harquebusiers, etc. These facts, taken from the work of a poet rather than from the writings of military experts, prove just how generalized the new methods of warfare were; even nonspecialists already knew about them in the second half of the sixteenth century.[76]

The new technique tends to close in the space on which the army depends. If it is a fortified place, this is done by curtains and bulwarks supported by strong, broad embankments; if it is an open space, the effect is achieved by trenches, which are the walls of the field, in the words of Francisco de Valdés. Can we imagine Don Quixote brandishing his weapons with the strength of his arm behind walls or in trenches?

For Don Quixote, as for any medieval Castillian, castles themselves are the warrior's residence, enclosed because private life was also in danger at any time and in any place, even in a kingdom. This was so until the State had completed the work of converting war and armed intervention into a public function. According to an expert on military architecture of the period, Fernández de Villarreal, a castle is an old-style fortress.[77] At the beginning of the seventeenth century they were to become an anachronism, replaced by powerful military fortifications whose structure had changed due to the invention of artillery and to the new political shape of the State.[78] For Don Quixote the inn of the Manchegan countryside, the flour mill on the Ebro, and the palace of the duke and duchess are all castles because his life as a man of arms is based on military assumptions according to which castles had an efficient function to fulfil, just as they did in the bygone chivalric world.

That world presupposed a system of social life in which the enemy, the *hostes,* was a private, personal enemy. It was neither a citizen of a foreign country nor a vassal of a king other than one's own who attacked the objective and public power of the State. It is true that Don Quixote says on occasion that the knight must above all be ready to fight for his king and his country; but this is due to his bond of fidelity with the king, a personal bond by virtue of which the enemy of the king is also a personal enemy of the knight. Here too it is curious to find a mixture of elements in writers of the fifteenth century: old ideas such as the *pro patria mori* which come from antiquity and are revived in the late Middle Ages, and others which proceed from Germanic tradition, such as the help and favor due to friends, to one's *conmilitones*. Pedro IV maintains that the knights must be disposed to die for their natural lord "and this they will do for the common good of the entire land." In the *Guillem de Vàroich* we read: "A sweet and lovely thing it is to die in defense of one's land and one's friends."[79] Don Juan Manuel asks that knights be equipped "for the defense of the land and the commonwealth in general."[80] Juan de Lucena has Juan de Mena—one of the speakers of his dialogue—praise knights (always identified with warriors), who bear the responsibility for the defense of the country. This praise should extend only to those "who spill their blood for the common good and not to those who, like dogs, fight among themselves over personal matters and who bite the royal hand that feeds them." They deserve honor who "did not hesitate to die, not just for the love of their country, but also to win everlasting renown."[81] But in addition he does not overlook the existence of the knight's own private enemies who have personal faults or defects: the unjust, the proud, the traitors, the criminal, or those with any other dishonorable vice whose guilt is decided by the knight himself. And this is what Don Quixote does: he fights against people whom he himself sets up as his own enemies, against wicked people deserving of punishment. Naturally, when the new monarchic State nationalizes both the concept of enemy and that of the delinquent or criminal, the knight's manner of conduct collapses at its very foundation.

When aiming his weapons at someone, Don Quixote does not in the least care whether or not the individual is a subject and servant of his own king. Indeed, if he always does battle in his king's lands, it is logical to assume that those he fights share his nationality. And this never stops him, nor is he even restrained by the consideration that those whom he is about to attack may be agents of the king engaged in some mission on the king's behalf. This is in spite of the fact that, according to the thinking of his time, there should be a close, strong bond of civil amity among all the monarch's dependents. Thus in the *Diálogo* of Jiménez de Urrea the speaker whose ideas are consonant with the new political climate tells the philosphically anachronistic knight: "If you wish to be considered a good and valiant soldier, turn the weapons and the fighting spirit with which you attacked your friends or relatives against the enemies of your king or your country."[82] This is what Don Quixote can never accept, because his sole intention is to effect his own justice. He even feels it is his duty to oversee the justice meted out by others, regardless of their political status. Thus only he can define who his enemy is, and it will be his own personal enemy, even if the individual has harmed somebody else, for Don Quixote has assumed as his responsibility the defense of those who need him. In Don Quixote's day, firearms thunder and swords clash in numerous wars in which the king of Spain and his armies are engaged, but it never once occurs to him to go into those battles. With his example and his arms he wishes to combat enemies in accordance with the moral code of the society whose restoration he seeks, not in accordance with law and politics. When he mentions the war of the Spanish monarch against the Turk, after setting forth the expedient which occurs to him, he does not feel even slightly moved to make any contribution of his own to the success of that undertaking and he even expressly declares his disinterest—"Therefore, I wish to remain at home, since the chaplain is not taking me out" (II:1)—and he announces that he will do exactly as he pleases. [I have used Walter Starkie's translation of this passage (New York: New American Library, 1964) rather than Putnam's, for it is based on the same text used by Rodríguez Marín for his edition, the one from which Maravall quotes, whereas Putnam follows the "no quiero quedar en mi casa" of the first edition.]

This method of understanding armed combat implies complete ignorance of all matters of tactics and strategy of concern to contemporary military writers and to the generals in charge of the campaigns. With what tremendous disdain would Don Quixote have listened to the advice of Cristóbal Lechuga, the great military expert in Flanders and a true scientist in martial matters, when he recommended practicing strategies of war and troop management with small harmless objects such as beans or pebbles, by means of which one could study the movement of squadrons, their placement in the field, their protection from enemy fire, the determination of the most effective fronts, and other matters. All of these are geometric problems foreign to the physical mettle and courageous heart which our champion admired.[83]

At the beginning of the modern age war had become in large part a question of science. What stands out as really new in the military sphere is how scientifically the affairs of war were directed. This is what leads the commanding officer Francisco de Valdés to recognize that "soldiering being as noble as it is, it must have its rules and precepts from which the art of war derives; just as we do not permit doctors, lawyers or theologians who are untrained and have not studied in the appropriate schools to practice in public, neither is it fitting for an individual unschooled in military discipline to order and control affairs of war."[84] War has its theory and praxis, both of which are necessary. The emphasis even seems to be on the former, in a period which witnesses the creation of the first military schools, such as the one Felipe II had established years earlier at El Escorial on the advice of Juan de Herrera. Against this situation, when Don Quixote bitterly enumerates the evils of the times, he will include among them the predominance of theory over practice of arms. For him the only possible training is pure and simple exercise of arms in the field, precisely that exercise which Alfonso de Palencia, imbued with the spirit of the early Renaissance, considered secondary and insufficient for military triumph.

Such a profound change in the modern period was due to the introduction of two decisive innovations: firearms and the spirit of analysis, both of which were manifestations of the rationalism of the modern age and its political creation, the State. That spirit of analysis is the one which gave rise to the new and efficient administrative organization of the State, the one which allowed the profit motive to develop and yield results in the economic sphere, and also the one which transformed the art of war into a science which ascertains "how a squadron can be strengthened, how wide a ditch should be, how trenches are best set up, what is a good spot in which to install artillery, how high and how wide gabions must be, how to shore up a mine and how to know if the enemy is searching it out, how to fortify a stronghold with its traverses and casemates, and the exact position each combatant should occupy, from the general to the soldier, when fighting becomes necessary."[85]

Rising up against that analytical, rationalistic spirit is the integral, total meaning of the adventure of Don Quixote. Don Quixote is neither willing nor able to follow his squire's computation of the salary he is owed. And in his battles he is so little given to calculation and measurement that at the end we see him criticize himself for not having taken into consideration the disproportionate strength of Rocinante and the powerful steed of the victor, the Knight of the White Moon.

The new firearms, whose use required increasingly complex mathematical operations, were also a creation of modern rationalism. Our spirited knight expressly declares himself against these fateful weapons:

> Happy were the blessed ages that were free of those devilish instruments of artillery, whose inventor, I feel certain, is now in Hell paying the penalty for his diabolical device—a device by means of which an infamous and cowardly arm may take the life of a valiant knight, without his knowing how or from where the blow fell, when amid that courage and fire that is kindled in the breasts of the brave suddenly there comes a random bullet, fired it may be by someone who fled in terror at the flash of his own accursed machine and who thus in an instant cuts off and brings to an end the projects and the life of one who deserved to live for ages to come. (I:38)

For the moment no more will be said on the subject of ancient and modern weapons, but later on it will be the axis on which my interpretation of the knight will turn. Don Quixote represents a deviation from established norms, as we see by the fact that the Cortes of Valladolid (1542) takes a contrary position, requesting "that the nobles as well as the commons of the kingdom [be armed] with pikes, harquebuses, rifles and crossbows."[86] This is something which Don Quixote would never accept, rejecting as he does all social guidelines of the sort.

All these historical factors brought about the disappearance of knights-errant. The preceding century had witnessed their displacement from one area to another, a circumstance still mentioned by Hernando de Pulgar.[87] The existence of these knights must have ended by the beginning of the seventeenth century and their presence at that time would only have been a product of Don Quixote's imagination (the residents of Utopia, of the New Atlantis, of Oceana, and of the country of the Felicians are equally imaginary). But this does not mean that the end obtained through their imaginary deeds may not have seemed really admirable to people of a certain mentality. Moreover, it could even inspire some to undertake the reform of a society whose historical elements made the obtainment of that end impossible. For this reason Don Quixote calls the age it was his lot to live in the "Iron Age" and he will lament over "this hateful age of ours" (I:11), "this degenerate age of ours" (II:1). He will have to make an effort not to renounce carrying out his venture "in an age so detestable as the one in which we now live" (I:38), proclaiming at every opportunity his rejection of his times.

Had Cervantes started from the simple facts in accordance with which chivalric doctrine was established, the *Quixote* would have been a very different book from what it is and its protagonist simply one Amadis among others, brought to life in more or less skillfully written pages. There would have been nothing in it of that nonconformity whose pulse we feel throughout the entire creation, a nonconformity on two levels: that of the knight vis-à-vis the world surrounding him, and that of the author concerning traditional, pseudoutopian reform movements with which some of the nobility wished to respond to the contemporary situation. In the novel we contemplate the knight, contrary to the false, idealized suppositions of chivalric doctrine, immersed in a society replete with historical density, very different from the one in which the hero fancies himself living merely by dint of wishing it so. A similar but less evolved phenomenon is observable in *La Galatea,* where the second level of nonconformity present in the *Quixote* went undeveloped. Cervantes presents his protagonist in a world of real people and things where the only unreal element is the pair representing the world of chivalry. And in that society composed of the widest variety of human types only knights are missing. Even when we encounter a duke among those people, he does not have the characteristics of a knight, in spite of the prevailing social system which always attributed the status of knighthood to a noble and thus identified knighthood with nobility. In this sense, neither is the famous Manchegan hidalgo a knight.[88] Cervantes simply gives us the figure of an impossible knight whom he charges precisely with the task of reforming the chivalric order. This must be interpreted as Cervantes's warning that evasive utopian reform based on the old-fashioned virtues of traditional society is incongruent with the present age. The reason is twofold: first, because those who at the time had the title of knights had abandoned their corresponding function and, given the deterioration of their ethical and social qualities, could not be the ones to reform a "detestable age" to which they themselves belonged; second, because in order to propose such a reform it would be necessary to count on knights as far removed from this world as are those who dream of that utopia with its impossible warriors, preachers, priests, villagers, and so on. They would be knights going through the countryside armed in the name of justice and peace and cutting the inappropriate and ridiculous figure of Don Quixote, hero of all failures.

Cervantes, who was very familiar with the degeneration into which the chivalric experiment in seignorial Europe had been falling since its inception, also knew the vices of the modern military, which he had been able to observe at close range. The latter inclined him to heed the voices of true utopian protest (such as Thomas More's) against the modern form of public life; but the former made him realize the inanity or, worse yet, the positive danger in a utopian program of restoration or return, that is, a utopia of evasion. Cervantes, thus, could not fail to see that the wrong road might be taken, namely that of the adventure of Don Quixote, which is, without question, the road of the great quixotic failure. Cervantes's brief statement of his esteem for the work of Pérez del Barrio leads us to believe that his inclination would be to reform modern society by accepting the historical level of its evolution and trying to improve it and purify it of its serious defects. Cervantes as a writer belonged to those who, like Pedro de Valencia, González de Cellorigo, Sancho de Moncada, Casca de Leruela, Martínez de Mata, and others, reflected on the way to straighten out the confused, inappropriate, and unreal state of Spanish society by modifying it along modern lines.[89]

It is necessary, therefore, to see Cervantes between two poles. Both have to do with the vocation of arms, a decisive aspect for the formation of European societies prepared to pass through the political-military stage of the Baroque period. On one side, he was aware of the decadence of the traditional moral code of chivalric society, swept along by the vices rather than by the virtues of bourgeois life in its beginnings; on the other side, he recognized the increasing corruption engendered at least in part by the new methods of warfare. As these methods were dependent on modern socioeconomic life, they necessarily inherited its defects and perhaps some of its benefits as well.

In order to understand Cervantes's rejection of chivalric life, let us examine a small anthology of passages which focus on its negative aspects. The criticism of corruption in chivalry had already appeared in the work of its principal definer (and those who follow Menéndez Pelayo's line of thought and exalt the chivalric ideal in Cervantes must remember this). I refer to Ramón Lull, whose book on the subject Cervantes knew either directly or through the work of Martorell. Lull, then, wrote at an early date: "[If] knights who today exercise the office of knighthood are abusive, warlike, and lovers of evil and disaster, I ask: what and who were the first knights who lived in harmony with justice and peace, pacifying men through justice and force of arms." And the truth is, in Lull's opinion, that "today's abusive war-loving knights" are very far from this proper chivalric behavior.[90]

After this Lullian antecedent, the Archpriest of Hita is the next to accuse them: "to collect their pay they are the first to arrive" (1254c)[91]— a charge of covetousness, the bourgeois vice par excellence and the one most criticized by those of traditional outlook. Covetousness is also the basis of the chancellor López de Ayala's denunciation:

Knights covet wars day in and day out
in order to grow rich and seize a fortune,
and they only rest when they've sacked the land. (337abc)[92]

Don Juan Manuel warned that in the military profession, contrary to the common view, for defenders or nobles, "there are many types of deceit and covetousness, and in wars, moreover, even though the war be just, many sins and wrongs are committed both during the conflict and afterwards; for this reason, therefore, the souls of those engaged in defense are in grave danger."[93]

Alfonso de Palencia provides evidence that the prestige of knights was falling and that the prevailing opinion regarding their bad qualities was becoming a source of conflict among social groups. Opposing the defender of the traditional doctrine of nobility and chivalry, the villager who is so skillfully debating him asks: "What decent work do our nobles perform? . . . Do present day nobles deserve any praise? I will grant you that they are indeed praised, but against our will." He attacks the attribution of nobility to knights: "You see, therefore, how the false nobility of our day destroys that notion; truly, it would be tedious to continue to expose this corruption in detail." In conclusion, the villager holds that "it would be more reasonable for us to abhor the customs of the nobles, who corrupt everything in every way possible, abusing their social superiority, for whatever they possess for the purpose of enlarging the republic they use instead to destroy it."[94] Diego de Valera, a contemporary of the Catholic Sovereigns who practiced chivalry in France, translated Bonet's *Arbre des batailles* and wrote original works on chivalry in addition to chronicles of historical events. He has given us a burning condemnation of the customs of the knights of his time:

> Now, for the most part, the purposes for which chivalry was founded have been altered. Before, knights would seek only virtue; now they seek knighthood to avoid taxation. Before, they sought to honor the order; now they wish only to appropriate its name. Before, their purpose was to defend the commonwealth; now they wish to rule it. Before, the virtuous sought to enter the order; now base people seek it merely to make use of its name. In our day the customs of chivalry have been turned into robbery and tyranny. Now we do not care how virtuous a knight is, but only how wealthy. Now the concern of knights, which used to be with carrying out great missions, has turned into sheer avarice. Today they are not ashamed to be merchants or to hold even less respectable offices but are, rather, inclined to find such things suitable. Their thoughts, which used to be centered on the common good, are now spent on acquiring riches on land and sea. What shall I say? Our ways are so contrary to former practices that I am ashamed even to think about it.[95]

At the same time (fourteenth and fifteenth centuries) a similar situation occurred in France, the cradle of chivalry, and gave rise to harsh criticism of knights' neglect of their basic purpose and obligations.[96] To conclude, let us recall the accusation of extreme violence hurled against that social group by a political writer acquainted with the struggle between the two factions of the *comuneros* and the tension of the first half of the reign of Charles of Austria. (This accusation of violence explains why the utopian writer Guevara gave secondary importance to the chivalric element.) We are referring to Alfonso de Castrillo, who affirms that at present,

> the world having been corrupted by various types of cupidity, we now see in our time that the entire order of nobility has been perverted and destroyed and we perceive that justice, faith, peace and virtue are slaves of greed. For those who are supposed to live by justice now live by self-interest, and those who are supposed to live by peace now steal, and those who may have been inclined to steal do not refrain from doing so mainly out of fear but rather because there is nothing left to steal. And knights, who are supposed to live according to virtue, do not so frequently ride their horses as they do their own advantage. The result is that all things which are born of virtue and which are hoped for from virtue are now possessed, along with virtue itself, by covetousness.[97]

The author of *El Crotalón*, as well as Doctor López de Villalobos and others, repeated more or less severe criticisms. In the world of Cervantes we thus find denunciation and also, inversely, fairly clear reformist aspirations of a utopian nature which connect the reinstitution of knighthood with social reform. (We have spoken of this in the preceding chapter and we shall deal with the subject again.) After Cervantes's time the criticism continued—Suárez de Figueroa, López de Vega, Ferrer de Valdecebro, Alvarez Ossorio[98]—but these figures remain outside the scope of our study.

Having examined evidence of chivalric decadence, we must now consider the second pole we indicated; in it we detect the discontent and occasionally deep irritation which the new military forms brought about, especially after the middle of the sixteenth century. The protests of El Crotalón strike out at this target too.[99] But it is an expert in the "art of war," like Diego de Salazar, who reveals the utter condemnation of those who practice it, that has arisen among the people, the very people for whose protection and defense, according to traditional doctrine, knights had to exist. "These opinions have taken hold in our day causing the people to despise the military and to flee from any conversation with soldiers because the military order is almost totally corrupt and its ancient mandate has been forgotten."[100] Marcos de Isaba's Cuerpo enfermo de la milicia española points out many of the evils which afflict the military profession, an aspect historians have tended to neglect in speaking of the Spanish "Golden Age." We mention this subject merely in passing, for our purpose is not a detailed analysis of that repertory of defects and vices (especially those to be found in the huge economic and administrative apparatus of a modern army) but only to point out the public mood and opinions which derive from such a situation. The complaints in the Cortes in the second half of the sixteenth century against the outrages of the soldiery have been cited more than once and those abuses constituted one of the factors which inspired the waves of pacifism spreading through Spain and the rest of Europe at the time.[101] Similar complaints about the state of the military can be found in a contemporary of Cervantes, Mateo Alemán, who shares many of his concerns about society, even though he approaches the issue from a different angle.[102] But in Cervantes himself we find two passages that sum up all the accumulated charges regarding conduct and neglect of obligations hurled against modern troops, those famous "companies" and their various component elements which formed the massive armies of the Renaissance. These passages are found in the Novelas ejemplares, which contain the most directly critical elements of Cervantes's work. When the dog Berganza tells how he joined the retinue of a company of soldiers, he says that it was full of bullies "who got out of hand in some of the places we passed, which led to curses being uttered against the man who did not deserve them. But it is the misfortune of a good prince to be blamed by his subjects for faults that other subjects are guilty of; some will steal from others, but this is not the fault of the ruler, since even when he wishes and tries, he cannot remedy such evils, for all or most circumstances arising from war are inevitably harsh, rigorous, and inconvenient."[103] And when the young man Tomás Rodaja, later to become *The Man of Glass* [*El licenciado vidriera*], enlists in a company of soldiers in order to travel to Italy, the author comments: "Already Tomás noted the authority wielded by the commissaries, the inflexibility of some captains, the rapacity of the quartermasters, the swindling of the paymasters, the complaints of the villagers, the trafficking in billets, the insolence of the recruits, the quarrels of the guests at the inns, the demands for more than the necessary luggage, and, finally, the almost inevitable necessity of doing all that he had noted and that appeared to him bad."[104]

Reflecting a current of opinion which he doubtless knew very well—the ideal of a rural society in accordance with the secular pastoral myth is a repeated element in his work and his life—Cervantes set up a utopian experiment: the restoration of the chivalric-pastoral world of which many people were dreaming (even though Cervantes may have been well aware of the error and insufficiency of such an ideal). That utopia, by its very nature, had an anarchical tone entailing the rejection of organized sovereignty. Cervantes wished to force people to reflect on the question of whether that restored world would be able to rest on the strength of a few solitary knights roaming the countryside (the assumed scenario for a natural life) and remaining almost entirely on the fringe of both the established political organization and what had formally come to be the chivalric estate. In what was this utopian restoration to consist? What road would lead to it, and what would its inevitable result be?

3

The Reform of Man and Society

Inner man. The role of love in his renewal. Adversity and virtue. His social mission. The forge of a new republic.

We constantly hear Don Quixote speaking, especially in part 1, about the order of chivalry, its laws and statutes. Every medieval person lived in an *ordo,* an estate which externally regulated and determined all activities. The new political climate did not eliminate this estate-based system. Indeed, the modern State in its first phase required the firm support of a society organized by classes. The spirit of the period unquestionably went beyond those old social boundaries but, still vacillating in its beliefs, needed the compensation of a firm social structure. In Camos's book *Microcosmia y gobierno universal del hombre cristiano* the class of knights is treated with all the inflexible ordering of the estate-based system, although thoughts of a more individualistic nature do appear frequently in its pages. Camos even defines the estate of beggars and lists its duties and rights.[1] In *De subventione pauperum* Luis Vives also speaks of the poor in a sense that is thoroughly class-oriented, and he even calls for the creation of an auditor's post in order to safeguard the purity of the profession.[2] Interestingly, this is one of the accomplishments of Sancho's short term as governor of the island: "He created and appointed a bailiff for the poor, not for the purpose of harassing them but to make an investigation of their real status, since many a thief or drunkard of sound body goes about as a make-believe cripple or displaying false sores" (II:51).

Thus, Don Quixote at first conceives his mission as subject to the order of knight-errantry. But as the book continues, he increasingly forgets to ask himself just what it is the rules of his class prescribe in the situations he faces, and his actions take on a more personal quality. In this sense also it would be possible to confirm the evolution of the knight's personality that Menéndez Pidal perceived in the composition of the *Quixote*.[3] Cervantes began his novel in accord with the traditional schema of the knight-errant, presenting him in a humorous vein, and he ended up creating a character who is much more than that. At the beginning Don Quixote is no more than an imitation knight-errant, and later we see him with a great reformist mission that individualizes his character and gives him a personality. In this, Don Quixote appears as a powerful individual, a product of that "discovery of the individual man" characteristic of the Renaissance. That discovery had as much to do with the beauty and perfection of the body as with the psychological and moral richness of the inner self. The Renaissance produced a series of works in defense of the qualities of the human being. Pérez de Oliva's *Diálogo de la dignidad del hombre* is typical. In it he affirms that painters prefer to represent the human body nude because of its harmonious perfection.[4] And it is easy to infer the enthusiasm with which man's inner qualities will be discussed in this work whose purpose it is to exalt his dignity. Corresponding to the triumphant display of human anatomy in the sculpture of Michelangelo, there are some similar passages in the *Quixote* which show a high regard for the human body: its beauty, grace, elegance, and strength are of great interest to Don Quixote and he frequently boasts of possessing such qualities. Recall the pride with which he describes his hand as he passes it through the hole of the wall of the inn to the young lass who he believes is the daughter of the castellan: "I extend it to thee, not that thou shouldst kiss it, but that thou mayest study the contexture of the sinews, the network of the muscles, the breadth and spaciousness of the veins, from which thou canst deduce how great must be the might of the arm that supports such a hand" (I:43). Yet that hand and that arm are not different from those of any other knight and are not individualized by their greater or lesser degree of mettle alone, but only by their usefulness for the particular and personal enterprises of an original moral personality.

Swept along by a modern individualistic emotion, Don Quixote comes to believe that each person is not what the order to which he belongs causes him to be, but rather whatever he makes of himself. The magnificent individualizing experience of the Renaissance was behind the renewal of the idea that works and not merely faith alone are important. (This reinvigoration of the Catholic concept of merit which occurs in Spanish thought of the time conformed in theory to the doctrine of Trent but also at times went beyond Tridentine orthodoxy.)[5] Don Quixote makes this principle his own and formulates it in sober and appropriate words: "Gratitude that consists only in the will to show it is a dead thing, just as is faith without works" (I:50).[6] For that reason, Don

Quixote will soon come to believe that lineage is something open and mobile, and that one's works are what finally determine one's social rank:

> All the people in this world may be divided into four classes: those who from humble beginnings have grown and expanded until they have attained a pinnacle of greatness; those who were great to begin with and who have since consistently maintained their original state; those who have arrived at a pyramidal point, having progressively diminished and consumed the greatness that was theirs at the start until, like the point of a pyramid with respect to its base or foundation, they have come to be nothing at all; and, finally, there is the vast majority who had neither a good start nor a subsequent history that was in any way out of the ordinary and who accordingly will have a nameless end, like the ordinary plebeian stock. (II:6)

Thus, some people manage to fall because of their works, even though they are descended from high nobility; others, starting from humble beginnings, reach the heights. What matters is what everyone has inside: "Virtue by itself alone has a worth that blood does not have" (II:42).

The Renaissance had so emphasized this force of personality that even Trent was unable to weaken it; as a result, it was possible for Don Quixote, agreeing with contemporary moralists, to reject or at least greatly relativize the concept of fortune, that other opposing force in which the first thinkers of the modern period (such as Machiavelli) firmly believed. For Don Quixote and the people of his time there is no fortune other than that which one makes for oneself: "There is no such thing as luck in this world, and whatever happens, whether it be good or bad, does not occur by chance but through a special providence of Heaven; hence the saying that each man is the architect of his own fortune" (II:66). The solution Cervantes provides to this problem of fortune coincides exactly with the one proposed in all Spanish literature of the period and maintained until the end of the seventeenth century. What is more, the hesitation and even the occasional patent contradiction between accepted doctrine on the subject and what is stated in some specific passage (a phenomenon which can easily be found in the *Quixote*) is common to all Spanish writers of the Counter-Reformation.[7] What is important to us here is to recognize individual force struggling against difficulties of fortune. Man is free and nothing can be an insuperable obstacle. Thus Don Quixote affirms the central thesis of the Counter-Reformation, in defense of which Erasmus too had taken the side of the Church by arguing against Luther. There is nothing in the world that "can move and compel the will... [for] our will is free" (I:22). Because we are free to do as we wish, merit is possible, for what each individual does may be imputed to him and to him alone. The unavoidable freedom of the human person, that colossal force of individuality, is consequently the great means by which one can reach, through one's own efforts, the highest level. Freedom, says Don Quixote, "is one of the most precious gifts that the heavens have bestowed on man; with it the treasures locked in the earth or hidden in the depths of the sea are not to be compared" (II:58).

Man, for Don Quixote, is what each person makes of himself; merit depends on what each individual accomplishes. The thought of the period insisted on giving preeminence to what is achieved over what is inherited. This theme was a necessary part of the chivalric construct and it coincided with the pastoral conception: as Jorge de Montemayor says, it is inadmissable to look for "valor and virtue beyond the person himself," and it is to be held that "he is quite bereft of the goods of nature who looks for them in his ancestors."[8] This is a line of thought which took firm hold. Overcoming the weight of his class beliefs, even Camos maintained, as did so many others, that "nobility acquired by one's own virtue must be held in greater esteem, with respect to the person who acquires it, than that which is inherited from one's ancestors."[9] The value of the person is connected to his very being. We can find an example of this idea in Pérez de Montalbán: "as if a diamond could lose its value because it were set in lead or surrounded by imitation stones."[10] A person is one thing or another because of his self; one is a better or worse person because of one's conduct, not blood. In an epoch in which the first experiences born of a new way of understanding science had demonstrated as a fact, and with all the probative force of fact, that there are no qualitative differences in the blood of individuals belonging to different estates, it was possible to set forth the moral belief, acquired earlier and independently of the scientific confirmation, that hidalgos do not have nobler blood than those who are not hidalgos and that everything depends on the individual's behavior. Elements of society now come to be recognized, on the other hand, as conditioning factors, and this explains the birth of a new genre dealing with the human condition: those utopias based on the nature of the individual, works which J. K. Fuz distinguishes as oriented toward the moral reform of humanity.[11] With good reason does Mucchielli hold that, whatever aspect of class struggle a utopian project may involve, its essence is always "the human condition in general."[12]

The principle of selection by individual merit began to spread through Europe and eventually reached Spain (although it never became firmly established, there or any place else, due to the weight of traditional class stratification). Martin has characterized it as a specific manifestation of the economically triumphant capitalist bourgeoisie.[13] In Spain and the rest of Europe (let us recall that France was still defining itself in the seventeenth century as a *société guérrière*)[14] this new way of thinking originated under the influence of other sociological assumptions, such as the contribution to military enterprises by large social sectors which were not necessarily the highest in terms of lineage. (It would be another matter, of course, for us in turn to connect this phenomenon with the erosion produced by the expansion of the bourgeoisie.) The conquest of America, in particular, made it necessary to give important positions in the royal service to a body of individuals considerably larger than the small group of grandees. These latter, moreover, would have nothing to do with the work of colonization, just as they would also abandon their participation in the military operations of the Old World, in violation of their traditionally established class obligations. When other individuals of less noble blood participated in these enterprises and demonstrated their worth and even their superiority over the old nobility, the principle of selection by deeds acquired extraordinary force. The ultimate and definitive support for this idea was, perhaps, to be found in theology, but the notion had already been secularized to a large degree. Of course all this was related to the new economic theory of personal success acquired by taking calculated risks in new commercial undertakings and financial activities.

Customs and conduct are what differentiate people and elevate one person over another: "One man is worth no more than another unless he does more," Don Quixote says (I:18), with a phrase having almost the character of a proverb. Every individual, therefore, depends on himself and can go as far as his energy for acting on his unique and irreplaceable individuality will allow him. "I have heard it said," exclaims the man of glass with Renaissance pride in individuality, "that out of men bishops are made."[15] One begins with people, that is to say, with being a human person and nothing else, equal by nature to any other individual, in order to reach any social state. "Being a man," Sancho affirms, "I may come to be pope" (I:47).[16] The only thing that matters is one's own merit or, at most, that it be recognized. As the century advanced, growing social pessimism would progressively bring about an emphasis on the importance of the recognition over the actual possession of virtue and merit. But at the end of the sixteenth century and even at the beginning of the seventeenth there was still a great deal of confidence in the possibility of success through one's own qualities.

All people, by being free, have an equal opportunity to merit through their works. Behind that position may be the Catholic theological concept of ordinary natural equality. Cervantes expresses it in the *Persiles:* "All souls are equal and have their origins in the same material, created and shaped by their Maker."[17] And in the *Quixote*—coincident with contemporary political aspirations—we see how this idea had recently been transposed into the social area (with a degree of secularization from which its efficacy proceeded), bringing about an equalizing of upper and lower classes. Sancho maintains, without Don Quixote correcting him, that he has seen governors around who are not to be compared to the sole of his shoe (II:3).[18] In this phrase we find not only a principle of equality, but the resounding affirmation of one's own opinion as a fully valid criterion for the determination of worth.[19]

There is nothing that is worth more than the individual, in whose personal deeds is found the cause of all merit. With the energy of his powerful individualism Don Quixote ends up breaking the mold of all social structuring by class, and he does this not just for himself but with an eye to his squire as well. Thus he is not inspired by an egotistical motive but rather by a general conviction. His squire could one day be elevated to the rank of knight or governor, or even attain status of nobility with the title of count or marquis. And he himself, the humble hidalgo of a Manchegan village, is transformed into a knight and sees himself as capable of becoming a king or an emperor; indeed, "a knight-errant, if he has two fingers worth of luck, has it in his power to become the greatest lord on earth" (II:39). In other words, simply through his own personal merit he can come to rule the world, it only being necessary that fortune favor him.

There is no medieval knight, in fact or fiction, who had similar aspirations to those of our jaunty knight of La Mancha. And the strong impetus of Renaissance individuality did not accept the temporal limitations of the present moment. In order to go beyond them and overcome them it aspired to something which became the ultimate object of human longing: fame. We shall presently see the role which fame played in the spirit characteristic both of the period and of the work of Cervantes.

For the moment let us keep in mind the extraordinary vigor chivalric personality acquires in Don Quixote. This is closely related to bourgeois aspirations and to the Counter-Reformation position of certain theologians, such as Luis de Molina. Both originated in the splendid rebirth of the human person occurring in the old societies of Latin culture during the period of humanism and were evidence of the expansive social conscience of the sixteenth century.[20] Having reached this point, let us ask: To what does humanism aspire and to what does Don Quixote aspire? That individual vigor did not come about overnight, as if at some given moment people decided to live as Renaissance individuals. Nor is it a question of being able to point out some isolated antecedent in this matter. We shall not make further reference to circumstantial economic factors, but must keep in mind that all of them (some more than others) may have had their part to play. We are in the presence of large and profound movements which took place throughout the Middle Ages and, conditioned by diverse factors, acquired new strength in the seventeenth century, ultimately making possible that maturity we see. With notable ups and downs, from the thirteenth century on there was growth in many aspects of Western social life. This growth, while not a continuous process (keep in mind plagues, wars, circumstantial phases deriving from the economy, etc.), can be seen in the flourishing of the cities and their bourgeois groups and in an awakening of new social energy. Here in this revival we find the energetic movements of the Victorines and the Franciscans and, on the heterodox side, the spiritualists, the Joachimites and other analogous sects. In all of them there seethed a religious zeal for the purification and perfection of man. Thus, humanism was formed within the context of the Renaissance from that multiple and many-sided heritage. We should not forget, nevertheless, that all those programs of reform which in some way Don Quixote attempted to synthesize, under the ironic gaze of Cervantes, rested on the survival of a traditional social structure, agrarian in nature. Agriculture has a wonderful effect on one's virtue, making people good and simple—and the cliché which Gutiérrez de los Ríos thus expresses is repeated (but without physiocratic intent) by everyone at the beginning of the Spanish seventeenth century who defends the superiority of agriculture. In the world of Don Quixote, as far as productive activity is concerned, agriculture is practically all there is, shepherding being subsumed under the category of agriculture in general.[21]

In reality, the whole chivalric movement of the late Middle Ages corresponded to that ideal of human betterment, and what the literature of chivalry offered society was a model of personal conduct based on the use of arms to improve human behavior. According to Campanella, the inhabitants of the "City of the Sun" say "that war should not be undertaken except to make men good, not to destroy them."[22] The originality of Don Quixote is to endeavor to have that reform include the protagonist himself.

What can one derive from histories, real or feigned, according to writers on chivalry? "Good examples and teachings," in the opinion of Garci Rodríguez de Montalvo,[23] and he consequently published the *Amadis* in order to inspire gallantry in young warriors. Conspicuous by its absence in those books is the internalization of the ideal, a phenomenon whose advent was prepared by medieval urban life and religious forms but which did not actually mature until somewhat later. Chivalric brilliance will gradually yield to an interior renewal. Petrarch's text in his epistle *De sui ipsius et multorum ignorantia* had a programmatic value for humanism: "You know, Lord, my every hope and desire, and that I have never desired anything more than to become good through the prudent study of letters."[24] The Pauline antecedent of "putting on the inner man" has occasionally been pointed out by historians of the humanist movement. And it is certainly significant that the moral symbolism on which the chivalric concept is based—arms and armor, for example—also corresponds to a "Pauline" source.[25]

The development of humanism in that direction was constant and continued to the end of the sixteenth century. Leonardo Bruni, in perhaps the most characteristic phase of Italian humanism, had already joyfully confessed in one of his epistles that "my special devotion is to religion and proper living,"[26] in which the "proper living" will signify both form and substance, because it is not only important to live well; it is also important that that living be in fact good and skillful. The moral perfection of man and society was the ideal which inspired so many treatises on the Christian man and the Christian woman, so many models of princes and perfect commonwealths. Spanish as well as foreign bibliography on these subjects is endless. At the head of all these authors is the supreme trilogy in the plenitude of humanism: Erasmus, Vives, More.

Erudition, literature, teaching, knowledge; all are means to a moral end: to be better. This is what we are to derive from the study of those who possess those means, the learned. "You will learn from wise people how to become better" was the advice of Vives.[27] The chapter "De litteris" of Mariana's *De Rege*, written long after "De eruditione," the sixth chapter of Vives's *Introductio ad sapientiam*, still aspires to that moral instruction. For humanism in its maturity, true humanist erudition, letters which really deserve the name, "not the silly pedantry of professional grammarians" of which Mariana speaks,[28] are not decorations but a preparation for life. (Mariana gives the example of Alexander, instructed by Aristotle.) Thus, Astudillo translates the chapter title "De eruditione" of Vives's work as "De la doctrina," for through doctrine [taken in its etymological sense of "instruction"] one learns to live properly. As Vives says: "This is the end of learning: that by recognizing vice and virtue we may more easily flee the one and pursue the other; otherwise learning is useless."[29]

True humanists properly so-called seek this renewal of humanity, which they consider the basis for other reforms, in the study of classical literature. They do not, of course, understand this literature apart from the Christian tradition still alive in them, nor can we comprehend fifteenth- and sixteenth-century interest in antique letters if we fail to consider its moral end: the spiritual perfection of man and society. To the study of Cicero the humanists almost at once added Seneca, and the fact that Erasmus believed in the salvation and sanctity of Socrates illustrates the moral content of his classicism.[30]

To believe fervently in the moral value of letters and in their sufficiency as a means to virtue is characteristic of humanism. The surest way to turn away from evil and pursue virtue is to be learned. Castiglione, reflecting these beliefs, spoke of the dignity and worth of letters: "Nothing is more naturally desired by men or more proper to them than knowledge, and it is a great folly to say or believe that knowledge is not always a good thing. And if I could speak with them or with others who hold an opinion contrary to mine, I would try to show them how useful and necessary to our life and dignity letters are, being truly bestowed on men as a crowning gift."[31] This should be sufficient illustration for us of how it is possible to reach the goal of human perfection by following the path of letters.

Letters and virtues, therefore, are connected in the thought of the period, with the understanding that we are referring to letters characterized by good style and cultivated art. To speak well and to say what is good are equivalents, or, at least, the second requires the first, which in its turn implies the obligation to be good. "Gentle," "delightful," and "sweet" are adjectives frequently applied to this literature, and they refer equally to the style and the solid doctrinal content. When Antonio de Guevara maintains that no hour is better spent "than by listening to a sweet-tongued man,"[32] that sweetness relates to what the man says as much as to the way he says it, to his diction and his content. (Guevara is alluding to Plato with these words, and that very fact confirms our interpretation.) Thus, for the humanist, rhetoric is a moral discipline: it teaches us not just to speak well, as does oratory, but also to move our listeners to good conduct. In one of the dialogues of Pedro de Navarra a noble and a farmer argue about the value of their respective ways of life, and the former, impressed by the sound doctrine and solid argumentation of his opponent, exclaims (perhaps ironically): "The rustic is waxing rhetorical." In the same dialogue it is held that virtues and letters can be cultivated in a desert but not among the worldly preoccupations of the nobility, clear evidence of the close connection that the thinking of the period saw between erudition and moral health.[33]

What the humanist asks of letters is a moral end; this is the basis of his interest in them. And that end is conceived dynamically, as leading to betterment and inner reform. Nobody is predetermined either to be good or not to be so by his social position, his family heritage, or by any other necessitating external causes. All are free progressively to achieve that good end, and since the means to reach it are known and easily obtainable, it is easy to understand the large-scale propagation of reformist ideas in Europe when these concepts came to maturity.

In Spain this reformative zeal took hold in the sixteenth century. The current of reformist spirituality among the Dominicans under the influence of Savonarola and other Italian spiritualists has been extensively studied.[34] It is not necessary to discuss the phenomenon of Erasmism, so admirably investigated by Bataillon.[35] Reform was the ultimate goal, reform of men and women,[36] of society and the commonwealth, of the Church and Christendom, of the military, of landholding, of studies and of the sciences. The goal was to bring new men into existence, as Alfonso de Valdés puts it.[37] Resounding throughout this entire movement (and any reform will emphasize the same point) is the Pauline admonition to "put on the new man." And, in the final analysis, such a bold and extraordinary aspiration does not stop until it has transformed the entire world. In another work of Alfonso de Valdés we hear the following exchange: "In other words, what you want is to change the whole world." And the answer: "I should like to leave in it what is good and take out what is bad."[38]

This reformative zeal probably did not spring from an intellectual conviction, critically formulated and set forth according to a logical system. It arose, contrarily, from the will and what the will desires. For this reason, from the moment the first symptoms of a new reformist spirit appeared, love acquired an extraordinary efficacy. In the field of religion, the mystics generally assumed a reformist attitude; the admirable work of Saint Francis and the first Franciscans was destined profoundly to shake the world of orthodoxy. And for the humanist, love is none other than the colossal energy which makes a man something other than what he was. Also, for all chivalric literature love is a source of abnegation and sacrifice, of the moral renewal of the hero. It figures just as prominently among the utopian conventions of the pastoral world.

Clearly it was by this double route that love's stimulus toward interior perfection, apparent on every page of Cervantes's masterpiece, reached Don Quixote. Juan del Encina sees in love the great transformer of the world, an ascesis that overcomes the defects and insufficiencies of coarseness.[39] Love estranges and removes one from one's self, as Fray Diego de Estella says; any great and true love "must drag a man out of his shell and out of his very self." Precisely for that reason it is a great means for the reform of man because it takes him out of what he has been, tears him from the roots of his vulgar, commonplace existence; and this is the first step—to be free of the old self—in becoming a new man.[40]

Because of love's function in the internal reform of man, a reform later to be reflected externally in his social intercourse, the pastoral world was incorporated into the chivalric, linking both forms of life together. Avalle-Arce observed this connection between them and noted its origin in the works of Feliciano de Silva, although he has made no attempt to explain the phenomenon.[41] Indeed, the *Amadís de Grecia* opened the way to the inclusion of the pastoral myth in chivalric literature (1530) through the utilization of the former's profound amorous values, values which had originated in the diffuse neoplatonism of the early Renaissance.[42] In pastoral literature, so strongly influenced by neoplatonism, we see just such a conception of love, very different from the goliardic or courtly love of the Middle Ages. Montemayor says: "Love is virtue, and virtue always resides in the best place." (Foreseeing the possibility that "the best place" might be understood in a socially traditional sense to mean the place of nobility, Montemayor immediately sets forth his theory of the value of the individual, quoted above [n. 8].)[43] In the axiology of the pastoral world love has a principal position conferred by its role of perfecting those who truly feel its power. This is the theory which Cervantes reinforces in the chivalric doctrine he inherited. Love refashions the knight according to the nature of the beloved. Don Quixote, therefore, says of Dulcinea: "She fights and conquers in my person, and I live and breath and have my life and being in her" (I:30).

Love, thus, brings out the inner man. It enriches him within and brings his soul to its center; it enables him to penetrate himself. This is precisely the meaning of Fray Diego de Estella's exhortation, and it is also part of the lesson of the mystics which the knight utilizes, even though the latter operates in the earthly sphere. Naturally, in the old books of chivalry all this was developed on a very superficial level; but as the inner being matured under the humanists, that zeal for reform and that love which impels one to become a better person gradually took deeper root. In order to take man outside himself and his banal and ordinary existence, it gave him a new being, which was none other than his true being, that of his inner self, the being of his innermost moral sense. Out of that profound being in which he was sustained by love, the knight drew strength to face danger in the service of good and in the aid of the weak and needy whenever he found himself in difficult situations. Whence the fact that the knight commends himself to his lady, not to seek her real and external aid, but rather so that by his remembrance of her the power of love may elevate him to his maximum energy. Therefore, Don Quixote notes that the knight, even though nobody may hear him, "is obliged to utter certain words between his teeth, commending himself to her with all his heart" (I:13), precisely so that that heart, casting aside all evil inclinations, may be inflamed in the noble struggle.

There is no efficacy comparable to that of love for leading a man away from his mundane, defective self, because nothing else can inspire such unheard-of deeds. And since everyone is what he does, there is no doubt that a love that brings us to such a level of action can also lead to an extraordinary level of being. Not even the force of law and punishment enables us to reach that goal. "This is the marvellous thing about love," Malón de Chaide said, "that what laws, decrees, codes, duties and

so many innumerable volumes of legislation have never been able to accomplish, love accomplishes in the briefest of moments."⁴⁴ Pastoral novels, clearly influenced by Renaissance platonism, are full of cases of the
effectiveness of love for making people gentle and benign, even those
who are not touched by it themselves but are only spectators of those
who feel its power. This is a frequent literary resource for Cervantes,
especially in *La Galatea* and the *Persiles*. We all know how, through the
invocation of Dulcinea, Don Quixote throws himself into the most tremendous undertakings (although in Don Quixote there are other operative factors of renewal which we shall take up later).

Not all of this need be attributed to Erasmism, for within the Erasmist side of Cervantes other prior and later experiences also carry
weight; yet there is no doubt that a colossal reformer is at the heart of
his inspired creation of Don Quixote. The knight recognizes that what
he has achieved by throwing himself into his extreme and unheard-of
behavior is simply this: to be "brave, polite, liberal, well-bred, generous,
courteous, bold, gentle, patient, and long-suffering when it comes to
enduring hardships, imprisonment, and enchantments" (I:50). That is to
say, Don Quixote considers himself fulfilled because he has renewed
himself according to a scheme of moral values that is truly exemplary,
not just for his own chivalric profession but for people in general. He
has become a new man, for he did not have those qualities before, and
he tells us he has acquired them through his personal and heroic effort.
Don Quixote wishes to provide a universal example of how one can be
somebody other than who he was, of how it is possible for human beings to change.

Bickermann noted the reformative character of Don Quixote but interpreted it in the sense of a "sacrificial victim." His mishaps, according
to this theory, would be an expiatory sacrifice for others to which the
hero lends himself, and his misfortune would serve as a recrimination
against society at large for a kind of behavior which drags the good man
down to so sorry a state. Our view, on the other hand, is very different
and closer to the research Luis Rosales has done on the double theme of
effort and failure in the knight. According to Rosales, humiliation and
failure constitute the counterpoint to Don Quixote's heroism, accompa-
nying it and in fact forming part of the same entity: his is a heroism of
will, a moral heroism.⁴⁵ What we are contemplating is at bottom the
problematic transformation of the inner man, and that problem is evidence of the fact that we have before us a reform of an ethical sort. Don
Quixote endures adversity not to move and excite others but as an ascesis
for his own personal betterment. It is not that he is happy to emerge
from an adventure with his body beaten to a pulp simply because sacrifice is his purpose, for we clearly hear him lament his pain and setbacks;

what makes him endure his misfortunes is the belief that at least something in him has come out triumphant: his courageous spirit. The blows which rain down upon his gaunt frame are an ascetic method of perfection for him, as is martyrdom for the saint. They are the sufferings which reform and morally ennoble the knight. And thus the word *trabajo* [travail] preserves the traditional meaning of laborious effort, of struggle against adversity, and even becomes a synonym of anguish, calamity, anxiety, something which puts a person's character to the test. In the *Quixote* and the *Persiles* Cervantes makes use of this meaning, ignoring the tendency to identify the word with the activity of the salaried individual who uses his hands as a means to economic productivity. (Covarrubias documented this latter meaning of *trabajo* in his *Tesoro de la lengua castellana*.)

Adversity, thus, can be at least as effective as success for a renewal of virtue. This was certainly the view of late medieval doctrine. In its attempt to construct the figure of the knight spiritually, it pointed out the difficult life to which the knight voluntarily had to submit; his willing acceptance of trials and tribulations have the same doctrinal function as poverty in the mendicant orders. It is a thoroughly purifying ascesis. Díez de Games, speaking of the real knights of his day, explains it in these terms in *El Victorial*:

> Knights in battle consume their daily bread with suffering; their indulgences are in pain and sweat, with one good day among many bad ones. They submit to all tribulations, they suffer great fear, they are in constant danger, they risk their very lives. Moldy bread or biscuits, poorly cooked meat; sometimes they have food and sometimes they do without. Little or no wine. Water from pools or wineskins. Wearing coats of mail laden with iron; always surrounded by enemies. Bad inns and worse beds. Houses of rags or rubbish; poor beds and poor sleep.[46]

All of this effects an inner transformation of the knight in his moral resistance and virtue. We know how far this position was from the corruption already being denounced everywhere in the fifteenth century and even more in the sixteenth. Cervantes, well aware of this corruption, makes Don Quixote an isolated knight without a chivalric society, something impossible in the real world of the time.

These virtues which Don Quixote believes he has acquired, renewing his soul through works, do not represent a moral scheme which Cervantes capriciously invented for the occasion. They are the ideal of the period, held by real knights who fought on innumerable battlefields for the Spanish monarchy. For one of them, Don Jerónimo Jiménez de Urrea, the title of "honorable" is achieved "by being virtuous, just, long-suffering, well-bred, truthful, liberal, decent, modest, strong and energetic in all adversities that may come to you."[47] The parallelism with Cervantes's text is patent. Don Jerónimo de Urrea, an Aragonese knight descended from the counts of Aranda, fought valiantly, according to the testimony of his contemporaries, serving the Emperor in the wars in Flanders, Italy, and Germany, earning a special reward from the ruler and eventually getting to be viceroy of Apulia. This perfect military man was a friend of Garcilaso and of the muses, and, a fine humanist as well, he translated the *Orlando furioso* of Ariosto and the *Arcadia* of Sannazaro. In imitation of the latter he wrote *La famosa Epila* as a kind of pastoral novel. A typical man of his age, he also composed a heroic poem (somewhat lacking in epic feeling), *El victorioso Carlos*. (Once again we see the attraction of the chivalric and the pastoral world together.) He is also the author of one of the last books of chivalry written in Spain, *Don Clarisel de las Flores*.[48] He is, thus, a living example of literary humanism and of the traditional heroic spirit, and in this latter capacity he is also the translator of a strange book, *El discurso de la vida humana y aventuras del caballero determinado*, to which we shall refer subsequently. Here, then, in Don Jerónimo de Urrea, is a fine example of the generations out of which Don Quixote emerges. He is also the author of the work we have just cited, *Diálogo de la verdadera honra militar*, a work which Cervantes could very well have known, not just because it had been reprinted several times in the years before the publication of *Don Quixote*, but because it was mentioned by Juan de Mal Lara, whose *Filosofía vulgar* is a known source of Cervantes's thought. We shall return to this work and connect certain passages with others from the *Quixote*. But let us first make an observation on the text cited.

Certain ways of living and acting allow one to acquire virtues, and these in turn, according to Urrea, bestow on one the quality of being honored. "True honor," as Pedro de Navarra also says, "does not derive from social status but from virtue," not from power and wealth but from being worthy.[49] This affirmation could be supported by a hundred other testimonies. We have seen a few of these, such as that of Montemayor, who shows us the same doctrine in the pastoral world. There existed, indeed, an entire process of interiorization of honor, which was made to depend on moral qualities and which was seen as a reward enjoyed preferentially by the soul. But no matter how thorough this inner penetration of honor may have been, there was still an external dimension through which one's honor came into contact with other people and was equivalent to the esteem with which they regarded the individual's name. In this sense the honorable person was the one who had a good reputation.[50] The tension and even outright opposition which could occur between the concepts of honor and reputation, that is, between one's own inner value and the external appreciation of it, was resolved in definitive harmony for sixteenth-century Spaniards on the basis of a Christian providential vision of history. In this view, sooner or later merit will be recognized, whatever the difficulties against which it may have to struggle.

For all powerful personalities from the Renaissance on, fame will be the object of the most energetic and widespread striving, and it will also be the prize of the renewed man. He who holds fast to virtue will attain fame. That union of moral renewal and fame is what produces Don Quixote's extraordinary drive. It is for that reason, he says to his squire, that they have to roam through the world "in search of opportunities that may and do make of us famous knights as well as better Christians" (II:8). The force with which fame operates in modern men is such that even moralists make use of it to serve their own ends. In a book which narrates, in Cervantes's words, "the greatest occasion that the past or present has ever known or the future may ever hope to see," that is, the battle of Lepanto, Mosquera de Figueroa writes: "Nothing is held in such high esteem by one and all as is the burning desire for fame and praise.... And this is something which all have engraved in their souls to such a degree that neither by force nor law nor custom would it be possible to take away this desire, acquired by right of inheritance from our mother Nature."[51] If, therefore, this force is natural, one can do nothing other than accept it and channel it. This gave rise to a Catholic transformation of the concept of glory and fame to which people so impetuously aspired; the idea was to allow it to lose none of its energy but simply to direct it morally. Moralists criticized Machiavelli's unlimited desire for fame as a pagan influence. But those same serious writers tried to stimulate that desire once they had placed it at the service of virtue (as they understood it). "I shall perform deeds that will be written down in the book of fame for all centuries to come," Don Quixote declares in an emotional ecstasy (I:18). So strong is the power with which fame dominates his will that he often seeks adventure "solely for the purpose of winning a glorious and enduring renown" (II:17). Fame for the Renaissance man is the driving force of history and politics. "What I mean to say, Sancho, is that the desire of achieving fame is a powerful incentive" (II:8). It was one so powerful and unavoidable that a military writer, Cristóbal Lechuga, recognized that "the desire for glory in a prudent man must last much longer than the course of his life."[52] And this is in a prudent man!

What is the reason for this general exaltation of fame and for its endurance beyond death? In the numerous praises written by the first humanists of princes, captains, and other personages, fame had no more value than that of satisfying pride of personality; in the hands of moral-

ists and reformers it later acquired another very different and more profound meaning. Fame was to become a powerful inducement for the
emulation of virtuous people. The desire for it would be stimulated as a
means of turning men away from evil and putting them on the path
followed by the outstanding figures whose renown they hoped to equal.
In this way the example of the superior individual would spread and the
favorable and meritorious self-renewal which he had achieved would be
more widely propagated. This is how, consequently, fame functioned as
a factor in moral-social reform. Pedagogical and political theory of that
time was based on example, and the whole psychological conception of
example was built, in turn, on this idea of renown.

Cervantes, in line with the mentality of his period, always keeps
within this framework and presents the glory and fame of the knight as
a result of his virtues, in the Christian sense of the word. His stance
corresponds to that baptism of fame carried out by Christian moralists
and utilized by all Spanish political writers. The point of departure is
the harmony between fame and virtue. Those who have achieved glory
in the world have been outstanding in virtuous deeds. And in the final
analysis, by acting in this manner, even if it should happen that fame
among mortals were not achieved, there would still be the certainty of
obtaining and enjoying it in perfect bliss *in vitam venturi seculi*. Many of
Don Quixote's talks with Sancho are prompted by his hope of future
rewards. In one such, after quoting various examples of people whose
reputation for virtue demands emulation, he says: "All these and other
great deeds of various sorts are, were, and shall continue to be a manifestation of the mortal desire for fame as a reward for notable achievements that confer upon man a portion of immortality. We Christians,
Catholics, and knights-errant, on the other hand, are more concerned
with the glory that, in ages to come, shall be eternal in the ethereal and
celestial regions than we are with the vanity of that fame that is to be
won in this present and finite time" (II:8).

None of this appears in the initial plan of the knight-errant as he
describes it to Sancho in the chapter on the adventure of the helmet of
Mambrino.[53] Don Quixote winds up taking on an enterprise, which is
what distinguishes him from the traditional version of the knight. The
way to carry out that mission is through the perfecting of mankind. And
that mission arises from his discontent with the age in which it is his lot
to live and from his yearning for a better life. "Sancho, my friend, . . .
you may know that I was born, by Heaven's will, in this our age of iron,
to revive what is known as the Golden Age" (I:20).[54] There is here a
whole social and concretely political mission arising from the interplay
of three factors: first, discontent with the present age; second, a zeal for
reform which rises powerfully over that discontent; third, the ideal of

the Golden Age whose very name reveals its optimum quality. For the fusion of these three factors to occur in an articulated way, it was unquestionably necessary for man to pass through the experience of the Renaissance. Only under the influence of this new spirit could he have developed a sufficiently critical sense to be able to reject the conditions in which he found himself. It was also only after the Renaissance that he could conceive of social and political organization as a human artifact, one of his own works, a product of art, using the medieval scholastic term or, in modern parlance, of technique. Finally, only after that decisive historical crisis, that momentous cultural experience called the Renaissance, could man, laden with personality, find the necessary energy to promote that reform which would bring about better conditions and make of the *aurea aetas* not just a literary or historical recourse but a paradigm for the future. Of all this a man of the Middle Ages, a typical traditional knight, could have had no idea. This is what makes Don Quixote much more than a traditional knight and, even were he only to function on the level of humanism, much more than a parody of the knight-errant; it is what confers on him a mission casting him in the role of a son of modernity, albeit a fundamentally maladjusted son.

For, in point of fact, this "aspiration of a more beautiful life" did exist in the Middle Ages, and Huizinga has made an interesting study of it. But Huizinga himself observed that "three different paths . . . have seemed to lead to the ideal life." One path is "that of forsaking the world. The perfection of life seems here only to be reached beyond the domain of earthly labor and delight." Another path leads through the land of dreams: "We have only to colour life with fancy, to enter upon the quest of oblivion, sought in the delusion of ideal harmony." The last path "conducts to the amelioration of the world itself." And about this path Huizinga says: "In the Middle Ages Christian faith had so strongly implanted in all minds the ideal of renunciation . . . that there was scarcely any room left for entering upon this path of material and political progress. The idea of a purposed and continual reform and improvement of society did not exist. Institutions in general are considered as good or as bad as they can be."[55]

We have seen what Don Quixote has in mind for the improvement of man through our examination of his personal scheme of virtues. Beyond that he seeks an ever-improving transformation of his age, not via an immediate reorganization of customs, government, and society, but through the beneficent influence of individual action. It is the individual who is to change, and anything which depends on him will also be modified. Through his deeds and his example (which is also a kind of personal action) that better world he wishes to revive will necessarily come into existence. If he was born for the mission we have announced, it is because he possesses sufficient personality for it. "I am he," he tells us, "for whom are reserved the perils, the great exploits, the valiant deeds" (I:20). And that heroism of his, those personal virtues, accredit him for his mission.

We have seen evidence of Don Quixote's aversion to his age. The lack of truthfulness, of martial courage, and of a sense of justice are, along with many other forms of social behavior, defects which Don Quixote finds offensive. Medieval man may think the world good or bad, but he does not really know anything about historical ages. Don Quixote, on the other hand, is forever comparing them, and although his own does not appear to him to be the worst, he continually denounces it and highlights its defects. "Today, sloth triumphs over diligence, idleness and ease over exertion, vice over virtue, arrogance over valor, and theory over practice of the warrior's art, which only lived and flourished in the Golden Age and among knights-errant" (II:1).

This first critical element—discontent with one's own time, with "this hateful age of ours" (I:11), in the words Don Quixote uses with the goatherds—has a second one as a corollary in Don Quixote's mind: the possibility of reforming his society, especially in its public affairs.

"It is a troublesome matter, a proud matter, an imprudent matter and even a dangerous matter for one to wish to put the commonwealth in order with a quill,"[56] Antonio de Guevara admitted. Guevara is a writer whose thinking reveals Renaissance elements as well as a considerable admixture of medieval vestiges, and he soon realized the utopian possibilities offered by the modern period. In his opinion, if foreigners were to "know and debate about the conditions and customs in our republics, I am certain that they would find more vices to criticize than virtues to praise."[57] This attitude can also be seen to some degree in the author himself. He notes the anxiety and unrest characteristic of the present day. The individualism of modern man brings him to desire changes; with anxiety and unrest ever present in modern life, all such malcontents would "like to find out what it is like to be king, to be a knight, to be a squire, a married person, a religious, a merchant, a farmer, or even a shepherd."[58] A traditionalist would surely condemn this substantial increase in social mobility, but the discontent thus expressed reveals the sorry state of the present and is a warning that it is necessary to remake a society on the point of dissolution, ruined by desires, frustrations, and falsehoods. Like Don Quixote later on, Guevara opts for the formula of the centuries-old pattern of village life. "A privilege of the village is that there men are more virtuous and less inclined to evil, which is certainly not true in the court and the great commonwealths where there are a thousand who will prevent you from doing good and a hundred thousand who will incite you to evil."[59] There is no doubt that the words of Guevara (his caveat regarding the difficulties and the risks notwithstanding) reveal an attitude one must keep in mind while studying this period, that of wishing to remake society, a tendency accentuated in the following decades. For example, did not the doctor Miguel Sabuco dare to write no less than a *Coloquio de las cosas que mejoran el mundo y sus repúblicas*? For him too the key to the restoration of nature is in country life.[60] We shall analyze the utopian meaning of Cervantes's work later, our concern at the moment being to situate it in the current of social reform. In another work Guevara speaks against the vices and dangers of the court, and although he does not have an active plan for change, his sermon against courtly life has an undeniable reformist thrust. It is not a simple and typical case of the medieval *de contemptu mundi*; at least in some aspects it is complicated by a more modern view of the gentle pleasures of country life and the superior moral worth of the villager, which together constitute the myth of the Golden Age. It is in his famous text *El villano del Danubio* that Guevara succeeds in conveying this attractive image of rural life.[61]

Others have also testified to the "aspiration of a more beautiful life," such as Pedro de Navarra, for example, in his *Diálogos entre el rústico y el noble*. His doctrine, however, is less disquieting and is closer to a medieval attitude. In the literature of the sixteenth and seventeenth centuries references to the Golden Age are frequent but they usually mean no more than an aspiration to an ideal. The mythical Golden Age is generally seen in most cases (as with the readers of Ovid) as something past, and it does not occur to anyone to try to revive it. When Guevara alludes to it, it appears as a declamatory motif: "oh past centuries, desired centuries, golden centuries!"[62] In any case, Guevara did teach his readers to aspire to this ideal. Only Don Quixote proposes to use it as a target to orient the entire course of the arrow of his life, as something for whose restoration he must use all the energy of his invincible spirit. This is also the aspiration of utopian writers (More, Campanella, and all the way to William Morris).

This reform—to exchange one age for another—is our knight's whole purpose. On occasion people have pointed out the manner in which Don Quixote discusses public affairs as an armchair statesman, a political dreamer, but this is inherent in a reformer, according to the thinking of the time. Don Quixote believes that the commonwealth is something organized by men, not a given, and that, consequently, they may reorganize it. He also believes that one's personal criterion is valid to judge that reform. This is the meaning of that passage in the *Quixote* in which we are told how the knight, the priest, and the barber have gotten together to do what is so common in our day and was then just beginning to occur in ever-widening social circles: discuss politics.

Cervantes describes the scene: "In the course of their conversation they came to touch upon what is known as statecraft and forms of government, correcting this abuse, condemning that one, reforming one custom and banishing another, with each of the three setting himself up as a new lawgiver, a modern Lycurgus or newly fledged Solon. In this manner they proceeded to remodel the State, as if they had placed it in a forge and had drawn out something quite different from what they had put in" (II:1).

4

The Humanism of Arms

Factors in the reform of the knight. The role of old-fashioned armor in inner renewal. The baptismal significance of chivalric rites and Don Quixote's name.

To pursue an end implies, at the very least, that some means will be found to attain it, that there will be a way or (in its etymological sense) a method that will enable us to reach it. Otherwise what we strive for will not be an end, properly speaking, but an illusion or something impossible to attain regardless of effort expended. The end presupposes the means by definition, and if Don Quixote aspires to the perfecting of humanity, it must be because he believes that it is possible to reach such a lofty goal.[1] We shall now examine how the means of reform we studied in chapter 3 are manifested in the case of Don Quixote and how they affect the knight as an individual, finally becoming for him the principal path for knighthood. Keep in mind that if Don Quixote has defined his mission as the restoration of the Golden Age—a way of life for society— he has also claimed that his desire is to restore knight-errantry—a social way of life for the individual. Between these two there must be some link. It is my belief that in Don Quixote's view the latter is a means to achieving the former. We shall therefore try to see how the knight's reform is presented and what role it plays.

We have already said that love, in the chivalric world, was a means of arriving at the human model set forth by books of knight-errantry at the end of the Middle Ages and that the influence of mysticism here was also in evidence. During the entire sixteenth century the preeminence of love held sway in religious circles; thus, for Malón de Chaide, "all the advantages love brings, while they are many, ultimately come down to this: that fleeing and avoiding evil we pursue good,"[2] and consequently we remake ourselves by means of love according to the requirements of virtue. Love comes to be a source of new and rigorous demands upon oneself, the origin of obligations which the lover assumes. Therefore, provided that love remain within the boundaries of virtue and chastity, the way Don Quixote conceives it, it is the stimulus for an individual effort which leads toward the ideal of the reformed person.

To journey toward perfection is a striking way to travel, one which consists not in trying to smooth the way but rather in seeking all kinds of obstacles and challenges in order to have to overcome them. One of the challenges Don Quixote utilizes in the face of the pursuit of the maiden Altisidora, or the duenna Rodríguez's presence in his room, or the nighttime visit of the servant girl in the inn, is his vow "never to fail in the fidelity which he owes to his lady."

Undoubtedly, the love which rules Don Quixote's will is a powerful aid to him to keep his vow of chastity; ultimately, however, an elevated love of such uncommon rigor requires the heart of an equally extraordinary knight. Thus, the problem remains: What power could have so renewed a human heart as to keep it constant in a love which was, in the view of the period, so virtuous? This is proper only to a knight, but what is it that gives a knight these noble qualities?

Observe, for the moment, that the knight is, in Don Quixote's case, a knight-errant. Naturally, merely roaming highways and byways will not suffice, for when Sancho tells his master that many such knights are errant, Don Quixote does not lose a moment in answering that few of these deserve the name of knight (II:8). Even so, however, there is no doubt that knowing different lands and peoples has its effect. For Renaissance people, travel occasions inner enrichment and fruitful acquisition of wisdom. In every educational program of the period it is portrayed as a means of perfecting oneself. Fernando de Herrera, referring to no less an authority than Strabo, wrote of how "poets showed that heroes were unusually wise, for they travelled through many lands on long journeys."[3] And in this matter the knight-errant, who spends his days travelling from one place to another, enjoys some obvious advantages. All that knowledge and, as its harmonious result, all that moral superiority of which Don Quixote boasts are acquired from having dealings with the most diverse peoples, each offering the possibility of comparing and choosing those of its customs which seem best. In a clearly Renaissance frame of mind Cervantes affirms that "extensive travel makes men shrewd,"[4] and, repeating this idea as something which he sees clearly and of which he is firmly convinced, he tells us again in another work that "visiting various lands and staying among various people makes men keen-witted."[5] This view of the new phenomenon of travel is something that Cervantes transfers to his character.

There are two sides to this interest in travel which the author wishes
to reflect (not without a touch of humor) in the errant nature of knighthood. In the Middle Ages—a period certainly not lacking in travel literature, especially from the thirteenth century on—we already see the
beginnings of that relative frequency of journeying, a need created by an
insufficient commercial network which obliged people to move to try to
obtain the resources they needed to maintain themselves. (This was, for
individuals, a necessity similar to the one which gave rise to the itinerant
monarchy or to that which brought about the creation of the Mesta to
control the movement of sheep; it is a vestige of a migratory civilization
that still inspires Don Quixote.) But we must also recognize in that interest in travel the intellectual repercussion of social territorial mobility
which the economy and the consequent opening up of new economic
relations created in the Renaissance. It is this that accounts for the
words of Cervantes just quoted and also for Don Quixote's opinion of
the value of his travels among different peoples. Cervantes thus gives
expression to an aspect of Spanish life that was intensely felt from the
fifteenth century on due to frequent communication with Italy and later
with Flanders and the vast regions of the American continent; nor
should we overlook the frequent cases of interpeninsular migration that
the famous *Relaciones geográficas de los pueblos de España* ordered by Felipe II continually point out.[6] Alfonso de Palencia, Furió Cerol, Saavedra
Fajardo, and Suárez de Figueroa exalt the intellectual and moral as well
as the formative and informative value of travel. Both aspects of the matter are visible in Don Quixote, as frequently happens.

But what is new and most interesting here is that the trip is consequently not a mere physical adventure, a material displacement, but
something which happens to a person and causes him to be something
that he was not before. And what does it cause him to be? More prudent. For a sixteenth-century Spanish humanist, prudence is the ultimate
word, the one used to designate the overall character of the ideal human
type. [The word I translate as "prudence" is *discreción,* a word rich in
connotations in sixteenth century Spain.] It expresses a series of intellectual, moral, and social qualities the well-balanced possession of which is
sought above all else.[7] We should remember the innumerable times the
words "prudence" and "prudent" are used in the *Quixote* as the highest
possible praise of an individual. And let us especially keep in mind that
when Don Quixote is in Barcelona living the life of high society with
others and is at that very point in his development, consequently, when
others will be able to appreciate all the qualities he has acquired, he
stands out precisely as a knight of admirable prudence. This happens
when Don Quixote reaches the shores of the Mediterranean after long
travels through what were at that time considered very diverse peninsu-

lar lands, and after learning about customs, conversing with people, and visiting the most different sorts of places.

This moral and educational value of travel is comparable to that of letters, since "to converse with those of other centuries is almost the same thing as to travel," said Descartes[8] in words which express with the greatest clarity what people had been thinking since the Renaissance. We have already mentioned what humanism required of letters and the end it hoped to obtain through them. Cervantes himself holds (although only in part, as we shall see) the same view. Half-jokingly he writes in one of his novels that "if the itch and hunger were not so closely identified with the student's life, there would be none more agreeable in the world, since virtue and pleasure go hand in hand."[9] The praise of knowledge, which is what the expression "letters" still means in sixteenth-century Spain, is frequent in the work of Cervantes and is the occasion of some of Don Quixote's most beautiful statements. For Don Quixote, too, letters are a cause of distinction and ennoblement, lifting the individual above the masses. If "noble" and "virtuous" are comparable, both must rest on wisdom, that is to say, on one's being an educated person. Observe what Don Quixote says on the subject: "And do not think, sir, that I apply the term 'mob' solely to plebeians and those of low estate; for anyone who is ignorant, whether he be lord or prince, may, and should, be included in the vulgar herd" (II:16). Learning and study are for everybody: soldiers, lawyers, ecclesiastics, etc.

But we must add something more to this. The optimistic hope in the humanities had, for the most part, already dissipated in the time of Cervantes, and it was not to be believed that just because a man admired Cicero he would be virtuous. The "sweet tongue" of which Guevara spoke could easily conceal a bitter message. "A silly word may be spoken in Latin as well as in the common tongue, and I have seen . . . stupid professional men and tedious grammarians."[10] It is evident that the connection between goodness and knowledge had broken down (at least relative to the strong connection formerly taken for granted). But what could not be tolerated was that studies should be applied to dishonest occupations, or should be inspired by malice, because "learning without virtue is like pearls on a dunghill" (II:16).

This very point indicates a certain difference between the humanism of the *Quixote* and that of the preceding century, in spite of the undeniable Erasmist inheritance studied by Bataillon. Just as Cervantes had distinguished in the *Viaje del Parnaso* between a crude and base poetry and an elevated and noble type, Don Quixote bases his speech about poetry (to which Don Diego's son is strongly inclined) on the same distinction, rejecting the kind that runs wild in "bawdy satires" or "soulless sonnets" and praising the poetry of "prudent, virtuous, and serious-minded sub-jects." If it is true that "humane letters [are] an accomplishment that is altogether becoming in a gentleman, one that adorns, honors, and dis-tinguishes him," it is equally true that they cannot give him more good-ness than he already possesses: "The pen is the tongue of the mind," Don Quixote proclaims, and it cannot express anything other than what is in the soul: "Whatever thoughts are engendered there are bound to appear in his writings" (II:16).

Only with considerable difficulty would a pure humanist believe that erudition in letters did not inherently exclude vice. Yet Cervantes's period rejected this automatic equation. The class-based society allotted its highest moral esteem to the military (not just in Spain but elsewhere as well, especially in France), doctrinally elevating the interests of the seignorial class. In the sixteenth and seventeenth centuries privileged society, *toute guerrière*, held this view and even objected to any diver-gence on the subject. Montaigne felt that "the study of the sciences soft-ens and unmans the spirit more than it strengthens and braces it for conflict."[11] This also is the view of Don Quixote; he sees an unquestion-able efficacy in study as a path to goodness, and he would not hesitate to admit that one who is learned even has a predisposition to do good, but he puts his trust in other means to bring about his great aspiration of reforming man, society, and the commonwealth, means still based on the idea of "courageous effort." This is what inspires the quixotic enter-prise of restoring the age of chivalry, identified with the Golden Age, a utopian vision which Cervantes skillfully takes from a certain social sec-tor and portrays in the *Quixote,* turning it in the end into an object of ridicule.

This is the meaning of Don Quixote's return to an archaic ideal. Those other means that the knight wishes to put into use are, simply, a certain kind of arms. Thus we call the interior purification to which he aspires "humanism of arms": the personal qualities the knight attributes to himself by virtue of his inner *renovatio* are, for the most part, the human values that humanists with their learning also wish to attain, but by other means. Bataillon, approving of my use of a number of works on military doctrine in the first edition of this book, wrote: "Spain at that time had an entire literature written by soldier moralists or by mor-alists receptive to a humanism of arms and Maravall was right to re-search this literature in connection with Cervantes."[12]

The idea that the practice of arms ennobles the individual was of ancient origin, was very long-lived, and was at the basis of the whole medieval social system. Those who fought constituted the class of no-bles. They were the most valuable members of society and the most virtuous.

There was such a close connection between virtue and preeminence for the medieval mind that to affirm the first was to secure the second and vice versa. Finding an individual situated at the peak of the social pyramid was sufficient reason to be sure that in some way he had attained virtue. For this reason the knight was obliged to externalize his moral quality. King Pedro IV in his *Tractat* holds that knights necessarily "should see to it that their vestments and the arms they bear are attractive and elegant, and this for their own good, so that they will be respected and recognized by those who see them."[13] At the end of the fifteenth century, individuals of the military class in Valencia sought advice from a master in the art of chivalry, and he answered them with a little treatise published under the title of *Lo Cavaller* (1493). In it we can see that the image of war and the warrior's function had become formalized and converted into a spectacle in which its violent aspect had been toned down. Menaguerra's little book is a code for tournaments, duels, etc., and he therefore states as an obligation of the knight that "the gracefulness and arrangement of his splendid beauty should be a source of delight and admiration." He stipulates that the knight "not forget to bear well-decorated armor, the trappings covered in metal, brocade or silk, as rich and splendid as possible; his arms clean, burnished, well adorned with gold and silk; his shield embroidered or painted in elevated and gallant style."[14] Virtue was thus conceived as oriented toward external manifestations. It required the performance of acts of strength, valor, or loyalty at most, qualities useful in the war which medieval man always had at the very doorstep of his existence. The profession of arms gave rise to the class of knights, membership in which implied the waging of war and the possession of certain virtues. Hence this class was considered superior and was therefore granted social preeminence. All the treatises on chivalry, from the thirteenth century to the sixteenth, included one or more chapters (until eventually this came to be their principal content) in which were explained the moral symbolism of the different parts of armor and how each component puts the knight in touch with a specific virtue. Thus one understands why Lull said that "to keep his armor polished and to take care of his horse" are moral obligations of the knight.[15]

This idea continued in the first centuries of the modern period and was the basis of the respect for nobility in the majority of sixteenth- and seventeenth-century authors. "This is what it is to be a knight: to be a soldier," Camos said,[16] accepting the equivalence of what had come to be a merely moral term (and was already so considered at the time, although not exclusively) for the designation of a social class. For him "the military and the estate of noble knights and hidalgos" are one and the same thing,[17] and both presuppose virtue. Of course, the old hereditary nature of the nobility at the time, along with the existence of cases in which it was no longer connected with the military profession, made it necessary to add another reason for the virtue of the noble: his long family example of integrity. "Speaking, thus, of the military or noble estate, this is a quality which proceeds from the purity of famous blood, originating in parents and in their ancestors and extending to legitimate children by natural descent. . . . It is always assumed that nobility of blood accompanies the virtue of which it gives promise and, for this reason, the quality of the genuine noble has been and still is preferred and held in great esteem as something founded and for long years centered on virtue and honor."[18] In short, even though nobility is now admired only for its presumed virtuousness, in the final analysis what there is in it of human superiority derives from the use of arms and from heroic deeds which were military in their origin.

From the beginning of the sixteenth century there was criticism of the knight and his alleged virtues precisely because these virtues depended on arms external to him, on weapons which anybody could wield. And there was also criticism of the showy appearance which left the inner man untouched and, by adorning him pompously and perhaps even blurring his true nature, presented a banal polish, a trivialization of courtly manners. Sánchez de Arévalo has a low opinion of "present-day knights, who spend more on clothing or a small ring than on their arms . . . which they purchase at little cost."[19] Lucas Fernández offers us a humorous dialogue between two rustics on this theme, which has now reached the lower social strata:

> Shepherd: And just what is a knight?
>   Is it some verminous pest?
>   Or a fierce predatory wolf?
>   Or a dog who guards vineyards?
>   Or is it perhaps a little mouse?
>
> Maid: It's a man of the palace,
>   highborn, of high quality,
>   with fine features.[20]

This was a result of the nobility's progressive and effective abandonment of arms and of changes in the nature of the weapons themselves. Don Quixote wishes to return to old-fashioned weapons as a means of personal fulfillment; but this is not even the most interesting aspect of his undertaking, which is instead to be found in the fact that he emphasizes ancient weapons as a means to a kind of internalized, spiritual virtue in the modern sense.

Vossler has perceptively spoken of the transition from a nobility of blood to a nobility of soul. In an earlier period, merely belonging to an aristocratic social order was sufficient grounds for considering oneself endued with its moral ideal. But

> this perfect state could only be maintained by the avoidance of reflection on these ideals. A certain class of people, however, with the talent and the ability to represent things artistically, artists, poets and troubadours, could not help but meditate on them. How could they praise and sing the virtues of this society without first determining what these were and defining them? The works of the troubadours and the *courtois* novelists are full of doctrines, discussions, and sophisms of moral-social and ethico-political nature. The concepts of courtesy, moderation, fidelity, valor, love and nobility could not escape having their spiritual foundations examined and studied in depth. By way of that intellectual elaboration, little by little an abyss was created between intimate beliefs and external conduct, between knowledge and convention, between authenticity and hypocrisy. These differences became even deeper because of the zeal of the poets and cultivators of that social and conventional poetry; by the end of the Middle Ages all the splendor of chivalric, courtly reality and character had been left devoid of meaning, not just from the ideological point of view, but also because a new force had meanwhile made its appearance in political life: the bourgeoisie of the craftsmen and the commerce of flourishing cities.[21]

That new bourgeoisie, according to Vossler, posited nobility of soul in opposition to nobility of birth as a new ideal. Of course this means that it is impossible to reduce the phenomenon to ideological factors: behind it was the displacement of economic power toward a group we may by extension call bourgeois; this group empowered the individual seeking to justify his success in the face of the past, and therefore from its inception the bourgeoisie highlighted inner values.

In Spain, of course, coinciding with the process we have pointed out, the social appreciation of the values which make one noble penetrated the regions of the inner self. The sociological base was different, at least in part. But the new ideal would not depend exclusively on the new bourgeois patterns of life, an ever present connection in any case, but on the opposition to these innovations sustained by a large sector of the lower nobility who, seeing their base wobble and feeling themselves controversial, reacted by accentuating their stance and trying to shore up tradition. Of course what they lacked to accomplish this was their former real base, that is, the martial "travails" they had been led to abandon almost completely. For this reason they came into conflict with the new groups participating in the military profession (in Italy, Flanders, and Germany) who frequently assumed the services that the absolutist kings repaid with ennoblement. There was an increasing extension of the profession of arms to social elements who did not possess hereditary nobility and for whom true nobility had to be based on the intimate acquisition of virtue in the service of arms or other services redounding to the benefit of the absolute majesty of the divine right sovereign, in accordance with the new concepts of modern monarchical absolutism. It was these virtues which made one noble, not heredity; the latter, indeed, could even be an obstacle to continued military service.

Why does Don Quixote, an insignificant Manchegan hidalgo, not content himself with the leisurely uselessness of the anachronistic starving group to which he belongs, but instead try actively to reestablish a lifestyle that will open doors to the highest levels of society (society, that is, as Don Quixote envisions it in the future)? Because being a product of humanist experience (this must not be forgotten), he feels himself swept along by the individualist initiative to be something more, he accepts the humanist ethic of inner virtue as the means to this end, and he finds himself attracted to the Renaissance ideal of the natural life (in accordance with the pastoral myth). All this occurs under the form of the chivalric ideal, held in high esteem by not a few humanists. It came to be accepted that the alleged nobility of soul (defended by the new ethos) was closer than the modern military to the old chivalric ideal. The ideal of the knight and the concept of moral nobility went together in the visible, external use of old-fashioned arms, an exercise having direct personal application and therefore verifiable in its authenticity. Thus, while the emphasis was placed on virtue obtained by arms, and while the process of interior renewal opened the door to other means of access to noble virtue, there would always be a preference for means that preserved certain external forms of honor. In this sense there is nothing comparable, for the traditional mentality, to the spectacle of the knight in armor mounted on his charger: every piece of the ensemble is a symbol which reconnects him to a complete aretological system. And this is what people of archaistic mentality—comically portrayed by Cervantes in Don Quixote—wished to revive.

Undoubtedly, the fact that such a strange, archaic way of viewing things should take hold at the end of the sixteenth century and the beginning of the seventeenth, to the point that Cervantes would be inspired to put a stop to it, was due to an economically important set of interests: in the first place, the interests of the new groups who had entered the system of nobiliary privilege and were attempting to enhance the traditional force of nobility, then in crisis, in order to stimulate their own economic activities; in the second place, the interests of the wealthy upper nobility who, although economically more powerful than at the end of the century, began thinking of a return to that tradition which had attributed moral superiority to them; they thought that in this way they would be better able to defend their position against all the subversive movements and popular protests of the period. Neither the newly wealthy bourgeois nor nobles with huge, tax-free patrimonies participated in the quixotic vision, but they did contribute to maintaining an attitude which could inspire that hope among the lesser nobles in need of improving their status. In the face of the latter's desperate situation—which had obtained for more than half a century—the only possibility was to support the utopia of traditional restoration (whose potential nonconformist aspects, part of every utopia, were not particularly virulent at the time); this utopian tactic would help maintain the repertoire of social values on which the system of full nobiliary privilege had been based. Were that restoration not achieved, they would perhaps have to deal with the social rancor of poor hidalgos like the one Lazarillo had encountered in Toledo. Many such had participated in social disturbances, and they could constitute support for rebellious popular movements.[22] In the refeudalization initiated at the end of the sixteenth century, the nobles and rich landholders had thought to lend greater support to renewed agrarian life by revitalizing the chivalric-pastoral utopia of the beginning of the century as a way to benefit the classes dependent on them for a living. The *Quixote* builds on this mentality in order to present the utopian figures of the knight and squire. (We have already mentioned how Cervantes soon realized what direction this idea could take and thereby altered the meaning of his work.)

In this attempt at chivalric reconstruction it was supposed that, just as there was a more intimate *devotio moderna,* so also was there a more personal "modern" use of arms. By means of it one sought to demonstrate not only strength of body but also of soul; not only courage in the attack but courage to be just and to do one's duty.[23] In the process one acquired all the other qualities which distinguished the good man from others. Such an ideological sublimation pleased the lower nobles, for it favored their integration into the new seignorial society and was not prejudicial to the powerful; rather, it provided some moral-social support in favor of all the privileged.

This new moral sense of arms was part of the thought of the period, inherited from the Middle Ages, although a process of transformation began from the very moment in which virtue and honor started to penetrate the interior of consciousness, and from this there was no turning back. There is in this respect a marked difference between the books of chivalry and the *Quixote.*[24]

Nevertheless, traditional chivalric doctrine was an antecedent of the quixotic focus. Ramón Lull already states that the knight must have the four cardinal and the three theological virtues.[25] Again sounding a Pauline note, he confers upon him the mission of succoring widows, orphans, and invalids, and aiding those who are inferior in nobility and strength, especially peasants (as was to be expected in that society); his task is to support justice by aiding judges whenever he himself cannot act as judge.[26] Pedro IV requires of knights, in addition to good intelligence and the regular exercise of their profession, the four cardinal virtues and good habits.[27] We could put together an ample anthology on this subject using late medieval texts, but we cite here just a few examples. The translator and commentator of Egidio Colonna, Juan García de Castrojeriz, admonishes the knight "vigorously to defend widows and men who are too weak to protect their rights."[28] Sánchez de Arévalo agrees, for his friendly relations with Italian humanists resulted in influences of this sort in parts of his work: according to this bishop, who was castellan of Sant'Angelo in Rome, the knight's duty is "to protect and defend widows, orphans and the wretched."[29] The fragment of *Guillem de Vàroich* we have already mentioned offers an ample picture: "It is meet, thus, that a knight be braver and have in his person wisdom, loyalty, sincerity, liberality, fortitude, mercy, and that he assume the care of orphans and defenseless widows, for our Lord God will help him at all times."[30] Finally, Díez de Games gives us a systematic vision of his moral compendium:

> What qualities must the good knight possess? He must be noble. What does "nobility" require? That his heart be ruled by virtues. By which virtues? By the ones I mentioned above. These four virtues are sisters; they are so connected that he who has one has all of them; and he who lacks one of them lacks all of them. Thus the virtuous knight must be cautious and prudent, just in his judgments, temperate and restrained, strong and brave; and along with these virtues he must have great faith in God and hope in his glory, believing that he will receive the reward for any good he may do, and he must have charity and love for all.[31]

Virtue, thus, was the goal of arms as much as of letters, regardless of the exceptions to this rule which might occur. The very possibility of comparing arms and letters (which is, as we know, a frequent topic of humanist literature) indicates that for humanism they possessed a basic homogeneity, for only similar things can be compared. Thus, in a work as representative as Castiglione's *The Book of the Courtier*, when the subject is broached, the one who defends arms notes that their use requires not only good physical condition but noble spiritual qualities as well, for "the practice of arms pertains to both the soul and the body."[32] And the Renaissance author Pérez de Oliva holds that the job of those who bear arms is similar to the purpose of learning, namely "to sweat in the fields in the service of virtue."[33]

These words seem to define the enterprise of Don Quixote. Otherwise, why would he have chosen such a difficult profession? He explains why: "I am aware that the path of virtue is a straight and narrow one, while that of vice is a broad and spacious highway. I realize that the ends and goals are different in the two cases, the highroad of vice leading to death, while virtue's narrow, thorny trail conducts us to life, and not a life that has a mortal close, but life everlasting" (II:6). This, as Don Quixote tells his niece, is the only reason he has chosen such a difficult way of life, for difficulty is, paradoxically, the easiest road to virtue. In previous chapters we have already given passages which clearly elucidate this idea, passages which we have taken from Díez de Games and Juan de Lucena. Even among humanists the renewal of ascesis in modern centuries has this sense of personal reform, of becoming virtuous. Luis Vives wrote: "It frequently happens that harm to one's body or material possessions is a pathway to the acquisition of virtue."[34] What is admirable and extraordinary about service to virtue is the fact that one serves her in order to acquire her and make her one's own. One must fight both on her behalf and in order to possess her, and there is nothing better, therefore, than to make of one's entire life a combat and so obtain her in that way. Thus, what Petrarch asks of letters is what Don Quixote believes he has achieved through arms. It is the same thing that García de Paredes asked of the good captain in real army life: he should be "merciful, affable, kind, humane and gentle." He had previously said that he should be humble, and he later added, among other things, chaste and modest.[35] But nobody forms such a complete and personal picture of internal *renovatio* as does Don Quixote: "As for myself, I may say that, since becoming a knight-errant, I am brave, polite, liberal, well-bred, generous, courteous, bold, gentle, patient and long-suffering when it comes to enduring hardships, imprisonment, and enchantments" (I:50). This passage bears frequent repetition.

Charismatic elements play only a small role in that resulting moral perfection; on only one incidental occasion can we speak of the knight as sent forth by God, and the affirmation (in another section) that it is a sin to oppose a knight is merely rhetorical. For Don Quixote moral perfection is the result of a very difficult human effort: he possesses those virtues "since becoming a knight-errant," as he tells us. And what does this mean? Since he has taken up arms. For this reason his work as a combatant has certain limits which are determined by the end he pursues:

> And so, Sancho, our deeds should not exceed those limits set by the Christian religion which we profess. In confronting giants, it is the sin of pride that we slay, even as we combat envy with generosity and goodness of heart; anger, with equanimity and a calm bearing; gluttony and an overfondness for sleep, by eating little when we do eat and by keeping long vigils; lust and lewdness, with the loyalty we show to

those whom we have made the mistresses of our affections; and sloth,
by going everywhere in the world in search of opportunities that may
and do make of us famous knights as well as better Christians. (II:8)

Don Quixote's arms and the enterprise to which he applies them typically respond to a moral ideal. If the lance he uses and the arm that
wields it are strong, it is because spiritual fortitude is a personal quality
of heroes. If the helmet or buckler with which he endures enemy blows
are resistant, it is because effort sustains his will. Naturally, therefore, it
is quite fitting that the result of those arms and that energetic combat
should also be a moral end. Whence that symbolism of the arms of the
knight we mentioned earlier,[36] which occurs (significantly for the point
we have been making) even in a work such as Erasmus's *Enquiridion* and
is still very much alive in the *Quixote*.

The progressive internalization of the arms of the knight is a characteristic of the modern era which dates from the origins of the humanist movement and became increasingly pronounced. It would be useful
to study the degree to which this internalization depended on Augustinian spiritual influence on the chivalric world, which it ultimately over-
came and eliminated.[37] Petrarch's moral works were extremely popular
in Spain during the sixteenth century and their author was praised not
only as a poet and orator but also as an admirable philosopher. In the
Spanish translation of one of the dialogues of his often reprinted *De los
remedios contra próspera y adversa fortuna*[38] we find the following exchange under the expressive title "Dialogue on the Dignity of Knighthood":

"I am a man of arms."
"Why arm yourself on the outside? The war, after all, is within
our souls, attacked and put to siege by the vices."
"I'm known for my triumphs and victories."
"Many times it happens that evil is better known than good, and a
threatening storm more noticed than the calm. In any case, what you
mean is that you have won titles you can leave to your bones, things
for the masses to talk about, but nothing for yourself."[39]

The interior battle, fought with equally interior weapons, is the one
that counts. A person will emerge remade from it, and this idea, with
roots in stoicism, combines perfectly well with the moral basis of culture
and with the whole understanding of life on the part of sixteenth-
century moralists. These writers exalted the value of works, but at the
same time they did not measure this value in terms of external results, in
part because they were offering an alternate solution that would correspond with the constant military defeats suffered by Catholic Christians
since the middle of the century. In this context that process of internal-

ization in the Spanish sixteenth and seventeenth centuries was closely connected to religious feeling. In Salas Barbadillo's portrayal of the perfect knight (1620) some external features remained, such as enjoying the hunt, dancing gracefully, having useful and suitable knowledge of natural and moral philosophy, mathematics, and politics, and acquiring skill in arms. All this, however, merited scant attention from the author. Only something entirely different would free the knight from a disordered life and allow him to safeguard his noble condition. He would not be able to hold fast to a perfect line of conduct "if he did not have in his spirit and understanding just as many interior weapons with which to defend himself."[40]

Precisely in relation to this, certain social sectors of the period believed (and Cervantes shows this in his novel) that it was necessary to add to that inner energy an external application in the use of chivalric arms, for the latter were the mainstay of those inner resources, strengthening them and stimulating their development. Once the arms of the chivalric profession were abandoned, it would be easy to fall into idleness, which engenders all those vices so repeatedly pointed out in the false courtier knights of the day.

Only the active work of a knight who fights and exerts himself makes virtue secure. Perfectly compatible with this is the condemnation (in Guevara and others) of the forces of conquest, which are contrasted with the idea of chivalry as a vehicle of personal renewal.[41] In this sense, one cannot merely repeat what Mosquera de Figueroa assured us about the military and the orders of knighthood, namely "that they are what resists the violence of the barbarous, represses the tyranny of the proud, and punishes and subjugates the impious";[42] it must be held, rather, that the profession of arms achieves all those effects within the person who dedicates himself to it by overcoming the inclinations to evil which may subjugate the soul if we are not properly vigilant. Thus, a professional military man such as Jiménez de Urrea noted that the first victory a good soldier has to win is over himself. The theme of "victory over self" is typical of the period, and Melchor Cano dedicated an extensive treatise to the topic (an amplification of an earlier one mainly on a different subject).[43] The idea was even taken up by military literature. That is the main battle in which Don Quixote engages, and it is with good reason that Sancho presents him as the victor when he finally returns to his native land: "Open your arms and receive also your other son, Don Quixote, who returns vanquished by the arms of another but a victor over himself; and this, so I have been told, is the greatest victory that could be desired" (II:72).

In short, in the appreciation of martial exercises external success came to have strictly secondary importance. The important thing, no

matter what the visible results might be, was whatever may have tran-
spired within the combatant and that he should have exerted himself,
arms in hand, until he was able to defeat his evil inner inclinations. At
the end of the fight enchanters or other enemy forces "may take my luck
away, but to deprive me of my strength and courage is an impossibility"
(II:17). What matters to Don Quixote in those cases in which he for-
goes a potential battle is not that this or that enemy may go undefeated,
but that his virtue—and his honor, its public manifestation—remain un-
stained; in other words, that he win a moral victory. The historian and
captain Don Luis de Avila had praised Charles V, victor of the Schmalkaldic League, with the same words used by Don Quixote: everything
on that occasion had been performed by the Caesar "with that vigor and
energy which are necessary so that he will deserve to surpass former
captains in fame just as much as he is their superior in virtue and
goodness."[44] Note that in these lines we see a scheme of values parallel
to the one utilized by Cervantes.

This is nothing other than traditional heroism renewed by the experience of humanism while keeping its previous basis. A daring feat of
arms is not in itself heroic. Heroism is an internal and total condition of
the person; the concept had transcended the sphere of martial activities
and was applied to all labor or effort of high ethical tension. When the
Petrarchist Don Pedro de Portugal spoke of the "heroic degree" of virtue, he added the following gloss: "Four grades or steps may be attributed to all virtue by means of which we ascend to happiness and eternal
glory. . . . The last and highest is called heroic, for it partakes more of
the divine than of the human; it does not feel the passions, nothing
harms it; adverse fortune does not shake it nor does prosperous fortune
disturb it; vices do not wear it down nor do temptations combat it."[45]
Do not these words seem to describe to us the moral quality to which
Don Quixote aspires?

Thus we can understand something which at first glance seems absurd: that an individual in Don Quixote's profession would boast, as he
does, of being patient, long-suffering, and gentle. We should remember
that Urrea also required those characteristics in the truly honorable military man. The fact is that the victory over self, the triumph of the courageous soul, is *tranquilitas animi*. On more than one occasion Don
Quixote praises such a lofty state, and he himself will strive to reach that
spiritual calm. One of the characteristics of the sixteenth-century Spanish mentality is that the virtue of tranquillity began to be held in very
high esteem. The moralists of the period gave it a name: Christian patience. Fray Fernando de Zárate wrote a treatise on this subject which
we shall cite momentarily. Thus, Don Quixote is, in a Christian sense,
patient and long-suffering.

Patience is the very foundation of virtuous reform. It is not passivity in the face of events; rather, the belief was that patience actually increases one's ability to act (and Don Quixote claims to offer definitive testimony on this) because it frees one from fear of adversity. It is not a petty way of killing time, like that of someone who carves figures inside an ivory ball. Strictly speaking, it increases time because it avoids crippling setbacks and permits us to hope to return to action on a higher level. For this reason the other virtues, all of which require a tranquil spirit, must be combined with Christian patience.

> Patience may be compared to bread with respect to the other foods which sustain the body, for just as they are good in themselves but are incapable of properly sustaining the body without bread, so that in order for fruit to give sustenance we need fruit and bread, and, similarly, vegetables and bread, meat and bread, and so on with all other foods, in like manner the virtues, although they are good in themselves and sustain the soul, have patience as their bread, so that in order to be temperate we need temperance and patience, and to be just, justice and patience, and so on in the other virtues.[46]

Fray Fernando de Zárate did well to explain the fundamental character of life (in a long and monotonous treatise) by choosing as a term of comparison the most basic food in a land where wheat was the most common source of wealth and well-being.

The profession of arms and his dedication to life as a knight-errant have led Don Quixote to achieve certain moral values which are not merely professional military qualities but basic human virtues. He starts, therefore, from the premise that these virtues are not class-based by nature. While there was in fact an entire class-based concept of virtue which attributed this or that quality permanently to one or another social class and which effectively recognized those qualities in members of the respective classes, Quixote can no longer accept that concept of the knight because he is aware of the existence of a courtly nobility which is not to be confused with that of knights who wield arms in real wars. Courtiers may, indeed, possess the qualities of a good Christian, but the esteem which their lives deserve, simply because they are courtiers, is always very inferior and even alien to that which is merited by knights who acquire real titles of personal virtue and authentic honor. Don Quixote admits that such courtiers "divert and entertain, and, if one may say so, honor the courts of princes" (II:17). There is no reason to suppress them, for they have their own function, even though it is a much lower one than that of knights who perform military exercises which are real and do not merely "appear to be such" (II:17). "It is right and proper that there should be [knights at his Majesty's court], to set off

the greatness of princes and to show forth the majesty of royal power"
(II:6). But their function has nothing to do with the high destiny of the
human person. "There have to be all kinds in the world, and even
though we may all be knights, there is a great deal of difference between
us" (II:6).

Don Quixote's theory of lineage and his concept of virtue rest on
the idea that human value depends entirely on the merit of one's own
works. The congruity of knighthood with such a concept and the role
that that institution plays for Don Quixote in this view of meritorious
action are undeniable. Knighthood was an appropriate means by which
to seek the reform of the person, not just because of its parareligious
nature and its moral inspiration, but also because it introduced an individual element into the Germanic medieval system of hereditary nobility.
The quality of knighthood, even though one might possess all the pre-
requisites for it (including nobility), was not inherited but was conferred by means of individual "ordination" in recognition of merit. In
France even kings, upon reaching a certain age and after demonstrating
their worthiness, were dubbed knights by a lord who already was one
and who could very well have been one of the king's vassals. (This occurred from the time of Louis VI to Francis I.) Knighthood and nobility, although closely related, interdependent entities, never came to be
seen as fully identical. And unlike nobles, who always had a feudal bond
of vassalage to the king or some other lord, the knight, as such, was not
a vassal of anybody. He owed his status to his merits and his works,
whose effects disappeared along with him. This demanded, consequently, a kind of action which would permit him to raise himself to the
possession of that superior, knightly quality. And what kind of action
does Don Quixote believe will be effective and sufficient to achieve such
a result?

We have already noted that a knight's activity is none other than
military endeavor. But if we recall what we previously said concerning
the changes that had taken place in the art of war, then we can ask ourselves the following question: Was that modern warfare, which made
use of technical devices that anyone could operate regardless of his personal qualities or lack thereof (as traditionally understood), the type
which would make possible the profound personal renewal Don Quixote
desired? Let us bear in mind that both More and Campanella applauded
the skill of the Utopians and the Solarians in the new art of war, and
they welcomed the invention of gunpowder. Cervantes had to reject that
element of reasonable acceptance of the present because his purpose was
to show the absurdity of a utopia of return or evasion, based on the
pattern of an individual who is "outside the natural order."

Cervantes was at Lepanto and therefore participated in one of the
naval engagements which made extensive use of new military techniques.

He had soldiered with those modern troops who depended mainly on gunpowder. He knew and personally had taken part in the new style of military life, and in some of his other works (mentioned in chap. 2) he shows how disillusioned he was by it.[47] Undoubtedly a bitterly pessimistic personal recollection throbs beneath the surface of those works. But that is not all. In the *Quixote* he needed to condemn the new military experience which on other occasions he had come to admire.

It is easy to understand that the modern military (portrayed as a cesspool of vice), if viewed from the perspective of a pseudoutopia of evasion, would not exactly be considered an ideal means for developing virtue in a soldier. This gloomy opinion was common in the period. It is worth pointing out the tremendous disillusionment with which another soldier, Diego Núñez Alba, speaks of the military profession in its new form. His work is a dialogue between a veteran returning from Germany where he had taken part in the emperor's Lutheran campaign and a young countryman of his who was heading for the battlefields of the north with high hopes and who was ultimately convinced by the older man to change his plans. In their discussion we hear the following:

> *Cliterio:* You don't want me to persevere? Why, I've heard that if reason, good breeding and charity were to disappear from view, they could be found among soldiers. Besides, that life strikes me as the freest and proudest in the world. And, as you know, freedom is proper to man and, as such, he desires it and spares no effort of will to obtain it. Anyway, it doesn't seem to me that this life is as difficult as other much more depressing ways to earn a living.
>
> *Milicio:* Happy are they who are able to learn a lesson from somebody else's misfortune, and this can happen to you if you'll just listen to what I say and heed my advice. As a person who has been schooled by experience, I am a competent physician to cure you of this madness, for I am sure that you will recognize it as such when I've enlightened your understanding with the light of truth. Charity and reason and those virtues you mention used to be found among soldiers.
>
> *Cliterio:* And why not now?
>
> *Milicio:* I'll tell you. When the king used to give special pay to good soldiers, many poor hidalgos who in their own land couldn't sustain their ancestors' way of life decided to try to sustain it in the wars in order not to see others who were not their equals getting ahead of them. These hidalgos spread so much virtue around that those who were not like them by nature imitated them in order to compete with them; and since all were motivated by a spirit of virtuous emulation, every day they behaved more and more virtuously.[48]

Thus, in the old days when a person—"the poor man of Spain"— went into the army, "they gave him such excellent moral instruction that anyone who saw him a year later would swear he was a noble."[49] According to Núñez Alba, however, nothing of this was left by the middle of the sixteenth century, and for many people—those whose outlook Cervantes portrays in Don Quixote—everything suggested that the problem would continue to worsen in a steady moral decline toward the final years of the sixteenth century and the beginning of the seventeenth.

The root of the evil, for Núñez Alba, was to be found in the profit motive and the corruption of the system of remuneration by the king for services rendered under his banners. Hurtado de Mendoza would stress the poor quality of municipal troops. Marcos de Isaba denounced the shoddy administration of the money used to maintain the troops and the corruption of the functionaries, which finally infected even the officers themselves. Our interest at the moment, however, is not to pursue a detailed analysis of these and many other causes of moral decline which were even then the object of more or less veiled denunciations. What is of interest, on the other hand, is to point out that for Cervantes, in the closed utopian sphere which he presents in the *Quixote,* one of the most serious causes of the decadence of heroic morality and of noble virtues (which some wished to support by making them dependent on the former) was to be found elsewhere, namely in modern weapons. All other causes ultimately derived from the negative effects which those new arms had on people who used them. Remember Don Quixote's aversion to these new machines of war and his condemnation of the abominable destruction of the moral fiber of the knight which they occasioned: an exemplary, faultless knight can die from a shot fired by a coward who perhaps fled from the sound of his own weapon.

At a time when military technique based on the use of gunpowder (which had had such a slow development in the late Middle Ages) was still in its relative infancy, Machiavelli held that modern artillery was no obstacle to old-style warfare and the valor it required.[50] In 1557 the author of *Viaje a Turquía* continued to believe that "artillery can do little damage," but he does offer this warning: "May God deliver you from the little pellets when the harquebuses are being fired, for it is like a swarm of bees, and if one does not hit us, along comes another that cannot miss."[51] To fight against harquebus shot or against heavy artillery balls is what Don Quixote cannot accept and what makes him almost doubt that he made the right choice of profession in the reckless age of modern weapons, for they discourage him by invalidating his whole purpose.

A long discussion in this period centered on the respective valor of ancient and modern warriors in relation to the weapons they used when they carried that valor into the fray. A representative Renaissance writer, the poet Fernando de Herrera, chose to defend the modern soldier. If it is an act of courage boldly to hurl yourself into danger of death, then the greater this danger is, the more courageous and meritorious your act will be. And in this respect those who go into battle against modern weapons have a decided advantage. "While [the ancients] had instruments and weapons of war, these were more frightening because of their horrible names and their fearful and imposing appearance than because of their real effects." Now, on the other hand, "Who can assess the force and cruelty of modern artillery, which the ancients did not have?"[52]

In principle, the greater the potential for mortality in the use of arms, the more suitable they are for making high demands on personal valor because in such circumstances the art of war requires greater bravery. Focusing the question from the point of view of the one who might be a casualty of war, there is no doubt that this position is logical; the traditional mentality, however, concentrated more on those who would be doing the killing and thus held that the wars in which the most people could be killed were the least propitious for the display of valor. The courageous man fights to win, not to kill, and the coward does exactly the reverse. This view was still held at the time of Calderón de la Barca, as shown by the following pertinent lines from *Amar después de la muerte* (act 3, scene 3):

> For valor is more commonly shown
> in forgiving, for killing is not valor.[53]

This is so, according to the thinking of the period, because the courageous man is sure that no matter how many times he must do battle with someone he has already defeated, he will always emerge victorious and he therefore does not need to eliminate him. Cervantes de Salazar clearly expresses this viewpoint: "Brave and courageous people never think that those whom they have once defeated will ever dare to attack them again, and the generous soul is content to conquer without killing, which is a recourse to be used only when victory or defense cannot be achieved in any other way."[54] To understand the connection of this idea with the period of humanism, let us listen to Montaigne: "Cowardice is the mother of cruelty.... Valour... stops when it sees the enemy at its mercy."[55] This was affirmed on the political, not interindividual level, in the case of wars whose outcome depended on personal qualities that would normally be the same on every subsequent occasion, thus making elimination of the enemy unnecessary. Of course those who took into account the value of the human person would affirm it in any event. This constituted another of the moral foundations of the utopia which sought to reestablish, along with heroic-chivalric society, the old-fashioned style of warfare as the most noble and effective path to virtue. Cervantes chooses to cast doubt on the entire enterprise.

Contrarily, viewing the issue from the perspective of the individual who risks his life, enthusiasm for modern war is the new and characteristic feature of society from the end of the sixteenth century on. Mosquera de Figueroa proclaims with open admiration that in his time the art of war has reached its highest level and is, he says, "more sophisticated than it has ever been." He adds that "no Spaniard, or anybody else, for that matter, ever raised it to a higher level than did Count Pedro Navarra, a stupendous inventor of war machines and mines; mining the fortifications of the island of Megara, he tore them up and sent them flying, the earth split open with mighty tremors, the shattered buildings flew through the air, and the men were thrown into the sky only to come back down to earth torn to shreds; a deadly and astonishing invention that causes horror just to think about it."[56] Here we have an early description of modern war, as opposed to the style of bygone chivalric conflicts with which Don Quixote identifies.

Because they hurt the royal ears, it was necessary to dispense with the gunshots that had been prepared as part of the festival in Valladolid in 1565.[57] But it is also true, as Mosquera de Figueroa says, that the squadron of the Marquis of Santa Cruz entered Lisbon, after the victory in the Azores, "with the orderly and pleasant thunder of artillery pieces and harquebuses."[58]

These texts we have just given date from 1556. In them one sees clearly the element of frightened admiration (or admiring fear) in the assessment of modern arms, but the literary cliché of referring to them as an infernal invention would last for a long while. A first-rate military man like Marcos de Isaba, although very much a part of the ambience of modern war, nevertheless accuses those who, not satisfied with inventing ever more deadly weapons, "sought and invented gunpowder and artillery, harquebuses, muskets, mines, mortars, powder horns, and so many devices of this kind that the only thing we can say is that some devil sent forth from hell put these inventions into people's hands in order thereby to witness the destruction of the world and more easily populate the wicked court with lost souls."[59] It is also true, however, that the consciousness of the period was deeply impressed by the heroes who fought with those weapons and by the knowledge and science which regulated their use. Lupercio Leonardo de Argensola praises captain Cristóbal de Rojas and asks what honors and titles can do justice to Rojas's book *Teórica y práctica de la fortificación*,[60] in which Spain is introduced to that sophisticated and difficult art of artillery, the art of using with rigorous precision that tremendous weapon, the modern cannon; for "even though it spews forth hell every day," this does not prevent Argensola from praising those who, like Rojas, understand how to use it, and he extols the good that comes from it:

This is your first son, oh Mother Spain,
who has added this science,
by study and experience
acquired, to your blazon.
With it you will bow the untamed
heads of a thousand barbarous nations
and impose, against their will,
just laws.[61]

Argensola, writing in 1597, anticipated the thinking of Saavedra Fajardo: firearms, far from being a diabolical invention, were an instrument of Providence ennabling Spain to carry out the conquest and colonization of America.[62] Gracián also admired the superior sophistication of firearms and the greater courage of the modern soldiers who fought with them.[63] Why, then, does Cervantes make that aversion to new weapons part of Don Quixote's consciousness? Because it is an essential aspect of the whole approach (somewhere between utopian and evasive) that Cervantes offers, basing his portrayal on observations of one sector of the mentality of his period. Thomas More was a stated enemy of the new methods of combat,[64] and Ariosto, Shakespeare, and Milton also concur with Cervantes in their opposition to firearms. Cervantes does not allow his knight ever to take up one of those powerful gunpowder-based weapons, he eliminates them from the world of Don Quixote's adventures, and he presents his hero armed and protected with old-fashioned armor. He does not even allow him to possess a single firearm in the collection of weapons in his house, and this in spite of the fact that they were so common that they frequently appeared in everyday speech: thus, Don Quixote himself will say that something is "a gunshot away."

Old-fashioned weapons had not yet become uncommon at the time, and in this sense Don Quixote's armor did not have for his contemporaries, and specifically for the author, the strangeness that they have for us. Among the things which an hidalgo living in a village ought to possess, Antonio de Guevara enumerates the following: "a lance behind the door, a nag in the stable, a buckler in his room."[65] Thus, there is nothing strange in the fact that Don Quixote should have such arms in his Manchegan house nor that someone should appear in the countryside with arms of that type. Although the following words appear in a novel, the passage nonetheless demonstrates, in its coincidence with Guevara's statement, that this was part of the reality of contemporary customs; we refer to what Cervantes says in *The Dogs' Colloquy*: "Just then, the owner of the flock came riding up on a dapple-gray mare with short stirrups, and carrying a lance and buckler, so that he resembled a coastguardsman rather than a sheepowner."[66]

But the interesting consideration is not that certain isolated elements of the ancient art of combat should have survived but rather that those old weapons had not been banished. In modern armies the pikemen subsisted along with the harquebusiers and artillerymen; and the desire to preserve the former influenced the thinking of a knowledgeable person in military matters, Sancho de Londoño, who proposed measures to guarantee that pikemen would never be lacking, even though most soldiers might prefer to be harquebusiers in order to be able to dress more comfortably.[67] Of course the massive use, Roman style, of companies of pikemen no longer had anything to do with the art of cavalry.

Naturally, the new military techniques had not caused the old armor to disappear because, among other reasons, old weapons such as the pike, mace, and sword had not disappeared either. Regarding this mixture of different types of arms in the period, we mention again the curious fact that the representative from Cordoba requested of the Cortes of Valladolid (1542) "that the nobles as well as the commoners of the kingdom [be armed] with pikes, harquebuses, rifles and crossbows."[68] A real debate took place regarding whether or not the armor composed of individual pieces had lost its usefulness. One of the most interesting writers on this subject, Diego de Alava y Viamont, resolved the question by saying that it was necessary to protect oneself not just from gunshots but from blows with percussive weapons as well, and for this reason defenses against the latter must be preserved. "And since I have heard some soldiers who were discussing modern methods of armament deprecate the corselet and other arms I have mentioned because they are no remedy against the fury of artillery and harquebuses, I say that their opinion would be valid if one did not fight against other offensive weapons as well, but as there are so many different types (and in reality harm from firearms is the least thing against which we need to be protected), I reject their point of view."[69] The extraordinary thing about Don Quixote, leaving aside the comic elements in the situation, is not so much that he hangs on to the old-fashioned armor (although he undoubtedly does so in an extreme way), but rather that he totally and systematically excludes every modern offensive or defensive weapon. He goes out into the countryside armed exclusively with those ancient weapons and never thinks of attacking anyone or defending himself by any other means. Our knight is not slowed down in the least by Herrera's warning about "the fury and violence of rifles and harquebuses, against which no resistance is possible and a well-tempered corselet offers no protection." To fall victim to a weapon of that type is of no concern to Don Quixote nor does he consider it a defeat, because his personal valor plays no role in it. "Supposing that they kill you in the first skirmish or encounter, or that you are struck down by a cannon ball, blown up by a mine, what does it matter? You die, and that is the end of it" (II:24).

Cervantes presents Don Quixote completely clad in the chivalric armor. How does this parallel his hero's entire martial concept? Cervantes, while wrapping the subject in irony, clearly sees the close relation between the pastoral-chivalric utopia and that particular concept of arms and armor. But what purpose does this restoration of the military world of chivalry have?

Naturally, there is a first and most obvious answer: It occurs by way of imitation of the old books of knight-errantry. But then one could ask why Cervantes limits himself to such an imitation, given the wide margin of freedom with which he moves, especially as the book progresses, with regard to the conventional and outdated pattern of that sort of book.

We can now see that the rejection of modern weapons, in addition to being part of the world of chivalry, corresponded to the reformist ideal of Don Quixote. The chivalric military conception is preserved because it is considered a means to the moral-heroic ideal which lives in our hero: the knight's method of doing battle is maintained as an exercise which leads to the acquisition of virtue and, with it, the moral quality proper to the knight.[70]

Whence the reinstitution of the knight's armor. Let us add to this Cervantes's disdain for new military dress. "Tomás had dressed himself in bright colors," he tells us in *The Man of Glass* when the protagonist exchanges his student clothes for those of a soldier.[71] Clothes, Cervantes seems to think, have a great deal to do with what the man is.

Interestingly, the very same rejection of firearms we find in Don Quixote is also found in a book which examines the renewed moral-heroic ideal of the knight in an almost academic manner, setting it on a traditional foundation but with an individual and reformist intent characteristic of humanism. There is here no ironic undertone, as in Cervantes, but only direct and full acceptance. I am referring to the *Tratado del esfuerzo bélico heroico* of Palacios Rubios.[72] According to this author, knights may fight with the agreed-upon weapons or, lacking an agreement, with whatever arms they wish, "provided they not be of the kind called machines or artifices, such as crossbows or gunshots, which kill men by traps they can neither see nor avoid."[73]

It is not permissible to make use of those inventions because they destroy the purpose of the knight and what he is fighting for. Palacios

Rubios himself warns us that "the devil invented such an evil thing, with the result being that now no one can recognize the virtue and mettle of knights in battle."[74] Don Quixote rejects them, for he does not seek in battle some good for the State or any kind of technical-military result, but a human and moral ideal: courage and virtue as individual values.

Since, however, "stratagems and tricks became licit once war was reduced to an art," as Mosquera de Figueroa confessed, we can see why, in Don Quixote's understanding, that method of doing battle is simply not possible for one who pursues the moral end that he does. To obtain that end it is essential that there be no obstacle to the realization of an act of personal courage, at least none aside from the shortcomings of the individual. And this act of personal courage is the only path to virtue.

What he desires is a knight who roams the open fields with no help other than his personal gifts and no arms other than those in which personal initiative has a direct and voluntary application, one who energetically and repeatedly seeks to perform courageous acts. Such acts transcend the martial sphere strictly understood and include everything the knight is obliged to undergo. Only by constant repetition of deeds of this kind can virtue be reached. Virtue is not a natural inclination but a habit acquired voluntarily. It is not, as Jiménez de Urrea will say, "a potency of the soul nor an effect of any kind, but a habit of freely choosing to do good."[75] Natural inclination has no merit because it is not something that a person has achieved but is a free gift and can incline one to good as well as to evil and to what is just and reasonable as well as to what is unjust and irrational. Let us return to Palacios Rubios: "Only habitual inclination, however, inclines man to put himself into arduous, great, difficult and dangerous situations, in accordance with moderation, justice, and ordered reason."[76]

The ideal of the courageous knight, according to Palacios Rubios, rests on three pillars: (1) free choice, "for while fortitude or courage are virtues, we can never accede to them except through free election";[77] (2) repetition, "for although one may write, sing or paint imperfectly at the beginning, if he continues writing, singing or painting, he acquires the art in his soul so that in the future he may quickly and perfectly write, sing or paint whenever he wishes. It is just the same with the virtue of courage, so that after a man has performed a courageous act once, then twice, and then again, continuing these courageous acts, he becomes more skilled at it and quicker to act until he acquires the habit of courage and can then truly and perfectly be called courageous";[78] and (3) reason, by which the author emphasizes the proper mean between extremes, "because everything must be done with moderation and reasonable prudence,"[79] "in accordance with ordered reason," as we have said. Along these lines, we should recall that on more than one occasion Don Quixote declares that in choosing this thorny path for a career he only follows his power of free choice, that he never lets pass an opportunity to perfect himself by taking part in martial adventures, which he conceives to be essential to his profession, and that in any situation it is his intention never to exceed the limits of reason; therefore, even after the "rash" adventure of the lions, when he explains his point of view, the calm and reasonable Knight of the Green-Colored Greatcoat cannot fail to recognize that "everything your Grace has said and done will stand the test of reason" (II:17).[80] And, through this efficacious combination of those three factors, what he attains is not merely the performance of this or that type of deed, but the alteration of his very being. Not to perform acts of courage but in fact to be courageous is his achievement. Thus "a man can and ought to be called courageous, not just when he performs one or several feats of courage, but also when he does not perform them, either because there is no reason for him to do so, or because it is not desirable, or because he does not have the materials he would need, or because he is unable, or because somebody prevents him; and thus we say that even if he is sleeping, he can and will be called courageous."[81]

The knight, therefore, manages to acquire a good habit by repeated good acts, and virtue consists in this. There is no reason to rely on what people are by their first and natural inclination. "How much more effective is practice for the performance of good works than nature!" A habit, the scholastics said, comes to be a second nature. By means of it an individual reforms the being which had been given to him and makes himself into a second being.

Through the tireless repetition of feats of arms in the anachronistic manner in which Don Quixote (together with a certain sector of Spanish society) understands them, he is going to develop a virtuous habit, a second nature, a transformation of his first being into another one which completely erases what he originally was. But this is a new being that is precisely what he essentially was before in his innermost being, the being which indicated his authentic destiny. For that reason our hero says that he was born for his high enterprise of knighthood.

To erase that interval of inauthenticity when he was no more than a petty hidalgo in a small Manchegan village and to testify publicly to his renewal, making people forget what he appeared to be in his years of falsification, our knight changes his name. That these name changes are common to chivalric literature does not invalidate our interpretation. They also were (and are) the rule in the most demanding religious orders. For that reason some people, such as Sánchez de Arévalo[82]—and Don Quixote picks up this thesis—maintain that the reception of the Order of Chivalry is "like a strict religion" which one professes (even though the Church never recognized a sacramental value in the ordination of knights, despite the participation of ecclesiastics in the ceremony). In any event, that ritual has a similar meaning in both types of ordination: to express a radical change from what one used to be, an inner renewal achieved through dedication to an enterprise. The difference is that in Don Quixote this has a much deeper, more intimate and human value than in books of chivalry. Without doubt, that sense of baptism derives from Catholic liturgy as reformed by the decree *De Justificatione* of the Council of Trent, according to which the sacrament not only frees from sin but also promotes the *renovatio interioris hominis*. In the *Guillem de Vàroich* it is required that anyone entering the Order of Chivalry, in addition to performing the vigil of arms before the altar, begin by bathing himself, for water cleanses us of our sins[83] (a secularized vestige of baptism by immersion). The Castillian Cortes of Madrigal (1476) had requested that solemnities such as bathing and washing the head continue to be observed by those wishing to be dubbed a knight.[84]

Don Quixote, when he sallies forth to fight in the countryside, is going to be somebody other than Alonso Quijano, and since he is going to be somebody else, he will also refer to himself differently.[85] What will his new name be? Simply this: Quixote.

Quixote ["cuisse" in English], a word of French or Catalan origin, is a part of the knight's armor, specifically the metal plate that protects the thigh.[86] It had not yet gone out of use at the beginning of the seventeenth century, and thus Alava y Viamont, writing on the proper attire for the three kinds of mounted combatants, required that men of arms and mercenaries wear cuisses and that fast horses be covered with half cuisses. But this was no more than a vestige, just as in the armies of the time pikes, swords, and even slings were still being used as offensive weapons.

Unquestionably the cuisse (and with this observation we bring our line of interpretation of the knight to a close) belonged to the armor of that military harness which corresponded to and symbolized personal courage. Don Quixote remakes himself internally and socially at the same time through the habitual use of old-fashioned arms, and for that very reason he chooses to name himself with the word for a piece of that old and, for him, glorious armor.

There is a work by a friend of Cervantes published in 1614 which supports my interpretation of the *Quixote*. I refer to *El caballero puntual* of Salas Barbadillo, a powerful satire on the typical courtly life of knights. Any rogue could pass for a knight in Madrid because the level of demands and obligations associated with the knight's social existence was so low. And that life at court was nothing more than a series of humiliations, effronteries, and misfortunes to which the author sarcastically refers by saying that "his every word and action was a chapter in the art of chivalry."[87] The norms and decrees to which knighthood was subject could not have been a more pathetic conventionalism. "He was of the opinion that it was the knight's duty to carry a rosary in his hand from ten to twelve in the mornings and a toothpick in his mouth from one to three in the afternoons." And as the author bitterly castigates this state of affairs, his memory goes back to the heroic character his friend Miguel de Cervantes created, inspired by his fond recollection of the chivalric ideal, but also convinced of its uselessness to contemporary society. By way of contrast Salas Barbadillo inserts into his chivalrous-picaresque novel a letter from Don Quixote to his own character in which the former requests that the latter, who has become famous for his deeds in Madrid, inform him about his adventures at the court. The rogue answers that they are more sad and pitiful than those which dragged Don Quixote all over God's creation from one failure to another, because in the court if one fights against malice, anger, and pride, he does so accepting beforehand the moral defeat of having to employ the very same ignoble weapons.[88] The "scrupulous knight" of Salas Barbadillo dies in a hospital, not in a kind of regenerative expiation, but as a sad end to a society that has lost its inner fortitude.

Contrarily, the individual who goes about the highways and the countryside exercising his valor and personal virtues through the employment of old-fashioned weapons as the final step in the apprenticeship of true knighthood may expect to be "chaste in his thoughts, decorous in words, ... generous in good works, valient in his deeds, long-suffering under hardships, charitable towards the needy. And, lastly, a maintainer of the truth, although its defense may cost him his life" (II:18). [The last sentence of the quote is Starkie's rendition.] This illustrates once more that what Don Quixote seeks is not to conquer others, but to create himself in his own ethical mold in accordance with certain ends and utilizing the means we have attempted to define. Concerned with the unrealistic paths which some people were attempting to follow, Cervantes's stern response is that such an attempt is impossible and, in the society of his time, leads only to ridicule and ruin.

Cervantes perhaps allows us to hear an echo of melancholy with regard to Don Quixote's reason. Don Quixote's reason! The ingenious phrase of Chesterton is apropos here: A madman is not somebody who has lost his reason; he is somebody who has lost everything but his reason.[89] With nothing but his reason Don Quixote was going to construct a world. And this, for Cervantes, was the mistaken utopia of so many unreasonable Spaniards.

5

The Transmutation of Reality

Sorcery and enchantments. Will as a power to transform reality. The external world as pretext.

As part of the social crisis of the period under study, many indications of abnormality appeared, from highly integrated fanaticism to anomy and deviance. As the process of secularization moved forward everywhere (although more in some places than in others), there were fewer heretical mystics, visionaries, pseudoprophets, and victims of possession, while the number of lunatics, on the other hand, actually increased. The latter were cases of natural disorder, bereft of the mission of revelation that medieval faith, basing itself on passages in St. Paul, had attributed to them. Rosen observes that "the period of the sixteenth and the first half of the seventeenth centuries was one of intense spiritual and psychological stress and strain derived from alterations that were taking place in the political, social, religious, and intellectual structure of Europe. . . . It is certainly no coincidence that the literature of the late sixteenth and the early seventeenth centuries is so rich in the portrayal of distraught and insane characters." Rosen mentions a long list of these, among whom Don Quixote occupies the first place. And he adds: "All of them are in some way an endeavor to understand human nature and behavior, to answer the question 'What is man and what is wrong with him?'"[1] It seems undeniable that a general answer to that question is found in Cervantes's work, which owes its universality to that very fact. But Cervantes poses distressing questions about those he saw around him, Spaniards who, in one of the most spectacular and apparently paradoxical crises of the time,[2] engaged in conduct that strayed from the path of rationality. It is only in connection with these circumstances that we can come to understand what the abnormality of Don Quixote's behavior means.

Don Quixote, a member of a social group that really was without operative power, is committed to a utopia of return to an idealized past. At the same time, because of his inevitable receptiveness to the society surrounding him, he is an individual whom we can properly call a Renaissance man. Impelled by a zeal for effective action, by a desire to mold his surroundings, he does not limit himself to rhetoric but works actively for the implementation of his vision. Cervantes took the old heroic tradition, which in Spain had been so long-lived[3] (and at that moment was alive throughout Europe), and linked it to a living example of modern activism. On that double foundation he thrusts his hero into the world to fight for his ideal. Whence Don Quixote's criticism of so many ecclesiastics who, unlike him, merely preach about political morality and enfeeble the spirit of those whom they should be sending forth to perform noble actions, and whence, also, his harsh criticism (which we have already mentioned) "of those . . . who, not having been born to the nobility themselves, are unable to instruct their charges in proper behavior . . . ; of those who would measure the greatness of great men by their own narrow minds . . . ; of those who, desirous of inculcating economy, merely succeed in making misers" (II:31).

But certain specific conditions are necessary so that this great feat Don Quixote proposes for himself may appear actually achievable to him. What does Cervantes do, then, in order to thrust his hero into such an extraordinary action as that required by his enterprise? He effects a transmutation of reality. This theme, the transmutation of the real world as a precondition of a chivalric vocation, is of fundamental importance for understanding the *Quixote*. We cannot, however, do more here than provide a few pertinent facts on the subject in order to continue the development of our interpretation.

There is a double transformation of reality in the *Quixote*: (1) that which causes the protagonist to suffer the effects of not perceiving things as they really and truly are; (2) that other transformation, much more profound, which he carries out in order to create the conditions of reality necessary to enable him to realize his heroic action. The former on many occasions causes Don Quixote to have doubts about reality. That incertitude is the shifting ground upon which people of the Baroque stood so unsteadily. As Guzmán de Alfarache says, "everything deceives and we all deceive. . . . Time, circumstances, and the senses deceive us, and, especially, even the most careful thoughts."[4] In a certain sense the theme of the false appearance of reality, the deception of the senses [*engaño a los ojos*] which external objects can cause us, derives not from the new Renaissance climate but rather reaches the modern period via the ascetic tradition. Here the powerful theme of worldly deception and false appearances occasioned a loss of confidence which was utilized by ascetic writers in order to incline people to detachment and even aversion to the things of this world.

The world of human affairs became altered not just because things pass and decay, but because weak human faculties for apprehending reality are easily sidetracked into error. Reality is not merely transitory but actually uncertain, at least from the point of view of its possible apprehension by the human mind. This incertitude regarding reality led Calderón pathetically to proclaim:

> For our eyes may be deceived,
> and things so differently perceive
> from what they in essence are,
> that they play tricks on our souls.[5]

Examining those verses carefully, we see that the incertitude resides in the perceiving agent and not in the things themselves. It consists, at bottom, in a weakness in the human being that always entails the agonizing possibility of error. But going hand in hand with this susceptibility to error was a deep and intense sense of the variability of things, a feeling which became a characteristic of the Baroque period. Baroque man, reaffirmed by his deep sense of the concrete and the mutable, of the incomplete, the imperfect and the real, rediscovered the edifying tendency to distrust what we see: what seems to us to be a beautiful maiden is, when she reveals her true self, a figure of death; what we hold to be a rich and desirable acquisition later turns out to be a useless object worthy of disdain.

> What further evidence, witness or proof
> do we need than the blue heaven we see?
> Is there anyone who does not believe,
> as is the common opinion, that it's
> a sapphire showing off its lovely rays?
> Well, it's neither heaven nor is it blue.[6]

That lack of confidence in reality had its roots in the "dream of life," that strange condition of our existence that makes it consist in an appearance, a mere representation in which things do not exist in reality but only as images, in which everything is just a part of the human comedy. That appearance of reality, that dream of life in which we are living, resembles nothing so much as the theater, whose actors, Don Quixote understands, do us a great service "by holding up a mirror for us at each step we take, wherein we may observe, vividly depicted, all the varied aspects of human life; and I may add that there is nothing which shows us more clearly, by similitude, what we are and what we ought to be than do plays and players" (II:12). And, just as it does in the medieval ascetic tradition, the "dream of life" terminates, according to Don Quixote, in the "dance of death." Just as we see in scenes acted on stage, "the same thing happens in the comedy that we call life, where some play the part of emperors, others that of pontiffs—in short, all the characters that a drama may have—but when it is all over, that is to say, when life is done, death takes from each the garb that differentiates him, and all at least are equal in the grave" (II:12).

Unquestionably, the moral-literary theme of the dance of death reappeared and was reaffirmed in the Baroque period, in conjunction with the thesis that "all life is a dream." But, on the one hand, Cervantes is still far from the spirit of Baroque "undeception" [*desengaño*], from that severe revelation of the true face of things, from that "light of undeception" of which Calderón spoke. (I wonder if Cervantes is not much more Renaissance than Baroque in his outlook, although the two terms, in the context of Spanish and European culture, are very closely related.[7] Perhaps, as we do in European culture, we should speak of an intermediate phase of mannerism.) And, on the other hand, in Don Quixote's view, the mutations of reality to which he so frequently alludes (and to which we refer here) are not the sort that derive from the fugacity of things or from the deception suffered by a person who takes life to be something more than a dramatic representation. Don Quixote believes in the existence of changes with respect to the way things appear to us, whatever their essence may in fact be at the definitive moment of truth, when our lives are removed from temporal flux.

In his interaction with the things of the world around him, Don Quixote presumes that enchanters are active. Burkhardt has aptly noted that there were enchanters in Renaissance Italy.[8] And the truth is that in the Renaissance the burning passion for the natural world had led to a considerable understanding of it, but in such a way that the discovery of new and formerly hidden natural phenomena, along with an inability to fathom the internal connections among them, produced a new flowering of belief in the control of natural occurrences by occult forces. If Cervantes has Don Quixote believe in enchantments and sorcery and in the intervention of extranatural powers, it is not because he is inconsiderately mocking his hero: he simply inserts him into a current of opinion that was on the increase throughout Europe at the turn of the century, as Trevor-Roper has documented.[9] Indicative of the period is the extensive bibliography on an "occult and secret natural philosophy" which controls extraordinary events in the world. It was a fundamental science for Rabelais himself and for his exceptional creatures, real and imaginary characters very representative of the time.[10] And with it there was also a revival of belief in enchanters, magicians, astrologers, etc., whose science, by delving into usually unknown aspects of things, allowed them to obtain results quite unexpected by ordinary standards.

Once it becomes possible for our relation with the world to be affected by strange powers that can alter the normal course of events, we must necessarily take such changes into consideration, because they can either facilitate or hinder our activity. Don Quixote intends to do battle with knights whose conduct he deems unworthy, but if at the moment he attacks them an enchanter who is his enemy gives them the appearance of sheep, the glorious victory he planned to claim over them will go up in smoke. Therefore, Don Quixote's main doubt about reality is his justified uncertainty as to whether or not enchanters have transformed the appearance of things and people at the moment when he comes face to face with them. Thus, his lack of confidence in what things look like is due to the intervention of sage enchanters in the world. Don Quixote's inexhaustible supply of energy and courage consoles him for his misadventures and enables him to overcome his perceptual misgivings, which, far from inclining him to desist, actually spur him on to overcome all discouragement. "No notice is to be taken of such things where enchantments are concerned, nor should one be angry or annoyed by them" (I:17).

We should bear in mind that Don Quixote's attribution of changes in reality to enchantment must not be judged from the standpoint of today's thinking but from that of the convictions current in his own period. The belief in goblins, monsters, and devils, in sorcerers and enchanters, was firmly held and people saw them as something that must be taken into account, for evil elements such as these diabolically interfered with things, altering their appearance.[11] "It cannot be denied," says Antonio de Torquemada,

> that there is an art of necromancy and that there have been many who have practiced it in ancient times (both the faithful and the infidels as well) and that there are many who use it now. But this art can be practiced in one of two ways. The first is natural and employs things which have the requisite natural properties and the ability to accomplish what is desired, such as herbs, plants, stones and other things (all of which have certain natural powers), and also constellations and other celestial influences. And this method is licit and may be performed, without any moral reservations or misgivings, by those who have penetrated and comprehended secrets which are a closed door to other people.... The other kind of necromancy or magic is that which is performed with the help of devils, and, as we have seen, this has also been known and used in the world since ancient times.[12]

One type can be permissible and the other sinful, according to Torquemada, but what is certain is that both types of necromancy exist and that things in their physical state are subject to that power. Thus sorcerers and enchanters exist and have the power to alter reality. These names, Torquemada says, are to be applied to those who, in addition to natural magic, rely also on other illicit means as well. Lope de Vega, in order to explain the Catholic myth of the three Magi, alluded to the common distinction between natural magic which was part of natural philosophy and therefore licit, and an infernal, malignant magic which was damnable.[13]

It is not strange, or at least not as strange as it might seem to us today, that Don Quixote should assume the reality of enchantments. As many have noted, the same recourse is utilized by Cervantes in the *Persiles,* where the adventure, rare and strange as it may be, is always composed of natural ingredients. Moreover, in that novel there is a character who speaks of enchanters with the ability to turn into wolves, and we hear him confess with astonishment: "How this can be, I don't know, and, as a Catholic Christian I don't believe it, but experience demonstrates just the opposite."[14] It is nothing less than experience, the maximum surety of knowledge, which asserts the existence of this power of transformation. Torquemada also includes in his book (which does not claim to be a novel but a true account of extraordinary events) the story of individuals in certain northern countries who can turn into wolves, and although he is filled with doubts on the subject, he ends up admitting that it may be possible due to the intervention of sorcerers and enchanters.[15] Cervantes may or may not have believed—probably he did not—in enchantment as a means of transforming things, but what we must keep in mind is that in using this particular recourse he was not operating in the region of pure fantasy. Not only is the belief in these extranatural beings common in literary works until the eighteenth century, but studies continued to appear in which the types and characteristics of these beings were examined in all seriousness.[16] That strange solution to the highly debated problem of magic we have just seen in the *Persiles* is repeated verbatim in *The Dogs' Colloquy.* In this story a witch believes she is looking at her own son transformed into a dog, even though she admits that those who are most knowledgeable in these matters claim that men cannot be transformed into beasts by magic. She tells the poor little animal: "But in you my son, experience shows the contrary, for I know that you are a rational being and I see you in the form of a dog."[17] That is to say, she sees him under the appearance of a dog, but she does not say that he is one, because this power to alter things is limited to the realm of appearances. It is a product, Cervantes will say, of "the art they call *tropelía,* which makes one thing appear to be another."[18]

This ability to make objects appear to be other than what they are is no minor branch of learning but a full-blown science. It presupposes, therefore, a set of rules and principles which are knowable and, consequently, capable of being taught. Throughout all of Europe at that time there were students of necromancy, of transformations, and of witchcraft.[19]

It is not enough to deal with what happens normally and naturally; one must also confront the element of the extraordinary. Don Quixote frequently says that things happen to him outside the boundaries of normality, and he points out to Sancho that "all these happenings... are outside the natural order" (II:41). Torquemada also devotes the first treatise of his work to informing us about "many things worthy of admiration which nature has done and continues to do in people outside her common and natural order."

Because this idea was so insistently repeated from the end of the sixteenth century, scholars have spoken of a confusion regarding the frontier between reality and illusion.[20] I do not believe, however, that people stopped distinguishing between one and the other so that Mannerist or Baroque man failed to recognize the passage from the real to the unreal; I think that it would be more exact to say that the sense of reality changed.

Undoubtedly, Cervantes utilizes the intervention of enchantments as a literary recourse. He does so from a perfectly ironic vantage point, thus functioning as a formidable deflater of the widespread credulity at the time. But even so, we must consider these enchantments a living element that corresponded to a real situation.

One more observation. The rural settings, those in which Don Quixote habitually operates, were also the ones where the belief in enchantments and their attendant evils was most firmly rooted. At that time, demented and deranged people, those considered very close to madness, were commonly brought to sanctuaries and other pious places so that through prayer they and their relatives and neighbors might be delivered from so serious an evil; or else people resorted to the practice of exorcisms or violent measures (incarceration, whippings, etc.). Yet, the country folk who come into contact with Don Quixote and readily see in him signs of madness or derangement by enchantment do not once respond to him in that way. They do nothing to free themselves from the evil influences which such an abnormal character can carry. This allows for the possible interpretation that in Spain, even in the villages, the level of secularization was greater than has been suspected (something I discussed while commenting on certain points in the *Re-*

laciones geográficas de los pueblos de España from the period of Felipe II). But in any case it shows that Cervantes, in order to give us a pseudoutopia as close as possible to the utopian genre (fundamental to a utopia is that it be capable of realization in this world), had to eliminate the religious element, which is so carefully pushed aside in the *Quixote*. The extraordinary treatment of reality he places before us via the madness of Don Quixote remains within a naturalist line or a "physicalization" of events which depart from normalcy, a treatment of madness as a natural phenomenon reminiscent of Ben Jonson. This facilitates the passage from one to the other of the two planes of unreality in Cervantes's creation, that is, from enchantment to madness, and gives it its unique human intensity.

But at this point let us note that what we can properly call transmutation of reality in Don Quixote should not be thought of as having been produced by enchantment. Don Quixote never believes that through the work of enchanters certain objects can come to be other than what they are. The power of enchanters is limited strictly to the external aspect of the world which we behold; it cannot change its essence. "I have already explained to you how enchanters change and transform things from their natural shape. I do not mean that they actually change them from one shape to another, but they appear to do so, as experience has taught us in connection with the transformation of Dulcinea, sole refuge of my hopes" (II:29). Yet the enchantment does give rise to an extraordinary reality in its victim, for it does not destroy the ordinary existence of things but changes it only for the person subject to its operation. Thus we can say that the enchantment is real, in the sense of being empirically existent, and its consequences are unreal or, better put, not natural, since they do not alter the true existence of things, so that for everybody else the objects can continue to be what they are. Whence the possibility of doubt regarding the locus of truth. Don Quixote, accepting all this, addresses his companions in the inn which he takes for a castle at the end of the first part. The issue is whether an object in view of all of them is a saddlebag or a horse's trappings, and Don Quixote, suspending his judgment, says:

> When it comes to declaring whether that is a saddlebag or a horse's trappings, I shall not venture to make any definite statement but shall leave it to your Worships' own good judgment. It may be that, inasmuch as you have not been dubbed knights as I have been, your Worships will not be subject to the enchantments of this place and, accordingly, your judgment being unimpaired, will be able to form an impression of things in this castle as they really and truly are and not as they appear to me to be. (I:45)

The item in question may be a saddlebag or a horse's trappings, the wheat Dulcinea was winnowing may be fine and white or of the reddish variety, because the enchantment is beyond reason; but what is real and true, although on occasion the enchanters can make it seem otherwise, is that Dulcinea exists in order to temper and strengthen the soul of the knight with her love, that Don Quixote exists in order to revive the Golden Age, and that knights-errant have existed so that for a time justice might reign on earth. In order to demonstrate the real existence of that world to whoever might deny it, Don Quixote resorts to the rational criterion of experience: Is not the pin of the wooden horse of valiant Pierres in the royal armory and Babieca's saddle and Roland's horn right alongside it? Have not bones been discovered in Sicily so large that they could only be those of a giant, as has been proved geometrically? Have not the histories of knights-errant been published and, what is more, received the approbation of strict censors?

What Don Quixote has done by this approach is point out a change of reality or, in more precise terms, a different reality from the one we daily contemplate, and thus bring about the most extraordinary transmutation of reality imaginable. Reality is going to be something other than what it has been. And this is not a problem of appearance but of being. As he himself has become another who is now his true person and who exists, as his name implies, in order to wield ancient weapons, he will also completely change the world as it existed and make another world out of it, one in which the activity of a knight-errant armed in that antique harness is a real possibility. And this world will be so real and, therefore, so normal that its authenticity will rest not on any extraordinary alteration of appearances but on reason itself. Concerning the truth and reality of the world he has created, that is, of things the way he assumes them to be, Don Quixote points out that, just as with the existence of giants, "it is a simple matter of geometry" (II:1).

Observe that we cannot consider Don Quixote mad for maintaining a chivalric ideal. His thoughts about honor, virtue, justice, valor, and love do not in themselves make him abnormal. Before losing his reason he was enamored of the world of chivalry and an admirer of what he considered the eminent virtues set forth in it. All of this might be something perfectly normal. The extraordinary thing is the way in which he tries to make those convictions prevail within the reality of the period in which he lives. On this the observation of Lissarrague is apt: "What he gets from his madness is not the substance of chivalry but the method of projecting it into the world."[21]

What is surprising in the *Quixote* is the perfectly reasonable development of the world of the hero once the premises have been accepted. The knight constantly amazes people with his flawless and coherent reasoning and on several occasions his interlocutors are reduced to perplexity regarding the nature of his madness. Speaking with him, the Knight of the Green-Colored Greatcoat "took him now for a sensible individual and now for a madman, since what Don Quixote said was coherent, elegantly phrased, and to the point, whereas his actions were nonsensical, foolhardy, and downright silly" (II:17). That wise and prudent Castillian hidalgo sums up for his son the nature of this strange character he has met on the way home: "I can only tell you that I have seen him do things that would lead one to believe he is the greatest madman in the world, yet his conversation is so sensible that it belies and causes one to forget his actions" (II:18). And Don Quixote himself, who never loses a distant awareness of other people's normal, everyday manner of perceiving things, says to him: "Undoubtedly, Señor Don Diego de Miranda, your Grace must take me for a fool and a madman, am I not right? And it would be small wonder if such were the case, seeing that my deeds give evidence of nothing else" (II:17).

These two texts, which reveal another's opinion as well as that of the knight himself, coincide: his reasoning is intelligible, expressed in an orderly fashion and in accord with normalcy; his deeds, on the other hand, are crazy and do not conform to what a normal person feels can be done given the reality at hand. This highlights the fact that what we have in Don Quixote is not a case of loss of reason, properly speaking, but something else. Don Quixote has brought about a prior and total twisting of the data of the empirical world. Windmills are giants, the inn is a castle, the flocks are armies, the basin a helmet, and the water mill on the Ebro a hateful prison. Given these presuppositions, this transformation of experiential data, everything goes along rationally. The extraordinary element resides in an operation which to a certain degree occurs prior to the reasoning process and which alters the reality of the world; or, if we prefer, an operation by which he utilizes the elements of the world and breaks them up and puts them together again in a different way in order to construct his own world.

There is even an instance in which he reveals that he is aware of this procedure. Sancho has dared to deny the existence and attributes of Dulcinea, and Don Quixote, on the subject of this absolutely essential element in his system and his conception of the world, clearly confesses how he operates: "I am content to imagine that what I say is so and that she is neither more nor less than I picture her and would have her be" (I:25). Don Quixote is not opposed to others' perceiving things differently, because, on the one hand, he has to keep in mind the power of enchantment which can cause him to doubt what he sees, and, on the other hand, anyone who does not wish to play his game should just stay out of it; to such an individual he directs his expression of utter disinterest: "And let anyone say what he likes; if for this I am repre-hended by the ignorant, I shall not be blamed by men of discernment" (I:25). Nothing destroys the reality of his world for him, and when oth-ers refuse to see things that matter to him the way he says they are, then it is the others, in his opinion, who are under the power of enchant-ment, not he. What is more, while he recognizes that in a few cases Sancho is right about what some of the things in his adventures seem to be, he points out that this is only a matter of appearances due to mo-mentary changes effected by enchanters. In real truth, however, things are what he claims them to be and not what they merely appear to be to Sancho and others. Therefore he tells Sancho that although what just passed before them seemed to be nothing but sheep, they were in fact the knights he had seen initially and against whom he tried to use his lance. This is so true, he claims, that if Sancho just follows them a short distance, he will see how they return to their authentic being once they are out of Don Quixote's reach and the magician who enchanted them feels sure he has snatched from him the possibility of gallantly defeating such powerful champions. He has the same reaction in the adventure of the enchanted bark, for he ends up by admitting that the prison unwor-thy of highborn people appears to him as well as to Sancho to be a water mill, but he does not on that account cease believing in its real essence. Thus, when he cannot achieve his mission due to that external mutation, he resignedly bids farewell to the illustrious prisoners who he is convinced are groaning within the walls of that prison: "Friends, . . . whoever ye may be who are locked within these prison walls, forgive me. It is my misfortune and yours that I am unable to rescue you from dire peril. This enterprise must doubtless be reserved for some other knight" (II:29). And he continues believing this, even though he may have accepted what he judges to be mere appearances, up to the point of agreeing to pay the fishermen for their boat.

Now then, in what does this operation of transmutation of reality consist? Simply this: a complete act of will. Rather than controlled rea-son in the Cartesian fashion, which comes later, what Renaissance man possesses above all is a powerful will. Don Quixote, a new Atlas, sup-ports by force of will the world he has created for himself out of the broken remains of everyday life. Thus when his niece asks him to give up what we might in synthesis refer to as his way of seeing things, Don Quixote, in order to affirm his position and his intention to persist in the world he has made, adduces the definitive justification: "My own will desires [it]" (II:6). Don Quixote, correctly speaking, is not de-mented but arbitrary to a colossal degree.[22] He positions his existence and that of the things which surround him upon a grandiose, colossal arbitrariness. We may say about Don Quixote what Nietzsche said about

Spain (in words which Fernando de los Ríos so loved to repeat): he willed too much. Upon the basis of an energetic will our hero endeavors to sustain a universe in the same way it was said that "the Monarchy of Spain is what upholds the weight of the world, which is about to collapse." He labors to support a broken world, one whose pieces were to be arranged very differently from the former archaic ensemble.[23] In the nineteenth century an idealist like Fichte assured us that what we call reality is nothing more than the limits of intelligence which intelligence itself has imposed. Similarly, reality for Don Quixote is the horizon of means and devices, of things, which his will has placed before him to make his activity possible. "The world," said Fichte, "is material for the fulfillment of obligation." The world, Don Quixote could say, is material with which to carry out a mission. Heine relates that those who heard Fichte speak, astonished by his prideful denial that things had any reality other than that posited by his ego, asked themselves, And what must Mrs. Fichte think of all of this? We know very well what Don Quixote's niece and his housekeeper thought of his extreme voluntarism.

Don Quixote practices a frank idealism, not in the banal sense in which the word is commonly used, but in a deep philosophical sense. A theoretician of science, Hans Reichenbach, has said in our own day: "Idealism is the philosophical brand of escapism; it has always flourished in times of social catastrophes which have shaken the foundations of human society."[24] Cervantes hit the mark in his portrayal of extreme idealism in a hero whose exterior world depends on his consciousness. This idealism correlates perfectly with the utopian evasionism of a group of people about whom their contemporary González de Cellorigo said that "it appears that they wish to reduce these kingdoms to a republic of enchanted men who live outside the natural order."[25] In order to shock them back into reality Cervantes invented the fiction of the *Quixote*.

In his discourse on Dulcinea, Don Quixote clearly reveals the primacy of will in his way of viewing the world and in connection with so essential a component as the lady of his passionate and chaste love. "I am content to imagine," he tells Sancho, "that . . . she is neither more nor less than I picture her and would have her be" (I:25). That is to say, what comes first is what the will desires. Then comes the act of painting, that is, of representing things to ourselves, making them be for us the way we want them. In the adventure of Mambrino's helmet we see clearly the willfulness of Don Quixote. He sees an individual approaching who in the testimony of any ordinary person—in this case, Sancho—is simply a man on a donkey with a shiny object on his head, but his will decrees that this shiny item is the helmet of Mambrino "which I have so greatly desired" (I:21), and for Don Quixote it comes to be so, really and authentically, even though once he gets his hands on it he admits to Sancho that it "appears, as you have said, to be a barber's basin" (I:21). When he has it before him, his very reason vacillates between somebody else's testimony, with which his own reason coincides completely, and what his will orders him to see in the object. It is from this vacillation that the so-called basin-helmet [*baciyelmo*] enters Cervantes's text. But will ultimately triumphs, and so fully is Don Quixote convinced that the object he has won from his opponent is a helmet, in spite of what it might seem to him to be, that he is not afraid to present his view to the large group of people in the inn-castle.

Reason yields to will and ends up accepting its judgment. If Don Quixote refuses to make a pronouncement on the issue of the saddlebag or horse's trappings because it is a question that really has nothing to do with his desire, he does at the same time manifest his firm conviction regarding the helmet: "As to the charge that this is a basin and not a helmet, I have already answered that" (I:45). In such a case those who believe the opposite are the ones who suffer the deception of enchanters, but "I recognize its value, and the transformation that it has undergone makes no difference to me" (I:21).

It is also true that Don Quixote, at times remotely aware of his formidable arbitrariness in ordering the reality of things, does not like to be constantly subjecting these questions to merely rational criteria. Thus, when the duchess expresses doubts about Dulcinea, Don Quixote responds: "God knows whether or not there is a Dulcinea in this world or if she is a fanciful creation. This is not one of those cases where you can prove a thing conclusively" (II:32).

Don Quixote, thus, has been able to construct for himself a world made to his own specifications. Cervantes does not choose to cure him of this unique mental disturbance in the same way he cured the Man of Glass, by means of the intervention of someone knowledgeable in the medical treatment of the insane.[26] In Don Quixote's case, since the illness resides in the will, for the cure to take effect it will suffice for his will to lose its extraordinary capacity for arbitrariness. Thus, when the knight is conquered and his will collapses completely and what he thought was his invincible courage fails without hope of recovery, he regains the habitual and ordinary way of perceiving the world. In spite of this, however, he still has energy left for a feeble attempt to turn himself and others into shepherds, who are the other key characters in the arbitrary construction of his world.[27]

The purpose of that voluntaristic creation of the world by Don Quixote was to make a particular mission possible, and we may define that mission, using the knight's own words, as the revival of the Golden Age. The critical spirit of the modern age and its creation, the State, had reduced and almost eliminated the possibilities for heroism and chivalric virtue. In order to return to them Don Quixote had no alternative but to annul existing reality and turn it into something else. In that way and only in that way does he obtain the resources to be able to formulate his enterprise and put it into practice. For that reason, out of all the occasions upon which others radically deny his position, there is only one on which Don Quixote does not give a definitive answer. It is when Sancho is on the verge of convincing him that in the normal world and in the circumstances of their historical period it is still possible to carry out an enterprise which is, if not identical to his, certainly very similar: that of the heroes of religion, the saints. Were this so, were it possible for such a heroic action to occur in the real context of his epoch, Don Quixote's conduct would be meaningless. He then could have become an Alonso de Contreras, for example, but with the inspiration of a divine purpose.

In Don Quixote's view, however, this is not possible because the world of his time, by its very structure, did not permit the program of life which he had chosen for himself. Things, what we call things, are nothing more than means with which to carry out the task of a life, that is, they are only possibilities with which to perform one or another activity. Given a limited repertory of things, the tasks we can perform will be equally limited. Outside those possibilities, if we attempt to do something which things around us do not allow, our only options will be to renounce our goal or to change the totality of objects at our disposal with which to realize that goal. We cannot cross the oceans, no matter how hard we strive, if we do not have something that floats or flies over the water. Neither, then, will we be able to demonstrate our fortitude and vigor if we do not confront an extraordinarily strong being whom we can attempt to conquer, and we will not be able to free a noble person from a despicable prison if there are no incarcerated princesses or knights. And since Don Quixote does not wish to renounce such virtuous deeds, he has no other alternative than to create a world in which those things exist and allow the realization of such extraordinary undertakings.

What Don Quixote does is comparable to what Saint Augustine meant by *volo ut intelligam*. He wants things to be one way and not another because he requires this condition in order to comprehend the world he has conceived. If things were not the way his determination forms them, the world in which he lives would have no rational meaning. If there were no giants, castles, knights, or princesses, what would be the meaning of all those deeds which the histories narrate, and, what is more, what would be the purpose of the heroism, love, and fortitude in the hearts of courageous men? What would be the purpose of so many virtues obtainable only through chivalric combat? Why would there be oppressed people to set free, the weak to defend, damsels to love, and aggrieved people for whom justice must be obtained? For all these reasons and because all of these things exist, the knight exists also; and because the knight exists, these things must be what they need to be in order for the knight to perform his admirable feats. This is why, if Don Quixote's will orders him to become a knight-errant, it must create those things which allow the world around him to have a sufficient and rational connection with what the knight is supposed to do in it.

Things are means which enable us to live in one way or another, to formulate this or that program of existence. And things as they were in Don Quixote's time did not allow him to realize his life's work, his human enterprise. He was obliged, therefore, to transmute them into something else in order to fulfill his destiny.

6

The Utopia of Natural Reason

The myth of the Golden Age. The paradigm of nature. The image of agro-pastoral society and the role of the knight. Government by natural man. The negation of this system of beliefs in the work of Cervantes.

In several pertinent passages of *Don Quixote* we have seen how the protagonist proclaims his mission in its dual aspect: on the one hand, to restore the order of knight-errantry and, on the other, to bring about a rebirth of the Golden Age. They are two sides of the same enterprise and are joined by their relationship of means to end. The intrepid courage of the knight, utilized within the strict laws of chivalry, will bring the world to a new and happy state which is none other than the Golden Age. As is usual in so many programs of reform, the element of newness is, in fact, a restoration: once again to bring to the present the image of a perfect society barely glimpsed in a vague, undefinable distance virtually outside time and space. Bonilla noted this mission of Don Quixote and recognized the important role it plays. According to him, the powerful attraction of the quixotic ideal is due to "the conviction that if this ideal were put into practice, the Golden Age would return and the world would be happy."[1] This is something that a number of Cervantes's contemporaries perceived in his inspired literary creation.

We are dealing, thus, with a program of restoration which, leaving aside psychoanalytical interpretations, we need not attribute to weakness or senility on the part of the social group that supports it. Marx observed that when each ascendent class appears with proposals for social change, it legitimizes its program by an appeal to the ancients. Are not the literary characters in a utopian writer such as William Morris, who lived at the height of the industrial revolution, closer to the Middle Ages

131

than to his own nineteenth century? Through the *Quixote* Cervantes points out that, given the current situation in Spain (despite strong traditional vestiges), the methods propounded by the ruined and isolated petty nobility are worthless. The Golden Age will continue to be a valid paradigm in European utopianism with its orientation to the future, but it was not valid in the hands of stagnant feudal remnants seeking refuge in the antiquated heroic customs of a bygone epoch that they thought could be reintroduced in a new Golden Age. Thus, in the *Quixote* everything becomes a pseudoutopia, a pure utopia of evasion.

We already know how the human and social renewal which Don Quixote seeks affirms the Golden Age. But what is the significance of this matter of the Golden Age? It is a concept which today we easily connect to the names of Saint-Pierre, Rousseau, and other primitivists of the eighteenth century but which had been present in European thought since ancient times. At this point we need not go back too far nor do we need to search out this idea in the Stoics or in the earlier Greek philosophers. The myth has considerable importance in Vergil, Ovid, Seneca, and Boethius, and its presence in such admired writers could not have gone unnoticed by those who were on the verge of a new critical approach to society and culture. The theme can be found in the prehumanists, as we see in *Lo Somni* by Bernat Metge and the *De optima politia* of Alonso de Madrigal. This dream, present to a greater or lesser degree in all ages, was alive in the sixteenth century and up through the time when Cervantes was writing. The strong influence on the Spanish Renaissance of the above-mentioned Latin writers, in whom the concept of the *aetas aurea* is so prominent, and the constant reading and discussion of their works probably inspired sixteenth- and seventeenth-century Spanish writers to take up the theme and include it in their social and political thought. Erasmus, too, brings it up in his letters. It is, so to speak, in the inkwell of Spanish humanists, and Luis Vives uses the idea in his commentary on Augustine's *De Civitate Dei*. The representatives to the Cortes of Valladolid (1518) trumpeted it in the presence of the Emperor.[2] For many people it would be a very important element of their conception of society and history, just as it had been a key piece in the philosophy of history of the classic writers of antiquity. Though in its revival during the humanist period the theme began as simply a rhetorical imitation, it soon developed into something very different: taken together with the experience of primitive life that the discovery of indigenous peoples in America made possible, the theme of the Golden Age once again came to be a way of understanding the origins of historical development. For that reason, and also because of the paradigmatic role which every image of "origins" has played for European reformist thinking, the idea naturally had an influence that was utopian in character.

It is also visible in sixteenth-century writers as an element of their philosophy of history (a philosophy which always ends up by influencing their view of the present, although sometimes in inverse directions). For evidence of this rejuvenation of the myth it should be sufficient to recall the names of Guevara, Torquemada, Mariana, and so many others. Pastoral dialogues and novels rest on this golden myth, which is normally tied to the rustic existence of shepherds and farmers; the image of the pleasantness of their life and their natural prudence and virtue forms the basic material, the cornerstone of this unique and special topic of the early modern period, a topic to which Cervantes, along with many others, renders homage.[3] Pedro Sánchez de Viana, the translator and commentator of Ovid, focuses the question when he writes: "I take gold to mean virtue and innocence." A further example: Balbuena's pastoral novel, clearly combining the two motifs mentioned—the genre of the pastoral novel and the myth of the Golden Age—is appropriately called *El Siglo de Oro en las selvas de Erífile*.

It became customary for historians and chroniclers to explain the first stage of the lives of the peoples whose past they were narrating in terms of an image of golden, primeval happiness. This was frequent among those writing on the Indies, from Oviedo, Las Casas, and Acosta to the Inca Garcilaso, who is a fine example of this school of thought. A friar of the Order of Our Lady of Mercy, Fray Martín de Murúa, still stressed this approach in his history of primitive Peru, completed in 1590, in which he claimed historically to find the Golden Age in the remote origins of that country.[4] The allusions to it are very frequent both in literature and in political treatises of the period; they normally apply the concept to the state of one primitive people or another. Painting seeks to portray it in visual form, and in the Museum of Troyes there is a canvas by Brueghel the Elder that has all the essential ingredients of the theme.

As to whether this constituted a mere literary recourse, we must conclude that it did not. Leaving aside its persistence in the human spirit, what is certain is that in Cervantes's period we find the myth in very close relation to a set of beliefs held by certain social sectors, just as happens in the post-Enlightenment Rousseauistic ideology.

Before the end of the sixteenth century voices would be raised to oppose the wide dissemination of this concept, either by altering its meaning or by refuting it head-on. In a poem dedicated to the secretary Martín de Morales, Barahona de Soto writes: "Golden indeed is this age of mine and yours," but he goes on to explain that it is so only with respect to the power of gold, the damnable lust for wealth.[5] In France Jean Bodin (*Methodus ad facilem historiarum cognitionem*) rejects any interpretation of the course of human events that starts from a premise of the superiority of a Golden Age in a remote and indeterminable past.[6] This is the line which Cervantes's counterutopia follows: he articulates perfectly the two sides of the utopian coin, the pastoral and the chivalric, in order to turn them inside out by reflecting them in the mirror of irony.

We need to unravel the component elements of the theme in Cervantes's thought, where it is so prominent. The relationship between the speech to the goatherds and the passage in Ovid's *Metamorphoses* dealing with the Golden Age is well known. We shall quote the latter so that the reader may compare the texts:

> In the beginning was the Golden Age, when men of their own accord, without threat of punishment, without laws, maintained good faith and did what was right. There were no penalties to be afraid of, no bronze tablets were erected, carrying threats of legal action, no crowd of wrong-doers, anxious for mercy, trembled before the face of their judge: indeed, there were no judges, men lived securely without them. Never yet had any pine tree, cut down from its home on the mountains, been launched on ocean's waves, to visit foreign lands: men knew only their own shores. Their cities were not yet surrounded by sheer moats, they had no straight brass trumpets, no coiling brass horns, no helmets and no swords. The peoples of the world, untroubled by any fears, enjoyed a leisurely and peaceful existence, and had no use for soldiers. The earth itself, without compulsion, untouched by the hoe, unfurrowed by any share, produced all things spontaneously, and men were content with foods that grew without cultivation. They gathered arbute berries and mountain strawberries, wild cherries and blackberries that cling to thorny bramble bushes: or acorns, fallen from Jupiter's spreading oak. It was a season of everlasting spring, when peaceful zephyrs, with their warm breath, caressed the flowers that sprang up without having been planted. In time the earth, though untilled, produced corn too, and fields that never lay fallow whitened with heavy ears of grain. Then there flowed rivers of milk and rivers of nectar, and golden honey dripped from the green holm-oak. [Trans. Mary M. Innes (New York: Penguin Books, 1955), pp. 31–32.]

In spite of all that Cervantes's "discourse" has in common with this passage, there is no doubt that he has effected a personal reelaboration of the theme.[7]

Cervantes transforms this classical legacy by means of everything that makes the literary myth a political utopia, which is the way it had come to be utilized in the sixteenth century: elimination of all mythological references; reduction of Ovid's four ages to two, in order to intensify the contrast between them; explicit identification of the Iron Age with the present; introduction of the chivalric element; and, above all, conversion of the myth into the goal of a reform movement which seeks its restoration, not as an impossible reproduction of a classical model but rather as a new vision of a natural society to be established in the context of present reality. Cervantes, however, denies his hero any success in this latter enterprise, forcing him instead to go from one failure to another.

The basic idea is that a natural goodness resided in the human heart before it was corrupted by vices originating in organized society. "Fraud, deceit, and malice had not yet come to mingle with truth and plain-speaking," Don Quixote says (I:11). Mariana too, in spite of his approval of his own politically constituted society, writes: "There was no occasion for fraud or mendacity of any kind."[8] The idea of the fallen nature of man subsequent to original sin was certainly a Christian principle. But this is a long way from the pessimism about the human condition that is the basis for modern political thought from Machiavelli on. The fall does not annihilate nature, which retains its ability to reach virtue in the order proper to it (although not in the order of grace, as the Counter-Reformation reminds us). The thinking of the period finds this element of virtue in the simplicity of primitive peoples. For this reason the pagan thesis concerning the virtues of peoples constrained to live a simple life could be assimilated without any contradiction by traditional Christian society of the late Middle Ages and the Renaissance.

It is worth noting that there is already a picture of rustic simplicity—and therefore of virtue—in a fifteenth-century work narrating the life of a real knight, *El Victorial* or *Crónica de don Pero Niño,* a book impregnated with chivalric mentality. The author says that when Alexander was going through the world conquering lands, he was told of people living beyond the mountains who spoke and lived very wisely and who possessed great treasures. Alexander found the place and asked its inhabitants to recognize him as king and render the appropriate tribute. This he justified by explaining to them with the true spirit of a knight (not of *imperator totius mundi*) that "I mete out justice to unjust kings and to corrupt judges." To which they replied:

> Sir, we have our king in God, whom we know and serve. If you have been empowered by him and wish to take his place on earth and do justice as he does, you may well do so and it would please us greatly. Concerning the tribute, all our treasure is wisdom; we have nothing else. If you desire wisdom, ask God for it, for only he can give it to you. We have nothing else, for we neither sow nor reap. When we get up in the morning, we give praise to our Creator. Then we go into the countryside in search of our food for the day. We do not worry about what we are to eat the next day. And then we spend the rest of the day in our houses until the morrow.[9]

This picture of a primitive economy based merely on gathering is the most extreme image of simplicity. Generally other activities are accepted, such as shepherding, cheese making, farming, and grinding wheat, but with a tendency to simplify economic operations in accordance with the virtuous simplicity of country people.

Fray Martín de Murúa also believed that, for similar reasons, there was no envy or other vice among the ancient subjects of the Incas, so that "they lived in a very pure and simple way." It has been the passage of centuries, of civilization, in a word, which has corrupted men and caused them to have evil passions, banishing "that time when the world, not so wrapped up in wickedness and vice, held out the promise of a less restrained and more peaceable life," in the words of Balbuena.[10] Life was free then, and free too were the noble sentiments which arose naturally from its enjoyment, when it was not necessary to shut yourself off from others defensively, trying to acquire (through craft and the elimination of competition) what the present age erroneously considers "goods." Then people knew what the good really was:

Oh good!, truly to be envied
where freedom from ambition
nurtures tranquil hearts
free from a thousand vain preoccupations.[11]

Thus this age is perceived to be golden not because of any extraordinary brilliance deriving from the presence of great sages but due to a kind of rough wisdom within the grasp of all and to the absence of evil people who might tarnish the sheen of natural goodness. As Guevara says, "that most ancient century of Saturn, also known as the Golden Century, was certainly very highly esteemed by those who lived in it, praised by those who wrote about it and greatly desired by everybody who was unable to enjoy its goodness firsthand, and it is important that we know that it was not golden because of any sages who gilded it, but rather because there were no wicked men to ungild it."[12] There is nobody in the *Quixote* who treats the knight more generously or who listens to him with more unselfish attention than do the goatherds to whom he delivers his speech on the Golden Age, of which they themselves are a living image, in accordance with their representation in the literature of the period. In his *Comentarios* on the works of Garcilaso, Fernando de Herrera refers to the pastoral world of the eclogues saying that "these customs are a reflection of the Golden Age."[13] In the Italian classicism of Garcilaso, however, the social dimension of the myth is still quite weak and will only begin to be emphasized later on, although the continuity in its development is clear.

It is obvious, consequently, that in the *Quixote* the Golden Age is very much present in that image of the knight and the shepherds. It is not just that Don Quixote evokes it at that moment but that the reader actually contemplates it in the whole picture of the simple goatherds and guardians of the flock and the knight with his traditional arms, the only source of spontaneous and equitable natural justice and the only stay of a like government. Those shepherds of the *Quixote* are like the ones in Balbuena's poem, generous, simple, spontaneously hospitable and friendly toward those they meet, especially people in distress, for in that case they comfort them by sharing their hopes or their grief. As we read in Balbuena, "we all came to his aid with compassionate tears."[14] Remember what happens to Don Quixote with the people he meets in his wanderings through the Sierra Morena: they either have always lived in a natural state or they have returned to it in a flight from civilization (an early example of the tendency we will observe in more modern times). Fleeing to remote places in order to have a rest from the sophistication of cultured society is a well-known phenomenon. Seneca provides an interesting example from his own period,[15] and Ruiz de Alarcón, in the Spain of the first half of the seventeenth century, tells us in *The Truth Suspected* that it was fashionable for one to abandon hectic court life from time to time and remain "concealed or retired in his village, or resting in his house" (act 1).[16] Lope makes an interesting observation: "Country property generally pleases princes more than all the riches of their palaces."[17]

We should recognize that in the country or pastoral topos there were echoes, somewhat weak by that time, of something else: a confrontation between rural and urban existence, between the familiarity of small groups and the anonymity of city life, and between self-reliance and dependence on a system of stores and markets; for traditionalists it was, in simple terms, a confrontation between the truth of simple life and the falsity of artificial, urban life. In the former there can be joy or sorrow. Speaking of the sentimental novels of Diego de San Pedro (in which the literary version of this real situation had its beginnings in Spanish literature), Vossler observes that the countryside is the ideal place for the sorrowful.[18] Such a setting makes possible a certain authenticity in feelings of grief which palliates them and actually makes them pleasant. Diego de San Pedro's characters retire to the countryside to shed their tears, just as Don Quixote will do later. The frequent tears in the *Quixote* (tears which the knight, as we said in chapter 1, will not wish his chronicler to pass over in silence) are already a literary motif of the period and an external sign of man's natural, innate goodness. To what extent we see here and in other areas the beginnings of the spirit which ultimately will lead to romanticism is not a subject into which we can enter without interrupting our interpretation. Perhaps the proximity of the two positions might be found in the intimacy which was restored through a return to natural, primitive simplicity; both periods aspire to this, at least in some very typical instances.

That natural, primitive goodness of man is preserved in those who hold to a lifestyle based on *simplicity*. When Sancho expresses his deep admiration for the virtues of the Knight of the Green-Colored Great-coat, a paradigm of the humanist gentleman, the latter answers: "It is you, brother, who are the saint; for you must be a good man, judging by the simplicity of heart that you show" (II:16). The theme of *sancta simplicitas* had been revived and transmitted to the sixteenth century by Erasmus, who had found it in Saint Jerome (*Ad Pammachium,* 57.12).[19] Literature on the myth of the Golden Age and on pastoral life had become the focus of a moral restoration. Speaking not of his shepherds but of sailors who live in rustic and isolated circumstances, Gil Polo describes them as "naturally compassionate men of kind and simple feelings."[20] Cervantes used the topos as part of a gilded picture of ideal social intercourse because in his day it was the image, projected into a nonexistent time, of a utopia of evasion utilized by some who were social outcasts (or who thought they were) because they saw themselves as defenders of purity.

Our consideration of the *simplicity = goodness* equation leads us to examine another aspect: the preference for *spontaneity* over sophisticated society, and thus the consequent preference for rustic and even primitive life. All those inhabitants of the Golden Age, as Don Quixote describes them to the goatherds, are in fact people who live an uncultured existence isolated in the countryside. The taste for "the unrefined solitude of pleasant meadows," in the words of Céspedes y Meneses,[21] is a theme representative of that modern sensibility.[22]

Here the elements of solitude and spontaneity are linked. As we have said, Petrarch's *De vita solitaria* was much appreciated and translated in the Spanish sixteenth century. This is not a harsh and difficult solitude. "The first thing someone who wishes to follow this life should find is a cool, delightful spot, verdant and lush, where there are springs and hills as well as trees and a variety of plants."[23] In such a lovely setting it will be possible to spend a gentle life conversing with a few wise companions in a program of inner renewal, a life which is "protection for the soul, a cure for bad habits, a renewal of the affections, a purifier of evil thoughts and defilement, . . . a life of philosophy and poetry."[24]

This desire for solitude does not mean a total renunciation of the world nor an elimination of all social dealings. As we read in lines by Tasis y Peralta:

He lives in solitude among people
and all alone in delightful company.[25]

It is in fact a simplified life which will allow people to dedicate themselves to the cultivation of their inner person by freeing them from occupations which alienate them from their true self. The "pleasant solitude" of meadows, forests, and mountains is not harsh isolation but a delightful conversation among people who exist for each other, joined by wisdom and friendship. As a place for cultivating that enriched, select company, the countryside is thus the means for entering into oneself, as Vossler has shown in his study of the characters of Diego de San Pedro. For this reason solitude, freedom, and intimacy go together. When this myth was at its height in the first half of the sixteenth century, Agostino Nifo published a work in which he held that only the solitary person is truly free.[26] In praising the isolation of rural dwellings Guevara maintains that those who retire there "will discover that they never knew what life was until after their retreat." That life is truly free: "There is no other life like it in the world: to arise freely and go where you want and do what you should." Guevara goes to the heart of the matter when he connects aspects of rural life with the first appearance of themes of alienation. The individual is alienated by society, authority, and the conventions that weigh heavily on him in the city. Only the freedom of the countryside allows him once again to get in touch with himself and, as Guevara observes, "nobody finds such a great treasure as the man who finds himself and, on the contrary, no loss is greater than the loss of oneself."[27] This is an aspiration which was to last for a long time. After its appearance in Cervantes it would intensify in the full Baroque and become a vehicle for the expression of one of the social tensions of the epoch. The feminine protagonist of Vélez de Guevara's *La serrana de la Vera* says:

> I do not want anyone to subject me;
> I do not want anyone to consider himself
> my master; freedom is what I seek.

Solitude, freedom, and intimacy in which one becomes master of oneself and experiences the full joy of living: this is a common theme of the period and may be found in the poetry of Aldana or the essays of Montaigne.

Castro makes an interesting point which will help us to understand the historical and social meaning of the myth of the Golden Age and to refine our thinking about the literary phenomenon of the pastoral novel: he claims that in the latter the seed of the portrayal of the individual soul is to be found and that pastoral solitude is "the individual being alone with himself, at which time he feels that he is himself and only himself."[28] Of course, this view of solitude applies not just to the genre in question but to the entire thought and literature of the Spanish

Renaissance from its very inception, as we might suspect from the references we have collected for this study. Following this line of interpretation, Vossler says: "In solitude we brush off the dust from the marketplace, the falsity of the business world and everything which is deceit and prejudicial to human dignity and the life of grace. This ethical-aesthetic tonality of solitude, a legacy of Vergil, Horace and Petrarch, begins to show up in the Spanish language. Hidden in Castillian tranquillity virile echoes of the Horatian *beatus ille* are clearly audible."[29]

This solitude of Cervantes is the vindication of the countryside as opposed to the city. In the rustic eclogues of Juan del Encina the shepherds and shepherdesses make fun of people who come from the city: "Oh you city people," the shepherdess says to the squire, laughing at his flattery; and the shepherd disdainfully says to the foppish hidalgo: "you city slickers."[30] Fernando de Herrera did not much care for Garcilaso's use of the unpoetic word "city" in his second eclogue, to which his own critic Fernández de Velasco—using the pseudonym of Prête Jacopín—replied: "And if the shepherd goes every day to the city to buy food and clothing and sell his sheep, wool and cheese, why should he not use the word?"[31] (We see here a much higher level of commerce than that found in the ideal of the pastoral myth.) Vázquez de Menchaca's legal analysis (inherited from late medieval jurists) according to which townsmen are more noble than villagers is curious.[32] Nevertheless, for the moral-political reform sought by humanism only the countryside is the apt setting for the development of moral values and only there, in solitude, can a person realize his full potential. "In the cities it is especially difficult to embrace solitude," as Suárez de Figueroa tells us.[33]

The image of rural economy and society are behind all this. As we have said, it is what the myth of the Golden Age represents at bottom and it implies, as does the concept of utopia, an element of insularity. We find this from More to Cervantes, with Las Casas as an intermediate stage. In the formation of the pastoral myth, which includes isolation as an essential ingredient, this element is always present. In one phase we see the appearance of the myth of the "pastoral island," which Avalle-Arce highlighted[34] as a parallel idea to Hans Freyer's "politische Insel."[35] The centuries were not long past in which social life was centered on the countryside, and the complex, busy, and worrisome life of the cities was a new reality. Indeed, in some sectors it could be said that they had not yet disappeared. We should keep in mind that the life of the knight was traditionally counted among modes of existence proper to the countryside, not the court. In the middle of the fifteenth century Juan de Lucena attempted to discover the social strata in which happiness might be attained. After rejecting the notion that princes, courtiers, and the rich can ever be happy, he turns to another sector and says: "If you are willing, let us not abandon our search for the happy life until we find out where it is. And if we have lost the track in the city, let us see if we can pick it up in the countryside."[36] The first people Lucena encounters in rural areas are precisely those who dedicate themselves to chivalric life.

Country life, of course, does not just mean a refuge in the mountains or in lands cut off from all communication; that is only its extreme, mythical manifestation. More commonly it means life in a village. The moderate rusticity which Fernando de Herrera sublimates poetically becomes the moral and social ideal of a certain type of individual. It is true that with the rise of the mendicant orders—an urban phenomenon—a negative view of the rural world likewise developed.[37] Nevertheless, the preference for humane and completely natural values that people perceived in peasant life continued to develop vigorously under the double stimulus of stoicism and Christianity. Saint Jerome's appreciation of *sancta rusticitas* (*Ad Paulinum*, 53.3)[38] spread through Europe from the late Middle Ages and was reinforced by the humanists. In Spain, López de Ayala has praise only for farmers in his review of social classes in his *Rimado de Palacio*. The Marquis of Santillana, as a knight and member of the nobility, considers peasants to be people of low office, but he nevertheless believes that their labors lead to virtue and are a corrective to the evils of urban life.[39] The doctor and moralist López de Villalobos writes: "If they understood and were grateful for the life they lead, they would not exchange it for any other in the world."[40] An early agrarianist (using the word in both its technical and its economic sense), Gabriel Alonso de Herrera, holds that a merchant's life is difficult and full of moral and physical dangers, while "working the land is a holy life, safe and innocent and free from sin. What tongue could ever recite the benefits and excellence of life in the country? Just as it makes for strong bodies, so does it fortify our souls."[41] We are already familiar with the example of Guevara. But let us note that in referring to the court with its vices and evil ways, he identifies the court with the metropolis as something opposed to the countryside and villages.[42]

Hence those who maintain the myth of the Golden Age praise the village as a way of life. In that passage from the deserted forest to the rural world we see the difference between an extreme, theoretical formula and prudent, practical implementation. It is the same difference that we observe in the reformer Rousseau between certain ideas he expresses in the *Reveries* and others contained in *Considérations sur le gouvernement de la Pologne*.

Thus, solitude in Cervantes is the relative solitude of the village, in which one of the most beautiful ways of life imaginable (in the view of the period) flourishes:

> I, Sir Knight of the Mournful Countenance, . . . am a gentleman and a native of the village where, please God, we are going to dine today. I am more than moderately rich, and my name is Don Diego de Miranda. I spend my life with my wife and children and with my friends. My occupations are hunting and fishing, though I keep neither falcon nor hounds but only a tame partridge and a bold ferret or two. I am the owner of about six dozen books, some of them in Spanish, others in Latin, including both histories and devotional works. As for books of chivalry, they have not as yet crossed the threshold of my door. My own preference is for profane rather than devotional writings, such as afford an innocent amusement, charming us by their style and arousing and holding our interest by their inventiveness, although I must say there are very few of that sort to be found in Spain. Sometimes . . . I dine with my friends and neighbors, and I often invite them to my house. My meals are wholesome and well prepared and there is always plenty to eat. I do not care for gossip, nor will I permit it in my presence. I am not lynx-eyed and do not pry into the lives and doings of others. I hear mass every day and share my substance with the poor, but make no parade of my good works, lest hypocrisy and vainglory, those enemies that so imperceptibly take possession of the most modest heart, should find their way into mine. I try to make peace between those who are at strife. I am the devoted servant of Our Lady, and my trust is in the infinite mercy of God Our Savior. (II:16)

Vicente Espinel portrays a virtuous man much like the Knight of the Green-Colored Greatcoat living similarly in a rural environment and attaining virtue by meditating on Fray Luis de Granada's *Memorial de vida cristiana*.[43] It was a common theme in the period.

Those moral values of village life and the superior physical qualities it makes possible (whence the unusual strength of knights) are closely related. Like the utopian mentality of the eighteenth century, the sixteenth also set forth the triple equation nature = virtue = health, using sociomedical ideas that the Enlightenment would take over. According to Juan de Lucena, the farmer's life with its regular, sensible diet is the most suitable for keeping human nature free from undue anxiety or grief. "They do not get sick or have much pain. They are healthy, brave, content, and more than happy." While it does not provide perfect happiness, which is impossible, "rustic life is the highest delight of the soul and a source of great enjoyment for the body."[44] A political writer such as Alfonso de Castrillo sees primitive, elemental ways of life as desirable and healthful,[45] and the writer who was perhaps the first in Spanish literature systematically to defend agrarian society and economy—the sine qua non for a quixotic existence—tells us that in the countryside "people stay healthier and live longer."[46] Guevara, logically, takes this theme and makes it the center of his thesis: "The man who is busy and hard-working is always healthy, stout, merry, ruddy, happy and content, for good exercise leads to healthiness and a good complexion. . . . It is a privilege of the village that its inhabitants are much healthier and are sick less frequently."[47] Doctors picked up on this thinking and dedicated increasing attention to concepts of hygiene. The goodness of nature and country life and the healthfulness of the village were all considered an effective tonic and as such they played a role in medical prescriptions for the conservation of physical, mental, and moral health. Long before a Rousseauistic kind of philosophe would do so, a doctor like Miguel Sabuco prescribed: "Take this advice: enjoy the fresh, clean, humid air of the countryside. Take pleasure in the freshness and the natural renewal of the environment, restored by the proximity of cool streams and refreshing rainfall, by the coming of every new dawn, and by successive changes in the air; this renewal is food for the brain, providing health and rejuvenation." There is also a remedy against the evils and illnesses which fear brings in its wake (which is why the knight can be so courageous): "to seek gaiety, sweet aromas, music, the country, the murmur of trees and water, good conversation, and, in a word, to enjoy pleasure and contentment in every way possible."[48]

Don Quixote's ideas thus correspond to a vision of village life and society that was already present in fifteenth-century Spain before the arrival of Erasmism, which later reinforced it; when that vision was supplanted by urban life (which always had an agrarian base, although that is another question), it became a factor in the utopian escapism of certain social sectors. When Salas Barbadillo recalls Cervantes's protagonist and contrasts him with his own pseudoknight of the court, he calls the former the "Knight of the Villages." This term is never used in Cervantes's text, but its use by Salas Barbadillo indicates clearly how the meaning of Don Quixote was grasped by kindred spirits in Cervantes's time who saw, as he did, the errors of those who would attempt to arrest historical evolution. Don Diego de Miranda is a village hidalgo who represents an ideal of civilian life; Don Quixote, on the other hand, is the expression of a different ideal, that of the warrior knight who defends certain archaic political views. Both reach the "heroic degree" of virtue of which Pedro de Portugal speaks in his *Sátira de felice e infelice vida*. Their lives are not equal, of course, but they are in perfect harmony.

Such was the importance of solitude for Spanish humanism that there were those who wished to turn this solitude from a remote source of moral inspiration into the basis for a stand against modernity. This was the case in Antonio de Guevara's "praise of the village." Humanism believed that its aristocratic and learned tendency was not incompatible with a true devotion to rusticity, in which the primitive, original nature of humankind is expressed at the same time that the false artificiality of the present is condemned. (These two sides of the coin of social value are a presupposition in every utopian attitude.) Pedro de Navarra wrote *Diálogos de la diferencia que ay de la vida rústica a la noble: Doctrina muy útil para los errores de nuestro tiempo.*[49] Guevara had similarly exclaimed: "Oh, how many prudent men are plowing the fields and how many fools are wandering around palaces! How many men with good judgment and cool heads live in villages and how many witless, brainless courtiers reside at the court!"[50] But some members of Cervantes's generation knew, as he did, that that idea would subvert contemporary society.

It is true that Petrarch himself had observed that "solitude is death to the unlettered."[51] Humanism of the sixteenth century, nevertheless, considered people in possession of the spontaneous prudence of natural man to be very learned indeed. In Torquemada's *Colloquios satíricos* the individual who converses with the shepherd says to him admiringly: "Everything you say is so correct and so elegantly and prudently expressed." And what is it that he sees in the peasant? "Above all, good character and clear judgment."[52] At that time the belief was already firmly established that the more old-fashioned a person is, the closer he is to his origin where his authentic self resides, while the more modern he is and the more influenced by civilization, the farther he is from his true nature. For that reason peasants, upon whom history has had less effect, are closest to man's original goodness, and their wisdom, being more ancient, is more natural and therefore more sound. Antonio de Guevara thinks that the villager "lives in accord with reason and not with opinion."[53] In the dawn of the new age (which in Spain coincided approximately with the reign of the Catholic Sovereigns), when old cultural forms were withering and were reborn in new ones, when a society under the influence of the spirit of modernity sought to begin a new epoch, Hernando de Pulgar—a good representative of that attitude—remembered that "in order to promote virtue and repress vice, authors wrote in a variety of ways. . . . Some poets composed plays and rustic songs and other similar literary forms."[54] In a reformist spirit he discusses some verses about shepherds, in whom he sees reflected the natural virtue of common people in contrast with the vices and crimes of powerful tyrants. (This is just one more example among many of those who see in simple, primitive society a model for the future which might be able to remedy the evils of the present.) Also, when the doctor Miguel Sabuco wished to compose a Renaissance dialogue on health and happiness, he had as speakers a group of shepherds living in solitude in the countryside, for only they could know anything about the subject.[55] There is a passage in the *Quixote* in which the reasonable and sensible priest admits that he knows from experience "that the woods breed men of learning and that many a philosopher is to be found in a shepherd's hut" (I:50). Letters and philosophy are not taken here in an academic, scholarly sense, but rather in their application to human behavior. What they mean is wisdom, in this case natural, uncultured wisdom, which is the most valuable kind and the most proper to the truly wise, for it is not dulled by passion, interests, or prejudice, all of which cloud the good judgment with which we order (or ought to order) our lives.

The Italianate influence in the Renaissance was able to dress pastoral material in sparkling literary finery and in that sense one can speak of an Italian phase in bucolic poetry and drama. However, the use of the figure of the shepherd surrounded by a world of virtues considered proper to him is a much older tradition. That idea of the shepherd as a model for life was familiar to the Hebrews and appears frequently in both the Old and the New Testaments.[56] Its importance in the New Testament makes it a key theme of primitive Christianity. The Christian moralist Hermas wrote *The Shepherd* in the second century; in it he refers to the book's Hellenistic antecedent, the Arcadia of ancient Greece. Vision V, the nucleus of this primitive Christian work, begins thus: "I had said my prayers at home and had just sat down on my bed when I saw a glorious looking man dressed as a shepherd come in. He was wrapped in the skin of a white goat and he had a knapsack on his shoulder and a staff in his hand."[57] This topic of shepherds as exemplars of a life of virtue dates, thus, from ancient Christian tradition and is reinforced every year by the liturgical cycle of the Church when it is recalled that the first to adore the child Jesus were shepherds. In relation to this episode in the life of Christ, E. Mâle was able to point out in medieval iconography and bibliographic sources the very favorable view of shepherds that had become established.[58] Thus it was absurd for Vossler to ignore these antecedents and claim that Spanish literature was unfamiliar with the topos of shepherds as sources of wisdom (as they appeared in French and Italian literature) and only portrayed them as rustic and boorish ignoramuses.[59] It is true that this kind of portrayal is found in Lucas Fernández and Juan del Encina, although their shepherds are never lacking in natural shrewdness and uprightness. But without waiting for examples of Italian influence, such as Garcilaso, we can find the praise of shepherds in our very first poet whose name is recorded by history: Gonzalo de Berceo.[60] In the middle of the fifteenth century the bishop and political writer Sánchez de Arévalo, examining the different states of human life, provided the following commentary: "This manner of life is pure, harmless to one's neighbor, and does evil to no one. It understands works of nature, serves the commonwealth, and is far from evils and occasions of sin. It is very suitable for contemplation and contrary to wasteful concerns. And the holy prophets followed this way of life and gave the name of shepherds to their kings and priests. And Christ our Redeemer took this glorious name for himself saying: 'I am the good shepherd.'"[61] Sixteenth-century Spain was well acquainted with the image of the "good shepherd" to characterize the perfect ruler. This means that writers like Alfonso de Valdés, Antonio de Guevara, Felipe de la Torre, Antonio de Torquemada, and Pedro de Navarra adopted the political-moral interpretation of the pastoral myth, taking it far beyond the literary version predominant in Garcilaso and others of the Italianist school. (Even in the latter there are, of course, nuances concerning the recognition of moral values; such is the case, for example, in Francisco de Aldana.)[62] Philosophers, political theorists, moralists, and doctors in the sixteenth century found in the image of the shepherd the hidden *integumenta* of a reformist literature offering lessons in exemplary living which it was the scholar's job to clarify. At the end of the century the literary theorist Carvallo held that "eclogues... are dialogues, speeches, treatises or competitions among shepherds in a rural setting, all of which must be taken allegorically to refer to very elevated subjects."[63]

Cervantes gives prominence to this in his works; he intuited that, as a result of an evolution in progress since the fifteenth century under the influence of what we might call a sociology of aspirations, the pastoral world and the chivalric world were not two separate things nor were they merely juxtaposed; they were the two hemispheres, perfectly fitted together, of one single ideal image of society. We know that the approximation of the pastoral and the chivalric myths, or the superimposition of one on the other, was possible in traditional social doctrine because of the compatibility of the aretological systems of chivalric and pastoral life. We have seen examples of this in Lucena, Valera, Díez de Games, and others. We also know that Feliciano de Silva incorporated pastoral material into books of knight-errantry, although he did not fully articulate the two elements. Thus, the possibility of connecting these two worlds was well established when Cervantes decided to make use of it. But nobody has enabled us to understand as well as he has the close connection between them, precisely at the historical moment when they had lost their efficacy and had become a deviation from the well-established norms of modern society.[64]

Cervantes's first serious literary effort was an "eclogue," a pastoral novel. (Remember what Carvallo's testimony tells us regarding the view of the pastoral genre commonly held at the time.) This was not a mere concession to literary fashion on Cervantes's part; the subject was very important to him, for he published the first part of *La Galatea* in 1585 and kept the work in mind throughout his entire career, promising the sequel until just before his death. As a young man he had shared to some degree in the inheritance of utopian ideas from the reign of Charles V, but this utopianism soon fell apart on him. In spite of his extensive literary output in those years and his repeated use of the pastoral motif in other works, he never wrote the second part of *La Galatea*. In our view this occurred because the social model which the genre implies and which many Spaniards living "outside the natural order" ardently desired had become invalid to Cervantes, who could not find a positive answer to the question. Cervantes, a prudent and reasonable man, a realist in fact, understood that the dream of a chivalric-pastoral society was senseless in the context of the real, historical world, for both positive and negative reasons: negatively, because of the serious defects of that world; positively, because of new technical, economic, military, and political resources. In the years immediately following the publication of *La Galatea*, Cervantes realized the impossibility and the absurdity of a program calling for government by a "good shepherd" in a traditional, economically rural society of knights and villagers. But this was precisely the kind of government of which many collaborators of Charles V had dreamed (Guevara, Las Casas, Alfonso de Valdés and others) and which some of Cervantes's own contemporaries were seeking to revive. What he did write was a brilliant refutation of that ideal. The second part of *La Galatea* is the *Quixote*, the demolition of the double chivalric-pastoral myth.

Hatzfeld correctly states that the pastoral element is present not just in the five episodes of the first and second parts of the Quixote but in fact exerts an influence throughout the entire work, showing up especially in Cervantes's stylistic use of language.[65] López Estrada has also pointed out the presence of pastoral elements in significant sections of the novel.[66] To our way of thinking, however, the question is much broader than this, manifesting itself in the focus and meaning of the entire work, that is, in its unity. Recall that at the beginning of the first part, in chapter 6, Don Quixote's niece expresses her fear that once her uncle is cured of his chivalry sickness, he might come down with another one transmitted by pastoral novels. The result is that these are thrown into the fire along with the books of knight-errantry. The possibility that Don Quixote's enterprise of restoration might take a pastoral turn was thus foreseen from the beginning. Had Cervantes continued with his impractical, evasive-utopian enthusiasm for an ideal society, the transformation of the chivalric environment into a society based on the bucolic model would have occurred at the beginning, perhaps after the encounter with the goatherds. But Cervantes abandoned that dream, so that the image of rural society only materializes in a precise manner in the final chapters, when Don Quixote's career comes to a melancholy end with his defeat, and at that point it can only have the appearance of farce.

Contrary to what Américo Castro believed, the appeal to the image of a pastoral world might not be a selection of elements taken from reality[67] but rather a transmutation of the real by means of a powerful Fichtean will. And just as for Fichte idealism does not annul history but in fact sets it in concrete order, the goal of the utopians of the pastoral myth (at least in one phase of that enterprise) was to bring historical reality to perfection. We observe in Cervantes a marked effort to stay on a historical level. Avalle-Arce has correctly noted that in *La Galatea* "the poetic, pastoral world is invaded by historical circumstances."[68] In this Cervantes is a direct heir of those who used the pastoral myth in the first half of the sixteenth century, and he must not be confused with people like Gabriel del Corral and Juan Pérez de Montalbán in the seventeenth who utilized inert, worthless vestiges of an already dead pastoral social literature. The meaning of this literature at the beginning of the hope-filled century of the Renaissance must be sought more in political, medical, and moral writers than in authors of pastoral novels as such, although in the earliest and most vigorous examples of the genre we can see elements of a moral-political line of thought. When people like Fray Cipriano de Huerga or Felipe de la Torre suggest to the king the image of the "good shepherd" (until around 1550–60), they are thinking in terms of the sensible imitation of a practical model for conduct.[69] Antonio de Torquemada systematically compares and contrasts social satire with praise of the pastoral life (especially in colloquia III and VII), declaring himself opposed to vanity, honor, sensuality, wealth, and the established professions, all of which we find in society, and in favor of the model of virtue he perceives in the rural, rustic existence of the shepherd. This must be understood as the clear choice of a proposal for reform in which that pastoral model functions as a remote inspiration to acquire a specific set of values. In his second colloquium Torquemada observes that his doctrine "will have the benefit of preventing people from despairing because of their poverty and placing their hopes for happiness and success in the possession of great wealth and high estate." It is, thus, extremely useful "for those who wish to follow it." We have already quoted similar words from Pedro de Navarra. Américo Castro cites an interesting passage from Mal Lara: Having encountered a group of shepherds in the mountains between Talavera and Salamanca, he exclaims: "Surely this is the Golden Age!"[70] This is the same thing that Erasmus longed for in a letter to a friend and that the Cortes of Valladolid of 1523 held up to Charles I of Spain as a worthy object of his desire.[71] The utopia of the Golden Age was possible. What is more, it was in existence; it could be found wherever groups like the American Indians or the isolated villagers of any country lived in virtuous mediocrity, in an economy based on strict necessity and a primary coexistence. Villagers and, especially, shepherds (who were more highly esteemed because of their importance in the Gospels) were the current repositories of the values of the Golden Age. Avalle-Arce is correct to deny that this is an artificial theme, "at least for these writers, all of whom connect it to essential elements in their thought."[72]

"What we do is make use of our reason," says the shepherd of Torquemada's dialogue, whereas city dwellers with all their hustle and bustle and conversations give themselves over to "a lot of nonsense and foolishness."[73] These are similar words to Guevara's, which we quoted a few paragraphs back: reason in opposition to capricious opinion. However, after writing the first part of *La Galatea*, Cervantes realized that this sort of reason was simply a kind of dreaming, and the dream of reason is madness, leading to mockery, impotence for action, and catastrophe.

Strictly speaking, the appeal to nature as a paradigm for individual and social life came from the medieval legacy, becoming consolidated and acquiring different nuances in the Renaissance. The late Middle Ages, with its more systematic (if not more accurate) information concerning the natural world, attributed to various creatures virtues which it felt they symbolized. (Thus, the lion, fox, serpent, etc. are animals which even today we connect with certain virtues or vices in our rhetorical use of language.) The Middle Ages even believed that nonrational beings—animate or inanimate—by lacking freedom of choice, follow the course that nature has set for them more faithfully than do humans and are thus much more effective examples of what we should consider natural behavior; they are, in other words, a more pure and constant manifestation of the paradigm of nature. This is why there are so many cases of animals in the repertory of *exempla* utilized by medieval moral literature: they are direct evidence of nature.[74] They are widely used by a Renaissance man like Leonardo, and there are also many instances in writers such as Guevara, Cervantes, Saavedra Fajardo, and others.

A writer of the late medieval period, Don Juan Manuel, explains the reason for the attention to subhuman beings in exemplary literature: "Animals obey the law of nature much better than do men."[75] The changes in outlook in the Renaissance did not alter this belief, without which Sancho's endless proverbs about animals would be meaningless. In the years just before Cervantes's time, Pedro Mexía affirmed that "all animals obey their nature perfectly" and for this reason their works are all "perfect in their class."[76] Francisco de Vitoria explains the reason for this: "What is natural in all things undoubtedly proceeds naturally from God."[77] Consequently, the closer a man is to nature, the more perfectly will he obey natural law. And, certainly, they are closer to nature who live within it: shepherds and villagers, naturally, but also knights who are in the countryside almost constantly and who, as we have shown, are obliged to eat, sleep, and fight exposed to the elements with nothing but rudimentary devices for their protection. Besides, in people such as these the damage done by culture to their natural goodness will never be as serious as it is in city dwellers who are always subject to the demands of ambition and covetousness, vices typical of an urban environment, in the view of a traditionalist.

The ideal way to restore society and return man to his original goodness is to introduce nature as the model to be followed: *sequere naturam* was the recommendation of both stoic and Christian doctrine, which together constituted the moral inheritance of the sixteenth century. Fernando de Herrera wrote that nature is "the tool of divinity,"[78] and as such it appears as a force conducive to rationality, a quality it never loses in later utopias where, although more secularized, it appears even more strikingly.[79] To adhere to the paradigm of nature was the basic principle of social intercourse and individual behavior in the Golden Age, whose restoration is Don Quixote's goal.

Around the middle of the fifteenth century the bishop Sánchez de Arévalo's advice was that "moral and political affairs ought to resemble the things of nature."[80] The countless writers of the fifteenth and sixteenth centuries who set forth the model of the Golden Age all agree in this stoic-Christian philosophy of moral naturalism. "There was a time when the world did not make use of such things and did not know about the aging of wine nor about the preparation of so many different types of food, nor about superfluous garments and offensive arms with which to perform evil deeds; rather, people then were given to the pursuit of knowledge and virtue. They rendered to nature what was necessary and avoided all excess and as a result lived happily in peace and concord. That century was golden in comparison with others which got progressively worse after men extracted from beneath the earth those costly dangers which they call riches."[81] This is the way Alfonso de la Torre presents to us the model that must be restored, a model which essentially is held in common by all writers who in the next century (the sixteenth) have a strong element of utopianism in their thought.

Nature is the principal subject of philosophical and moral dialogues and discourses in the Renaissance. It is the setting for books of knight-errantry, which contain a complete model of life in the country. (The seignorial palaces in those books are rural palaces located in the center of an agrarian society; they are, in fact, the element which rounds out the image of the shepherds' huts.) When the pastoral novel was incorporated into the novel of chivalry, a perfectly understandable process of literary evolution was brought to completion. Likewise, when Cervantes integrated the pastoral element into the chivalric world as one more piece of the whole picture, he brought out the deepest meaning of what it was that people sought in that genre. López Estrada has noted how in the much imitated works of Sannazaro "the protagonist is really nature extolled in opposition to the city."[82] And the system of values of every kind—ethical, aesthetic, economic, etc.—is patent in words such as those written by Jorge de Montemayor when he wished to lavish superlatives on something: "It seemed to be more a work of nature than of art or human industry."[83]

If in any system of belief there is one single idea which is the axis on which everything else hinges, that central idea in the period we are studying is the one which Torquemada defines thus: "The closer things are to what nature commands and loves, the better and more perfect they are."[84]

In that admirable golden state men's lives run their course in a natural setting. People live by eating the produce of the land and the fresh and delicious products of the flocks they tend, "cheese and acorns being common foods."[85] They have no food or protection other than what nature so prodigally provides, according to Mariana's portrayal. A frequent theme in sixteenth-century Spanish literature is the superiority of the rustic foods available in the countryside and small villages over what can be had in cities. Guevara was a sensualist, so enamored of the pleasures of food that he was more grateful to a friend for the shipment of some local cured meat than for sending him the *Dialogues* of Ockham, and he describes, in minute, mouth-watering detail, the advantages of the village over the court in this regard. And when we read Cervantes's description of the scene, we can have no doubt of the excellent appetite with which Don Quixote shares the bread and cheese of the goatherds. It is thus an error, one of Torquemada's characters notes, "for city dwellers and rich people to expend so much effort trying to add to their foods some flavor other than the ones they have, instead of following the order of nature as we shepherds do."[86] This approach logically leads to an idea which may be surprising to encounter in the sixteenth century, since its initial defense has so frequently been attributed to Rousseau: Children should be nursed by their own mothers rather than by wet nurses. The doctor Alvarez Miraval recognizes the medical advantages of maternal milk.[87] The theme is also echoed in the seventeenth century by moralists and political theorists. Francisco Santos holds that a mother "who gives birth but not suck can never be called a mother in the full sense of the word."[88] Saavedra Fajardo defends a similar thesis.[89]

It is not just that the basic foods consumed by people living in harmony with nature are more healthful and tasty; in addition, these people never lack what is necessary to satisfy hunger. For this reason they do not have the concept of property, that shackling of the possibilities of the human person. "No farmers worked the fields nor could they divide up the land with stone markers. They neither sowed nor took from the land more than what it freely offered, uncoerced and uncultivated. They erected no buildings but took their rest on the green grass and their houses were formed by the shade of tall trees."[90] Thus Jorge de Montemayor can inform us that in these circumstances "the shepherd never bothered to consider good or bad turns of fortune nor changes wrought by the passage of time. The covetous diligence of the ambitious courtier simply never occurred to him."[91] Mariana provides these same details in his version of the Golden Age. For Don Quixote that absence of private ownership will be the most characteristic feature of those happy centuries "to which the ancients gave the name of golden, and not because gold, which is so esteemed in this iron age of ours, was then to be had without toil, but because those who lived in that time did not know the meaning of the words 'thine' and 'mine'" (I:11). We must, however, avoid falling into a very easy and common misinterpretation of this statement. The aversion to the words "thine" and "mine" (the invention of which destroyed humanity, in Rousseau's opinion) can undoubtedly be documented in other writers of the period. According to Juan de Santa María, discord entered the first age of the world because of "those words 'mine' and 'thine,' laden with indifference (as Saint John Chrysostom says), the cause of all discord and evil."[92] Mateo López Bravo alludes in similar terms to these possessive pronouns.[93] Among Spanish Baroque writers the concept was in its twilight. For Cervantes it was part of the remains of a utopianism that the sixteenth-century chroniclers of the American Indians had surely helped encourage and that was about to be abandoned. In any case, there is in these passages, so similar to those of Cervantes, a clear reference to the elimination of private property such as that which later societies have experienced. In his speech to the goatherds Don Quixote adds that "in that blessed era all things were held in common" (I:11). This expression must not be interpreted strictly to mean a kind of collectivism. The image of the Golden Age implies the optimistic vision of natural production sufficient for human necessities; any excess that might occur need not be regulated. But all collectivism, in any of its forms, is an administration of insufficiency. The myth of the Golden Age tells us, on the contrary, that we are free to take whatever we need from nature because there will always be enough to go around. "To gain his daily sustenance no labor was required of any man save to reach forth his hand and take it," as Don Quixote explains (I:11). Neither do Torquemada's shepherds ever lack anything to satisfy their basic needs. Unlike later forms of collectivism which attempt to correct the abuses of a system of private property, what the Golden Age affirms is the freedom of individuals to take the goods of nature not because they are collective but because they are offered to all. The only limitation is a moral one, namely, willingly to refrain from taking more than what a person really needs. Seeing the issue in this way we can understand that the myth of the golden centuries entails the rejection of a socially organized economy, that is, of an urban, civilized economy which has brought about a scarcity of goods. All modern utopias, from More to Fourier and (later) Morris, rest on the notion of free and happy limitation to strict necessity, even though it may be a comfortable "necessity." We also have here the phenomenon of a return to the natural, receiving its extreme expression in the idea that in the blessed age there was no cultivation; the hand of man did not act upon nature or did so only in a very limited way. (We are dealing with a fable, and therefore all reasoning is on the basis of its unreality.) "The crooked plowshare had not as yet grievously laid open and pried into the merciful bowels of our first mother, who without any forcing on man's part yielded her spacious and fertile bosom on every hand for the satisfaction, sustenance, and delight of her first sons" (I:11). This beautiful picture which Don Quixote describes was ruined by the work of human beings "with all the rare and exotic tricks of fashion that idle curiosity has taught them" (I:11), words alluding to what we today designate more briefly: civilization. According to Sánchez de Arévalo, work in the fields is a school of sobriety and moderation, whereas all other work entails the risk of corrupting customs because, among other reasons, it tends to introduce new features which alter the social system of wealth.[94] Torquemada's shepherd also rails against "new inventions"[95] because "all things which come naked from Nature with only their essential being are more perfect than when their accidents are artificially acquired."[96]

Of course, when the utopia must be constructed and made socially effective, the problem becomes one of finding a way to organize work that will be freely done. (For Fourier work must be passional, while Marx opts for a vocational concept.) Work performed by free choice is more efficient and allows for a higher level of productivity with a shorter work day (six hours for More, four for Campanella). The new escapist utopia generally limits itself to urging the suppression of material labor, for it views such work as a painful and oppressive imposition. In any case, regardless of how work is conceived, both types of utopia reject the market system in favor of one which supplies only necessary provisions. In both of these aspects—natural work and natural production—we recognize the influence of the myth of the Golden Age.

Naturally, there is always a degree of human intervention to promote and facilitate nature's productive work. This activity is principally manual, with only a very limited use of rudimentary tools. Thus natural society can be seen (and this was in fact the view of the authors who made use of the Golden Age myth) as a system based on a life of work. For traditionalists or for reformers of the period seeking the restoration of distant or atemporal models, the culture of the countryside was a culture of work par excellence which did not allow for leisure, and this for two reasons: leisure deprives humans of energy needed to assist nature in a situation of scant population, and it also generates an increase in consumption by those who are not productively employed. Gabriel Alonso de Herrera holds that "the countryside does not allow for idle or lazy people; many evils and sins spring from idleness, for when men are not busy, they learn wickedness." The author consequently proposes that hidalgos and knights be obliged to work (in the country, of course, since that work is fit for nobles) and if they refuse, they should receive no food.[97] We should remember that writers on chivalry (treatises, dialogues, novels, etc.) consider a knight's labor with his weapons to be rural work, not because of the use of weapons, but because his life and his undertakings develop in the framework of nature.

Thus, while in the pastoral myth as well as in the broader myth of village life there certainly is a connection with the classical topos of *beatus ille*, the former is a larger concept and cannot be confused with the latter. The scope of the *beatus ille* motif is merely personal and does not go beyond the repertory of intimate, inner goods it provides its followers. On the other hand, the myth of rustic life aspires to a reform of society along traditional lines based on a static agrarian economy, a fixed, atemporal social order, and low, unchanging levels of production and consumption; these all work together to form the necessary basis for individual human virtue and for the inalterable means of social intercourse. This aretological image based on traditional society was understood to be the most desirable vision of human existence, and it should not surprise us that this myth of traditional restoration occurred as a reformist attitude oriented toward the future (the paradox is merely apparent) whose goal was the protection of the weak.

While not all literature of the period locates this myth in a historical phase prior to every form of cultivation, it is generally portrayed as having occurred at a time when human inventions had barely begun to develop and only made use of elements directly taken from nature. To be more precise, it is not a mere economy of gathering, but one based on rudimentary techniques of cultivation for the purpose of self-sufficiency, without any exchange of money with merchants. Miguel Sabuco, who uses the shepherd and farmer to represent the Golden Age and who has a clear concern for the welfare of the poor, refers to "the good times and golden age when everybody plowed the fields dressed in brown wool."[98] He thus reduces all economic activity to the basic and ancient operation of plowing, at the same time that he reinforces the idea of a natural state with his allusion to brown wool, so different from the fancy weaves and colors that civilization brings. Agriculture and shepherding were also the basic and most common activities of the Utopians and Solarians of More and Campanella.

The life of these rustics cannot properly be described as uncultured except in the sense that it is spontaneous. Their prudence, their clear understanding, and their taste for beautiful things may be equal or superior to that of learned people whose natural faculties are dulled by the detestable customs of modern society. The role attributed to music among those who lived in the Golden Age is noteworthy. Tacitus (*De Oratoribus*, 12) mentions the abundance of poets and singers in the *aureum saeculum*. Even the uncouth shepherd of Juan del Encina (sixteenth century) is delighted by the musical quality of the sounds of the countryside, particularly "the sound of crickets."[99] Music is an even more necessary component of the chivalric-pastoral world. The characters of Montemayor believe that there is no sadness that can resist music.[100] And for Fray Luis de León, making music is a function of a government modeled on the pastoral ideal.[101] In Gil Polo's comparison of life in the court and the countryside a lady familiar with the best music made in any palace or city of the world maintains that there are no melodies like the ones the shepherds sing: "These rustic shepherds' songs with such simple accompaniments give me more pleasure than the delicate airs composed in the palaces of kings and lords with their curious art, new inventions, and complicated novelties."[102] Returning to Miguel Sabuco, we see that a preference for the countryside and the joy that it occasions, along with a taste for the sounds of natural music, go together to form a medical concept of health.[103] It is not surprising that this idea was given social expression, becoming a characteristic aspect of the mythical Golden Age. In the literature of the sixteenth century there is nobody who knows how to make use of poetry and song as the shepherds and country folk do, nor is there anybody else who can astonish listeners with such elegant and prudent conversation. In the first phase of the period that inspires these myths, the chronicler Bernáldez commented on some real people in a primitive community (such as those that were being discovered in Africa or America), saying that they possessed such cleverness because they were shepherds and rustics.[104] As one element of the social image he offers us, Gil Polo maintains that in shepherds' huts there is no lack of clear understanding or lively wit: these qualities are easily encountered "in the deep woods and in rude huts."[105] Fray Luis de León insists on the same idea.[106] In Balbuena's pastoral council the "wit and skill" used by one and all in such places is much in evidence. And the songs and tales of the goatherds in Don Quixote are surprising for their pleasing sentiment, their prudent discourse, and the harmonious beauty with which they capture listeners' attention. All this derives from the sixteenth-century preference for a model based on nature rather than one learnedly fabricated by human effort. Gil Polo, a good source for commonplace themes of the period, exemplifies that idea in his contrast of these two models in his Diana enamorada.[107] On this matter the Baroque represents a radical change of attitude from the previous period, as we observe most notably in Gracián, a militant defender of the superiority of art over nature.[108] Cervantes finds himself in the middle of the tradition; initally a believer in Renaissance ideas regarding nature, he came to the conclusion that the great transformations of his period obliged him to go beyond them.[109]

Everything we have set forth has a political application, as we shall see. In the first place, this naturalism of chivalric-pastoral society leads to the belief that it might be possible to achieve a certain lack of coercion through coexistence in a natural state. G. Vida, widely read in sixteenth-century Spain, published a treatise titled De Reipublicae dignitate[110] in which he defended the idea that men are born free and exempt from law. "They were bound by law to no one, nor to the rule of any leader," Mariana says. There was no organized public power because, as Don Quixote tells us, "there was no one to judge or be judged" (I:11). Consequently, paternal guidance was all that was necessary, and the political utopia of the Golden Age did not go beyond this minimal element of law. And Murúa too, speaking of his noble barbarians, says that "among them there were neither judgments nor judges, other than their leaders, because there was nothing to correct; there were no laws because there were no excesses or crimes."[111] As we can see in the literature on the American Indians, sometimes the figure of the shepherd, a human type who represents rural society and presupposes upbringing, cultivation, rudimentary government, and spontaneous justice, is contrasted with the figure of the savage, a man of the wild and totally uncultivated jungle. We find this contrast in Montemayor's Diana and there are also echoes of it in the Quixote. But the characteristic feature of shepherds is for them to be sociable and capable of living together and having a political government in the way described by Fray Luis de León: Their life "shows the fullness of friendship and agreement among them, linking one to the other, allying and mixing, and by this mixture and alliance continually revealing and producing fruits which embellish the air and the earth."[112] In his commentary on shepherds Fray Luis frequently mentions their freedom. When Saavedra Fajardo takes up the myth years later, he says that "in the first age punishment and reward were unnecessary because there was no guilt, and glorious and decent things were loved for their own sake."[113] All this had the desired effect, whose precise meaning we shall examine later, of making it possible to claim that the consequence of the nature, habits, and virtues of Golden Age man was just what Don Quixote said: "All then was peace, all was concord and friendship" (I:11). In reference to the same natural state Mariana wrote: "Their way of life was based on peace." Balbuena, too, affirmed that at that time "the world still enjoyed the tranquillity and peace of its first summer."[114]

This means that the enterprise which inspires Don Quixote is clearly political. Is the goal of restoring knight-errantry and the Golden Age not essentially political? Do not both aspects of his activity refer directly to social intercourse and political government? The "myth of the village" had this projected application practically from the beginning. In Alfonso de Palencia's work, on the borderline between tradition and modernity, the rustic who debates with the defender of chivalric virtues says: "We have heard that there have been many residents of villages who have been called away to govern cities or who, after having ruled the republic well, have chosen to spend the rest of their days in their village."[115] And Fray Luis de León holds that government is proper to the shepherd, a government which "doesn't consist in issuing laws or in giving orders but in feeding and nourishing those whom He governs." If rulers are praised in accordance with the "good shepherd" image or if they are instructed through the many Renaissance "mirrors of princes" proposing this ideal, it is because good government is the shepherd's task. Fray Juan de los Angeles, like Fray Luis, tells us that the innocent and tranquil life of the shepherd has as its purpose "to govern, sharing with all his sheep and accommodating his government to the particular needs of each one of them." This text dates from 1607.[116] Cervantes agrees with these words and with other similar passages in his contemporaries and also in writers of the preceding century. Thus he tells us in *The Dogs' Colloquy* that the shepherd's "is a work involving the great virtue of protecting and defending the humble and feeble against the proud and mighty."[117] The nucleus of Don Quixote's world of villagers, shepherds, and knights is thoroughly political. It opposes the political forms that the social and economic transformations of the time bring with them, and, by proposing in their stead the restoration of something belonging to no particular space or time, it opens the way to an understanding of the values of the future.

Nevertheless, as happens with so many similar utopian visions, the paradox is immediately evident. All those beliefs which form the concept of the Golden Age are simply premodern. For this reason they clearly contrast with the modern State. And this gives us the key to the political world Cervantes constructs in order to overturn it in the end. It explains the nature of those ideas of Don Quixote we provisionally called medieval. They are medieval to the extent that they represent an effort to halt the advance of modernity; as such, it would be more precise to call them premodern. But Don Quixote does not represent the hope of a medieval restoration so much as he does a rejection of the modern State. For example, in the mentality of the modern State rusticity is condemned. This can be seen in Baroque writers who share the quasi-medieval ideology of Don Quixote.[118] Calderón suggests that one of the feats of Prometheus was to enable mankind to overcome its inability to be governed by formal laws.[119] What had been achieved in humanism along the lines of restoration or restitution, however, was simply an adaptation of beliefs which were really traditional in nature and were now articulated differently and supported by a new or partly new attitude. The end result was thus something which was not medieval, because it was combined with previously nonexistent ingredients, and which had nothing to do with the development of the modern spirit, either. It seems more an effort to force developments through a different channel, one closer to medieval ideas. This is what happened, to take one example, with the process of secularization begun in the thirteenth century but at times interrupted in the sixteenth because of humanism's deep sense of the religious dimension in life. Other examples: the arrival of modern political forms that the anachronistic imperial revival nearly eliminated; the development of a scientific spirit hinted at in the critical thinking of the fourteenth century but put aside in later decades at least until the mechanicalism of Galileo, with the result that today scholasticism is considered to be closer to the modern scientific outlook than the "rhetoric" and "letters" of humanism.

Later, in the final years of the eighteenth century and in the context of a very different system of beliefs, those elements of the Golden Age we have analyzed would again become an innovation in European thought. At the end of the sixteenth century, however, they were exactly the opposite: the trench from which the fight was carried on against modernity and its typical form of political organization, the State, already definitely established in other European countries.

In Don Quixote Cervantes symbolizes a current of opinion resistant to such a serious innovation, and it is precisely the modern State which Don Quixote in effect rejects. He is totally opposed to new political forms that in his view have destroyed religion, peace, happiness, and justice among people. In the long list which Angel Valbuena patiently put together of the authors cited in the *Quixote*[120] there is not a single mention of the name of Machiavelli, the symbol (for good or for evil, depending on one's point of view) of new-style politics. It is curious that Cervantes himself only mentions Tacitus once, in the *Viaje del Parnaso,* and even then only as a historian.

Yet in certain aspects Cervantes does have a politically modern outlook. A concrete example is his Spanish patriotism. Patriotism is a modern product; the word itself did not even exist yet.[121] That political vision of the unity of Spain was both recent and unstable, but in Cervantes it is a firm conviction—so firm, in fact, that he tends to attribute it to the primitive inhabitants of the Peninsula, even at the risk of falling into an anachronism. His *Numancia,* an epic of Spanish freedom, is one of the most beautiful plays of our classic theater, far superior in tragic power to the works of even our best dramatists. The play contains the very beautiful prophecy of the Duero, a paean to what Cervantes sees as Spain's high destiny. These verses recall Fray Luis de León's "Profecía del Tajo" not just because of the similar literary technique but because in both there is a common feeling for country which Fray Luis extends "to all of sad and spacious Spain." For him and for Cervantes the land has but one name: Spain. Cervantes's characters in the *Persiles,* for example, identify themselves as Spaniards and say that their burning desire, like the captive in the *Quixote,* is to return to Spain. His praise of Castillian, his admiration for Barcelona, and his defense of literary humanism in vernacular tongues (remember his high praise for *Tirant lo Blanch*) are well known. He admires and takes pride in the power of the kings of Spain, and there is no reason to doubt his sincerity when on occasion he celebrates and defends their enterprises.

But just what enterprises are they? Political writers of the seventeenth century closest to the theory of the modern State speak of the Catholic Sovereigns as exemplars for their successors. But long before those Baroque writers and even before Cervantes's birth Charles I had brought other ideals to Spain. (Or, more precisely, he had caused them to flourish in part of the country.) These ideals were not exactly those of the Middle Ages, for the titular head of the medieval Christian empire was the Germanic emperor, while the sixteenth-century Spaniards who hoped for a Christendom under the moral direction of chivalry expected that this mission would belong to Spain. This was the dream of humanists like the ambassador Lope de Soria or Alfonso de Valdés. Perhaps for Cervantes this could never be more than a dream, or possibly a delirium. (What the Spanish State did have, on the other hand, was the most modern military organization in Europe, whence its period of great victories.)

For Cervantes, of course, it is not a question of renovating the dead medieval structure of the Empire. For him the word "emperor" or the Dantesque term "monarch" (which we see in the famous sonnet of Hernando de Acuña) have lost all concrete political meaning, and the title of emperor even appears occasionally in the plural. This indication of his thinking can be verified in several passages of the *Quixote*. But what the quixotic utopia rejects is an expanding state organization attentive only to the particular interests of the kingdom. The world of the knight implies an indefinite and unobtainable universalism, with no institutional structure. If we see the *Quixote* in relation with other works of Cervantes, however, such as his "Canciones de la Armada Invencible" exalting his king as "the Lord of the vast Spanish homeland," we may wonder whether there is evidence for the existence of such heroic sentiments in his masterpiece. It is true that references to space and time are quite veiled in *Don Quixote*, which, as we have pointed out, is appropriate in works of utopian nature. But it is equally true that the novel alludes to concrete Spanish events, and we may infer from the discussion about the war with the Turks or the expulsion of the moriscos that Cervantes felt the king was obliged in justice to be vigilant in the defense of Christendom. In the final analysis Don Quixote, a knight-errant exercising his profession in Spain, is more interested in the interior reform of life and of the Christian republic than in battles with foreign infidels; this is not to deny a national element to his enterprise, but it is an imprecise one, as is typical of any utopia. This corresponds approximately to the intellectual world of certain Spanish collaborators of Charles V whom Cervantes portrays as spiritually akin to his hero. While Cervantes exalts the memory of the invincible Charles V, "which is and shall be eternal" (I:39), there is in all of his works only one brief reference to a king whose contemporary he was, Philip II, whom he simply calls "our good King Philip" (I:39, a few lines before the passage just quoted); this in spite of the fact that he mentions Philip in connection with the great battle of Lepanto.[122]

The author of the *Viaje a Turquía* speaks of "our civil wars" which prevent the Spanish king from taking on other enterprises and whose purpose, according to the thinking of the period, was to restore the Christian polity. That was a universal goal for Christendom. Thus Don Quixote will use his weapons to pursue an analogous moral end, the restoration of social life, and will only occasionally consider taking on a foreign war, and always with the same goal of moral correction, never for territorial expansion. Maldonado has correctly clarified the close relation between the formula which defines Don Quixote's action (set forth in the highly significant speech to the goatherds and in many other places) and the one that expresses the imperial policy of the Caesars, whose last representative was Charles V: "to be merciful to the down-trodden and to conquer the haughty."[123] This formula reveals the idea of justice in Don Quixote as the basis and even the content of the social and political life of Christians and, perhaps, at a certain moment, of Cervantes himself. We find the same formula enunciated in *The Dogs' Colloquy* with a meaning similar to that which it has throughout the *Quixote*.[124] Don Quixote tells the goatherds of his mission to bring justice to society and thus improve customs, reform souls, and correct evil desires, explaining that the order of knights-errant was instituted "for the protection of damsels, the aid of widows and orphans, and the succoring of the needy" (I:11). This is the chivalric formula with all its Pauline flavor. His enterprise is oriented toward the interior of the body in which he lives, of that world which on more than one occasion he calls the "Christian community" or the "Christian republic." For that reason, he confesses, "my sole endeavor is to bring the world to realize the mistake it is making in failing to revive that happiest of times when the order of knight-errantry was in the field" (II:1). Whatever that mistake may be (we shall not pursue the matter at the moment), it is an inner mistake that the knight tries to combat and in this way bring about the renewal to which he has committed all his effort.

López Estrada has noted the very limited, almost insignificant role allotted to the question of the "good prince" in *La Galatea*.[125] We believe, however, that this does not detract from the political significance that the pastoral myth has and from the role it plays in the totality of Cervantes's work. In a pastoral novel it is quite logical that the image of society should be a limited one and that questions of command and government should receive scant attention, for law and authority are but a thin veneer covering this quasi-anarchical world. Besides, Cervantes, at the midpoint of his work on *La Galatea*, realized the insufficiency and emptiness of the image of pastoral society in the concrete circumstances of his time; he therefore took up the whole political aspect of the problem in the *Quixote* and highlighted the uselessness and inadequacy of the anachronistic utopia in which that pastoral image found expression. As we have said, the *Quixote* is the novel-utopia of the chivalric-pastoral government in which a sector of society sought refuge against the natural course of history. In it Cervantes brings together the three paths which, according to Huizinga, came into being at the end of the Middle Ages in connection with the longing for a more beautiful life, an aspiration that acquired something like the status of an article of faith among certain social groups in sixteenth-century Spain.[126] And Cervantes shows with frank but not cutting humor (such is his art) that anyone following that road winds up in "quixotry."

Cervantes's *La Galatea* and its intended sequel, his warm portrayal of the world of village and chivalry in the *Quixote,* and his return to a similar image of government in the *Persiles* all suggest that he was sympathetic to that kind of belief. In the latter work, his last creation, the government of King Policarpo is similar (even in the names) to the episode of King Polidoro in the *Diálogo de Mercurio y Carón* of Alfonso de Valdés.[127] Valdés, Guevara, Las Casas, and others were all, from somewhat different points of view, proponents of that utopianism which Cervantes wanted stopped.[128]

The *Quixote* has a political purpose: to show the foolishness of those who choose to be part of a world of beliefs that leads to the unreal vision of Don Quixote. But Don Quixote and those who live in the world he symbolizes insist that that is precisely where human happiness is to be found. Cervantes had to elucidate that utopia thoroughly and seriously in order to show how it leads from one failure to another. This is why *Don Quixote* impresses us as a serious book in spite of its strong dosage of humor.

What is to be the universal task of righting the world, the effort that will bring about human happiness? Let us identify it with reference to its end. The so-called autumn of the Middle Ages, a period which is no longer medieval *sensu stricto,* saw peace as the primary political task. Luis Vives spoke of the golden times of the Saturnian kingdoms, "when people lived in great tranquillity, concord, and equality, without pride, anger, or envy; without doubt such were the people who obeyed the orders of God."[129] Strictly speaking, the end was the same during the centuries of political Augustinianism of the high Middle Ages, with the difference that the peace sought could only be the *pax Domini,* a spiritual matter and therefore under the aegis of the Church. The political theorists shifted the task to the Emperor. That was precisely what Alfonso de Valdés believed that Charles V, the great champion of Europe, was striving for, and it was also the hope of humanists like Erasmus and Luis Vives. Don Quixote longs for the same thing, and in its service he places the arms wielded by heroes formed according to his ideal of perfection. For Don Quixote the end of arms is peace, the greatest good people can desire in this life. (The curious thing is that he contrasts arms with letters, perceiving the latter to have nothing to do with the end he exalts.)

For the first good news that mankind and the world received was that which the angels brought on the night that was our day: "Glory to God in the highest, and on earth peace, good will toward men." And the salutation which the great Master of Heaven and earth taught his chosen disciples to use when they entered any dwelling was, "Peace be to this house." And another time he said to them, "Peace I leave with you, my peace I give unto you, peace be with you." It was a jewel and a precious gift given and left by such a hand, a jewel without which there can be no blessing whatsoever either in Heaven or on the earth. This peace is the true end of war, and for "war" you may substitute "arms." (I:37)

The idea of peace through arms had been a common theme in literature well before Cervantes and continued to be so long after him. It appeared repeatedly in the numerous "discourses on arms and letters" in vogue at the time, in keeping with a kind of pacifism that Bataillon says was widespread in Spain and that Cervantes shared up to a point, although he had different views about how it should be defended. In Camos's treatise, published ten years before the *Quixote,* we find the following statement: "The peace which the commonwealth enjoys is obtained by arms and the military; by those same arms prosperity is acquired and conserved; in fine, the end of war is peace."[130] This was also the thesis of Bartolomé Felippe, who affirmed that peace is "the end for which men take up arms."[131] The list of writers in agreement with this idea would be endless and would even include military theoreticians such as Vicente Mut. And to see how it has persisted we have only to refer to the great collector of commonplace ideas, Suárez de Figueroa, according to whom "war was invented to preserve peace."[132]

Nevertheless, in the midst of all that unanimity there is an interesting difference. For Suárez de Figueroa peace is preserved when an enemy, seeing that a province or town is well fortified and prepared to resist, abandons its plans for attack. Peace, in other words, is threatened by foreign forces who have targeted certain positions in an extensive territory. In opposition to this essentially modern concept of a threat to peace, Camos refers to "the insolence of those who disturb the peace." This is much closer to the premodern view that peace is disrupted from within the kingdom by violent types who have unjust designs on the rest of their community. This in essence is Don Quixote's understanding of the matter.

How, then, is it possible for arms to bring about peace? Because arms must serve justice and virtue. In the "Discourse on Arms and Letters" we are told that the object of letters "is to administer distributive justice and give to each that which is his and see that good laws are observed" (I:37). But even for this end arms are necessary, for through them justice is upheld. In the symbolism of the knight's arms as defined according to traditional chivalric theory in *Guillem de Vàroich* there is a symbol which alludes to that distributive justice, only mildly and occasionally coercive, which it is the knight's duty to uphold: "The horse symbolizes the people, whom the knight must uphold in peace and concord by maintaining justice; for just as the knight does all he can to care for his horses when he wishes to go into battle and allows no one to harm them, so is he also obliged to protect the public."[133]

The knight's function as a minister of justice is patent throughout the book and does not require further textual documentation. We should notice, however, that the ideal of justice which the knight (as he is conceived in the *Quixote*) attempts to realize does not involve the kind of justice proper to a closed political organization, but rather the type which by its very nature constantly makes its presence felt at an individual level. Although the justice of the *Quixote* may be called distributive, it is not legal justice but rather the kind in which the State appears more as an arbiter than as a directly interested party. And this reveals scant fondness for the modern state system. In keeping with traditional teaching, any political writer of the seventeenth century, as, for example, Juan de Santa María, speaks of two kinds of justice, "one which is common and orders man's relations with the commonwealth, and another which is individual and orders his dealings with his neighbor."[134] The latter is the type which concerns Don Quixote and contributes to the formation of his ideal. It is also the type in which the State is least directly interested. To a degree, the period was aware of this distinction. The same Juan de Santa María held that while Aristotle based his republic on the former, Plato opted for the latter. The humanists were very much influenced by Plato, whom they understood more or less correctly, and Cervantes, drawing once more on humanism in his presentation of an ideal society in the *Quixote,* also reveals Platonic influences. What is more, the justice of the State vis-à-vis individuals is also conceived by Don Quixote to be his own personal affair, as we see clearly in the episode of the galley slaves.

This connection between peace and arms, the agent of justice, explains a difficulty. One might consider it odd that a knight, whose profession is arms, should be enamored of an ideal time whose basic characteristic is peaceful life, and that he should go so far as to present himself as a restorer of that time whose concord and social amity he constantly praises. Revealing characteristics of the Golden Age myth, Mariana too tells us: "No tumult of war ever disturbed the peaceful life of those people." The fact is that arms, utilized in Don Quixote's way and with his purpose in mind, do not disturb the peace but rather make it possible. For no matter how good people in their natural state may be, there is always the possibility that some will commit acts of violence and injustice against others.

We have already mentioned that in pastoral life, in spite of everything, pain, violence, and even crime do exist. Pastoral or rustic life, no matter how idealized, does not mean that these evils are impossible, just that they are the exception. They are so exceptional, in fact, that they do not require an established organization to combat and punish them, as is the case in urban society where, in fact, some people claim that the bureaucratic system only serves to increase social evils. (Among the utopian literary works, William Morris's *News from Nowhere* describes a similar society.)

In natural society the persons charged with reacting, when necessary, to unfortunate situations in order to restore justice are equally natural and spontaneous. In the world of Don Quixote they are the practitioners of the order of chivalry whose natural virtues, brought to perfection by the exercise of arms under an oath to do good, guarantee the correctness of their judgment and behavior.

This is why there had to be knights-errant in natural society: to set evil people on the right path and to correct any offenses they might have committed. Thus, the arms or fighting which concern Don Quixote have nothing to do with battles between large organized armies; rather, they are individual actions by means of which one or at most a small group of prideful and lawless people are brought by force to that respect which all must have for each other in a peaceful society. Political interest is not involved, but only a pure criterion of justice on all sides, even when an action is not the national enterprise of a whole people but the just undertaking of a group of knights in defense of a particular kingdom. Did Charles V not view the opposition of Francis I as a matter susceptible to resolution by a duel rather than as a conflict between two large blocks of political power?

It should be noted that during the centuries in which the chivalric mentality reached its apogee, we see the beginning of the great political and territorial organizations, the precursors of modern or Renaissance monarchies. In the second half of the fifteenth century we find evidence of the coming nationalization of war, which occurs between extensive and solid concentrations of power, between monarchs who do not confront each other individually (unlike Charles V) but rather as sovereigns of large territories and great masses of people. The documents published by Luis Suárez Fernández provide some significant examples. Enrique IV of Castille, declaring war on the king of France, ordered all his subjects to sever relations with the French king and to give him no money, for otherwise their goods would be confiscated. On the same occasion he prohibited the cities of Guipúzcoa from signing truces with cities of the neighboring kingdom, although he did allow them to continue to trade so that they would be well stocked with grain.[135] War is a general undertaking of an entire political community and of its sovereign power.

The concept of war in the chivalric mentality is very different indeed. Here war is conceived as a limited encounter among individuals or small groups over matters capable of resolution by interindividual combat without the entire country suffering the harsh consequences of a large-scale conflict. It is not a public or "nationalized" affair, even though we use that word here anachronistically. This is why, among the militarily passive inhabitants of the Golden Age, knights acted as combatants and "took upon themselves the defense of realms, the protection of damsels, the succor of orphans, the punishment of the proud, and the rewarding of the humble" (II:1). Thus, given the close links among justice, arms, peace, and happiness, the age in which these knights were in the field was blessed indeed. There is nothing strange, therefore, in the fact that the premodern knight of Jiménez de Urrea's *Diálogo*, who believes it is the knight's duty to impose justice by means of duels, should buttress his argument with concepts both of the Golden Age and of knightly justice: "We read that in those golden centuries, when men earned nobility and eternal renown by their own valor, the world exalted and honored those who won hand to hand battles."[136]

This system of war, with triumph depending totally on the virtue of the knight, is the only one, in the traditional view, able to ensure peace through justice, in the universal and Christian sense of the word, free from the interference of private political interests. In the second half of the sixteenth century this was, of course, a thoroughly anachronistic scheme that Cervantes felt obliged to expose as impractical at best. This ideal of peace through justice comes from the Augustinian tradition. At its base is the concept of peace as spiritual calm and tranquillity in the public order, as Saint Augustine explains in *Civitas Dei*. This Augustinian link is the thread that leads us to a political interpretation of the *Quixote* as inconsistent with the modern State; it enables us to view the novel instead as solidly within the humanist tradition, a direct heir of medieval mentality.

That yearning for peace and justice led to the possibility of portraying a world in which they reign supreme. When Erasmus wrote his letters to Francis I and Charles V, and when Luis Vives wrote his *De concordia et discordia in humano genere*, they were not thinking about returning to a hierarchical structure for Christendom; nor, as we have made clear, was Cervantes. It is true that years earlier Antonio de Guevara had said that it was very beneficial "for an emperor to be monarch and lord of all the world," but he denied that Spanish kings had harbored this idea as their "secret and ultimate goal," and he assured us that hidden behind this claim was just another excuse for the widespread enmity toward Spain.[137] The imperial idea was no longer valid for Cervantes; at most, it was a mere echo inspiring a form of government based on *auctoritas* rather than on *potestas*. Thus, what Cervantes would seek was universality not in organization but in conduct, a universality based on the "Christian politics" he praised in Gabriel Pérez del Barrio's book on the new public function of secretaries[138] (although what this book really contains is not so much Christian politics as the beginnings of a new concept of administration):

> Your book shows us
> that only you have given
> beautiful and Christian form
> to the matter of State.[139]

Don Quixote has also stated that the deeds of the knight should not exceed those limits set by the Christian religion (II:8). He says, too, that they will serve as a model for general behavior; but he could never see religion incorporated into the realm of bureaucracy, which was acquiring so much importance in his time.

Notice that the life of the knight is not, properly speaking, the normal or common life of the Golden Age. His function is to resurrect that life, to watch over it, and to defend it against human malice. His job is to bring about conditions in which people can live in a happy, natural state; he does this by the example of his courage and virtue and by punishing and eliminating evils.

The Golden Age was a time in which natural goodness preserved peace, justice, and virtue and enabled people to live in harmony with nature. The modern age, however, is far removed from all of those goods. In the second half of the seventeenth century Ferrer de Valdecebro asked himself who caused this situation. His answer: "People, because they have apostatized from nature."[140] Martín de Murúa, on the other hand, tells of those primitive Peruvians who were so similar to the inhabitants of the Golden Age: "They had only one law: not to offend the rights of nature."[141] What Don Quixote's mission means to him, in terms of the restoration of nature, has already been analyzed here.

Thus Don Quixote's utopia of Fichtean will leads to the utopia of natural reason and culminates in the episode of the island of Barataria. The political key to the Golden Age is government by reason; but we must clarify that we are speaking of reason in the traditional sense, the kind which engenders wisdom, and not reason which in modern thinking produces positive science. Castiglione talks about "the manner and method of right rule: which of itself alone would suffice to make men happy and to bring back once again to earth that Golden Age which is recorded to have existed once upon a time when Saturn ruled."[142] It is that "republic of nature" which was still spoken of by Quevedo and in which all one has to do is pay attention to what natural signs tell us, for "these are lessons disguised as meteors."[143]

Don Quixote's purpose is to create in society those conditions which will make possible Sancho's government, that is, the utopia of reason in a natural state, the utopia of good reasoning, of justice in accord with good sense.[144] Max Weber has seen in Sancho's government of the island the rational administration of justice based on free and natural use of reason, as opposed to formal, organized justice.[145]

This utopia of Solomonic government is what Fray Luis de León finds in pastoral society: "The perfect government is inspired by the living law capable of judging what is best and always willing to judge in such a way that the law is nothing other than the sane and right judgment of the one who commands, who always adapts himself to the particular case of the one he governs."[146] That image of a pastoral or village utopia (similar in some ways to the "justice of the Cadi" which Cervantes recalls in another context) is better reflected in the qualifications which entitle Sancho to govern than in the knight's advice to the new governor or in the latter's judgments. At first Don Quixote requires heroism in his squire if he wishes to be a governor. And on another occasion the knight's thinking appears to be influenced by elements of political technique on a Machiavellian level:

> Come now, you sinner, supposing that the wind of fortune, which up to now has been so contrary a one, should veer in our favor, filling the sails of our desire so that we should certainly and without anything to hinder us be able to put into port at one of those islands that I have promised you, what would happen to you if, winning the victory, I were to make you the ruler of it? You will have rendered that impossible by not being a knight nor caring to become one, and by having no intention of avenging the insults offered you or defending your seignorial rights. For you must know that in newly conquered kingdoms and provinces the minds of the inhabitants are never tranquil, nor do they like their new lord so well that there is not to be feared some fresh move on their part to alter the existing state of affairs and, as the saying goes, see what their luck will bring. And so it is necessary that the new ruler possess the ability to govern and the valor to attack or defend himself as the case may be. (I:15)[147]

But this gradually disappears in the course of the novel. Sancho will govern not merely through the gracious concession of his lord, nor through the merit of his heroic deeds. Referring to his master with that admiration he has been developing, he says: "God willing, I'll be just such another as he is" (II:32). By this he does not mean he has the physical and moral energy to be another knight-errant, but rather that he feels he has been captivated by Don Quixote's world, imbued with his spirit, and enabled, therefore, to play a role in that world in his own capacity. Of course, as Alborg notes, Sancho is by nature a peace-loving villager, but when he finds himself in a situation that obliges him to fight, he is never cowardly.[148] On the other hand, we must guard against the tendency of the reader of the *Quixote* to undervalue the squire's social function in the world of chivalry. The squire is not a mere mechanical servant; he represents a rung on the ladder to knighthood. Thus Don Juan Manuel informs us that squires were usually sons of knights.[149] In any case, in the second quarter of the sixteenth century there was an evident change in the function and consequently in the social worth of the squire, which brought about certain changes in lexical usage.[150] Naturally the squire's role is altered in the *Quixote* because Sancho comes from a social group that no longer believes in chivalry; thus the tendency to translate his services into a salary.[151] Don Quixote's desire is to raise him to a another level within the hierarchy of his world. But, in any case, the factors which in various parts of the novel play a role in assessing whether or not Sancho should ascend to a position of governor are other than those we have already mentioned.

By what right, then, will Sancho be able to govern? Against those who doubt his capacity he repeatedly states what his merits are and what is the good and sufficient reason for him to ascend to such a high position, namely that he has the wits to do so. This implies that wits, good natural reason, common sense, if you will, are all that is required for the function of government and that Sancho, like anybody else, possesses that faculty. He asks his lord for the island and assures him that "however large it may be, I feel that I am indeed capable of governing it as well as any man in this world has ever done" (I:10). On another occasion he answers the ecclesiastic who doubts his ability to govern by saying, "I am one who deserves it as well as any other" (II:32). Why is this? Because to govern is merely to follow nature, and nature is equal in everybody and tells everybody the same thing. He will therefore rule over his subjects with judgment "more of the dull than of the sharp," as he himself admits (II:51).

There is in the belief of the period a basic conviction which allows people to believe that, in Descartes's words, "good sense is of all things in the world the most equally distributed."[152] The assumption is not only that this good sense can be utilized in the natural governance of a small society, but that in the area where intelligence is most necessary, in the development of knowledge, it will make possible the stupendous adventure of discovering a scientific method that can be used by ordinary people: the *novum organum* with which Bacon wished to replace the old Aristotelian *organon* is just such a method.

Long, painful study and a disciplined, complete preparation are not necessary in order to govern. Arguing in a very different direction, Simón Abril suggested that the study of moral philosophy be encouraged not just in universities and schools but in the towns themselves, "so that many men of government would be nurtured with a knowledge of this part of philosophy which is so pertinent for governance; thus, those who serve His Majesty would know what good government means and they would not go into something as serious and important as this so poorly prepared as they now do."[153] Sancho de Moncada, a contemporary of Cervantes, would go so far as to request that a secularized university be established in the capital in order to provide a supply of experts in government.[154] In truth, however, all that is required to follow the maxims of nature is a simple method that will sharpen the *lumen rationis* which we all possess. Thus Don Quixote says of Sancho:

> I discern in him a certain aptitude for governing, and with a little brushing-up of his wits he might make out as well with any government whatsoever as a king with his taxes. Especially since we know from long experience that neither much ability nor much learning is necessary in order to be a governor; for there are a hundred hereabouts who are barely able to read and who yet acquit themselves of their task like so many gerfalcons. The main thing is for them to be possessed of good intentions and a desire to do the right thing always, for they will never lack those who can advise and direct them in what they have to do, just as those who are knights and not scholars pass judgment with the aid of an assessor. (II:32)

According to the usual system of the period, exceptions notwithstanding, governing was a function of the learned. Thus, even though Sancho might reach a position of government without being highly educated, Don Quixote assumes that once he finds himself in such a distinguished position, he will naturally go on to acquire some learning. In a letter he sends the new governor from the duke's palace he says, apropos of a maxim he quoted in Latin: "If I quote Latin to you, it is because I assume that since becoming a governor you will have learned it" (II:51). Nevertheless, the utopia of Sancho's government is based on reducing principles and rules and, in general, limiting the knowledge needed for government to the level of natural reason and good Christian conscience. Sancho, whom we have seen declare himself fit for government, openly admits: "I don't know much about letters; ... in fact, I don't even know my ABC's; but to be a good governor, it's enough for me to be able to remember the Christus" (II:42). Rodríguez Marín notes that the "Christus" was the cross preceding the alphabet in school primers. Clemencín comments that Sancho "ingeniously applies this idea to the principle that to govern well it is more important to have God in mind than a lot of knowledge."[155] Above all, it is important to judge according to reason in its first, natural manifestation, once the precepts of faith have prepared it to follow the straight and narrow path, and not according to technical formulas and interpretations. Moments later, when Don Quixote expresses certain reservations regarding his squire's fitness to rule, Sancho offers to renounce his claim if it might lead to failure and endanger his salvation, for he places religion before all else: "I would rather go to Heaven as Sancho than go to Hell as a governor." This convinces Don Quixote of his merit once and for all, and he answers: "So help me God, Sancho, ... if only by reason of these last words that you have spoken, I hold you fit to be the governor of a thousand islands. You have by nature a good disposition without which no knowledge is worth anything. Commend yourself to God, then, and try not to lose sight of your main purpose; by which I mean, that you should make it your unswerving aim to do the right thing in all matters that come up for your judgment, for Heaven always favors good intentions" (II:43).

In good government one must hold fast to what is natural, to the good sense which all people normally possess. It is for this reason that in his example of a perfect government, in his *Utopia*, Thomas More held that the laws were accessible to everyone. Thus, "among them everyone is an expert in law," and in the interpretation of law "they are of the opinion that the most obvious [interpretation] is the fairest."[156] Sancho's method of government is also the plainest and the most plebeian, understood by anybody and based on a common sense which, in Don Quixote's words, has just been brushed up a bit.

Sancho can govern using a kind of wisdom within everybody's grasp because, in point of fact, everybody has had a hand in creating it: it is the wisdom of popular maxims, which carry more authority than anything else because "nobody is so wise that he can hit the mark as regularly as the people as a whole when they confer and pool the resources of their knowledge, unless it be a case of very dull-witted people."[157] While Don Quixote criticizes the incessant string of proverbs that flows from Sancho's lips, his criticism is limited to his squire's inability to use them in moderation and in an opportune manner, and to his lack of understanding of their meaning, especially at the beginning of their adventure. Don Quixote himself makes frequent use of proverbs, but he does so in a measured and appropriate way. He even goes so far as to praise them explicitly and attach great value to the knowledge they contain, for in the final analysis they are maxims based on long experience. "It is my opinion, Sancho," he says, "that there is no proverb that is not true; for they are all drawn from experience itself, mother of all the sciences" (I:21). Shortly afterwards the novel again insists, this time through the words of the captive, that all proverbs are true, "being wise maxims drawn from long experience" (I:39).[158] Don Quixote adopts the popular view, as expressed by one of Lope's characters: "These [proverbs] are all quintessential books of the world; they were composed by custom and confirmed by experience."[159]

And in what environment does that experience occur? The taste and high regard for proverbs became widespread in sixteenth-century humanism for two reasons: in the first place, because popular or rustic wisdom was considered ancient wisdom; secondly, because it was consequently held to be natural wisdom. Castillian proverbs were compiled and glossed, and whole books were written on them. Their authority derives from their antiquity, in addition to the fact that "the best thing about proverbs is that they are born among common people," as Juan de Valdés said.[160] Juan de Mal Lara's enormous tome *Filosofía vulgar*, a collection of a thousand proverbs with commentary, was widely read in Cervantes's time. And that "vulgar philosophy" (in which "vulgar" means of or relating to the common people) is what Sancho has. As Mal Lara says in classifying it, it is for the most part moral philosophy, a suitable discipline to lay the foundation for every type of government, from self-government of an individual to the government of society and the commonwealth.[161]

In the view of the period proverbs are philosophy, then understood to be the same thing as wisdom. "They are," in the words of León de Castro, "more than science and they belong to the wisdom and understanding which are so resplendent at that age [i.e., in old age]."[162] In Mal Lara's thinking on this subject we see the fundamental relationship already familiar to us: natural = primary = primitive. The first thing in man is what is natural, especially a knowledge of nature, and it is therefore what we discover in the first men or in those who are closest to them. "The goodness of our earliest forebears who had just been created by God" guarantees, in the view of Pedro de Medina, the validity of the proverbs which supposedly have their origin in them.[163] Proverbs are a branch of knowledge, properly speaking, and thus fit to be studied in books, but not in any book "which has been printed and copied, but in one which is natural and engraved in human memory and creativity." This is why they are so valued for their age; Mal Lara refers to them as "antiques, relics of ancient knowledge" which "place all the wisdom of antiquity before our very eyes."[164] León de Castro also holds that proverbs "are the most ancient philosophy." And for this very same reason Don Quixote praises them once again: "Proverbs are concise maxims drawn from the wisdom and experience of our elders" (II:67).

The authority of this knowledge is based on the belief to which we have alluded and which is perfectly expressed by Mariana: "Our first ancestors were people who were more sensible in their thinking, as would be expected from those who lived nearest to the very origin of the world, and they thus had a certain air of divinity about them and understood the truth and the demands of nature more clearly."[165] What is ancient is closest to what is natural and original in man, and, as we know from Torquemada, the more natural something is, the more perfect.

Applying psychoanalysis to the subject, Jung holds that the image of the Golden Age, like all myths involving a similar aspiration (the myth of the good savage, the blessed islands, even the spiritual Jerusalem), is a manifestation of the desire to return to the tranquillity of the maternal womb. Commenting on this thesis, Mucchielli sees in such ideal creations "an archetype of humanity, a theme of the collective unconscious in which the world is free from the frustrations, the impotence and the limitations that beset adult life."[166] One of our Erasmist writers with utopian leanings, Fray Alonso Ruiz de Virués, made a statement which is relevant to this approach: "Happiness for all men consists in returning to that glorious and beatific origin from which their natural being emanated."[167] He is referring, of course, to divine creation. This myth of "return" is always most noticeable in periods of great social transformations. We have attempted to present it here in its historic aspect, viewed from multiple angles, in order to understand how Cervantes conceived it and related it to the circumstances of his society and in the end highlighted its incongruity.

Sancho, thus, is an elemental, primary man whose basic qualities have been purified by the continual indoctrination of his master. He is the genuine representative of the people, the image of natural society and the repository of centuries of judicious and prudent understanding. With just a little extra light to help him to see clearly what he has within his grasp, he is, therefore, optimally qualified to govern. All he needs to do is follow the supreme maxims of nature, accessible not just to rustics like him but to any being who has not become separated from the womb of our first mother—like the animals, for example, whose behavior provides material for so many moralists of the sixteenth and seventeenth centuries. Sancho, as well as anybody else, can therefore be a governor whose subjects will sing with the shepherds of Balbuena:

> Sweet indeed is the story of our life;
> here the Golden Age is alive,
> a sweet treasure discovered by very few.

Dialogues and other types of humanist literature of the sixteenth century reveal to us the organized totality of beliefs on which the myth of the Golden Age was based. This myth is one of the most characteristic manifestations of humanist thought. Its underlying moral naturalism springs from Aristotelian and Stoic roots developed in the fertile soil of an early modern mentality we may call prebourgeois. Cervantes is perfectly familiar with the image of that vision which during the Renaissance combined the paradigm of antiquity with the aspiration to a program for the future. His presenting it as the goal of a renewed chivalric activity is the heart and soul of the *Quixote*. Undoubtedly, the reformist and expansive period of the sixteenth century had sought by the renewal of that myth to express its desire for a restoration of nature. On the one hand, the model of nature provided a paradigm for social life by which residual errors and defects of tradition could be corrected; it also made it possible to retain Christian belief thanks to the fact that Thomist theology had already declared the Aristotelian notion of *physis* to be a Christian idea. On the other hand, however, this idea opened the way to the secularization which the ascendent social forces created by the Renaissance and precapitalism ardently desired. (Note, contrary to the common view, the high level of secularization in the great century of Spanish literature: the *Celestina*, the poetry of Garcilaso, Huarte de San Juan, Furió Ceriol, Góngora, Cervantes, Gracián, and many others. Correlatively, the idea of nature as a paradigm for social or individual morality was always viewed negatively by those who held inflexibly to Church orthodoxy, because it finally relegated Church discipline with its rites and sacraments to secondary status and gave preference to the natural model. Don Quixote and Sancho pay no attention to the sacraments, they have no liturgical obligations, they do not attend Mass, and they do not pray. As people of the countryside they consider themselves free from all this discipline. Seeing what happened to books of chivalry after Trent, it is easy to understand the innumerable condemnations which fell on those books and frequently on pastoral books as well. Understandable, too, were the efforts to purify them by rewriting them from a religious perspective.)

Sixteenth-century utopian writers who best express the content of that nonconformist reform movement, writers such as Las Casas, Guevara, Alfonso de Valdés, Vasco de Quiroga, and the more or less systematic constructors of utopian worlds such as More, Rabelais, and even Campanella, all propose the restoration of nature as the system of the Golden Age in an agro-pastoral society. Cervantes skillfully uses the elements of that construction, but instead of adhering to it he highlights the deterioration the myth has suffered. For example, he criticizes the falsity of idealized pastoral novels. In *The Dogs' Colloquy* Berganza says that while he worked as a sheep dog all he saw among the shepherds was coarseness, filth, and vulgarity, "and this led me to conclude what I think must be the general belief, that all those books are dreams well written to amuse the idle, and not truth at all; for were it otherwise, there would have been some trace of that happy life of yore, and of those pleasant meads, spacious glades, sacred mountains, lovely gardens, clear streams, and crystal fountains."[168] But, what is more, Berganza relates that the shepherds themselves would shout at him "Wolf! Wolf!" so that he would run to the place where the wolf supposedly was. In the meantime they would kill a ram and eat it and tell the owner the next morning that the wolves had done it because the dogs were useless and would not attack. " 'God help me,' I said to myself; 'who can ever put down this villainy? Who will be able to bring it home to the people that the defense is guilty, the sentinels sleep, the trustees rob, and he who protects you kills you?' "[169]

Cervantes condemned the turn which so-called pastoral government—suggested as the ideal by the reformers of the time of Charles V—had taken toward forms of absolutism. Once supposedly paternal and attentive to the good of the people in the time of the Duke of Lerma, of Don Rodrigo Calderón, or of the Duke of Uceda, it became corrupt through the widespread practice of robbing, fleecing, and destroying the population whose guardianship it had usurped. But there was no possibility of solving the problems of the moment through an appeal for the restoration of that kind of Solomonic government, if indeed it had ever existed. Thomas More could believe, as did many Europeans, that the possibilities of government based on nature, as in the agro-pastoral myth, were valid. Decades later, Cervantes realized the fallacy of that ideal, even though he had shared it in his youth. What is more, with deep melancholy he discovered a distressing fact: There were individuals in his society belonging to a decadent social group, the poor, tradition-bound hidalgos, who were taking refuge in that fantasy which by now was no longer a utopia but a mere dream, perhaps even outright delirium. They were attempting to link up the alleged values of a frugal and immobile traditional agrarian society with those attributed in an earlier day to the members of the group of which they considered themselves the descendents, the knights (taking the word in the old, estate-based concept of *bellatores*). Cervantes understood that the driving force capable of inspiring efficient reform had come to an absolute end in the vision which he saw around him. We repeat: The utopia of reconstruction had degenerated into a mere utopia of evasion or perhaps even into something less, a kind of pseudoutopia. Cervantes took pains to construct this ideal with great precision so that through its reflection in the mirror of failure it could effectively serve as a counterutopia. The more or less nonconformist character of those misfits disappeared, although from the beginning this may have been, as we have suggested, a case of deviance occasioned by high social integration. A few isolated elements from the earlier, active phase always remain, of course, as an inert residue. The countryside will always be considered a source of physical and moral health (and this view has lasted up to the present), and the virtues of the peasant will be praised at least until the period of full social industrialization. In Lope de Vega, a conservative writer highly committed to the defense of the monarchical-seignorial system then in force, it is easy to detect praise for the virtues of the "rustic in his place" [*el villano en su rincón*], but without any reformist or even escapist intent. This is evident in the three kinds of agricultural plays he wrote, as classified by Salomón: Italianist pastoral plays; plays with nobles disguised as rustics, anticipating the eighteenth century; and plays about peasants who really were peasants.[170] If Spanish theater continued to use the village and pastoral theme well into the Baroque period, it is because this was in the seignorial interests of the great grain harvesters (of whom the Church was the most important) and of the owners of huge flocks who were seeking some early and still poorly defined protectionist measures. Salomón wrote that "the ownership of rural goods became recognized as a positive moral value."[171] In today's terminology we would say that the phenomenon was based on economic politics, not on a policy of social transformation. The utopian tendency proper to the latter was exhausted at the time of the society from which the *Quixote* emerged, a society whose progressive paralysis Cervantes confronted. That tendency would continue outside all natural order, as González de Cellorigo said, or in the clouds, pursued by people who were attempting to escape reality mounted on their own private Clavileño. There are similar commentaries in the *Avisos* of Barrionuevo and other sources. But let us recall especially, because of its similarity to the famous passage of González de Cellorigo, the commentary of another economist writing in the last quarter of the seventeenth century: Alvarez Ossorio denounced those who maliciously "cause people to live in a dream which seems a respite."[172] We have already seen how Campillo lamented in the eighteenth century the lack of "reality" in Spanish social life.

All these testimonies reveal a national mistake which lacked all reformist intent and did not even try to disguise itself as escapist illusion. For that reason the formerly disquieting chivalric-pastoral literature could become entertainment and even material for orthodox instruction in the Jesuit schools of the Baroque. There would remain only an occasional echo in certain economists such as Caxa de Leruela, who anachronistically stated, in order to convince people of the desirability of a stockbreeding economy, that he holds pastoral life to be "the happiest and most delightful."[173]

But Cervantes was not wrong in attributing to the myth of the Golden Age (with its paradigm of "nature" and its setting in agro-pastoral society) the influence it has in the *Quixote*. Its connection with chivalric tradition—with its gratuitous and even contradictory claim to moral values—would disappear soon. But its other aspect, that is, the model of a society which modernizes the way of life of primitive people and projects it into the future, would survive and recover its considerable ability to inspire reformist nonconformity for a long time to come. Its presence in eighteenth-century France is well known, from Bernardin de Saint Pierre to Rousseau and Morelly; in England there are Defoe and Swift, in spite of the great difference in their approaches; and in Spain we have Meléndez Valdés, Montegón, and a few other minor authors. Finally, in a fully industrialized country William Morris wrote a utopia in which he portrayed the life and customs of a collectivist society and found occasion to recall "the true and ancient ideal of the pastoral poets."[174]

The Novel of Chivalry as
Utopian Method

At the dawn of the Modern Age, men of science were just beginning to glimpse the possibilities of an empirical method which would enable them to rely on the certitude of factual knowledge. Historians sought to limit themselves to strict canons of truth in their accounts, even adopting a critical attitude toward documents, which until that time had been used without regard for scientific rigor. The world was soon to see, in just a few generations, a new, Baroque man, possessed of a dramatic sense of concrete, limited time and space. Yet at the same time a different and contrasting phenomenon was occurring in European culture: the appearance of a new type of social genre—the so-called utopias— destined to take its name from the felicitous title of one of these works. In this new social genre the most salient characteristic seems to be a denial of reality. Contrary to what has been believed for a long time (and Engels's polemical interpretation is the origin of this error), we now know that there is no radical contradiction between the new positive science and utopian thought.[1] Francis Bacon, after all, was an empirical scientist and one of the founders of the new experimental method. His profound respect for pure facts, so little valued before his time, is evident in his desire to compile a natural history as an empirical basis for higher intellectual tasks. And yet he also wrote a political work in which he did not limit himself to a typically modern observation of what things are or what they might be (a method on which Saavedra Fajardo was to insist years later) but instead let his imagination run free to portray an invented social organization without any apparent relation to reality.

We have already spoken of the factors which gave rise to this boom in utopian political thought. A sufficient answer to the question of why utopian philosophy reappeared with renewed vigor and certain special characteristics precisely at the beginning of the modern period requires consideration of several highly diverse causes. One of these was the discovery of new societies in America and, consequently, the realization that people do in fact govern themselves in ways very different from those commonly accepted in Europe. This was a powerful stimulus to the desire to imagine new, unheard-of social systems. Another cause was the powerful force of reason in the Renaissance, fully capable of constructing ex nihilo a previously unseen world. These factors were particularly operative among ascendent social groups who were not content with their position in the class system.

From the time of Leonardo to that of Descartes people utilized the instrument of reason with a degree of precision previously unobtainable, reserving their greatest admiration for the most independent and characteristically rational creation: mathematics. (This is not to deny that elements of magic were still influential.) While they did not yet attempt to make mathematics the model for all other knowledge including political and moral affairs (this would come later, with rationalism), they certainly held that it was a discipline without equal for training, sharpening, and developing the mind. This was the view of the humanist Pedro Simón Abril, according to whom mathematics has the advantage of "accustoming men to look for the solid truth of things and not to allow themselves to be swayed by the inconstancy of opinion, which is most harmful to learning."[2] And there is no doubt about this; but it is equally certain that the so-called exact sciences accustom the mind to seeing things as subject to a ruler and compass, to conceiving reality as something traced (or at least traceable) in a straight line. A good example of this in the area of social life could be those streets Descartes wanted to see regularly laid out by a surveyor left free to follow his own rational ideas, not like the ones we find in old (and real) cities where "it might be said that it was chance rather than the will of men guided by reason that led to such an arrangement."[3] In much the same way the utopias represent a corresponding effort to order and systematize social life.

While there was among Spanish writers an undeniable correlation with mainstream European thought of the early modern period, Spain never produced a complete, systematic utopian work. The name of Thomas More circulated among us relatively quickly, and his *Utopia* was read, quoted, and applied to real-life institutions by governors and proselytizers in America such as Vasco de Quiroga, Zumárraga, probably Las Casas, and others. In the last quarter of the sixteenth century this type of reference to More disappeared almost completely and we only see him mentioned, and with great admiration, as a martyr of the faith and an example for rulers and for all believers. Rivadeneyra spoke glowingly of him in these terms,[4] and Herrera, focusing on those same qualities, made him the subject of a short biography.[5] But in Spanish authors it is not easy to detect references to More's *Utopia* again until well into the seventeenth century. There are none in Rivadeneyra or Herrera, and although they both allude to the fact that "by his writings and his authority" he tried to keep German heretics from infecting England, there is no doubt that the word "writings" does not include the *Utopia*. Was there in Spain a kind of resistance to this type of thought at the theoretical level? Theory, in its utopian mode, took in Spain a different direction, which we shall briefly outline in the following pages, a direction already evident in the enthusiastic reception granted by many Spaniards at the time of Charles V to this type of political thought. A thorough study of the fate of utopian thinking in Spain and of the forms it has taken in our literature would be a most useful contribution to the history of Spanish culture.[6]

In a few books written in the sixteenth and seventeenth centuries there undoubtedly are occasional fragments that can be identified with this kind of Renaissance political literature, but they are circumstantial, theoretically unambitious, and only partially developed. (They are, on the other hand, clearly intended to have a practical application, an aspect that has been confirmed in a number of cases.) Spain does have, however, one work which presents an image of a world in its totality and which can, in our view, be connected to the literature of utopia (although only to a degree) in its specific and peculiarly Spanish manifestation: *Don Quixote*. The difference is that after he has designed his utopian world resting on the transformative willpower of his protagonist, Cervantes turns that point of view inside out, looks at his creation through the prism of irony, and makes it the opposite of what it might have been. He makes it, in a word, a counterutopia.[7]

We have said that at first glance one sees in the utopias a desire to turn away from reality, but the purpose of the separation is precisely to increase one's ability to transform that reality. The utopia does not radically depart from what is real but rather orients itself toward it. Horkheimer has written that "the construction of a nearby world which one can reach in this life is certainly a radical change relative to the times when men could only dream of ideal countries in the hereafter."[8] Utopias have by nature (as Campanella recognized) the element of aspiration to obtainable reform. This being the case, Cervantes has no problem with trying to detect what genuine utopian qualities the quixotic model might possess; he feels perfectly capable of judging a vision of an imagined world to decide if it is really utopian or merely a case of escapism which must be denounced as unworkable. That sense of reality in Cervantes is noticeable in his appreciation of the human body (referred to in another chapter) and, equally, in his sharp powers of psychological observation, so evident in all his works. His connection with the founder of experimental psychology, Huarte de San Juan, was pointed out some time ago.[9] Cervantes is so convinced of the relation between physiognomy and personality, a field seen by the Renaissance as one with vast potential for empirical research, that he has Don Quixote engage in a game of inverse psychological deduction: from what he knows of the personal qualities of famous knights-errant he will infer, without ever having seen them, their exact physical appearance. "And just as I have depicted Amadis for you, so I might go on, I think, to portray and describe all the other knights-errant in all the storybooks of the world. For I feel sure that they were what the histories make them out to have been, and from the exploits that they performed and the kind of men that they were it would be possible, with the aid of a little sound philosophy, to reconstruct their features, their complexions, and their stature" (II:1).

While this appears to be an extreme application of modern science, whose possibilities were just being discovered when Cervantes was writing the great Spanish masterpiece, it in fact reveals its author's proximity to a conception of reality that is based on transcendence and final causality, a conception, therefore, that is less Renaissance than it is scholastic-medieval, especially in those who write about human affairs. (Aristotelianism survived in the Renaissance to a greater degree than has generally been believed, and it took on renewed power in the Baroque [Nardi and Mopurgo Tagliabue have made rigorous studies of this phenomenon], thus guaranteeing the permanence of that philosophy of final causality in European culture.) Cervantes's vision of the world is essentially Aristotelian. Things are as they are due to a specific efficient cause and for an equally specific final cause. This means that an end known to us always leads us to a certain way of seeing things. (Not even Newton's philosophy escaped this legacy.)

What seems in utopias to be a withdrawal from reality is in fact no such thing. What they do is intensely focus attention on certain aspects of the real to the point of deforming them. In Curzio's view, the utopian thinker believes that the reality of ideas is supreme and he tries to remove from human affairs all the nonrational impurities and dregs imposed on them by daily life. His goal is to purify them according to ideas, and in human affairs "idea" always involves an element of purpose. This strikes us as rather too much Platonism. Our view is that reality is present in utopias because of their ties (not always acknowledged) with history. But we shall not get into polemics on this point.

Cervantes writes at all times with that sense of reality characteristic of reformers.[10] He believes that the real is not to be found in the relationships among the rational entities of mathematics but in the concrete and the historical, in the sufferings and triumphs of human affairs, always subject to ends. And therefore, even when Cervantes wishes to go beyond the ordinary appearance of reality in order to bring it to perfection, his new pretended or imagined reality will not be that of Descartes's surveyor but the creation of a human figure. This is why his utopia, far from a geometrical construct, is nothing other than a repertory of social behavior presented to us by a succession of human destinies. While Las Casas crossed the Atlantic to discover new men, Cervantes sought them in literary creation, and by conceiving a utopia he also created a new literary genre, the modern novel. He would reveal the utopian possibilities contained in the novel, as understood in its new sense. This is a discovery which would be exploited later by Diderot, Rousseau, and Sade. The utopian novel of Cervantes is simply the drama of a human existence with all its pain, imperfection, and impurity, for human perfection is achieved, according to the moral outlook of Cervantes—so close to the Baroque view—only through pain and even failure.[11] He has Don Quixote express with marvellous precision the deepest meaning of his utopian enterprise: "It has been my desire to revive a knight-errantry that is now dead, and for some time past, stumbling here and falling there, now throwing myself down headlong and then rising up once more, I have been able in good part to carry out my design" (II:16). This literary treatment is very well suited to Cervantes's purpose of later turning the enterprise upside down.

There are two ways to write about a human drama, as a poet or as a historian. "The former may narrate or sing of things not as they were but as they should have been; the latter must describe them not as they should have been but as they were, without adding to or detracting from the truth in any degree whatsoever" (II:3) Does Cervantes really fit into either of these categories? We may, of course, understand "should be" not as a moral norm but as something inherent in any work with aesthetic purpose, an exigency of a literary creation whose parts must have an inner coordination. But, as it concerns the *Quixote*, the question, even with this qualification, is far from exhausted.

Cervantes has high regard for historical truth and for the work of reliable historians, for as he says, "it should be the duty of historians to be exact, truthful and dispassionate, and neither interest nor fear nor rancor nor affection should swerve them from the path of truth, whose mother is history, rival of time, depository of deeds, witness of the past, exemplar and adviser to the present, and the future's counselor" (I:9). Nevertheless, Cervantes does not write the *Quixote* as a historian narrating real occurrences; instead he imagines events, dialogues, and thoughts of a knight which cannot be real because neither is the agent who performs them. But to increase the veracity of his narrative he resorts to the device of interposing the imagined work of an imagined Arab historian between his hero's deeds and his own account of them. What is certain, in any case, is that his readers know that he is not telling them about events that have ever occurred. Can we say then that he is writing about things as they should have been? (We use the phrase "should have been" with the meaning it has in the passage just quoted: things that have been beautifully imagined by the fantasy of a poet in accordance with aesthetic canons.) It is true that even in poetic inventions like *La Galatea* Cervantes is firmly grounded in reality. He himself has set limits to creativity in describing what could be a good novel of chivalry: "For in works of fiction there should be a mating between the plot and the reader's intelligence. They should be so written that the impossible is made to appear possible, things hard to believe being smoothed over and the mind held in suspense in such a manner as to create surprise and astonishment while at the same time they divert and entertain so that admiration and pleasure go hand in hand" (I:47). Often in utopian programs dealing with other worlds or other times the concern is not with social aspirations to reform but with sublimations that are, in Mucchielli's words, "a personal compensatory world." But usually this is all fused with the image of an "ideal society."[12] Both aspects can be detected in books such as those by Antonio de Guevara or Alfonso de Valdés. Nevertheless, the second element, the vision of an ideal society, is the strictly utopian one and is never lacking.

The transformations in sixteenth-century society as a consequence of greatly increased mobility caused serious frustration and gave rise to a level of anxiety which tended to foster escapism to dream worlds. At the same time, however, people had a strong tendency to try to put into practice a social order which would correspond more exactly to the aspirations shared, at least in theory, by many of them. A number of individuals felt increasingly competent to criticize society, and they sought reforms that would make it new, pure, and perfect, or at least perfectible in each succeeding situation.

But in the *Quixote* there are many more important things between these two attitudes than one might think at first glance, a fact which Cadalso was the first to notice. Cervantes is writing in a modality between poetry and history, that is, in that hinterland in which utopias are born, and he maintains a special relationship, as do all utopian writers, between what things really are and what they ought to be. As we know, that relationship has a double aspect in utopias: first, lack of adaptability to the real situation; second, a desire to bring it to perfection. What characterizes utopianism is to be found in the focus on the reality of human existence and not on a product of reason whose perfection is of a purely logical nature. Utopianism (at least until the contemporary period, when the attitude changes with Huxley and others) takes its inspiration and motivation from the belief in the rule of reason, which can say a critical "no" to given reality and then proceed to structure reality in some other way; but reason operates here as an instrument and not as a paradigm. This is why the utopias of the modern period are largely products of history, and it is also why the novel is such an apt vehicle with which to portray them.

Cervantes constructs that brilliant combination of a chivalric-pastoral novel first, on the negative side, to highlight the resounding "no" that the type of character he portrays says to "this hateful age of ours," and second, in a positive vein, to set forth the values of the Golden Age. Maladjustment and negation of the present are evident both in the negative and the positive aspect; the passage from negative to positive, however, is not guaranteed by any kind of historical determinism, but is only articulated by the protagonists' efforts to engage in efficient action.[13]

Mannheim has pointed out that an essential note of all utopian thought is incongruity with the social ambience in which it arises and disagreement with its goals. "An attitude is utopian when it is incongruous with the state of reality within which it occurs."[14] This maladjustment and nonconformity in the *Quixote* regarding its own social context abounds in every page of the novel. In fact, the early modern period was well aware that there is a condemnation of the given reality implicit in every act of composing fiction in which the events depicted have an exemplary quality. Alfonso de Palencia admits as much: "It was necessary for me to include certain reproaches in this little book, which could perhaps best be rendered palatable by giving the treatise a fictional format."[15] Much later Quevedo elucidated the meaning of Thomas More's *Utopia* in the same way: "He lived in a time and in a kingdom in which, in order to reprove the oppressive government, he was obliged to imagine a suitable one."[16] Cervantes also imagines the fiction of an impossible knight so that his very impossibility will reveal the distressing situation of a society in which noble purposes no longer have any meaning.

It would be hard to find a period like the first half of the Spanish sixteenth century, in which there was such a strong insistence on reproval of vices in everybody and everything: in men and women, in ecclesiastics and the laity, in the military, in civilians, in politicians, and in men of letters. Some examples, such as Fray Pablo de León's *Guía del Cielo,* can easily bear comparison with the most violent scourgings of other reformers of those decades.[17] The criticism continued in the second half of the century (with the exception of an occasional area of social harmony), and there are extreme cases in the works of Juan de Medina, Pedro de Valencia, González de Cellorigo, Caxa de Leruela, and others. While the situation had changed somewhat when Cervantes was writing, we need not attribute to hypocrisy or fear his use of the literary technique of reproval through fiction, even though he does occasionally reveal symptoms of depression and apprehensiveness. In any case, we have already seen that the period believed the critical intent to be inherent in certain types of fictional works; there are also cases of bitter, direct condemnations. But Cervantes has other reasons, which we shall mention shortly, for his particular method of expressing his displeasure with the current state of affairs.

Let us once again consider the subject from the other side. We have held that for a manner of thinking to be characterized as utopian, a second factor must be present: the idea of possibly improving the situation one castigates. Undeniably, the widespread Platonism of the sixteenth century was sufficient to bring about this second tendency in utopianism. Everything that exists is a manifestation of an idea in which that existent reality finds its perfection. A characteristically Renaissance Platonism (largely preserved in the fiction of Cervantes) is evident in the following remark by one of the speakers of Castiglione's *The Book of the Courtier:* "Still I do think that there is a perfection for everything, even though it be hidden; and that this perfection can be determined by someone reasoning about it who has knowledge of the subject."[18] When people imbued with that perfectionism which inspired Western culture came to realize that it was possible for them to change a great many things, this realization inevitably triggered in them a spirit of utopianism.[19]

The presence of that utopian element in the *Quixote* was pointed out long ago. Carreras Artau noted that "Cervantes sought to make his coarse squire the incarnation of the perfect ruler."[20] Ordinarily, those who speak of this factor in Cervantes's work (such as Hazard or Conde)[21] find it in the episode of the island of Barataria. Undeniably, this is the point at which Cervantes's utopia culminates. While islands appear frequently in books of chivalry (in *Amadís, Florisel,* and others), the island is an inherently characteristic device of utopian literature, beginning with the work of More which provided the name for the entire genre. This aspect has been noted by H. Freyer in *Die politische Insel.* It enables the author to remove the space in which his creation exists from all open and normal contact with the world of real countries. The island permits utopian writers to make their ideal societies to a greater or lesser degree closed and static (at least in relative terms), with a system of control strongly limiting the presence of foreigners. This is something which can be shown in More, Bacon, and Harrington,[22] as well as in the plans for real utopian experiments in the Americas of people like Las Casas and Fray Toribio de Motolinia. Yet the residents of these utopias are always deeply interested in the study of foreigners and in the information they provide. The village of peasants and shepherds implies above all an unpopulated area separate from civilization. On the other hand, it is the best way of indicating a place which really does not have any place, being only a creation of the author's imagination. It corresponds perfectly to that nonspatial condition of utopian thought, expressed in the very word "utopia," as Quevedo explained: " 'utopia,' a Greek word meaning 'there is no such place.' " The best way to form an image of such an entity is to situate it in the middle of a body of water. Thus, on the one hand Cervantes takes the idea of the island as a reward for his squire from chivalric literature, where there are such cases, and on the other hand he later turns it into the typical medium of utopian literature in order to represent the high point of a nonexistent form of social intercourse he has invented as an experiment in ideal living.

We have already pointed out, however, that this is only the culmination of a long and continuous utopian construction that runs through the entire novel. Whatever Cervantes's initial purpose may have been, his discontent with the Spanish social situation and the idea of bringing it to a higher level of perfection are developed very ingeniously throughout the book. Nor is it necessary that those two utopian characteristics be placed in an imprecise and unreal geographic setting, for the fundamental change Cervantes introduces into the utopian method is that, rather than create a place that is really no place, he invents a human figure whose activities occur in an undeterminable setting. (The references to the Sierra Morena, the Ebro, Barcelona, etc., do not detract from the knight's spatial flotation, among other reasons because of his own nonexistence.) There is a whole direction of utopian thought here—to form a model of an ideal ruler, an exemplary teacher, a perfect captain, etc.—which does not cease being utopian simply because of its relatively concrete setting.

By means of his creation Cervantes wishes to show "the astuteness of Ulysses, the filial piety of Aeneas, the bravery of Achilles, the woes of Hector, the treasons of Sinon, the friendship of Euryalus, the liberality of Alexander, the valor of Caesar, the clemency and truthfulness of Trajan, the fidelity of Zopyrus, the prudence of Cato—in short, all those attributes that go to make an illustrious man perfect, as shown sometimes in a single individual and other times as shared among many" (I:47). All this is what Cervantes, speaking through the canon who appears at the end of the first part of the novel, believes it is possible to achieve in a good novel of chivalry, written with sound understanding, pleasant style, and skilled inventiveness. This is the way he was to judge his own work, and this passage serves as a personal testimony regarding his real purpose in writing. It is clear that Cervantes sincerely saw the *Quixote* to be something more than a source of pleasant diversion: speaking of his masterpiece, he said he believed it would be eternal, while his opinion of the *Persiles* was that "it ought to be the worst or the best that has been written in our language—I am referring, of course, to books designed for entertainment." If we take into consideration that these words are spoken in the dedication of the second part of *Don Quixote* (p. 509), it seems not unreasonable to assume that Cervantes did not include the *Quixote* among "books designed for entertainment." In addition, when he replies to the attacks of the author who tried to take advantage of his glory by publishing the apocryphal *Quixote,* he thanks "this gentlemanly author for observing that my *Novels* are more satirical than exemplary, while admitting at the same time that they are good; for they could not be good unless they had in them a little of everything" (p. 506). At the very least this reveals that Cervantes's literary purposes are complex; this can be confirmed by a comparison of his work with the simplicity of motifs in the false *Quixote*.

We have just seen that Cervantes does not reject classification as a satirical writer but simply claims that he cannot be reduced merely to that. Pedro de Portugal, a prehumanist in the early years of the Catholic Sovereigns, had titled his work *Satire,* "which means reproval motivated by a friendly desire to correct."[23] The concept, thus, had two notes: a verbal whipping for some vice or defect and the desire to bring about its correction. This continued into the Renaissance, but with the emphasis more on the first note than the second. Thus the theorist Luis Alfonso de Carvallo says that "satire is a work in which some evil person or some vice is reproved or condemned."[24] The conflict and tension at the end of the sixteenth century and during the Baroque period gave rise to a kind of negative and threatening criticism; reacting to this situation, a number of kindred spirits such as Cervantes and Espinel condemn any satire directed against a particular individual. This is the thesis Cervantes defends in *The Dogs' Colloquy;* similarly, Espinel complains that "recently people have been described as satirical who are simply foul-mouthed." There is no equating this virulence with true satire, for the purpose of the latter is to "reprehend a vice," that is, to correct it.[25] Nevertheless, the condemnation of the vices of classes and social types of the period is very well developed in Cervantes's works, and that generalized social tendency he saw as proper to satire helped him to make use of the genre to express his nonconformity and his condemnation of a particular society; this is the most decisive and visible aspect of utopian thought. Alborg notes that *Rinconete y Cortadillo* is a relentless satire against the upper classes.[26] (I would have said against the middle and upper classes.) In *La ilustre fregona* and *La gitanilla* the targets are the agents of justice. A variety of groups are under attack in the entremeses, especially *El rufián dichoso, El juez de los divorcios, La guarda cuidadosa* and *La elección de los alcaldes de Daganzo.* In the entremés *El retablo de las maravillas* he denounces the conventional concept of honor, the monstruous invention of "purity of blood," the hypocrisy and the lies, all of which were mainstays of established society. [All these entremeses except the first have been translated by Edwin Honig in *Interludes,* cited in chap. 2, n. 45.] Thus the ground is prepared for the emergence of the utopian element in the *Quixote* as well as in a brief episode of the *Persiles,* although Cervantes, always reasonable, did not see it as the solution to social problems.

With this preparation the book of chivalry becomes in Cervantes's hands a magnificent method for the expression of utopian thought, even though he later turns it around. By means of it he can easily communicate the idea of a perfection that is to be desired. And by setting forth this model he can indirectly but eloquently expose the evils that require correction by showing how distant these things are from their potentially improved condition. The thousands of episodes offer an unparalleled variety of opportunities openly to state just what it is that needs correcting, and Cervantes does so profusely. Also, by pointing out the ideal of a perfect knight he criticizes in precise terms the useless courtly nobility of his time and the sad decline of the heroic ethos. In the profoundly melancholy Spanish society at the end of the sixteenth century and into the seventeenth (like that of the rest of Europe) Cervantes saw a whole complex of dreams, hopes, and aspirations as well as nonconformity, opposition, and criticism. These elements, heavy with utopian tension, were the building blocks for the utopia of the *Quixote,* a construct which at first attracted his sympathy but which he now, sincerely undeceived, reveals as impractical and necessarily doomed to failure. What he attacks at bottom is its inauthenticity, for genuine utopian thinking does not evade reality but is directly oriented toward it.

It must have seemed to a society structured principally on the aristocracy that the important task was to reform and perfect the knight, the axis around which the whole society revolved. This explains the attempt to utilize the already moribund genre of novels of knight-errantry in order to show what must be demanded of a true knight and what must be corrected in those who do not live up to this high ideal. Thus he adds a moral purpose to the many entertaining possibilities which that type of book offers the imagination. This moral purpose is closely related in many ways, as we know, to the chivalric spirit that was certainly the animating force of those works. By these means it is possible to attain "the most worth-while goal of all writing, which . . . is at once to instruct and to entertain" (I:47). Thus, from a book of chivalry one can derive the figure of courageous captain; a chaste, prudent, and modest lady; a valiant and reserved Christian knight; a courteous, careful, and valorous prince; and countless others. If it is maintained that the reading of heroic books written about real people will leave one "improved in manners and morals" and a model of virtue (I:49)—an expression which in the language of the period combines the two essential aspects of a utopian attitude—it is equally true that the canon who defends this point of view and exalts the world of heroes is not too demanding in his criterion of truth. It must be recognized that very similar results can be obtained from an imaginary novel of chivalry, provided the story is well done. The canon himself is so convinced of this that he was tempted to write one "observing all the points that I have mentioned," and he even confesses to having already written more than a hundred pages.

A book such as Cervantes's reflects not only the more or less questionable taste for novels of chivalry but also the desire of a certain sector to see society reformed in such a way that heroism (moral as well as military) will be a principle of life. In the *Quixote* Cervantes presents this desire to the hopeful reader and then, by means of occasionally cruel humor (we should not forget that this does exist in his pages), makes him see that the project is impossible. He chivalrously baptizes his hero "Don Quixote" and then invents the cruel word "quijotadas" (with an obvious intent to ridicule) in order to give some name to the necessarily frustrated acts of his senseless, or, rather, his incongruous hero.

Just such a book is what Salas Barbadillo inopportunely attempted to write in *El caballero perfecto*, "in whose sayings and deeds a moral and political example is to be found, worthy of imitation by nobles and necessary for the perfection of their manners."[27] We know that Salas Barbadillo was a good friend of Cervantes and that in another work he mentioned Don Quixote precisely as an exemplary knight. This is a clear illustration of what an outstanding talent of the time who was closely connected with Cervantes saw in his creation. And it is also what undoubtedly moved Salas Barbadillo to utilize Cervantes's method. But he could not capture the utopian nature of the *Quixote,* and he was even less able to perceive the dramatic inadequacy of the knight as social model. This is why his book also lacks another element, irony. Salas too wished to give us the image of a perfect knight in a chivalric novel. He has all the customary voyages, adventures, battles, and love affairs. The protagonist travels through Castille, Naples, Flanders, and Germania. He serves the king, challenges knights, settles disagreements, reconciles husbands and wives, protects worthy knights, shelters damsels, and defeats the Turk and the rebellious Germans. He is chaste, faithful, and loyal. But in the novel there is not even anachronistic evidence of the social group which Don Quixote symbolizes, not even a passive faith in the heroic ideal, and no feeling, not even a deviant one, for the chivalric spirit. This is why it is absurd to use this kind of novel to portray an ethic that no longer belongs to the chivalric world. In 1620 it was no longer possible for Salas Barbadillo to utilize the novel of knight-errantry, either as a literary form or even less as a vehicle to express his intimate beliefs. This is why his novel fails. In it he tries to give us, as a concession to the Baroque mentality of the day, the biography of a Castillian knight of the fifteenth century who is related to real noble families, with names like Pimentel, Córdoba, Cueva, and Mendoza, so that "by this likeness his example might be more persuasive." One detects here Saavedra Fajardo's protest against the method of biographical utopias: "Many have written the life of a prince not as it really was but as it should have been. A useless attempt, because imaginary events cannot lend authority to moral and political doctrine. Only the truth of the case can move and teach us."[28] So Saavedra Fajardo sought a real example and found him in Don Fernando el Católico. And what can be said of a prince is also applicable to a knight and, indeed, to anyone in whom we seek perfection.

But before Cervantes (and apart from the well-known cases of chivalric novels rewritten "a lo divino," from a spiritual point of view) this literary form had been put to moral, didactic use in *Le Chevalier délibéré* by Olivier de la Marche. This book was widely read and admired around the middle of the sixteenth century, having been translated by Hernando de Acuña and, two years later, by Jiménez de Urrea. It was among the favorite reading of Charles V himself and it shows the strong element of residual medievalism at the time. Seen from this angle, it enables us to attribute a traditional, medieval quality to the enthusiasm for the world of Caesar Charles and his knights that we see in the *Quixote*. That "Resolute Knight" is a genuine "mirror of human life" in the late medieval sense, and for this reason the Spanish version of *Le Chevalier délibéré* ends with an "Exhortation" of Juan Martín Cordero, a sermon on "the way and the end of the worldly."[29] Martín Cordero is also known as the translator of a *Summa de doctrina christiana,* a book with strong Erasmist and reformist flavor.[30] The difference between *Le Chevalier délibéré* and the *Quixote* is to be found in European culture's debt to humanism and to the Renaissance, specifically a greater valuation of the world and the individual, an inner enrichment of the human person, and an aspiration to reform, even though Cervantes winds up recognizing that such reform is incongruent with the situation in which his hero lives. But above this historical level there is in the *Quixote* a heroic Christian ideal with its own set of values, principally justice and peace understood in a universal, Augustinian sense. This was how people conceived the imperial idea of the Middle Ages, whose last representative Charles V judged himself to be. If Cervantes praises the Caesar as a "thunderbolt of war,"[31] he does so as a logical consequence of a traditional view of war, and he connects that view to a whole way of understanding life and society that we have tried to elucidate. (We saw earlier, however, how well informed Cervantes was about the new methods of warfare and how he judged them.)

It was not without good reason that Cervantes chose the well-known but somewhat extravagant vehicle of the chivalric-pastoral novel in order to pose the problem he intended to examine. In the first decades of the Renaissance the dialogue, the discourse, and the pastoral treatise were all clear examples of the utopian genre. But the pastoral novel, in the way Cervantes inserts it in the *Quixote,* is not, strictly speaking, a utopia. How can it be if we have just called it a counterutopia, which totally alters its genus? The pastoral novel is a late development, a secondary and derivative product of the utopian genre, a reflection (admittedly with a certain radiance) of the lively and energetic utopian will of the first half of the sixteenth century. With the failure of the utopian enterprise around the middle of the century and the consequent realization that it would be impossible to implement its plans for transforming society, refuge was sought in the idealized creation of the pastoral world. The shepherd, the savage, the primitive, and the rustic peasant all very easily become, in any given epoch, the receivers of elements that have been floating about from a previous and energetically utopian period, when reformers came to the conclusion that there was no road to Utopia. Thus there will always be strong utopian elements attached to the shepherd, the savage, and the solitary man of the countryside. Around the middle of the sixteenth century when people realized that a utopian society was impossible, among the thousand utopian elements distributed here and there—recall the final works of Las Casas, for example—shepherds appear as gratuitously idealized and intentionally falsified characters, the heirs and representatives of what the inhabitants of Utopia might have been. Thus pastoral literature continues to be utopian, but in a markedly evasive rather than an effective way. And this is why Cervantes includes it in his novel: in order to do away with it, to destroy it with laughter.

Finally, Cervantes complicates the factors we have mentioned in utopias with a third position. Perhaps, had he lived at the height of the era of Charles V and observed, as did others, the drift toward a new way of understanding the knight, his arms, and the society in which he lived, or had he seen peace and justice viewed as political tasks incumbent on every individual prince and connected to the special interests of his State, our author might have written a simple utopia containing only its two basic elements. In those days, when the king himself participated in battles, when he had his portrait painted in his finest armor and wielding a lance, when his campaigns were announced (at least externally) as a universal service to Christendom, when he personally challenged an enemy king to hand-to-hand combat, and when he appeared before the Pope seeing himself as the heir of the full imperial tradition of the Middle Ages, perhaps then it was possible to believe in the reform of innovations alien to that spirit. It is not our intention to suggest by this that such ideas really did exist in the Caroline imperial phase. My own view is that they probably never existed except, at most, as a sublimation that was false in the sense of having no basis in reality but sincere in its rhetorical formulation. (The latter, of course, is not to be discounted as a factor of historical importance in western Europe.) While Cervantes himself felt a certain nostalgia for that world, he insists on telling its anachronistic apologists that the hope is gone and that all that can be salvaged is a sense of melancholy tinged with appreciation and sadness. Without any bitterness whatsoever, he feels that he has been defeated by his period, and he serenely laughs at a dream he perhaps shared as a young man. But with his laughter he forces others to reflect on the state of a society in which a pure and noble intention always looks ridiculous, an era that has forgotten the knight and that has also forgotten the old soldier, allowing him to return home ignored.[32] That reference to the knight, a figure already imprecise in his historical existence, implied an allusion to an equally imprecise society, based on nature and equity, which would be the last level to be achieved.

The truth is that Cervantes says, more because he has hope than because he has actually seen any evidence of this, "provisions are now being made for giving aid and relief to old and disabled soldiers" (II:24). His mind drifted back to those soldiers who were his companions in his heroic years. They would not be rewarded at the end of their service with a domain or another honor that involved some wealth, but with the administrative recourse of a retirement pension. Nevertheless, the new age would also claim to have its own ethic, its own heroes, and would state, more or less sincerely, that it wanted to keep its deeds within "those limits set by the Christian religion" (II:8), just as Don Quixote does. But the coercive, repressive pressure of Baroque absolutism would leave little opportunity for utopianism; any nonconformity would be interpreted as subversion. While the sixteenth century is one of the richest in utopian thought, the seventeenth is one of the poorest, except in England, where the liberties obtained through the Revolution once again opened the way to Utopia.

In Cervantes's sublime creation, what corresponds to his hero's "errant" quality is the mythical element, that note of literary creation which is always present in utopias. And, in the final analysis, the rejection of modern arms and the use of the antique harness have the same meaning. All this is the equivalent of the imaginary city and the island setting in other utopias. Underneath we find genuine utopian thought in its double aspect of criticism and reform. It may be that Cervantes, in composing a counterutopia, really presents a utopia in reverse. It would be useful to see how much there is in common between the ideal Cervantes offers and then demolishes and the social organization certain Franciscan preachers proposed for New Spain or the one Las Casas attempted with his Knights of the Golden Spur.

In the future there was to be a continual contrast in Europe between utopian reformist impulses and the resistance offered by the hard facts of established society. The dynamism that has so powerfully moved and changed Europe was produced out of that deep dialectical tension. In Spain the repressive, chimerical structure imposed in the Baroque period[33] and repeated so many times afterward was to create long-lasting difficulties that would be very hard to resolve, precisely because an unreal illusion should not be mistaken for a desire for genuine utopian reform, and the latter has not always had sufficient vigor among us.

Notes

Translator's Introduction

1. José Antonio Maravall, "Los 75 años de José Antonio Maravall," with Carmen Iglesias, *El País* (Madrid), 14 August 1986, Libros (supplement), p. 1.

2. Maravall has stated that he has always eschewed the term "ideas" to refer to the type of history he wished to write, preferring instead the word *pensamiento* ("thought") to denote the subject of his books, although he also admits that there may be advantages to the current expression "mentality" (*Utopía y reformismo en la España de los Austrias* [Madrid: Siglo Veintiuno de España Editores, 1982], p. 1).

3. Maravall, *Utopía y reformismo*, p. 1.

4. In his article "Materials" in *Approaches to Teaching Cervantes' "Don Quixote"* (New York: Modern Language Association of America, 1984), Richard Bjornson lists this work, along with those of only six other authors, among fundamental studies of the *Quixote* not yet translated into English (p. 19). (Nonspecialists will find this a very helpful article as they attempt to orient themselves in the oceans of scholarship Cervantes's novel has generated.)

5. See, for example, Hatzfeld's article "Results from *Quijote* Criticism since 1947," *Anales Cervantinos* 2 (1952): 131–57, esp. 134–38.

6. Parr, *Hispanic Review* 48 (1980): 249.

7. Parr, *Hispanic Review* 48 (1980): 249.

8. Weisheipl, *Friar Thomas d'Aquino: His Life, Thought and Works* (New York: Doubleday, 1974), pp. 1–2. And Peter E. Russell, who might disagree with some of Maravall's conclusions, expresses full agreement with his method: "It seems to me that one can only make critical sense of the whole book, from whatever critical angle one chooses to approach it, by going back to Cervantes's declared intentions and to the assumptions of his age which went with them" ("*Don Quixote* as a Funny Book," *Modern Language Review* 64 [1969]: 325).

9. Parr, *Hispanic Review* 48 (1980): 252.

10. I have omitted many names from this list, especially those of well-known writers such as Alfonso de Valdés, Luis Vives, Fray Antonio de Guevara, and others with whom even those without a reading knowledge of Spanish might already be familiar.

11. *Liber de optimo Genere interpretandi,* ed. and study by G. J. M. Bartelink (Leiden, The Netherlands: E. J. Brill, 1980), p. 13.

12. Scholarly opinion differs greatly on the quality of available English translations of the *Quixote.* I have quoted from Samuel Putnam's translation simply because it is the most widely used and easily obtained. Readers wishing to pursue this question are referred to John J. Allen's article *"Traduttori Traditori: Don Quixote* in English" (*Crítica Hispánica* 1 [1979]: 1–13), and also to Bjornson's *Approaches to Teaching Cervantes' "Don Quixote"* (cited above, n. 4), pp. 8-11.

Prologue

1. *Carlos V, 1500–1558: Homenaje de la Universidad de Granada,* 2 vols. (Granada, 1958).

2. See my study "Utopía y primitivismo en el pensamiento de Las Casas," *Revista de Occidente* 47 (December, 1974): 311–88.

3. Maravall, *Carlos V y el pensamiento político del Renacimiento* (Madrid: Instituto de Estudios Políticos, 1960), p. 205.

4. Maravall, *El humanismo de las armas en "Don Quijote"* (Madrid: Instituto de Estudios Políticos, 1948).

5. Bataillon, "Publications cervantines récentes," *Bulletin Hispanique* 53, no. 2 (1951): 162.

6. Bataillon, *Erasmo y España,* 2nd ed. (Mexico, 1966), p. 794.

7. Ricken, "Bemerkungen zum thema *Las armas y las letras,*" *Beiträge zur Romanischen Philologie* (Berlin, 1967), p. 82.

Chapter One

1. *Poema de Fernán González* (356b), ed. A. Zamora Vicente, Clásicos Castellanos, 128 (Madrid: Espasa-Calpe, 1946), p. 108.—Trans.

2. Quotations from *Don Quixote* are taken from the translation of Samuel Putnam (New York: Modern Library, 1949). All source citations are included in the text with roman numerals indicating the part and arabic the chapter.—Trans.

3. Diego de Salazar, *De re militari* (Alcalá, 1556). This is a paraphrased version of Machiavelli's *Arte della guerra.*

4. Sabuco, *Nueva filosofía de la naturaleza del hombre* (Madrid, 1587).

5. Ortiz, *Memorial del contador Luis Ortiz a Felipe II* (1558; published by M. Fernández Alvarez as an appendix to his *Economía, Sociedad y Corona* [Madrid: Ediciones Cultura Hispánica, 1963]), pp. 375–462.

6. Author's prologue to the *Novelas ejemplares*, in *The Deceitful Marriage and Other Exemplary Novels*, trans. Walter Starkie (New York: New American Library of World Literature, 1963), p. xxxv (hereafter cited as *Exemplary Novels*). In *The Man of Glass* [*El licenciado vidriera*] Cervantes states that writers are necessary to the commonwealth, "as necessary indeed as flower gardens, avenues, and pleasure grounds" (*Exemplary Novels*, p. 167).

7. Antonio Tovar provides interesting references on this theme in "Lo pastoril y lo heroico en Cervantes" in the volume *Homenaje a Miguel de Cervantes en ocasión de su IV centenario* (Buenos Aires: Universidad de Buenos Aires, 1947), pp. 27–41.

8. Fray Gabriel Téllez [Tirso de Molina], *Cigarrales de Toledo*, ed. Said Armesto (Madrid: Renacimiento, 1913), p. 136.

9. Alcalá Yáñez y Ribera, *El donado hablador*, ed. Valbuena Prat in his *Novela picaresca española* (Madrid: Aguilar, 1968).

10. Santos, *Día y noche de Madrid* (Discurso XVI), in *Costumbristas españoles*, ed. E. Correa Calderón (Madrid: Aguilar, 1950), 1:332.

11. In his work *El caballero puntual*, which we cite in chap. 4, n. 87.

12. In *Obras completas*, ed. A. Valbuena Prat (Madrid: Aguilar, 1967), p. 81.—Trans.

13. Sainz Rodríguez has collected passages from thirty-seven authors who, prior to the seventeeth century, condemned books of chivalry (in the addenda to n. 12 of his article "Una posible fuente de *El Criticón*, de Gracián," *Archivo Teológico de Granada* [1962]).

14. Don Juan de Silva's *Don Policisne de Boecia* dates from 1602. For more complete and precise information see the work of H. Thomas, *Spanish and Portuguese Romances of Chivalry* (Cambridge: The University Press, 1920).

15. See his "Discurso preliminar" for the volume *Libros de caballerías*, BAE, 40:lvii. See also p. xlii, n. 4.

16. Alborg, *Historia de la literatura española* (Madrid: Gredos, 1966–80), 2:141.

17. See his lecture "Un aspecto de la elaboración del *Quijote*," delivered in 1920 and included in his *De Cervantes a Lope de Vega*, Col. Austral, 120 (Madrid: Espasa-Calpe, 1940), pp. 9–60.

18. Even the Estremenian obsessed with notions of jealousy and honor is an individual who has returned from America enriched by commerce and is presented by Cervantes as a source of humor, in *El celoso extremeño*, in *Novelas ejemplares*, ed. Schevill and Bonilla (Madrid, 1923), vol. 2.

19. Guevara, *Historia del famosísimo emperador Marco Aurelio, seguida del Relox de Príncipes* (Seville, 1532), fol. vi (hereafter cited as *Marco Aurelio*). The reader will easily identify the characters mentioned by Guevara. But we should perhaps indicate that the name Lucenda refers to the novel of Diego de San Pedro, *Tratado de amores de Arnalte y Lucenda*, now available in an edition prepared by K. Whinnom (Madrid: Castalia, 1973).

20. Between those dates there is the episode of the Cortes of Valladolid of 1555 in which the representatives request the prohibition and recall of *Amadís* and "all the books which subsequently imitated its quality and style," and this "because young people, principally because of their excess of leisure,

take up this kind of reading and they lose their wits and become so fond of the events these books narrate, be they amorous or martial or other such vanities, that when some incident in real life occurs which resembles these fictions, they throw themselves into it more freely than they would if they had never read about it" (*Cortes de los antiguos Reinos de León y Castilla* [Madrid: Sucesores de Rivadeneyra, 1861–1903], 5:688). It is interesting to observe that the Cortes correctly find no relationship whatsoever between the unique kind of "heroism" (we shall call it that, at least for the moment) inspired by the chivalric contagion and the conventions of military life at that time.

21. See F. Yndurain, "Relección de *La Galatea*," in the multiauthored volume *Homenaje a Cervantes* (Madrid: Cuadernos Insula, 1947), p. 112; the author indicates passages which reveal the literary influence of Guevara on Cervantes. I believe there is a deeper relationship: Cervantes wrote the *Quixote* with Guevara's mentality in mind, a mentality which had deteriorated in the later writers who came under its influence and one which Cervantes had come to see (perhaps with a touch of melancholy) as unreasonable.

22. In his article "La Epístola a Mateo Vázquez" (in *Homenaje a Cervantes* [Madrid: Cuadernos Insula, 1947], p. 191), A. Zamora Vicente presents it as a document of protest and concern for the state of the country, a document, in the author's own words, of "national anxiety."

23. A. Castro, *El pensamiento de Cervantes*, 2nd ed. (Barcelona: Editorial Noguer, 1972).

24. Sánchez Albornoz has insisted on presenting the "Raíces medievales del *Quijote*," an article included in his *Españoles ante la historia* (Buenos Aires: Losada, 1958), pp. 13–31. In reality, all the great European writers of the sixteenth century have deep medieval roots.

25. I have dealt with this subject in "Empirismo y pensamiento político (Una cuestión de orígenes)," published by the University of Granada in 1947 and now included in my volume *Estudios de Historia del pensamiento español*, 3rd ser., Siglo XVII (Madrid: Ediciones Cultura Hispánica, 1975), pp. 13–38.

26. See Bataillon, *Erasme et l'Espagne* (Paris: E. Droz, 1937), pp. 819ff. The author sums up his thinking with this formula: "The humanism encountered throughout the works of Cervantes is only intelligible if we know that it is a Christian humanism transmitted to the novelist by a master of the school of Erasmus" (p. 837). The presence of that conduit is without doubt an important fact. Of course Bataillon tends to interpret as Erasmism every case of nonconformity in Cervantes. (Something like this seems to happen frequently to everyone who has studied a theme as profoundly and admirably as has Bataillon.) But perhaps we should consider the multiple and diffuse activity of the varied lines of reformism in the time of Charles V. The case of the phrase "works of charity that are performed lukewarmly and halfheartedly are of no merit but are, indeed, worthless" (II:36), a phrase which the Inquisition ordered removed, was probably due, given the circumstances of that historical moment, more to echoes of the polemic regarding Lutheranism (which the theological debate about the "de auxiliis" issue was to keep alive at

the end of the sixteenth century and the beginning of the seventeenth) than to the already waning influence of Erasmus. Let us not forget, however, that the whole moral figure of Don Quixote is built upon the thesis, which Cervantes articulates on several occasions, regarding the value of works. This was the thesis of heroic-medieval tradition which Cervantes, whatever his sympathies, had to incorporate into his work. It was a necessary principle of the chivalric world and it imposed itself on the author for that very reason, rather than because of any dogma reinforced by the doctrinal discipline of the Counter-Reformation.

27. See the study of Bonilla, "¿Qué pensaron de Cervantes sus contemporáneos?" in his *Cervantes y su obra* (Madrid: F. Beltrán, 1916), pp. 165–84.

28. Hazard, *Don Quichotte de Cervantes, étude et analyse* (Paris: Mellottée, 1931), p. 241.

29. Hatzfeld, *El "Quijote" como obra de arte del lenguaje*, Spanish trans., 2nd ed. (Madrid: Consejo Superior de Investigaciones Científicas, *Revista de Filología Española*, anejo 83, 1972), p. 326.

30. Recall the study of E. Gilson, *Etudes sur le rôle de la pensée médiévale dans la formation du système cartésien* (Paris: J. Vrin, 1951).

31. Lewis Mumford, *The Story of Utopias. Ideal Commonwealths and Social Myths* (London, 1923).

32. A. L. Morton, *The English Utopia* (London: Lawrence and Wishart, 1952), chap. 1. (There is a Spanish translation under the inadequate title *Las Utopías socialistas* [Barcelona, 1970].)

33. Karl Mannheim, *Ideology and Utopia*, trans. Louis Wirth and Edward Shils (New York: Harcourt, Brace and Co., 1953).

34. Campillo, *Lo que hay de más y de menos en España para que sea lo que debe ser y no lo que es*, ed. and preliminary study A. Elorza (Madrid: Seminario de Historia Social y Económica de la Facultad de Filosofía y Letras de la Universidad de Madrid, 1969), p. 117.

35. Pierre Vilar emphatically points out how the effort to maintain the system of domination of traditional society brings about a degree of immoderation whose effect is to disfigure reality. And we must not forget contemporary criticism of that same social state. It is what Vilar calls "the social foundations of Spanish unrealism" ("El tiempo del *Quijote*," in his *Crecimiento y desarrollo*, trans. E. Giralt Raventós [Barcelona: Ediciones Ariel, 1964], pp. 342ff.).

36. For Mannheim Counterutopia is a manifestation of conservative thought (*Ideology and Utopia*, p. 206–7), arising from the comfortable acceptance of a given set of interests and closing the door to future reform, whether out of a desire to affirm the unique creative power of the past or out of respect for the efficacy of the status quo. Leaving aside the very different meaning of the term "conservative" in German and Spanish thought, let us observe that the fundamental nonconformity of Cervantes leads us to see in him a valid concept of counterutopia, not in the conservative but rather in a reformist sense of the word. He is thus able to perceive that the wrong direction of an ineffective utopia, a pseudoutopia, can be an obstacle to the recognition of social vices and their practical correction.

37. H. Ligier, *La politique de Rabelais* (Paris: G. Fischbacher, 1880).

38. G. Adler, *Idealstaaten der Renaissance: More-Rabelais-Campanella* (Munich-Leipzig: Annalen de Deutschen Reiches, 1899).

39. E. de Pompery, *Les thélemites de Rabelais et les harmonieux de Fourier* (Paris, 1892).

40. Nevertheless, the most recent work on Rabelaisian thought, N. Aronson's *Les idées politiques de Rabelais* (Paris: A. G. Nizet, 1973), is a step backwards in this point. For us its only interest lies in its bibliographic aspect.

41. Ciro Caversazzi, *Il Tasso e l'Utopia* (Milan, 1896).

42. Joaquín Casalduero, *Sentido y forma de las novelas ejemplares,* 2nd ed. (Madrid: Gredos, 1974), p. 107.

43. José Cadalso, *Cartas marruecas,* ed. J. Tamayo y Rubio, Clásicos Castellanos, 112 (Madrid: Espasa-Calpe, 1935), p. 147.—Trans.

44. Gil y Carrasco, in an article in *El Correo Nacional* (April 12, 1837), reporting on a modern literature course that Espronceda was giving in the Ateneo, says that the latter presented Cervantes as "the man who hastened the fall of a profoundly decrepit society, namely the chivalric, in order to replace it with a nascent society" (BAE, 74:571).

Chapter Two

1. In *La guarda cuidadosa* Alborg claims to detect an echo—wrapped in sarcasm, we should have to add—of this kind of internal contraposition in society at the end of the sixteenth century (*Historia de la literatura española,* 2:59).

2. See my *Carlos V y el pensamiento político del Renacimiento* (Madrid, 1960), pt. 2.

3. This is the term which the bishop Sánchez de Arévalo was already using for them in his *Suma de la Política* (BAE, vol. 116). The date of the work is 1454 or 1455, according to T. Toni.

4. On the subject of the Spanish mentality in relation with these themes, see the detailed exposition in my *Estado moderno y mentalidad social. Siglos XV a XVII,* 2 vols. (Madrid: Revista de Occidente, 1972), which provides in-depth background for a comparison of Don Quixote's attitudes with the thought of the period. Here we shall make only an occasional observation to orient the reader.

5. Richard Ehrenberg, *Le siècle des Fugger,* French trans. (Paris, 1955).

6. See Margarita Morreale, *Pedro Simón Abril* (Madrid: Consejo Superior de Investigaciones Científicas, *Revista de Filología Española,* anejo 51, 1949), p. 51.

7. *Exemplary Novels,* p. 52.

8. Pérez de Guzmán, *Generaciones y semblanzas,* ed. J. Domínguez Bordona, Clásicos Castellanos, 61 (Madrid: Espasa-Calpe, 1924), p. 49 and passim.

9. Hurtado de Mendoza, *Guerra de Granada,* ed. C. Rosell, BAE, 21:106.

10. Núñez de Alba, *Diálogos de la vida del soldado,* ed. Antonio María Fabié (Madrid, 1890), p. 8 (hereafter cited as *Vida del soldado*). The first edition was that of Andrés de Portonaris (Salamanca, 1552).

11. García de Paredes, *Diálogos militares* (Mexico, 1593 [facsimile edition, Madrid, 1944]), fol. 33.

12. Vives, *Introductio ad sapientiam,* in *Opera omnia,* ed. Gregorio Mayans (Valencia: Monfort, 1782–90), 1:4. García de Paredes says something similar in *Diálogos militares,* fol. 34.

13. Pedro de Navarra, *Diálogos muy subtiles y notables* (Zaragoza: Juan Millán, 1567), fol. 14.

14. Gutiérrez de los Ríos, *Noticia general para la estimación de las artes* (Madrid, 1960), bk. 4:227ff.

15. Céspedes y Meneses, *Historias peregrinas y ejemplares,* ed. Yves-René Fonquerne (Madrid, 1970), pp. 165–66.

16. Ferrer de Valdecebro, *Gobierno general, moral y político hallado en las aves más generosas y nobles, sacado de sus naturales virtudes y propiedades* (Madrid: Villadiego, 1683), unnumbered pages of the argument and prologue.

17. Juan Manuel, *Libro de los estados,* BAE, 51:304.

18. Juan Manuel, *Libro del caballero et del escudero,* BAE, 51:236.

19. Barahona de Soto, "Paradoja: A la pobreza," in Francisco Rodríguez Marín, *Luis Barahona de Soto* (Madrid: Sucesores de Rivadeneyra, 1903), p. 734.

20. Valera, *Espejo de verdadera nobleza,* BAE, 116:107 (hereafter cited as *Verdadera nobleza*).

21. Guevara, *Menosprecio de Corte y alabanza de aldea,* Clásicos Castellanos, 29 (Madrid: Espasa–Calpe, 1967), pp. 71–72 and 74 (hereafter cited as *Menosprecio*).

22. Torre, *Visión delectable de Filosofía,* BAE, 36:391.

23. Cervantes, *El celoso extremeño,* in *Novelas ejemplares,* ed. Schevill and Bonilla (Madrid, 1923), 2:152.

24. García de Castrojeriz, *Glosa castellana al Regimiento de Príncipes,* ed. Beneyto, 3 vols. (Madrid: Biblioteca Española de Escritores Políticos, 1947) (hereafter cited as *Regimiento de Príncipes*).

25. Sánchez de Arévalo, *Espejo de la vida humana,* Spanish trans. (Zaragoza, 1491), bk. 1, chap. 21.

26. Martín González de Cellorigo, *Memorial de la política necesaria y útil restauración de la República de España* (Valladolid, 1600), fols. 22 and 26 (hereafter cited as *Memorial*).

27. Luciana de Stéfano, *La sociedad estamental de la baja Edad Media española a la luz de la literatura de la época* (Caracas, 1966).

28. Felippe, *Tratado del Consejo y de los consejeros de los príncipes,* 2nd ed. (Turin, 1589), fol. 132 (hereafter cited as *Consejo de príncipes*).

29. More, *Utopia,* trans. H. V. S. Ogden (New York: Appleton-Century-Crofts, 1949), p. 21.

30. Pérez de Herrera, *Discurso al Rey Felipe III en razón de muchas cosas tocantes al bien, prosperidad, riqueza y fertilidad destos Reynos* (Madrid, 1610), fol. 31.

31. Guevara, *Menosprecio,* pp. 79, 83, 94. Guevara notes that in villages the law of ostentation and conspicuous consumption, absolutely binding in cities, is not in force (pp. 73 and 22). "It is a privilege of the village that in it the good man is honored as such while the base man is known for what he is" (p. 89).

32. See Lucena's *Libro de vida beata,* ed. Antonio Paz y Melia, in *Opúsculos literarios de los siglos XIV al XVI* (Madrid: Sociedad de Bibliófilos Españoles, 1892), p. 167 (hereafter cited as *Vida beata*).
33. Lucena, *Vida beata,* pp. 131–32. This interesting passage confirms the subsistence of the chivalric idea of "travail" and at the same time reveals its connection with life in the countryside.
34. Núñez de Alba, *Vida del soldado,* p. 5.
35. Hurtado de Mendoza, *Guerra de Granada,* p. 101.
36. In *Novelas ejemplares,* ed. Schevill and Bonilla (Madrid, 1923), 2:52ff.
37. In *Novelas ejemplares,* ed. Schevill and Bonilla (Madrid, 1923), 2:154–62.
38. Guevara, *Marco Aurelio,* fol. lxxi.
39. Torquemada, *Los colloquios satíricos, con un colloquio pastoril* (Bilbao, 1584), fol. 74. (An edition was published earlier in Mondoñedo, 1553.)
40. Núñez de Alba, *Vida del soldado,* p. 26.
41. Felippe, *Consejo de príncipes,* fol. 119. We previously quoted a passage of the same author representing a precapitalist, estate-based concept. The contradiction which this second fragment may imply relative to the former is characteristic of a period of transition. It is an analogous situation to what we see in the comendador Don Luis de Avila y Zúñiga when he writes that the Emperor sent "some money, which is the nerve of war" (*Comentario de la guerra de Alemania,* BAE, 21:435). On the subject of this phrase which becomes a cliché, see my *Estado moderno y mentalidad social. Siglos XV a XVII,* 2:518ff.
42. See Isaba's *Cuerpo enfermo de la milicia española* (Madrid, 1594) (hereafter cited as *Cuerpo enfermo*).
43. Guevara, *Menosprecio,* p. 93.
44. See my *Estado moderno y mentalidad social. Siglos XV a XVII,* 2:75ff.
45. *Choosing a Councilman in Daganzo,* in *Interludes,* trans. Edwin Honig (New York: New American Library of World Literature, 1964), p. 70.
46. Enríquez de Guzmán, *Libro de la vida y costumbres de Don Alonso Enríquez de Guzmán,* BAE, 126:83.
47. Basing himself on the work of Durkheim, Stuart Palmer has spoken of this interesting and infrequently studied sociological process in his article "High Social Integration as a Source of Deviance," *The British Journal of Sociology* (May, 1973), pp. 93–100. Certainly the case is not entirely comparable to the one we are studying here, but there are a few points of contact: these people are "deviates" because of their effort to keep themselves "pure" in the defense of a tradition perceived to be the only firm support contributing to the survival of a social order. Those who welcome, or have at least come to accept, the new developments introduced into a system see these people as eccentrics and, we do not hesitate to use the term, "deviates." On the other hand, Talcott Parsons, in elucidating the concept of deviance, observes that "ego must have some reaction to the frustration which alter has imposed upon him, some resentment or hostility" (*The Social System* [New York: Free Press, 1951], p. 253). Such an attitude is easily verifiable in Cervantes's hero. In a footnote to this statement Parsons adds: "Another very important phenomenon of reaction to strain is the production of phantasies" (p. 253, n. 1).

48. Jiménez de Urrea, *Diálogo de la verdadera honra militar* (1566). I quote from the 4th ed. (Madrid, 1642), fol. 32 (hereafter cited as *Verdadera honra militar*).
49. Jiménez de Urrea, *Verdadera honra militar,* fol. 6.
50. *Libre qui és de l'Orde de Cavalleria,* in *Obres essencials* (Barcelona: Editorial Selecta, 1957), 1:530. This collection of Lull's works was prepared by various specialists. The one here cited was done under the aegis of Pere Bohigas. (This treatise will subsequently be cited as *Orde de Cavalleria.*)
51. They were published with the *Avisos* of Barrionuevo and they appear thus in BAE, vol. 222.
52. March 2, 1661, BAE, 222:253.
53. Vives, *In Georgica Publii Vergilii Maronis Praelectio ad Antonium Bergensem,* in *Opera omnia,* 2:79.
54. Rabelais, *Gargantua,* ed. J. Plattard (Paris, 1946), chap. 57, p. 189.
55. Campanella, *La Città del Sole: Dialogo Poetico/The City of the Sun: A Poetical Dialogue,* trans. Daniel J. Donno (Berkeley: University of California Press, 1981), p. 101. The individual, humanist aspiration to a comfortable life is one thing. A very different matter, however, is an individual's social aspiration to an ideal society in which there occurs an amalgamation of elements that come from agrarian society, and even a utilization of literary formulas deriving from Stoic and Christian primitive sources. (This happens not only in the sixteenth century but also in the nineteenth, as we see in W. Morris.) Thélème has utopian elements, but the true Utopia is not in the construct of Rabelais but in that of More or Campanella, and perhaps also in that of Guevara or Alfonso de Valdés.
56. Alamos de Barrientos, aphorism 60 of bk. 2 of the *Historias, Tácito español, ilustrado con aforismos* (Madrid: L. Sánchez, 1614), p. 694 (hereafter cited as *Tácito español*).
57. Pedro IV, *Tractat de Cavalleria* (adaptation of Partida II), in *Tractats de Cavalleria,* ed. Pere Bohigas, Els Nostres Classics, Collecció A, 57 (Barcelona: Barcino, 1947), p. 147.
58. Sánchez de Arévalo, *Suma de la Política,* BAE, 116:278.
59. See García de Palacio's *Diálogos militares* (1583; facsim. rpt. Madrid: Cultura Hispánica, 1944), fol. 27.
60. Alamos de Barrientos, aphorism 407 of bk. 1 of the *Historias, Tácito español,* p. 672.
61. Bloch, *Les Clases et le gouvernement des hommes,* vol. 2 of *La societé féodale* (Paris: Albin Michel, 1940), p. 47.
62. "Without doubt anyone who considers the military discipline which the Romans practiced will not be surprised that they were able to extend their dominion to the ends of the earth. Because of their discipline the Romans were often able to conquer large batallions with few people, and with little wealth they destroyed very rich kings and trampled on the power of fortune; this they accomplished not through flowery speech and rich garments but only through the strength of their stout hearts. They were far from all apathy and desire for dishonest profit and were more interested in horses and arms than in clothing, jewelry or other pleasures. No labor was new to them, for

their energy and vigor had mastered them all. They lived free of expectations and fear, and their final end was glory and fame. Oh blessed time in which virtue flourished thus and in which vice was punished, merit praised, and the virtuous rewarded!" (Diego de Valera, *Verdadera nobleza*, BAE, 116:106)

63. Palencia, *Tratado de la perfección del triunfo militar*, BAE, 116:345–92 (hereafter cited as *Triunfo militar*).
64. Juan Manuel, *Libro de los estados*, BAE, 51:319.
65. See Ferdinand Lot, *L'art militaire et les armées au Moyen Age* (Paris: Payot, 1946).
66. Marcos de Isaba, *Cuerpo enfermo*, pp. 16–17.
67. Brussels, 1598. On this question see vol. 1, pt. 5, chap. 3 of my *Estado moderno y mentalidad social*.
68. Gutierre Díez de Games, *El Victorial, Crónica de don Pero Niño*, ed. J. de M. Carriazo (Madrid: Espasa-Calpe, 1940), p. 6.
69. Sánchez de Arévalo, *Suma de la Política*, ed. M. Penna, BAE, 116:277.
70. Quoted by Mesnard, *L'essor de la philosophie politique au XVIe siècle* (Paris: Ancienne Librairie Furne, Boivin, et Cie, 1936), p. 148.
71. Sabuco, *Obras* (Madrid, 1891), p. 192. From the second half of the fifteenth century this was a general opinion which never became established as law. The Cortes of Toledo (1462) shared Sabuco's views and requested prohibitions and restrictions on the right to bear arms (*Cortes de los antiguos reinos de León y Castilla*, 3:731).
72. Jiménez de Urrea, *Verdadera honra militar*, fol. 2.
73. Pedro de Salazar, *Crónica de Carlos V* (1548), chap. xc, fol. lxvi.
74. Sandoval, *Historia del emperador Carlos V*, BAE, 81:420.
75. Quoted by Antonio Gallego Morell, *Garcilaso de la Vega y sus comentaristas. Obras completas del poeta acompañadas de los textos íntegros de los Comentarios de El Brocense, Fernando de Herrera, Tamayo de Vargas y Azara*, 2nd ed. (Madrid: Gredos, 1972), p. 539 (subsequently cited as *Garcilaso de la Vega y sus comentaristas*).
76. Herrera, *Relación de la Guerra de Cipre y suceso de la batalla naval de Lepanto* (Seville, 1572).
77. Fernández de Villareal, *Arquitectura militar o fortificación moderna* (Paris: Jean Henault, 1649), p. 8.
78. See pt. 5, chap. 3 of my *Estado moderno y mentalidad social*.
79. Pedro IV, *Tractats de Cavalleria*, p. 143 for the passage from the Catalan-Aragonese king. On the fragment of the Catalan adaptation of a Franco-English poem (probably the work of Joanot Martorell, the author of *Tirant lo Blanch*, around the middle of the fifteenth century), see the ed. of Pere Bohigas, also in *Tractats de Cavalleria*. The quote is on p. 74.
80. Juan Manuel, *Libro de los estados*, BAE, 51:319.
81. Lucena, *De vita beata*, ed. Bertini (Turin, 1950), pp. 118–24. The chivalric transformation of the idea of fame which is implicit in the texts cited can be studied in María Rosa Lida de Malkiel, *La idea de la fama en la Edad Media castellana* (Mexico: Fondo de Cultura Económica, 1952).
82. Jiménez de Urrea, *Verdadera honra militar*, fol. 31.

83. Lechuga, *Discurso en que se trata del cargo de Maestre de Campo general y de todo lo que de derecho le toca en el exército* (Milan, 1603) (hereafter cited as *Cargo de Maestre de Campo*).

84. Francisco de Valdés, *Espejo y disciplina militar* (Brussels, 1589), p. 11.

85. Marcos de Isaba, *Cuerpo enfermo*, fols. 15–16.

86. *Cortes de los antiguos reinos de León y Castilla*, 5:175.

87. "I have certainly never seen in my own day nor have I read that in days past as many knights have come from other kingdoms and foreign lands to these our kingdoms of Leon and Castille courageously to practice arms as those Castillian knights who have left Castille to seek feats of arms in other parts of Christendom" (Hernando de Pulgar, *Claros varones de Castilla*, ed. R. B. Tate [Oxford: Clarendon Press, 1971], p. 56). He mentions eight and even forgets Rodrigo de Villandro and Pero Niño, count of Buelna.

88. Unfortunately there is still no in-depth study of the complex social world of Cervantes. Neither Julio Puyol y Alonso's *Estado social que refleja el "Quijote"* (Madrid: Imp. del Asilo de Huérfanos del S. C. de Jesús, 1905) nor the erudite comments of Ricardo del Arco Garay in *La sociedad española en las obras de Cervantes* (Madrid: IV Centenario, 1951) deliver all that we would expect from such a study.

89. To the two which we have already mentioned we must add a third level of nonconformism in Cervantes, namely his own vis-à-vis the society of his time. Olmos García (*Cervantes en su época* [Madrid: Ricardo Aguilera, 1968]) has gathered numerous passages of intense social criticism from Cervantes's works and, along these lines, has suggested an interesting nexus between Don Quixote's mishap in the Manchegan countryside with the galley slaves and what happens to Sancho in the port of Barcelona ("Acotaciones a los episodios de los galeotes en el *Quijote*," in *Mélanges offerts a Charles Vincent Aubrun*, ed. Haim Vidal Sephiha [Paris: Editions Hispaniques, 1975], 2:147–58). But I believe that as he wrote the *Quixote*, from the second sally on, Cervantes was convinced that in the face of that unfortunate social situation the only possible attitude was one of commitment to reasonable reform.

90. Ramón Lull, *Orde de Cavalleria*, p. 534.

91. Juan Ruiz, *Libro de Buen Amor*, ed. and trans. Raymond S. Willis (Princeton: Princeton University Press, 1972), p. 340.

92. López de Ayala, *Rimado de Palacio*, BAE, 57:435.

93. Juan Manuel, *Libro de los estados*, BAE, 51:337.

94. Palencia, *Triunfo militar*, BAE, 116:350–53.

95. Valera, *Verdadera nobleza*, p. 107.

96. See R. Lincoln Kilgour, *The Decline of Chivalry as Shown in the French Literature of the Late Middle Ages* (Cambridge, Mass.: Harvard University Press, 1937).

97. Castrillo, *Tratado de República* (1521; rpt. Madrid: Instituto de Estudios Políticos, 1958), pp. 196–97.

98. See my *Estado moderno y mentalidad social*, pt. 3, chap. 1.

99. *El Crotalón*, ed. A. Cortina, Colección Austral, 264 (Buenos Aires: Espasa-Calpe, 1942?).

100. See my *Estado moderno y mentalidad social,* 2:51.
101. Théodore Ruyssen, *Des origines à la paix de Wesphalie* (Paris: Presses Universitaires de France, 1954), vol. 1 of *Les sources doctrinales de l'internationalisme,* 3 vols. (1954–61).
102. Alemán, *Guzmán de Alfarache,* ed. S. Gili y Gaya, 5 vols., Clásicos Castellanos, 73, 83, 90, 93, and 114 (Madrid: Espasa-Calpe, 1926–64), 4:40.
103. *The Dogs' Colloquy,* in *Exemplary Novels,* p. 281.
104. *The Man of Glass,* in *Exemplary Novels,* p. 149.

Chapter Three

1. See dialogue 20, pt. 2 of Camos, *Microcosmia y gobierno universal del hombre cristiano* (Madrid, 1595), pp. 228ff. (hereafter cited as *Microcosmia*).
2. Vives, *De subventione pauperum,* bk. 2, chap. 5, in *Opera omnia,* 4:477–78.
3. Menéndez Pidal, *De Cervantes y Lope de Vega,* p. 28.
4. Pérez de Oliva, *Diálogo de la dignidad del hombre,* BAE, 65:392 (hereafter cited as *Dignidad del hombre*).
5. In general, Américo Castro is correct when he states that the emphasis on works over faith ordinarily serves the purpose of identifying the primacy of "works" with the "sacraments" of the Church; but this may not always be the case. It could be a personal affirmation about the practice of Christian virtues which was not exactly pleasing to the Inquisition. Let us take as an example a passage of Fray Dionisio Vázquez in which he speaks of "religious men, not Dominicans or Franciscans or anything of the kind, but religious men who lived in community, who sold all they had and brought it to the feet of the apostles and pledged and professed the holy Catholic faith and persevered in it until death" (*Sermones,* ed. F. de Olmedo, S.J., Clásicos Castellanos, 123 [Madrid: Espasa-Calpe, 1956], p. 85). Don Quixote aspires to an internal transformation, not identical to the one described but definitely similar, to be effected by means of "works" which in this case are his martial achievements on behalf of justice and inspired by mercy.
6. Long before Trent and even before Erasmus's anticipation of the idea—the datum is worth keeping in mind—Mosén Diego de Valera wrote (as a basis for his conception of knightly honor and virtue): "Faith without works is useless" (*Espejo de verdadera nobleza,* ed. M. Penna, BAE, 116:107). In some codices this work is titled *Tratado de Nobleza e Fidalguía.* Its first editor, Balenchana, dated it around 1441.
7. Hatzfeld maintains that the mentality of Cervantes is sincerely impregnated with the spirit of the Counter-Reformation. He relates the latter to the *Spiritual Exercises* of Saint Ignatius and the canons of Trent and makes his point by showing the influence of these factors on the language of the *Quixote* (*El "Quijote" como obra de arte del lenguaje,* 2nd ed., pp. 131ff.). Hatzfeld forgets that this is a frequently superficial aspect in most of the writers of the period and that, moreover, it does not exclude the presence of other more characteristic factors in Cervantes. We believe that it is necessary to clarify the spiritual qualities in Cervantes in a different way and with greater precision, as Rafael

Lapesa has done in his article "En torno a *La española inglesa* y el *Persiles*," in his *De la Edad Media a nuestros días* (Madrid: Gredos, 1971), pp. 242–63.

8. Montemayor, *Los siete libros de la Diana*, ed. López Estrada, Clásicos Castellanos, 127 (Madrid: Espasa-Calpe, 1954), p. 171.

9. Camos, *Microcosmia*, p. 174.

10. Pérez de Montalbán, *La villana de Pinto*, BAE, 33:528.

11. Fuz, *Welfare Economics in English Utopias* (London, 1952).

12. Mucchielli, *Le mythe de la cité idéale* (Paris: Presses Universitaires de France, 1960).

13. See Martin's *Sociología del Renacimiento*, Spanish trans. (Mexico, 1947), pp. 16ff.

14. See R. Mousnier, *Les hiérarchies sociales de 1450 a nos jours* (Paris: Presses Universitaires de France, 1969), p. 71.

15. *Exemplary Novels*, p. 146.

16. In this very same place Sancho uses the words so often reiterated by Don Quixote: "Each one is the son of his own works," just as Don Quixote himself maintains on another occasion: "The number of persons of lowly birth who have gone up to the highest pontifical and imperial posts is beyond counting" (II:42).

17. Cervantes, *The Trials of Persiles and Sigismunda*, trans. Celia Richmond Weller and Clark A. Colahan (Berkeley: University of California Press, 1989), p. 79.

18. There is here a criticism of the deplorable method of governing and electing people to high office practiced at the time, an idea expressed with complete clarity by Sancho later on: "Do not think, my lady the duchess . . . that there would be anything so strange in [taking my ass along with me to a government]. I have seem more than one ass go up to a government" (II:33).

19. I have dealt with the subjects of stratification and mobility in the period, pointing out the degree to which the latter existed and the limits within which it can be recognized, in my *Estado moderno y mentalidad social*, vol. 2, pt. 3, chap. 1.

20. See my study "La imagen de la sociedad expansiva en la conciencia castellana del siglo XVI," in the vol. *Histoire économique du monde méditerranéen. Mélanges Fernand Braudel* (Toulouse: Privat, 1973), 1:369–88.

21. Gutiérrez de los Ríos, *Noticia general para la estimación de las artes*, pp. 227–38.

22. Campanella, *La Città del Sole: Dialogo Poetico/The City of the Sun: A Poetical Dialogue*, trans. Daniel J. Donno (Berkeley: University of California Press, 1981), p. 79.

23. Montalvo's preface to *Amadis of Gaul*, trans. Edwin B. Place and Herbert C. Behm (Lexington: University Press of Kentucky, 1974), 1:19.

24. The 1554 Basel edition of Petrarch's *Opera quae extant omnia*, p. 1145.

25. See F. Lecoy, *Recherches sur le "Libro de Buen Amor" de Juan Ruiz, Archiprête de Hita* (Paris: Droz, 1938), pp. 179ff.

26. See Bruni's letter *De studiis et litteris* in the incunabulum in the Biblioteca Nacional of Madrid.

27. Vives, *Introductio ad sapientiam,* in *Opera omnia,* 1:14. Therefore the pen or *stilus* is "optimus dicendi magister" (1:14).

28. Mariana, *De Rege et regis institutione* (Toledo: Pedro Rodrigo, 1599), p. 171.

29. Vives, *Introductio ad sapientiam,* in *Opera omnia,* I:4.

30. The question of the sanctity of Socrates had already been formulated by the middle of the fifteenth century. The High Constable Don Pedro de Portugal says, speaking of that heroic level of virtue proper to the saints: "And among the pagans I believe that Socrates reached this level" (in *Sátira de felice e infelice vida,* ed. Antonio Paz y Melia, in *Opúsculos literarios de los siglos XIV al XVI,* p. 67). See my study "La estimación de Sócrates y de los sabios clásicos en la Edad Media española," in my *Estudios de Historia del pensamiento español,* 1st ser., Edad Media, 2nd ed. (Madrid: Ediciones Cultura Hispánica, 1973), pp. 287–354.

31. Castiglione, *The Book of the Courtier,* trans. Charles Singleton (Garden City, New York: Anchor Books, 1959), p. 68.

32. Guevara, *Marco Aurelio,* fol. 11.

33. Navarra, *Diálogos muy subtiles y notables,* fol. 28.

34. See Beltrán de Heredia, *Las corrientes de espiritualidad entre los dominicos de Castilla durante la primera mitad del siglo XVI* (Salamanca, 1941).

35. See Bataillon, *Erasme et l'Espagne. Recherches sur l'histoire spirituelle du XVIᵉ siècle* (Paris, 1937).

36. Recall that Cervantes suggests that in the education of a young girl an effort be made to teach her "to read and write with more than average skill," as this will constitute one of her most exquisite and attractive qualities (*La española inglesa,* in *Novelas ejemplares,* ed. Schevill and Bonilla, 2:6). We should also not forget what, inversely, as an example of the old seignorial mentality, Alfieri tells us in his autobiography concerning his parents' negative view of the role of letters in the education of a noble (*The Life of Vittorio Alfieri, Written by Himself,* trans. Sir Henry McAnally [Lawrence, Kansas: University of Kansas Press, 1953], p. 12).

37. New men from whom "all vices and evil inclinations would be banished" (Alfonso de Valdés, *Diálogo de Mercurio y Carón,* ed. José F. Montesinos, Clásicos Castellanos, 96 [Madrid: La Lectura, 1929], p. 235).

38. Alfonso de Valdés, *Diálogo de las cosas ocurridas en Roma,* ed. J. F. Montesinos, Clásicos Castellanos, 89 (Madrid: La Lectura, 1928), p. 183.

39. Encina, *Representación del amor,* in *Egloga de Plácida y Victoriano, precedida de otras tres églogas introductorias,* ed. E. Giménez Caballero (Zaragoza: Editorial Ebro, 1948), p. 37.

40. Estella, *Meditación del amor de Dios,* ed. A. García Ruiz, Clásicos de Espiritualidad, 36 (Madrid: Rialp, 1965), p. 54.

41. Avalle-Arce, *La novela pastoril española* (Madrid: Revista de Occidente, 1959), pp. 25-27.

42. H. Thomas, *Spanish and Portuguese Romances of Chivalry,* p. 75.

43. Montemayor, *Diana,* p. 170.

44. Malón de Chaide, *Libro de la Conversión de la Magdalena* (Alcalá: Viuda de Juan Gración, 1702), fol. 280 (hereafter cited as *Conversión de la Magdalena*).

45. See L. Rosales, *Cervantes y la libertad,* 2nd. ed., 2 vols. (Madrid: Ediciones Cultura Hispánica, Instituto de Cooperación Iberoamericana, 1985), 2:827ff.

46. Díez de Games, *El Victorial, Crónica de don Pero Niño,* p. 42.

47. Jiménez de Urrea, *Verdadera honra militar,* fol. 7. This work is representative of a spirit in which that belief to which we have already alluded is still held, viz. that merit and recognition of merit go together, while being honored and having honor [el ser honrado y el tener honra] already appear as two different things in that interesting passage of Mateo Alemán quoted by Rodríguez Marín (*Guzmán de Alfarache,* pt. 1, bk. 2, chap. 3): "And if you consider this correctly, you will find that people like this are not men of honor but rather men who are honored; for men of honor possess it themselves; nobody can pluck them but that they grow a new feather, fresher than the first one; whereas men who are honored receive their honor from others" (ed. S. Gili y Gaya, 5 vols., Clásicos Castellanos, 73, 83, 90, 93, and 114 [Madrid: Espasa-Calpe, 1926–64], 2:32). This disjunction makes Don Quixote possible as a creature of fiction.

48. The first part was published by the Sociedad de Bibliófilos Andaluces. The manuscript is in the library of the University of Zaragoza.

49. Navarra, *Diálogos muy subtiles y notables,* fol. 31.

50. "Honorable" becomes institutionalized in our sixteenth century and signifies both the moral-social quality of a person and a public title which carries with it certain formally recognized honors and privileges, due, one supposes, to personal qualities, and which comes to be the equivalent of a personal, lifetime patent of nobility. See Antonio Marichalar, "El cortesano. En el centenario de Boscán," in the journal *Escorial* 9, no. 26 (1942): 384.

51. Mosquera de Figueroa, in his "prefación" to Fernando de Herrera's book cited in chap. 2, n. 76.

52. Lechuga, *Cargo de Maestre de Campo,* p. 20.

53. Chap. 21 of pt. 1.

54. This is the cause of his effort and, at times, of his despair: "My sole endeavor is to bring the world to realize the mistake it is making in failing to revive that happiest of times when the order of knight-errantry was in the field." And without abandoning the thread of his discourse he tells us a moment later just what the benefits were that that blessed period enjoyed: "the defense of realms, the protection of damsels, the succor of orphans, the punishment of the proud, and the rewarding of the humble" (II:1), all of which are of a political and moral nature. We shall later return to the meaning of this aretological scheme.

55. *The Waning of the Middle Ages,* trans. F. Hopman (New York: Doubleday, 1954), pp. 37–38. What Huizinga does not sufficiently highlight is the conviction of many medieval nonconformists that what is indeed possible is to annihilate the present state of the world, annul history, and make way for the sudden coming of the millenium. On this subject see Norman Cohn, *The Pursuit of the Millenium,* 2nd ed. (New York: Harper Torchbooks, 1961).

56. Guevara, *Marco Aurelio,* fol. 111.

57. Guevara, *Menosprecio,* p. 137.

58. Guevara, *Menosprecio,* p. 36.

59. Guevara, *Menosprecio*, p. 92.
60. We shall return to this subject in chap. 6.
61. See my *Carlos V y el pensamiento político del Renacimiento*, pt. 3, chap. 2. Guevara's *El villano del Danubio* may be found in BAE, 65:160–66.
62. Guevara, *Menosprecio*, p. 139.

Chapter Four

1. This unrealistic exaltation of chivalric idealism was a necessary aspect of Cervantes's literary construction enabling him to condemn the false, merely apparent idealism of knights, whose vices he knew only too well. Many have committed the error of judging chivalry by its appearance rather than by its reality, from contemporaries of Cervantes right up to Menéndez Pelayo, Helmut Hatzfeld, and others. Pere Bohigas—the compiler of the brief anthology of *Tractats de cavalleria* (cited in chap. 2, n. 57)—is absolutely correct when he states that the sincerity of belief in chivalric ideals, encouraged and blessed by the Church, has been far too readily accepted. He notes (on p. 13) that the decline of medieval society in the fourteenth and fifteenth centuries gave rise to an imitation of the knight in accordance with the type found in idealized novels. Bohigas says that from that moment on (although I personally suspect that this was always the case), "beneath all that show lurked a great deal of moral depravity, and history teaches us what there was there of brutality, oppression and decadence concealed in that dazzling display of gallantry and feats of arms."
2. Malón de Chaide, *Conversión de la Magdalena*, fol. 279.
3. See Herrera's *Comentarios*, in A. Gallego Morell, *Garcilaso de la Vega y sus comentaristas*, 2nd ed., p. 321.
4. *The Man of Glass*, in *Exemplary Novels*, p. 148.
5. *The Dogs' Colloquy*, in *Exemplary Novels*, p. 280–81.
6. See my study "La imagen de la sociedad expansiva en la conciencia castellana del siglo XVI."
7. This concept of prudence was well established among Spanish writers of the fifteenth century, and the "prudent man" was seen as opposed to the uneducated and brutish commoners. That word designated an essential element of the profile of the Spaniard in our great centuries, but it became, like the profile itself, an inoperative cliché in the seventeenth century, a fact later denounced by Forner: "In the time of Felipe IV there was in use in drawing rooms, ceremonies and conversations a chimerical and extravagant entity which they baptized with the name of *prudence*, when in reality there was nothing more imprudent in the entire world" (*Exequias de la lengua castellana*, Clásicos Castellanos, 66 [Madrid: La Lectura, 1925], p. 157).
8. Descartes, *Discourse on the Method*, in *The Philosophical Works of Descartes*, trans. E. S. Haldane and G. R. T. Ross (New York: Dover Books, 1955), 1:84.
9. *The Dogs' Colloquy*, in *Exemplary Novels*, p. 264.
10. *The Dogs' Colloquy*, in *Exemplary Novels*, p. 266.

11. Montaigne, *The Essays of Michel de Montaigne,* trans. J. Zeitlin (New York: Knopf, 1934), vol. 1, chap. 25, p. 125.
12. Bataillon, "Publications cervantines récentes," p. 162.
13. Pedro IV, *Tractat de Cavalleria,* p. 146.
14. Menaguerra, *Lo Cavaller,* in *Tractats de Cavalleria,* p. 194.
15. Lull, *Orde de Cavalleria,* p. 534.
16. Camos, *Microcosmia,* pt. 2, fol. 175.
17. Camos, *Microcosmia,* pt. 2, fol. 171.
18. Camos, *Microcosmia,* pt. 2, fols. 171–72.
19. Sánchez de Arévalo, *Suma de la Política,* BAE, 116:277.
20. Fernández, *Farsas y églogas,* facsim. of the Salamanca ed. of 1514 (Madrid: Real Academia Española, 1929), p. 52.
21. Karl Vossler, *Formas literarias en los pueblos románicos,* Col. Austral, 455 (Madrid: Espasa-Calpe, 1944), p. 12.
22. See the last essay of my book *La oposición política bajo los Austrias,* 2nd ed. (Barcelona: Ediciones Ariel, 1974).
23. It is true that we already find in Lull the idea that chivalry consists more in strength of spirit than of body (*Orde de Cavalleria,* p. 532).
24. There is interesting information on the meaning of virtue in these works in the study of Félix G. Olmedo, *El Amadís y el Quijote* (Madrid: Editora Nacional, 1947).
25. Lull, *Orde de Cavalleria,* pt. 6, p. 540.
26. Lull, *Orde de Cavalleria,* pt. 2, p. 531.
27. Pedro IV, *Tractat de Cavalleria,* p. 117.
28. García de Castrojeriz, *Regimiento de Príncipes* 3:351.
29. Sánchez de Arévalo, *Suma de la Política,* p. 278.
30. *Guillem de Vàroich,* in *Tractats de Cavalleria,* p. 66.
31. Díez de Games, *El Victorial,* pp. 40–41. In order not to overload the text we shall place in the notes the following passage from Valera's *Verdadera nobleza,* which is a fine summary of the theoretical formula, so frequently confused with reality: knights are requested "to defend widows and orphans; to answer for the poor and the feeble; to serve and honor sacred churches; to treat priests with kindness and reverence; to keep within the limits of strict chastity with duennas and maidens; and, above all, always to practice truthfulness, under which all other virtues are contained. And for all these things and for any single one of them they should be prepared willingly to surrender their lives if need be. To knights of such character very noble horses and arms suitable for exercise of their profession have been given, and these knights are further exhorted to practice with their arms in times of peace so that they will be ready for war" (p. 106).
32. Castiglione, *The Book of the Courtier,* p. 72.
33. Pérez de Oliva, *Dignidad del hombre,* p. 395.
34. Vives, *Introductio ad sapientiam,* in *Opera omnia,* 1:8.
35. García de Paredes, *Diálogos militares,* fols. 32ff.
36. See Carlos Clavería, *Le Chévalier délibéré, de Olivier de la Marche, y sus versiones españolas de siglo XVI* (Zaragoza: Institución "Fernando el Católico," 1950), p. 94.

37. This would explain the perfect harmony of Augustinian elements in Cervantes's thought and in the chivalric models he uses. We shall again (in chap. 6) focus on an Augustinian aspect in Cervantes: his ideal of peace through justice. Once again, the agreement with the humanism of Vives and Erasmus is patent.

38. There was an extraordinary number of translations and editions of Petrarch in sixteenth-century Spain, especially in the first half, a fact which must be kept in mind in the history of Spanish literature and thought. There were editions of this work published in Valladolid, 1510 and 1548; Seville, 1513, 1524, and 1534 (which is the one we are using); Zaragoza, 1518 and 1523. His *Triunfos* were published in Logroo, 1512; Seville, 1526 and 1532; Valladolid, 1541; Medina, 1554; Salamanca, 1581. There was also a translation by Peña of the *Vida solitaria* to which we shall later refer. In addition there are abundant translations of the sonnets and canzoni.

39. Francesco Petrarch, *De los remedios contra próspera y adversa fortuna*, trans. Francisco de Madrid (Seville, 1534), fols. 36–37.

40. Salas Barbadillo, *El caballero perfecto* (Madrid, 1620), fol. 10.

41. Guevara, *Marco Aurelio*, BAE, 65:178ff.

42. Mosquera de Figueroa, *Comentario en breve compendio de disciplina militar* (Madrid, 1596), fol. 2 (hereafter cited as *Disciplina militar*).

43. Cano, *Tratado de la victoria de sí mismo*, BAE, 65:303–24.

44. Avila, *Comentario de la guerra de Alemania*, BAE, 21:449. The quotation is taken from the last sentence of the book.

45. Pedro de Portugal, *Sátira de felice e infelice vida*, p. 67.

46. Zárate, *Primera parte de los Discursos de la paciencia cristiana* (Madrid, 1597), fol. 7.

47. *Exemplary Novels*, pp. 149 and 281.

48. Núñez de Alba, *Vida del soldado*, pp. 6–7.

49. Núñez de Alba, *Vida del soldado*, p. 8.

50. Machiavelli, *Discourses on the First Ten Books of Titus Livius*, trans. Christian E. Detmold, bk. 2, chap. 17, in *The Prince and the Discourses* (New York: Random House, 1950), pp. 331–38, esp. 335–36.

51. *Viaje a Turquía*, ed. Solalinde (Buenos Aires: Colección Austral, 1942), p. 260. This work is generally attributed to Cristóbal de Villalón. According to Bataillon, however, the author was probably the physician Andrés Laguna (*Erasme et l'Espagne*, pp. 712ff.).

52. Herrera, *Relación de la Guerra de Cipre y suceso de la batalla naval de Lepanto* (Seville, 1572), last page.

53. Calderón de la Barca, in *Dramas*, ed. Valbuena Briones, vol. 1 of *Obras completas*, 5th ed. (Madrid: Aguilar, 1966), p. 377.—Trans.

54. Cervantes de Salazar, *Crónica de la Nueva España*, bk.1, chap. 22, in BAE, 244:137.

55. Montaigne, *The Essays of Michel de Montaigne*, vol. 2, chap. 27, 348–49.

56. Mosquera de Figueroa, *Disciplina militar*, fols. 4–5.

57. Alenda y Mira, *Relaciones de solemnidades y fiestas públicas de España* (Madrid, 1903), 1:64, no. 211.

58. Mosquera de Figueroa, *Disciplina militar*, fol. 12.

59. Isaba, *Cuerpo enfermo,* fol. 3.
60. Published in Madrid by Luis Sánchez in 1598.
61. This poem was published in the initial unnumbered pages of Rojas's work.
62. Diego de Saavedra Fajardo, *República literaria,* BAE, 25:394.
63. Baltasar Gracián, *El Criticón,* ed. Romera-Navarro, 3 vols. (Philadelphia: University of Pennsylvania Press, 1938–40), 3:259.
64. Quoted by Mesnard, *L'essor de la philosophie politique au XVIe siècle,* p. 148. This is in spite of the fact that More praises artillery technically.
65. Guevara, *Menosprecio,* p. 94.
66. *Exemplary Novels,* p. 253.
67. Londoño, *Discurso sobre la forma de reducir la disciplina militar a mejor y antiguo estado* (Brussels, 1589).
68. *Cortes de los antiguos reinos de León y Castilla,* 5:175.
69. Alava y Viamont, *El perfecto capitán* (Madrid, 1590).
70. We should once again remind the reader that our claim is not to provide a real version of the situation, but to present objectively the variety of opinions (either imagined or taken from a current of anachronistic thinking) utilized by Cervantes. His ultimate purpose, of course, is to dismantle that anachronistic philosophy and to bring the utopia he has built crashing to the ground.
71. *Exemplary Novels,* p. 149. In one of the colloquies of Erasmus a Carthusian who is chatting with a soldier whom he has not seen in some time greets him with the following: "How many colors are you painted with? No bird changes his feathers as much as that" (*The Colloquies of Erasmus,* trans. Craig R. Thompson [Chicago: The University of Chicago Press, 1965], p. 128).
72. The work dates from 1524. We are quoting from the splendid reedition of Franscisco Morales (Madrid: Sancha, 1793) (hereafter cited as *Esfuerzo bélico heroico*).
73. Palacios Rubios, *Esfuerzo bélico heroico,* p. 65.
74. Palacios Rubios, *Esfuerzo bélico heroico,* p. 65.
75. Jiménez de Urrea, *Verdadera honra militar,* fol. 78.
76. Palacios Rubios, *Esfuerzo bélico heroico,* p. 19.
77. Palacios Rubios, *Esfuerzo bélico heroico,* p. 71.
78. Palacios Rubios, *Esfuerzo bélico heroico,* p. 81.
79. Palacios Rubios, *Esfuerzo bélico heroico,* p. 17.
80. In this risky situation to which we have just referred, Don Quixote has said: "I well know the meaning of valor: namely, a virtue that lies between the two extremes of cowardice on the one hand and temerity on the other. It is, nonetheless, better for the brave man to carry his bravery to the point of rashness than for him to sink into cowardice" (II:17). This is also the opinion of Palacios Rubios who, after dealing in respective chapters "with the two extremes, which are cowardice and temerity," dedicates two more to proving that temerity is the lesser of two evils and that "the daring man should be more esteemed and respected than the timorous" (*Esfuerzo bélico heroico,* p. 45).
81. Palacios Rubios, *Esfuerzo bélico heroico,* p. 19.
82. Sánchez de Arévalo, *Suma de la Política,* p. 278.
83. *Guillem de Vàroich,* in *Tractats de Cavalleria,* p. 67.

84. *Cortes de los antiguos reinos de León y Castilla,* 4:78.
85. This chivalric practice, used for reasons very different from those which inspire Don Quixote, was corrupted by becoming a recourse of delinquency. Luque Fajardo informs us that it was "common for soldiers, in order to have maximum anonymity in the military, to change not only their Christian names but their surnames as well" (*Fiel desengaño de la ociosidad y los vicios,* ed. Martín de Riquer [Madrid, 1955], 2:21).
86. It appears in Spanish in the fourteenth century; its meaning evolves, and at the beginning of the sixteenth century Bernáldez uses it to refer to an item of nonmilitary masculine attire (*Memorias del reinado de los Reyes Católicos,* ed. Gómez Moreno y Carriazo [Madrid, 1962], p. 170).
87. Salas Barbadillo, *El caballero puntual.* We are using the Madrid edition of 1614. This quote and the following are from fol. 19.
88. Salas Barbadillo, *El caballero puntual,* fols. 81ff.
89. Gilbert Keith Chesterton, *Orthodoxy* (Garden City, New York: Image Books, 1959), p. 19.—Trans.

Chapter Five

1. George Rosen, *Madness in Society. Chapters in the Historical Sociology of Mental Illness* (Chicago: University of Chicago Press, 1968), pp. 150 and 158.
2. We have dealt with the historical novelty which the Spanish crisis presented at the dawn of modernity in our works *Estado moderno y mentalidad social. Siglos XV a XVII* and *La cultura del Barroco. Análisis de una estructura histórica,* 2nd ed. (Barcelona: Ariel, 1980).
3. Regarding this extraordinary phenomenon which transcends the literary sphere and acquires the status of a national historical value, see Menéndez Pidal, *La epopeya castellana a través de la literatura española* (Madrid: Espasa-Calpe, 1959).
4. Mateo Alemán, *Guzmán de Alfarache,* ed. S. Gili y Gaya, 5 vols., Clásicos Castellanos, 73, 83, 90, 93, and 114 (Madrid: Espasa-Calpe, 1926–64), 3:113. On this topic, see Luis Rosales, *El sentimiento del desengaño en la poesía barroca* (Madrid: Ediciones Cultura Hispánica, 1966).
5. Calderón de la Barca, *Saber del mal y del bien,* act 3, scene 6. In *Dramas,* p. 240.
6. Calderón de la Barca, *Saber del mal y del bien,* act 3, scene 6, p. 240. On the Baroque sense of the reality of time and space, see Orozco Díaz, *Temas del Barroco* (Granada: Universidad de Granada, 1948). Regarding the expression used by Calderón in the last verse, see Otis Green, " 'Ni es cielo ni es azul.' A Note on the *Barroquismo* of Bartolomé Leonardo de Argensola," *Revista de Filología Española* 34 (1950): 137–50.
7. Aubrey Bell, "Notes on the Spanish Renaissance," *Revue Hispanique* 80 (1930): 528–36.
8. Jacob Burkhardt, *The Civilization of the Renaissance in Italy,* trans. S. G. C. Middlemore (New York: Harper and Brothers, 1958), 2:484–509.
9. See Trevor-Roper's study *The European Witch-Craze of the Sixteenth and Seventeenth Centuries and Other Essays* (New York: Harper and Row, 1967), pp. 90–192.

10. L. Febvre, *The Problem of Unbelief in the Sixteenth Century: The Religion of Rabelais,* trans. B. Gottlieb (Cambridge, Massachusetts: Harvard University Press, 1982).

11. See Caro Baroja, *Las brujas y su mundo* (Madrid, 1961).

12. Torquemada, *Jardín de flores curiosas* (Salamanca, 1570), fols. 135–36.

13. Vega, in *Pastores de Belén,* in *Obras escogidas,* ed. F. L. Sáinz de Robles, 4th ed. (Madrid: Aguilar, 1964), 2:1289–90.

14. Cervantes, *The Trials of Persiles and Sigismunda,* p. 48.

15. Torquemada, *Jardín de flores curiosas,* fols. 230 and 243.

16. See Caro Baroja, *Algunos mitos españoles* (Madrid: Editora Nacional, 1941).

17. *Exemplary Novels,* p. 286.

18. *The Dogs' Colloquy,* in *Exemplary Novels,* p. 286.

19. This was the first appearance of the idea that man does not have to limit himself to contemplating the world of things but can actually alter it. The attitude was, thus, a prelude to modern science. On the relation of this idea with magic, see E. Cassirer, *The Individual and the Cosmos in Renaissance Philosophy,* trans. Mario Domandi (New York: Harper and Row, 1963).

20. Alborg, *Historia de la literatura española,* 2:165.

21. Salvador Lissarrague, "El sentido de la realidad en el *Quijote,*" *Escorial,* no. 31 (May, 1943): 207.

22. In the seventeenth century "unreason, and with it insanity, were related primarily to the quality of volition and not to the integrity of the rational mind," according to G. Rosen, *Madness in Society,* p. 165.

23. This would be the opinion of any hidalgo of the period, as, for example, Don Antonio de Toledo, Lord of Pozuelo de Belmonte. See his prologue to the book of Alava y Viamont (cited in chap. 4, n. 69).

24. Hans Reichenbach, *The Rise of Scientific Philosophy* (Berkeley: University of California Press, 1951), p. 254.

25. González de Cellorigo, *Memorial,* fol. 25v.

26. In that incurable madness which can lead to no understanding of ordinary people Foucault perceives the passage to the literary experience of madness in the seventeenth century. In any case, his comments regarding the theme of madness in Cervantes strike us as rather unconvincing. Cervantes does not follow the accepted medical beliefs of his period, as the discrepancy between Don Quixote and the Man of Glass proves. (The latter, incidentally, is not mentioned by Foucault.) See his *Folie et déraison. Histoire de la folie à l'âge classique* (Paris: Plon, 1961).

27. In the following chapter we shall see how the free pastoral society belongs to the same compensatory and evasive world conceived by Don Quixote.

Chapter Six

1. Bonilla y San Martín, "Don Quijote y el pensamiento español," in his *Cervantes y su obra* (Madrid: F. Beltrán, 1916), p. 40.

2. See my *Carlos V y el pensamiento político del Renacimiento* (Madrid: 1960).

3. Not just in *La Galatea* and the *Quixote* but in the play *Los tratos de Argel* as well.

4. Murúa, *Historia del origen y genealogía de los Reyes Incas del Perú,* ed. P. Bayle (Madrid: Consejo Superior de Investigaciones Científicas, 1946) (hereafter cited as *Reyes Incas*).

5. Barahona de Soto, "Paradoja: A la pobreza," in F. Rodríguez Marín, *Luis Barahona de Soto,* p. 737.

6. Jean Bodin, *Methodus ad facilem historiarum cognitionem,* ed. P. Mesnard, in *Corpus géneral des philosophes français* (Paris, 1951), chap. 7, pp. 223ff.

7. [Note that the version of Ovid I have given is not my translation of the Bustamante rendition used by Maravall and to which he alludes in this note, but rather Mary Iness's direct translation of the passage. Readers who wish to consult Bustamante's version will find it on page 173 of *Utopía y contrautopía en el "Quijote."*] On the other hand, the free prose version of Bustamante, although he identifies himself as being "from a foreign nation," fits in very well with the literary climate of Spain's sixteenth century in which the classics were highly valued but also freely altered by the spirit of the time. This version of Bustamante had its second printing in 1546, in which Gothic characters were still used, and it was again reprinted in Antwerp, 1551; Huesca, 1577; and Antwerp, 1595. The latter is the edition from which we have quoted; the passage is on fol. 3. In addition, the *Metamorphoses* were translated in verse by Antonio Pérez (Salamanca, 1580); by Felipe May, into *octavas reales* (Tarragona, 1585); and by Pedro Sánchez de Viana (Valladolid, 1589). Of these, the first and the last have annotations or "allegories" in prose. These glosses superimpose on Ovid a moral factor which is foreign to him, and the passage from one age to the other is interpreted as proof of how "men are more inclined to stray from virtue than to follow it," as Pérez says (fol. 25), an idea which Viana picks up. Viana is the only one who utilizes the metaphor of the "bowels of the earth," which appears in Cervantes: "And without having its pure bowels / rent by the plow, freely did earth / provide them with sweet and ripe fruit."

8. Mariana, *De Rege et regis institutione,* p. 16. The remaining quotes from Mariana come from the following page of this work.

9. Díez de Games, *El Victorial,* pp. 317–18. Américo Castro noted the connection between a simple, natural, rustic life of shepherding as in the Golden Age myth on the one hand and the chivalric world on the other, but without mentioning the utopian nature of this material (*El pensamiento de Cervantes,* pp. 173–81).

10. Bernardo de Balbuena, *El Siglo de Oro en las selvas de Erífile* (Madrid: Martín, 1608), fol. 18.

11. Balbuena, *El Siglo de Oro en las selvas de Erífile,* fol. 46. Mariana also held that "nulla solicitudine gravis" ("no serious concern") oppressed these people.

12. Guevara, *Marco Aurelio,* fol. xxxvii.

13. Quoted by Gallego Morell, *Garcilaso de la Vega y sus comentaristas,* 2nd ed., p. 474.

14. Balbuena, *El Siglo de Oro en las selvas de Erífile,* fol. 34.

15. L. Annaeus Seneca, *De tranquilitate animi,* 2.13 (Paris: Les Belles Lettres, n.d.), p. 78.

16. Juan Ruiz de Alarcón, *The Truth Suspected*, trans. R. C. Ryan, in *Spanish Drama*, ed. Angel Flores (New York: Bantam Books, 1962), p. 150.

17. Lope de Vega, *Las fortunas de Diana*, which forms part of the *Novelas a Marcia Leonarda*, BAE, 38:9.

18. Karl Vossler, *La soledad en la poesía española*, trans. J. M. Sacristán (Madrid: Revista de Occidente, 1941).

19. Saint Jerome, in *Lettres* (Paris: Les Belles Lettres, 1953), 3:72.

20. Gaspar Gil Polo, *Diana enamorada*, Clásicos Castellanos, 135 (Madrid: Espasa-Calpe, 1962), p. 123.

21. Gonzalo Céspedes y Meneses, *El español Gerardo y desengaño del amor lascivo*, BAE, 18:170.

22. Perhaps, in addition to what we say on the following pages, we might see here a case of the type of deviance which R. Merton calls "retreatism." See his *Social Theory and Social Structure* (New York: Free Press, 1957), pp. 187ff.

23. Petrarch, *De la vida solitaria* (Medina del Campo, 1553), fol. 37. (A very different matter is the solitude of despair, which Petrarch is also one of the first to describe [in Canzone XIII]: "Per alti monte e per selve aspre trovo / Qualque riposo; ogni abitato loco / E nemico mortal degli occhi miei" [in *Canzoniere*, ed. Piero Cudini, 2nd ed. (Milan: Garzanti, 1976), p. 188].)

24. Petrarch, *De la vida solitaria*, fol. 61.

25. Juan de Tasis y Peralta, soneto amoroso 107, in *Poesías de Juan de Tasis, Conde de Villamediana* (Madrid: Editora Nacional, 1944), p. 56.

26. Nifo, *De vera vivendi libertate* (Venice, 1535).

27. Guevara, *Menosprecio*, pp. 33, 53, and 58.

28. Castro, *Lo hispánico y el erasmismo. Los prólogos al "Quijote"* (Buenos Aires: Instituto de Filología, 1942), pp. 110ff. Quote on p. 111.

29. Vossler, *La soledad en la poesía española*, p. 74. Lope de Vega exalts the "solitary life" in *Pastores de Belén* (*Obras escogidas*, 2:1190), and in his novel *Las fortunas de Diana* he speaks of the intimacy of the forests, saying: "for I find my own company / in your solitude" (BAE, 38:11). In his *Cigarrales* Tirso has a young woman say that, as one customarily takes delight in the countryside, "I took advantage of this to begin to acquire a taste for solitude" (ed. Said Armesto [Madrid, 1914], p. 49). And in *La estatua de Prometeo*, act 1, Calderón holds that "there is no / safer company / than solitude" (*Dramas*, p. 2069).

30. Encina, *Pastoral de amores*, in *Egloga de Plácida y Victoriano, precedida de otras tres églogas introductorias*, ed. E. Giménez Caballero (Zaragoza: Clásicos Ebro, 1948), pp. 29–30. This was an intermediate stage in which the rural ambience and rustic life reflected in part of our sixteenth century theater fell into disrepute, as José María Díez-Borque has observed in his *Aspectos de la oposición caballero-pastor en el primer teatro castellano* (Bordeaux, 1970).

31. Juan Fernández de Velasco, *Controversia* (Seville: Sociedad de Bibliófilos Andaluces, 1870), p. 36.

32. Fernando Vázquez de Menchaca, *Controversiarum illustrium*, bk. 1, praefatio (Valladolid, 1932), 1:131.

33. Cristóbal Suárez de Figueroa, *El pasagero*, ed. F. Rodríguez Marín (Madrid: Biblioteca Renacimiento, 1913), p. 320.

34. Avalle-Arce, *La novela pastoril española,* p. 35.
35. Freyer, *Die politische Insel. Eine Geschicte der Utopien von Plato bis zur Gegenwart* (Leipzig, 1936).
36. Lucena, *Vida beata,* p. 130.
37. Max Weber, *Protestant Ethic and the Spirit of Capitalism,* trans. Talcott Parsons (New York: Charles Scribner's Sons, 1958), p. 212, n. 8.
38. Saint Jerome, in *Lettres* (Paris: Les Belles Lettres, 1953), 3:11.
39. See B. Isaza y Calderón, *El retorno a la naturaleza* (Madrid: Bolaños y Aguilar, 1934), pp. 78ff.
40. Francisco López de Villalobos, *Los problemas de Villalobos,* BAE, 36:426.
41. Alonso de Herrera, *Obra de Agricultura* (Alcalá, 1524), prologue. We note in passing that St. John of the Cross, unaffected by the myth we are studying, did not prefer nature and mountains to churches and art as places for prayer (*Ascent of Mount Carmel,* trans. E. Allison Peers [Garden City, New York: Image, 1958], p. 377).
42. Guevara, *Menosprecio,* pp. 67, 69, 71, and passim.
43. Espinel, *Vida del escudero Marcos de Obregón,* Clásicos Castellanos, 43 and 51 (Madrid: Espasa-Calpe, 1959), 2:255–56.
44. Lucena, *De vita beata,* ed. Bertini, pp. 129–35.
45. Castrillo, *Tratado de República,* p. 108.
46. Gabriel Alonso de Herrera, *Obra de Agricultura,* prologue.
47. Guevara, *Menosprecio,* pp. 62 and 81.
48. Sabuco, *Nueva filosofía de la naturaleza del hombre,* BAE, 65:354 and 337. [Perhaps a word of explanation is in order here. Readers who look up this reference will be surprised to find the work attributed to Doña Oliva Sabuco de Nantes and titled *Coloquio del conocimiento de sí mismo.* In the first place, the attribution to Doña Oliva is erroneous, as Benjamín Marcos has demonstrated in his *Miguel Sabuco (antes Doña Oliva),* published in Madrid by Biblioteca Filosófica in 1923. Her evidently doting father, wanting his intelligent and well-educated daughter to receive the esteem he felt she deserved, allowed her to pass as the author of one of his own works. Secondly, *Nueva filosofía de la naturaleza* consists of three separately titled sections: *Coloquio del conocimiento de sí mismo, Coloquio en el que se trata de la contextura del mundo, tal como está formado,* and *Coloquio de las cosas que mejoran este mundo y su república.* Maravall sometimes gives the title of the whole work and sometimes the title of one section.]
49. Second part of the *Diálogos muy subtiles y notables* (Zaragoza, 1567). The date indicates that this was one of the times when it was common for nobles to become courtiers.
50. Guevara, *Menosprecio,* p. 142.
51. Petrarch, *De la vida solitaria,* fol. 26.
52. Torquemada, *Colloquios satíricos,* fol. 70.
53. Guevara, *Menosprecio,* p. 70: "A privilege of village life is that there everyone takes honest pleasure in their houses, lands and farms, for they have no extravagant expenses, the women do not make their men jealous and the men harbor no suspicions about their women. Go-betweens do not disturb them, the lovesick pay no calls; people simply go about the business of raising their

children and living honorably with their relatives, and there everybody is related. He who lives content in a village enjoys no small measure of happiness, for he lives in tranquillity and is rarely disturbed; he lives in a way that benefits him but yet does not harm anybody else; he lives according to obligation and not inclination, in accord with reason and not with opinion."

54. Pulgar, *Glosas a las Coplas de Mingo Revulgo,* in *Letras,* ed. Domínguez Bordona, Clásicos Castellanos, 99 (Madrid: La Lectura, 1929), p. 159.

55. Sabuco, *Coloquio del conocimiento de sí mismo,* in *Obras* (Madrid, 1888).

56. Vinzenz Hamp, "Le motif du Pasteur dans l'Ancien Testament," in *Festschrift Kardinal Faulhaber* (Münster, 1949).

57. Hermas, *Le Pasteur,* critical edition with annotated bilingual text by R. Joly (Paris: Editions du Cerf, 1958), pp. 51 and 141.

58. Mâle, *L'art religieux de la fin du Moyen Age en France* (Paris, 1925), p. 53.

59. Vossler, *Formas literarias en los pueblos románicos,* p. 61n.

60. Berceo, *Vida de Santo Domingo de Silos,* ed. Teresa Labarta de Chaves (Madrid: Clásicos Castalia, 1972), pp. 63–64.

61. Sánchez de Arévalo, *Espejo de la vida humana,* chap. 30, bk. 1.

62. Aldana, *Poesías,* Clásicos Castellanos, 143 (Madrid: Espasa-Calpe, 1957), pp. 99–100.

63. Luis Alfonso de Carvallo, *Cisne de Apolo,* ed. A. Porqueras Mayo, Biblioteca de Antiguos Libros Hispánicos, ser. A, 25–26 (Madrid: Consejo Superior de Investigaciones Científicas, Instituto "Miguel de Cervantes," 1958), 2:103.

64. I am grateful to Professor Bataillon for a reference which, as he pointed out in the Berlin colloquium of 1966, was lacking in the first edition of this study. The work, unobtainable by me at the time, is the *Discurso de las armas y las letras,* authored by Francisco Miranda Villafañe, and it contains this very same fusion of chivalric and pastoral society as an echo of the Golden Age myth. I think it would be very interesting to relate this theme to the renewal of the privileges of the Mesta and the restoration of the economic power of the nobility, as Werner Krauss has suggested, but I also feel that it would not be well to put aside completely the ideological survival of traditional society. Miranda Villafañe's *Discurso* was published as part of his *Diálogos de la fantástica filosofía* in Salamanca in 1582 and the entire work was translated into French in 1587. The fact that today there are copies of this translation in France, England, and Germany is an indication of the extent of its acceptance and of the survival of traditional attitudes in Western Europe.

65. Hatzfeld, *El "Quijote" como obra de arte del lenguaje,* 2nd ed., pp. 249ff.

66. Francisco de López Estrada, *"La Galatea" de Cervantes. Estudio crítico* (La Laguna de Tenerife: Universidad de La Laguna, 1948), pp. 174ff. See also his outstanding work *Los libros de pastores en la literatura española. La órbita previa* (Madrid: Gredos, 1974).

67. Américo Castro, *El pensamiento de Cervantes,* p. 179.

68. Avalle-Arce, *La novela pastoril española,* p. 212.

69. See my *Carlos V y el pensamiento político del Renacimiento.*

70. Américo Castro, *El pensamiento de Cervantes,* p. 181.

71. Both of these facts are mentioned in my book cited in n. 69 above, pp. 61 and 225.
72. Avalle-Arce, *La novela pastoril española*, p. 9.
73. Torquemada, *Colloquios satíricos*, fol. 80.
74. See J. T. Welter, *L'exemplum dans la littérature religieuse et didactique du Moyen Age* (Paris: E. H. Guitard, 1927).
75. Juan Manuel, *Libro de los estados*, BAE, 51:292.
76. Mexía, *Silva de varia lección* (Madrid: Sociedad de Bibliófilos Españoles, 1933), 2:156.
77. Vitoria, "De potestate civili," 6, in *Relectiones theologicae*, ed. L. G. A. Getino (Madrid: Publicaciones de la Asociación Francisco de Vitoria, 1934), 2:181.
78. Quoted by Gallego Morell, *Garcilaso de la Vega y sus comentaristas*, 2nd ed., p. 504.
79. Mannheim, *Ideology and Utopia*, pp. 190ff. I believe that Jacqueline Savoye-Ferreras is correct when she relates the renewal of the pastoral topos with tendencies to secularization and worldliness. See her article "El mito del pastor," *Cuadernos Hispano-Americanos*, no. 308 (February, 1976): 30–43.
80. Sánchez de Arévalo, *Suma de la Política*, BAE, 116:280.
81. Alfonso de la Torre, *Visión delectable de Filosofía*, BAE, 36:391.
82. López Estrada, ed., *Los siete libros de la Diana*, by Montemayor, Clásicos Castellanos, 127 (Madrid: Espasa-Calpe, 1954), prologue, p. xlix.
83. Montemayor, *Los siete libros de la Diana*, ed. López Estrada, p. 165.
84. Torquemada, *Colloquios satíricos*, fol. 64r.
85. Barahona de Soto, "Paradoja: A la pobreza," in Rodríguez Marín, *Luis Barahona de Soto*, p. 734.
86. Torquemada, *Colloquios satíricos*, fol. 79. From the end of the fifteenth century until the seventeenth there is a curious literature regarding this aspect of diet: moralists condemn it as a corrupting expense; doctors think it unhealthy; and economists view it as a negative factor upsetting sound economic order. Among the latter, however, there are a few, perhaps the most perceptive (such as Moncada and Martínez de Mata) who consider it a stimulus to production and a potential growth factor.
87. Blas Alvarez Miraval, *Libro intitulado la conservación del cuerpo y del alma* (Medina del Campo, 1597).
88. Santos, *Día y noche de Madrid*, p. 378.
89. Diego Saavedra Fajardo, *Idea de un príncipe político y christiano representada en cien empresas*, in *Obras completas*, ed. González de Palencia (Madrid: Aguilar, 1946) (hereafter cited as *Príncipe político*).
90. Alfonso de Castrillo, *Tratado de República*, pp. 79–80.
91. Montemayor, *Los siete libros de la Diana*, p. 10.
92. Juan de Santa María, *Tratado de República y policía Christiana* (Valencia: Mey, 1619), fol. 96.
93. López Bravo, *De Rege et regendi ratione* (Madrid, 1627).
94. Sánchez de Arévalo, *Espejo de la vida humana*, bk. 1, chap. 21.
95. Torquemada, *Colloquios satíricos*, fol. 74.
96. Torquemada, *Colloquios satíricos*, fol. 72.

97. Alonso de Herrera, *Obra de Agricultura,* prologue, in the first (unnumbered) folios.
98. Sabuco, *Coloquio de las cosas que mejoran este mundo y sus repúblicas,* in *Obras,* p. 191.
99. Encina, *Cancionero,* ed. facs. (Madrid: Real Academia Española, 1928), fol. cxv.
100. Montemayor, *Los siete libros de la Diana,* p. 30.
101. Luis de León, *The Names of Christ,* trans. Manuel Durán and William Kluback (New York: Paulist Press, 1984), p. 90.
102. Gil Polo, *Diana enamorada,* p. 116.
103. Sabuco, BAE, 65:337.
104. Andrés Bernáldez, *Memorias del reinado de los Reyes Católicos,* p. 139.
105. Gil Polo, *Diana enamorada,* pp. 77, 83, and 116.
106. Luis de León, *The Names of Christ,* p. 89.
107. Gil Polo, *Diana enamorada,* p. 120.
108. See my book *La cultura del Barroco.*
109. This is why we said earlier that Cervantes never found the inspiration to finish *La Galatea.* It is true that he wrote the *Persiles,* a formidably insincere work but one which does contain occasional moments of intimate self-reflection. For evidence that *La Galatea* proceeds from the model we have presented, see the edition of Schevill and Bonilla (Madrid: B. Rodríguez, 1914), 2:33–34.
110. Cremona, 1556. See especially pp. 22–23.
111. Murúa, *Reyes Incas,* p. 156.
112. Luis de León, *The Names of Christ,* p. 89.
113. Saavedra Fajardo, *Príncipe político,* p. 263.
114. Balbuena, *El Siglo de Oro en las selvas de Erífile,* fol. 84.
115. Palencia, *Triunfo militar,* BAE, 116:350.
116. Luis de León, *The Names of Christ,* p. 90. Fray Juan de los Angeles was quoted by Avalle-Arce, *La novela pastoril española,* p. 13.
117. *Exemplary Novels,* p. 253.
118. Suárez de Figueroa, for example, says that "rusticity is not an ornament of virtue but a manifest imperfection" (*El pasagero,* p. 137).
119. Calderón, in *La estatua de Prometeo,* act 1. Prometheus, speaking to a group of peasants, tells them it is his desire "that your uncouthness / submit to the precepts / of civil government, / offended by the coarse / barbarism which keeps you / from laws which could make you / rational" (*Dramas,* p. 2069).
120. In Valbuena's edition of Cervantes's *Obras completas* (Madrid: Aguilar, 1967), pp. 1747–1801.
121. See my *Estado moderno y mentalidad social,* 1:461ff.
122. There is no contradiction between Cervantes's loyalty to the sovereign and his deep and bitter nonconformity. Was not Thomas More the chancellor of a king in a society which he castigated severely, and was this not in fact the cause of his downfall?
123. See Maldonado de Guevara, "La espiritualidad cesárea de la cultura española," *Revista de Estudios Políticos* 18, nos. 33–34 (1947): 1–22, esp. 14.

124. *Exemplary Novels,* p. 253. Laín Entralgo has called attention to the importance of this novel for Cervantes's social thought in his lecture "Coloquio de
dos perros, soliloquio de Cervantes," reprinted in his *Obras* (Madrid: Plenitud, 1965), pp. 914–32.

125. López Estrada, *"La Galatea" de Cervantes. Estudio Crítico,* pp. 115–16.

126. Huizinga, *The Waning of the Middle Ages,* pp. 37–39.

127. Alfonso de Valdés, *Diálogo de Mercurio y Carón,* pp. 195–96. The passage
of the *Persiles* may be found in the Weller and Colahan translation, pp. 92–
93. Regarding the thought of Alfonso de Valdés, see my *Carlos V y el pensamiento político del Renacimiento,* pp. 206ff.

128. Américo Castro discusses the connection between Cervantes and Alfonso
de Valdés in *El pensamiento de Cervantes,* p. 354. Above all, see Bataillon,
Erasmo y España, 2nd ed. (Mexico, 1966).

129. Vives, *In Allegorias bucolicorum Vergilii,* in *Opera omnia,* 2:32–33.

130. Camos, *Microcosmia,* fol. 132.

131. Felippe, *Consejo de príncipes,* fol. 116.

132. Suárez de Figueroa, *El pasagero,* p. 186.

133. Guillem de Vàroich, in *Tractats de cavalleria,* p. 71.

134. Juan de Santa María, *Tratado de República y policía Christiana,* fol. 103.

135. Suárez Fernández, *Política internacional de Isabel la Católica* (Valladolid: Instituto "Isabel la Católica" de Historia Eclesiástica, 1965), 1:269–70.

136. Jiménez de Urrea, *Verdadera honra militar,* fol. 2.

137. Guevara, *Marco Aurelio,* fol. xxxiii.

138. Pérez del Barrio, *Secretario y consejero de señores y ministros* (Madrid, 1613).

139. Cervantes, *Poesías sueltas,* in *Obras completas,* ed. Valbuena Prat (Madrid:
Aguilar, 1967), p. 48.—Trans.

140. Ferrer de Valdecebro, *Gobierno general, moral y político hallado en las aves
más generosas y nobles,* in the unnumbered pages of the argument and prologue.

141. Murúa, *Reyes Incas,* p. 160.

142. Castiglione, *The Book of the Courtier,* p. 303.

143. Francisco de Quevedo, *Marco Bruto,* in *Obras en prosa,* ed. Astrana Marín
(Madrid: Aguilar, 1945), p. 702.

144. This thirst for natural justice based on human will enlightened by common
sense is found in many texts of the period, among them the *Viaje a Turquía.*
Laguna praises the justice he found among the infidels, saying: "Judges and
lawyers there, like our own, have their books of law, but what they do not
have is so much barbarity and Babylonian confusion. One who does not have
justice on his side will not find anybody to argue and adduce sophisms in his
defense. They have few books, for the most important thing is judgment" (p.
242). Examples from Vives, Montaigne, and More have already been given.

145. See Weber's *Economy and Society,* trans. E. Fischoff et al. (Berkeley: University of California Press, 1978), 2:845.

146. Luis de León, *The Names of Christ,* p. 97.

147. This analysis of the conditions prevailing in a new seigniory derives from
Il Principe, albeit indirectly.

148. Alborg, *Historia de la literatura española,* 2:167.

149. Juan Manuel, *Libro de los estados,* BAE, 51:336.
150. See R. Menéndez Pidal, "Sobre un arcaísmo léxico en la poesía tradicional," in his *De primitiva lírica española y antigua épica,* 2nd ed., Col. Austral, 1051 (Madrid: Espasa-Calpe, 1951), pp. 131–33.
151. In connection with the progressive degradation of the concept of "squire," there is a passage in Suárez de Figueroa that is worth remembering. He is again complaining about the behavior of the powerful: "Flee from the great lords, for as you know, they honor all who are not of their own house or, more exactly, who are not their equals with the title of rogues or, at best, squires" (*El pasagero,* p. 300).
152. Descartes, *Discourse on the Method,* in *Philosophical Works of Descartes,* 1:81.—Trans.
153. Pedro Simón Abril, *Apuntamiento de cómo se deben reformar las doctrinas y la manera de enseñallas,* BAE, 65:296.
154. See my article "Un primer proyecto de Facultad de Ciencias Políticas en la crisis del siglo XVII: el Discurso VIII de Sancho de Moncada," included in my *Estudios de historia del pensamiento español,* 3rd ser., Siglo XVII (Madrid: Ediciones Cultura Hispánica, 1975), pp. 125–60.
155. Quoted by Rodríguez Marín as part of his commentary on this passage of the novel in his ten-volume edition of *El ingenioso hidalgo Don Quijote de la Mancha* (Madrid: Patronato del IV Centenario de Cervantes, Ediciones Atlas, 1947–49), 6:226.
156. More, *Utopia* (Cologne, 1629), p. 206.
157. Maestro León de Castro's prologue to *Refranes o proverbios en romance,* written by the Comendador Hernán Núñez Pinciano (Salamanca, 1555). Some editions referred to the author of the prologue simply as "maestro León," which has caused it to be erroneously attributed to Fray Luis de León.
158. See M. Joly, "Aspectos del refrán en Mateo Alemán y Cervantes," *Nueva Revista de Filología Hispánica* 20, no. 1 (1971): 95–106.
159. These words are spoken by the go-between Gerarda in *La Dorotea,* ed. E. S. Morby, 2nd ed. (Berkeley: University of California Press, 1968), p. 391, n. 17.
160. Juan de Valdés, *Diálogo de la lengua,* (Madrid: Calleja, 1919), pp. 45 and 67. On sociohistorical aspects of the spread of proverbs, see my *Antiguos y modernos. Visión de la historia e idea de progreso hasta el Renacimiento,* 2nd ed. (Madrid: Alianza Editorial, 1986), pp. 407–13.
161. Regarding the nexus between the image of natural government, as we have tried to present it here, and the taste for proverbs, everyday wisdom in simple language, see Romera-Navarro, "La defensa de la lengua española en el siglo XVI," *Bulletin Hispanique* 31 (1929): 204–55.
162. León de Castro, prologue to *Refranes o proverbios en romance.*
163. Medina, *Libro de las grandezas de España,* ed. González Palencia (Madrid: Consejo Superior de Investigaciones Científicas, 1944), p. 11.
164. Juan Mal Lara, *Philosophia vulgar* (Seville, 1568), preamble in the first (unnumbered) pages.
165. See Mariana's *Historia de España,* bk. 20, chap. 3, BAE, 31:64.

166. Mucchielli, *Le mythe de la cité idéale,* p. 285.
167. Ruiz de Virués, "Apología de Erasmo," published by Bonilla as app. 1 to his *Luis Vives y la filosofía del Renacimiento,* Nueva Biblioteca Filosófica, 32–34 (Madrid: Bruno del Amo, 1929), 3:123–28.
168. *Exemplary Novels,* pp. 255–56.
169. *Exemplary Novels,* p. 258.
170. Noël Salomón, *Recherches sur le thème paysan dans la comédie espagnole au temps de Lope de Vega* (Bordeaux: Féret et fils, 1965).
171. Noël Salomón, *Recherches sur le thème paysan dans la comedie espagnole au temps de Lope de Vega,* pp. 755ff.
172. Alvarez y Ossorio y Redin, *Discurso Universal de las causas que ofenden esta Monarquía y remedios eficaces para todos,* published by Rodríguez Campomanes in the five-volume appendix to his *Discurso sobre la educación popular de los artesanos y su fomento* (Madrid: Antonio de Sancha, 1775), 1:315.
173. Miguel Caxa de Leruela, *Restauración de la abundancia antigua de España* (Naples, 1631), p. 286.
174. William Morris, *News from Nowhere; or, An epoch of rest. Being some chapters from a Utopian romance* (Boston: Roberts Brothers, 1890), chap. 22. (The Spanish translation of this work [*Noticias de ninguna parte* (Madrid, 1968)] was done by Juan J. Morato, a socialist and a historian of socialism.)

Chapter Seven

1. R. Ruyer perceived a connection between modern science and utopianism on the basis of their common roots in hypothesis. See *L'Utopie et les utopies* (Paris: Presses Universitaires de France, 1950).
2. Simón Abril, *Apuntamiento de cómo se deben reformar las doctrinas y la manera de enseñallas,* BAE, 65:296.
3. Descartes, *Discourse on the Method,* in *Philosophical Works of Descartes,* 1:88.
4. Pedro de Rivadeneyra, *Historia del cisma de Inglaterra,* BAE, 60:212ff.
5. Herrera, *Thomas Moro* (Madrid: Luis Sánchez, 1617), p. 35. Herrera follows Rivadeneyra here.
6. There was a study written along these lines some time ago but to my knowledge the attempt has not been repeated. I refer to the work of Vida Nájera, *El concepto y la organización del Estado en las utopías* (Madrid, 1928). I have written a few partial studies on the subject which have been included in my *Utopía y reformismo en la España de los Austrias* (Madrid: Siglo Veintiuno de España Editores, 1982).
7. A counterutopia based on sarcasm (which we also see in Cervantes more than occasionally) was written by Jonathan Swift in 1729 [*A Modest Proposal*]. See Mucchielli, *Le mythe de la cité idéale,* pp. 92–94.
8. Max Horkheimer, "La utopía," in Neusüss, ed., *Utopía,* trans. María Nolla (Barcelona: Barral Editores, 1971), p. 97.
9. Rafael Salillas, *Un gran inspirador de Cervantes: el doctor Juan Huarte y su "Examen de ingenios"* (Madrid: E. Arias, 1905).
10. I reject all those oft-repeated appeals to the realism which is erroneously supposed to be a characteristic of our writers. Dámaso Alonso has dealt with

one aspect of the problem in "Escila y Caribdis de la literatura española," in his *Ensayos sobre poesía española* (Buenos Aires: Revista de Occidente Argentina, 1946), pp. 9–27.

11. Consider that the seventeenth century not only lays the basis for modern mathematical physics but also is known as the century of moral issues. See Paul Bénichou, *Morales du grand siècle* (Paris: Gallimard, 1948).

12. Mucchielli, *Le mythe de la cité idéale*, pp. 274ff.

13. On this problematical connection between negative present and positive future see F. L. Polak, "Cambio y tarea persistente de la utopía," in Neusüss, ed., *Utopía*, p. 175.

14. Mannheim, *Ideology and Utopia*, p. 173.

15. Palencia, *Triunfo militar*, BAE, 116:345.

16. Quevedo, in "Noticia, juicio y recomendación de la *Utopía* de Tomás Moro," published as a prologue to the Spanish trans., 2nd ed. (Madrid: Aznar, 1790).

17. *Guía del Cielo* (Alcalá: Juan de Brócar, 1553). On Fray Pablo de León see Beltrán de Heredia, *Las corrientes de espiritualidad entre los dominicos de Castilla durante la primera mitad del siglo XVI* (Salamanca: Biblioteca de Teólogos Españoles, 1941). [His edition of the *Guía del Cielo* (Barcelona: Juan Flors, 1963) also has a useful preliminary study.]

18. Castiglione, *The Book of the Courtier*, pp. 27–28.

19. At the basis of the perfectionist dynamism animating western culture are the myth of a "better country" beyond the boundaries of the world known to Christendom and also the fundamental pluralism of our culture. See Myron Piper Gilmore, *The World of Humanism* (New York: Harper, 1952). Also see my essay "El pensamiento utópico y el dinamismo de la historia europea," *Sistema. Revista de Ciencias Sociales* (Madrid), no. 14 (July, 1976): 13–44.

20. Tomás Carreras Artau, *La filosofía del derecho en el "Quijote"* (Gerona: Tip. de Carreras y Mas, 1905), p. 146.

21. Francisco Javier Conde, "La utopía de la ínsula Barataria," *Escorial* 3 (May, 1941): 169–202. Hazard's work was cited in chap. 1, n. 28.

22. Harry Elmer Barnes and Howard Becker, *Social Thought from Lore to Science*, 3rd ed. (New York: Dover, 1961), 1:309–14.

23. Pedro de Portugal, *Sátira de felice e infelice vida*, in *Opúsculos literarios de los siglos XIV al XVI*, p. 48.

24. Carvallo, *Cisne de Apolo*, 2:621.

25. Vicente Espinel, *Vida del escudero Marcos de Obregón*, 1:239.

26. Alborg, *Historia de la literatura española*, 2:93–94.

27. Salas Barbadillo, *El caballero perfecto* (Madrid: Juan de la Cuesta, 1620).

28. Saavedra Fajardo, *Introducciones a la política y razón del Estado del rey don Fernando el Católico*, in *Obras completas*, ed. González Palencia (Madrid: Aguilar, 1946), p. 1242.

29. Martín Cordero, *Discurso de la vida humana y aventuras del caballero determinado*, trans. Jiménez de Urrea (Antwerp: Martín Nucio, 1555). This version is done in hendecasyllabic tercets. The translation of Hernando de Acuña, in "coplas castellanas" (octosyllables in stanzas of ten verses), was published two years earlier in the same city by Juan Steelsio. Martín Cordero's "Exhortaciòn" was published with Urrea's version.

30. Published in 1558. Martín Cordero also translated Seneca and Flavius Josephus and, good humanist that he was, *Prontuario de las medallas de todos los más insignes varones*.
31. *Exemplary Novels,* author's prologue, p. xxxiv.—Trans.
32. Protests against this shabby treatment of ex-soldiers joined with condemnations of warmongering in general and led to an increase of pacifism among Erasmist military men or nonconformists such as Núñez de Alba and Marcos de Isaba.
33. See my *La cultura del Barroco. Análisis de una estructura histórica.*

Works Cited

Adler, George. *Idealstaaten der Renaissance: More-Rabelais-Campanella.* Munich-Leipzig: Annalen des Deutschen Reiches, 1899.

Alamos de Barrientos, Baltasar. *Tácito español, ilustrado con aforismos.* Madrid: L. Sánchez, 1614.

Alava y Viamont, Diego de. *El perfecto capitán.* Madrid, 1590.

Alborg, Juan Luis. *Historia de la literatura española.* 4 vols. Madrid: Gredos, 1966–80.

Alcalá Yáñez y Ribera, Jerónimo de. *El donado hablador.* In *Novela picaresca española.* Ed. Angel Valbuena Prat. Madrid: Aguilar, 1968. Pp. 1197–1339.

Aldana, Francisco de. *Poesías.* Clásicos Castellanos, vol. 143. Madrid: Espasa-Calpe, 1957.

Alemán, Mateo. *Guzmán de Alfarache.* 5 vols. Clásicos Castellanos, vols. 73, 83, 90, 93, 114. Madrid: Espasa-Calpe, 1926–64.

Alenda y Mira, Jenaro. *Relaciones de solemnidades y fiestas públicas de España.* 2 vols. Madrid, 1903.

Alfieri, Vittorio. *The Life of Vittorio Alfieri, Written by Himself.* Trans. Sir Henry McAnally. Lawrence, Kansas: University of Kansas Press, 1953.

Alonso, Dámaso. "Escila y Caribdis de la literatura española." In his *Ensayos sobre poesía española.* Buenos Aires: Revista de Occidente Argentina, 1946. Pp. 9–27.

Alonso de Herrera, Gabriel. *Obra de Agricultura.* Alcalá, 1524.

Alvarez Miraval, Blas. *Libro intitulado la conservación del cuerpo y del alma.* Medina del Campo, 1597.

Alvarez y Ossorio y Redin, Miguel. *Discurso Universal de las causas que ofenden esta Monarquía y remedios eficaces para todos.* Vol. 1 of the five-volume appendix to Rodríguez Campomanes, Pedro. *Discurso sobre la educación popular de los artesanos y su fomento.* Madrid: Antonio de Sancha, 1775.

Arco Garay, Ricardo del. *La sociedad española en las obras de Cervantes.* Madrid: IV Centenario, 1951.

Aronson, Nicole. *Les idées politiques de Rabelais.* Paris: A. G. Nizet, 1973.

Avalle-Arce, Juan Bautista. *La novela pastoril española*. Madrid: Revista de Occidente, 1959.

Avila, Luis de. *Comentario de la guerra de Alemania*. In vol. 1 of *Historiadores de sucesos particulares*. Ed. Cayetano Rosell. Biblioteca de Autores Españoles, vol. 21. Madrid: Ediciones Atlas, 1946. Pp. 409–49.

Balbuena, Bernardo de. *El Siglo de Oro en las selvas de Erífile*. Madrid: Martín, 1608.

Barahona de Soto, Luis. "Paradoja: A la pobreza." In Francisco Rodríguez Marín. *Luis Barahona de Soto. Estudio biográfico, bibliográfico y crítico*. Madrid: Sucesores de Rivadeneyra, 1903. Pp. 731–40.

Barnes, Harry Elmer, and Howard Becker. *Social Thought from Lore to Science*. 3rd ed. 3 vols. New York: Dover, 1961.

Bataillon, Marcel. *Erasme et l'Espagne: Recherches sur l'histoire spirituelle du XVIe siècle*. Paris: E. Droz, 1937. Spanish trans., *Erasmo y España: Estudios sobre la historia espiritual del siglo XVI*. Trans. Antonio Alatorre. 2nd ed. Mexico: Fondo de Cultura Económica, 1966.

———. "Publications cervantines récentes." *Bulletin Hispanique* 53, no. 2 (1951): 157–75.

Bell, Aubrey F. G. "Notes on the Spanish Renaissance." *Revue Hispanique* 80 (1930): 319–652.

Beltrán de Heredia, Vicente. *Las corrientes de espiritualidad entre los dominicos de Castilla durante la primera mitad del siglo XVI*. Salamanca: Biblioteca de Teólogos Españoles, 1941.

———, ed. *Guía del Cielo*. By Fray Pablo de León. Barcelona: Juan Flors, 1963.

Bénichou, Paul. *Morales du grand siècle*. Paris: Gallimard, 1948.

Berceo, Gonzalo de. *Vida de Santo Domingo de Silos*. Ed. Teresa Labarta de Chaves. Madrid: Clásicos Castalia, 1972.

Bernáldez, Andrés. *Memorias del reinado de los Reyes Católicos*. Ed. Gómez Moreno y Carriazo. Madrid, 1962.

Bloch, Marc. *Les Clases et le gouvernment des hommes*. Vol. 2 of *La societé féodale*. Paris: Albin Michel, 1940.

Bodin, Jean. *Methodus ad facilem historiarum cognitionem*. Ed. P. Mesnard. Corpus géneral des philosophes français. Paris, 1951.

Bohigas, Pere, ed. *Tractats de Cavalleria*. Els Nostres Classics, Collecció A, vol. 57. Barcelona: Barcino, 1947.

Bonilla y San Martín, Adolfo. "Don Quijote y el pensamiento español." In his *Cervantes y su obra*. Madrid: F. Beltrán, 1916. Pp. 11–40.

———. "¿Qué pensaron de Cervantes sus contemporáneos?" In his *Cervantes y su obra*. Madrid: F. Beltrán, 1916. Pp. 165–84.

Bruni, Leonardo Aretino. *De studiis et litteris*. Incunabulum. Madrid: Biblioteca Nacional.

Burkhardt, Jacob. *The Civilization of the Renaissance in Italy*. Trans. S. G. C. Middlemore. 2 vols. New York: Harper and Brothers, 1958.

Cadalso, José. *Cartas marruecas*. Ed. Juan Tamayo y Rubio. Clásicos Castellanos, vol. 112. Madrid: Espasa-Calpe, 1935.

Calderón de la Barca, Pedro. *Dramas*. Ed. Valbuena Briones. Vol. 1 of *Obras completas*. 5th ed. Madrid: Aguilar, 1966.

Camos, Fray Marco Antonio de. *Microcosmia y gobierno universal del hombre cristiano.* Madrid, 1595.

Campanella, Tommaso. *La Città del Sole: Dialogo Poetico / The City of the Sun: A Poetical Dialogue.* Trans. Daniel J. Donno. Berkeley: University of California Press, 1981.

Campillo, José del. *Lo que hay de más y de menos en España para que sea lo que debe ser y no lo que es.* Ed. A. Elorza. Madrid: Seminario de Historia Social y Económica de la Facultad de Filosofía y Letras de la Universidad de Madrid, 1969.

Cano, Melchor. *Tratado de la victoria de sí mismo.* In *Obras escogidas de filósofos.* Ed. A. de Castro. Biblioteca de Autores Españoles, vol. 65. Madrid: Ediciones Atlas, 1953. Pp. 303–24.

Caro Baroja, Julio. *Algunos mitos españoles.* Madrid: Editora Nacional, 1941.

———. *Las brujas y su mundo.* Madrid: Alianza Editorial, 1961.

Carreras Artau, Tomás. *La filosofía del derecho en el "Quijote."* Gerona: Tip. de Carreras y Mas, 1905.

Cartas anónimas. In vol. 2 of *Avisos de Don Jerónimo de Barrionuevo.* Ed. A. Paz y Melia. Biblioteca de Autores Españoles, vol. 222. Madrid: Ediciones Atlas, 1969.

Carvallo, Luis Alfonso de. *Cisne de Apolo.* Ed. A. Porqueras Mayo. 2 vols. Biblioteca de Antiguos Libros Hispánicos, Ser. A, 25–26. Madrid: Consejo Superior de Investigaciones Científicas, Instituto "Miguel de Cervantes," 1958.

Casalduero, Joaquín. *Sentido y forma de las novelas ejemplares.* 2nd ed. Madrid: Gredos, 1974.

Cassirer, Ernst. *The Individual and the Cosmos in Renaissance Philosophy.* Trans. Mario Domandi. New York: Harper and Row, 1963.

Castiglione, Baldassare. *The Book of the Courtier.* Trans. Charles Singleton. Garden City, New York: Anchor Books, 1959.

Castrillo, Alfonso de. *Tratado de República.* 1521; rpt. Madrid: Instituto de Estudios Políticos, 1958.

Castro, Américo. *Lo hispánico y el erasmismo. Los prólogos al "Quijote."* Buenos Aires: Instituto de Filología, 1942.

———. *El pensamiento de Cervantes.* 2nd ed. Barcelona: Editorial Noguer, 1972.

Castro, León de. Prologue. *Refranes o proverbios en romance.* By Hernán Núñez Pinciano. Salamanca, 1555.

Caversazzi, Ciro. *Il Tasso e l'Utopia.* Milan, 1896.

Caxa de Leruela, Miguel. *Restauración de la abundancia antigua de España.* Naples, 1631.

Cervantes y Saavedra, Miguel de. *The Deceitful Marriage and Other Exemplary Novels.* Trans. Walter Starkie. New York: New American Library of World Literature, 1963.

———. *La Galatea.* Ed. Rudolph Schevill and Adolfo Bonilla. 2 vols. Madrid: B. Rodríguez, 1914.

———. *The Ingenious Gentleman Don Quixote de la Mancha.* Trans. Samuel Putnam. New York: Modern Library, 1949.

———. *Novelas ejemplares.* Ed. Rudolph Schevill and Adolfo Bonilla. 3 vols. Madrid: B. Rodríguez, 1922–25.

————. *Poesías sueltas*. In *Obras completas*. Ed. Angel Valbuena Prat. Madrid: Aguilar, 1967. Pp. 41–63.

————. *The Trials of Persiles and Sigismunda*. Trans. Celia Richmond Weller and Clark A. Colahan. Berkeley: University of California Press, 1989.

————. *El Viaje del Parnaso*. In *Obras completas*. Ed. Angel Valbuena Prat. Madrid: Aguilar, 1967. Pp. 65–104.

Cervantes de Salazar, Francisco. *Crónica de la Nueva España*. Ed. Manuel Magallón. 2 vols. Biblioteca de Autores Españoles, vols. 244–45. Madrid: Ediciones Atlas, 1971.

Céspedes y Meneses, Gonzalo de. *El español Gerardo, y desengaño del amor lascivo*. In *Novelistas posteriores a Cervantes*. Ed. C. Rosell. Biblioteca de Autores Españoles, vol. 18. Madrid: Ediciones Atlas, 1946. Pp. 117–271.

————. *Historias peregrinas y ejemplares*. Ed. Yves-René Fonquerne. Madrid, 1970.

Chesterton, Gilbert Keith. *Orthodoxy*. Garden City, New York: Image Books, 1959.

Clavería, Carlos. *Le Chévalier délibéré, de Olivier de la Marche, y sus versiones españolas del siglo XVI*. Zaragoza: Institución "Fernando el Católico," 1950.

Cohn, Norman. *The Pursuit of the Millenium*. 2nd ed. New York: Harper Torchbooks, 1961.

Conde, Francisco Javier. "La utopía de la ínsula Barataria." *Escorial* 3 (May, 1941): 169–202.

Cortes de los antiguos reinos de León y Castilla. 5 vols. Published by Real Academia de la Historia. Madrid: Sucesores de Rivadeneyra, 1861–1903.

Descartes, René. *Discourse on the Method*. In *The Philosophical Works of Descartes*. Trans. E. S. Haldane and G. R. T. Ross. 2 vols. New York: Dover Books, 1955. 1:78–130.

Díez-Borque, José María. *Aspectos de la oposición caballero -pastor en el primer teatro castellano*. Bordeaux, 1970.

Díez de Games, Gutierre. *El Victorial, Crónica de don Pero Niño*. Ed. J. de M. Carriazo. Madrid: Espasa-Calpe, 1940.

Ehrenberg, Richard. *Le siècle des Fugger*. French trans. Paris, 1955.

Encina, Juan del. *Cancionero*. Ed. facs. Madrid: Real Academia Española, 1928.

————. *Pastoral de amores*. In *Egloga de Plácida y Victoriano, precedida de otras tres églogas introductorias*. Ed. E. Giménez Caballero. Zaragoza: Clásicos Ebro, 1948. Pp. 22-34.

————. *Representación de amor*. In *Egloga de Plácida y Vicoriano, precedida de otras tres églogas introductorias*. Ed. E. Giménez Caballero. Zaragoza: Clásicos Ebro, 1948. Pp. 35–48.

Enríquez de Guzmán, Alonso. *Libro de la vida y costumbres de Don Alonso Enríquez de Guzmán*. Ed. H. Keniston. Biblioteca de Autores Españoles, vol. 126. Madrid: Ediciones Atlas, 1960.

Espinel, Vicente. *Vida del escudero Marcos de Obregón*. 2 vols. Clásicos Castellanos, vols. 43 and 51. Madrid: Espasa-Calpe, 1959.

Estella, Fray Diego de. *Meditación del amor de Dios*. Ed. Alberto García Ruiz. Clásicos de Espiritualidad, 36. Madrid: Rialp, 1965.

Febvre, Lucien Paul Victor. *The Problem of Unbelief in the Sixteenth Century: The Religion of Rabelais*. Trans. B. Gottlieb. Cambridge, Massachusetts: Harvard University Press, 1982.

Felippe, Bartolomé. *Tratado del Consejo y de los consejeros de los príncipes.* 2nd ed. Turin, 1589.

Fernández, Lucas. *Farsas y églogas.* Salamanca, 1514. Ed. facs. Madrid: Real Academia Española, 1929.

Fernández de Velasco, Juan. *Controversia.* Seville: Sociedad de Bibliófilos Andaluces, 1870.

Fernández de Villareal, Manuel. *Arquitectura militar o fortificación moderna.* Paris: Jean Henault, 1649.

Ferrer de Valdecebro, Andrés. *Gobierno general, moral y político hallado en las aves más generosas y nobles, sacado de sus naturales virtudes y propiedades.* Madrid: Villadiego, 1683.

Forner, Juan Pablo. *Exequias de la lengua castellana.* Clásicos Castellanos, vol. 66. Madrid: La Lectura, 1925.

Foucault, Michel. *Folie et déraison. Histoire de la folie à l'âge classique.* Paris: Plon, 1961.

Freyer, Hans. *Die politische Insel. Eine Geschichte der Utopien von Plato bis zur Gegenwart.* Leipzig, 1936.

Fuz, Jerzy Konstanty. *Welfare Economics in English Utopias.* London, 1952.

Gallego Morell, Antonio. *Garcilaso de la Vega y sus comentaristas. Obras completas del poeta acompañadas de los textos íntegros de los Comentarios de El Brocense, Fernando de Herrera, Tamayo de Vargas y Azara.* 2nd ed. Madrid: Gredos, 1972.

García de Castrojeriz, Juan. *Glosa castellana al Regimiento de Príncipes.* Ed. Beneyto. 3 vols. Madrid: Biblioteca Española de Escritores Políticos, 1947.

García del Palacio, Diego. *Diálogos militares.* 1583; facsim. rpt. Madrid: Cultura Hispánica, 1944.

García de Paredes, Diego. *Diálogos militares.* Mexico, 1593. Ed. facs. Madrid, 1944.

Gil y Carrasco, Enrique. "Revista de cursos literarios y científicos. Liceo literario y artístico." *El Correo Nacional,* no. 420, April 12, 1839. Reprinted in *Obras completas de Don Enrique Gil y Carrasco.* Ed. Jorge Campos. Biblioteca de Autores Españoles, vol. 74. Madrid: Ediciones Atlas, 1954. Pp. 569–71.

Gil Polo, Gaspar. *Diana enamorada.* Clásicos Castellanos, vol. 135. Madrid: Espasa-Calpe, 1962.

Gilmore, Myron Piper. *The World of Humanism.* New York: Harper, 1952.

Gilson, Etienne. *Etudes sur le rôle de la pensée médiévale dans la formation du système cartésien.* Paris: J. Vrin, 1951.

González de Cellorigo, Martín. *Memorial de la política necesaria y útil restauración de la República de España.* Valladolid, 1600.

Gracián, Baltasar. *El Criticón.* Ed. Romera-Navarro. 3 vols. Philadelphia: University of Pennsylvania Press, 1938–40.

Green, Otis. " 'Ni es cielo ni es azul.' A Note on the *Barroquismo* of Bartolomé Leonardo de Argensola." *Revista de Filología Española* 34 (1950): 137–50.

Guevara, Fray Antonio de. *Historia del famosísimo emperador Marco Aurelio, seguida del Relox de Príncipes.* Seville, 1532.

———. *Menosprecio de Corte y alabanza de aldea.* Clásicos Castellanos, vol. 29. Madrid: Espasa-Calpe, 1967.

————. *El villano del Danubio*. In *Obras escogidas de filósofos*. Ed. Adolfo de Castro. Biblioteca de Autores Españoles, vol. 65. Madrid: Ediciones Atlas, 1953. Pp. 160–66.

Guillem de Vàroich. In *Tractats de Cavalleria*. Ed. Pere Bohigas. Els Nostres Classics, Collecció A, vol. 57. Barcelona: Barcino, 1947. Pp. 43–77.

Gutiérrez de los Ríos, Gaspar. *Noticia general para la estimación de las artes*. Madrid, 1960.

Hamp, Vinzenz. "Le motif du Pasteur dans l'Ancien Testament." In *Festschrift Kardinal Faulhaber*. Münster, 1949.

Hatzfeld, Helmut. *El "Quijote" como obra de arte del lenguaje*. Spanish trans. 2nd ed. Madrid: Consejo Superior de Investigaciones Científicas, *Revista de Filología Española*, anejo 83, 1972.

Hazard, Paul. *Don Quichotte de Cervantes, étude et analyse*. Paris: Mellottée, 1931.

Hermas. *Le Pasteur*. Critical ed. with annotated bilingual text by R. Joly. Paris: Editions du Cerf, 1958.

Herrera, Fernando de. *Comentarios*. In A. Gallego Morell. *Garcilaso de la Vega y sus comentaristas. Obras completas del poeta acompañadas de los textos íntegros de los Comentarios de El Brocense, Fernando de Herrera, Tamayo de Vargas y Azara*. 2nd ed. Madrid: Gredos, 1972. Pp. 305–594.

————. *Relación de la Guerra de Cipre y suceso de la batalla naval de Lepanto*. Seville, 1572.

————. *Thomas Moro*. Madrid: Luis Sánchez, 1617.

Horkheimer, Max. "La utopía." In *Utopía*. Ed. Arnhelm Neusüss. Trans. María Nolla. Barcelona: Barral Editores, 1971. Pp. 91–102.

Huizinga, Johan. *The Waning of the Middle Ages*. Trans. F. Hopman. New York: Doubleday, 1954.

Hurtado de Mendoza, Diego. *Guerra de Granada*. In vol. 1 of *Historiadores de sucesos particulares*. Ed. C. Rosell. Biblioteca de Autores Españoles, vol. 21. Madrid: Ediciones Atlas, 1946. Pp. 65–122.

Isaba, Marcos de. *Cuerpo enfermo de la milicia española*. Madrid, 1594.

Isaza y Calderón, Baltasar. *El retorno a la naturaleza*. Madrid: Bolaños y Aguilar, 1934.

Jerome, Saint. *Ad Pammachium*. In *Lettres*. Paris: Les Belles Lettres, 1953. 3:55–73.

————. *Ad Paulinum*. In *Lettres*. Paris: Les Belles Lettres, 1953. 3:7–25.

Jiménez de Urrea, Jerónimo. *Diálogo de la verdadera honra militar*. 4th ed. Madrid, 1642.

————. *Don Clarisel de las Flores*. Unpublished novel. MS is in library of University of Zaragoza.

————, trans. *Discurso de la vida humana y aventuras del caballero determinado*. By Olivier de la Marche. Antwerp: Martín Nucio, 1555.

John of the Cross, Saint. *Ascent of Mount Carmel*. Trans. E. Allison Peers. Garden City, New York: Image, 1958.

Joly, Monique. "Aspectos del refrán en Mateo Alemán y Cervantes." *Nueva Revista de Filología Hispánica* 20, no. 1 (1971): 95–106.

Juan Manuel. *Libro del caballero et del escudero*. In *Escritores en prosa anteriores al* siglo XV. Ed. Pascual Gayangos. Biblioteca de Autores Españoles, vol. 51. Madrid: Ediciones Atlas, 1952. Pp. 234 –57.

———. *Libro de los estados*. In *Escritores en prosa anteriores al siglo XV*. Ed. Pascual de Gayangos. Biblioteca de Autores Españoles, vol. 51. Madrid: Ediciones Atlas, 1952. Pp. 278–364.

Juan de Santa María, Fray. *Tratado de República y policía Christiana*. Valencia: Mey, 1619.

Kilgour, R. Lincoln. *The Decline of Chivalry as Shown in the French Literature of the Late Middle Ages*. Cambridge, Mass.: Harvard University Press, 1937.

Laguna, Andrés. *Viaje a Turquía*. Ed. A. Solalinde. Buenos Aires: Colección Austral, 1942.

Laín Entralgo, Pedro. "Coloquio de dos perros, soliloquio de Cervantes." In his *Obras*. Madrid: Plenitud, 1965. Pp. 914–32.

Lapesa, Rafael. "En torno a *La española inglesa* y el *Persiles*." In his *De la Edad Media a nuestros días*. Madrid: Gredos, 1971. Pp. 242–63.

Lechuga, Cristóbal. *Discurso en que se trata del cargo de Maestre de Campo general y de todo lo que de derecho le toca en el exército*. Milan, 1603.

Lecoy, Félix. *Recherches sur le "Libro de buen amor" de Juan Ruiz, Archiprêtre de Hita*. Paris: Droz, 1938.

León, Fray Luis de. *The Names of Christ*. Trans. Manuel Durán and William Kluback. New York: Paulist Press, 1984.

León, Fray Pablo de. *Guía del Cielo*. Alcalá: Juan de Brócar, 1553.

Lida de Malkiel, María Rosa. *La idea de la fama en la Edad Media castellana*. Mexico: Fondo de Cultura Económica, 1952.

Ligier, Hermann. *La politique de Rabelais*. Paris: G. Fischbacher, 1880.

Lissarrague, Salvador. "El sentido de la realidad en el *Quijote*." *Escorial*, no. 31 (May, 1943).

Londoño, Sancho de. *Discurso sobre la forma de reducir la disciplina militar a mejor y antiguo estado*. Brussels, 1589.

López de Ayala, Pero. *Rimado de Palacio*. In *Poetas castellanos anteriores al siglo XV*. Eds. T. A. Sánchez, P. J. Pidal, and F. Janer. Biblioteca de Autores Españoles, vol. 57. Madrid: Ediciones Atlas, 1952. Pp. 425–76.

López Bravo, Mateo. *De Rege et regendi ratione*. Madrid, 1627.

López Estrada, Francisco de. *"La Galatea" de Cervantes. Estudio Crítico*. La Laguna de Tenerife: Universidad de La Laguna, 1948.

———. *Los libros de pastores en la literatura española. La órbita previa*. Madrid: Gredos, 1974.

———. Prologue. In *Los siete libros de la Diana*. By Jorge de Montemayor. Ed. F. López de Estrada. Clásicos Castellanos, vol. 127. Madrid: Espasa-Calpe, 1954. Pp. ix–ciii.

López de Palacios Rubios, Juan. *Tratado del esfuerzo bélico heroico*. Ed. Francisco Morales. Madrid: Sancha, 1793.

López de Villalobos, Francisco. *Los problemas de Villalobos*. In *Curiosidades bibliográficas*. Ed. A. de Castro. Biblioteca de Autores Españoles, vol. 36. Madrid: Ediciones Atlas, 1950. Pp. 403–60.

Lot, Ferdinand. *L'art militaire et les armées au Moyen Age*. Paris: Payot, 1946.

Lucena, Juan de. *De vita beata*. Ed. Bertini. Turin, 1950.

————. *Libro de vida beata*. In *Opúsculos literarios de los siglos XIV al XVI*. Ed. Antonio Paz y Melia. Madrid: Sociedad de Bibliófilos Españoles, 1892. 105–217.

Lull, Ramón. *Libre qui és de l'Orde de Cavalleria*. In *Obres essencials*. 2 vols. Barcelona: Editorial Selecta, 1957. 1:527–45.

Luque Fajardo, Francisco de. *Fiel desengaño de la ociosidad y los vicios*. Ed. Martín de Riquer. 2 vols. Madrid, 1955.

Machiavelli, Niccolò. *Discourses on the First Ten Books of Titus Livius*. Trans. Christian E. Detmold. In *The Prince and the Discourses*. New York: Random House, 1950. Pp. 99–540.

Mal Lara, Juan. *Philosophia vulgar*. Seville, 1568.

Maldonado de Guevara, Francisco. "La espiritualidad cesárea de la cultura española." *Revista de Estudios Políticos* 18, Nos. 33–34 (1947): 1–22.

Mâle, Emile. *L'art religieux de la fin du Moyen Age en France*. Paris: A. Colin, 1925.

Malón de Chaide, Fray Pedro. *Libro de la Conversión de la Magdalena*. Alcalá: Viuda de Juan Gración, 1702.

Mannheim, Karl. *Ideology and Utopia*. Trans. Louis Wirth and Edward Shils. New York: Harcourt, Brace and Co., 1953.

Maravall, José Antonio. *Antiguos y modernos. Visión de la historia e idea de progreso hasta el Renacimiento*. 2nd ed. Madrid: Alianza Editorial, 1986.

————. *Carlos V y el pensamiento político del Renacimiento*. Madrid: Instituto de Estudios Políticos, 1960.

————. *La cultura del Barroco. Análisis de una estructura histórica*. 2nd ed. Barcelona: Ariel, 1980.

————. "Empirismo y pensamiento político (Una cuestión de orígenes)." In his *Estudios de historia del pensamiento español*. 3rd ser. Siglo XVII. Madrid: Ediciones de Cultura Hispánica, 1975. Pp. 13–38.

————. *Estado moderno y mentalidad social. Siglos XV a XVII*. 2 vols. Madrid: Revista de Occidente, 1972.

————. "La estimación de Sócrates y de los sabios clásicos en la Edad Media española." In his *Estudios de Historia del pensamiento español*. 1st ser. Edad Media. 2nd ed. Madrid: Ediciones Cultura Hispánica, 1973. Pp. 287–354.

————. *El humanismo de las armas en "Don Quijote."* Madrid: Instituto de Estudios Políticos, 1948.

————. "La imagen de la sociedad expansiva en la conciencia castellana del siglo XVI." In *Histoire économique du monde méditerranéen. Mélanges Fernand Braudel*. Toulouse: Privat, 1973. 1:369–88.

————. *La oposición política bajo los Austrias*. 2nd ed. Barcelona: Ediciones Ariel, 1974.

————. "El pensamiento utópico y el dinamismo de la historia europea." *Sistema. Revista de Ciencias Sociales* (Madrid), no. 14 (July, 1976): 13–44. Reprinted in his *Utopía y reformismo en la España de los Austrias* (q.v.), pp. 27–77.

————. "Un primer proyecto de Facultad de Ciencias Políticas en la crisis del siglo XVII: el Discurso VIII de Sancho de Moncada." In his *Estudios de historia del pensamiento español*. 3rd ser. Siglo XVII. Madrid: Ediciones Cultura Hispánica, 1975. Pp. 125–60.

———. "Utopía y primitivismo en el pensamiento de Las Casas." *Revista de Occidente* 47 (December, 1974): 311–88.

———. *Utopía y reformismo en la España de los Austrias.* Madrid: Siglo Veintiuno de España Editores, 1982.

———, et al. *Carlos V, 1500–1558: Homenaje de la Universidad de Granada.* 2 vols. Granada, 1958.

Mariana, Juan de. *De Rege et regis institutione.* Toledo: Pedro Rodrigo, 1599.

———. *Historia de España.* In vol 2 of *Obras del padre Juan de Mariana.* Biblioteca de Autores Españoles, vol. 31. Madrid: Ediciones Atlas, 1950. Pp. 1–411.

Marichalar, Antonio. "El cortesano. En el centenario de Boscán." *Escorial* 9, no. 26 (1942): 377–409.

Martin, Alfred Wilhelm Otto von. *Sociología del Renacimiento.* Spanish trans. Mexico, 1947.

Martín Cordero, Juan. Exhortación. *Discurso de la vida humana y aventuras del caballero determinado.* By Olivier de la Marche. Trans. J. Jiménez de Urrea. Antwerp: Martín Nucio, 1555.

Martín Cordero, Juan, trans. *Summa de doctrina christiana.* Anon. 1558.

Medina, Pedro de. *Libro de las grandezas de España.* Ed. González Palencia. Madrid: Consejo Superior de Investigaciones Científicas, 1944.

Menaguerra, Ponç de. *Lo cavaller.* In *Tractats de Cavalleria.* Ed. Pere Bohigas. Els Nostres Classics, Collecció A, vol. 57. Barcelona: Barcino, 1947. Pp. 177–95.

Menéndez Pidal, Ramón. "Un aspecto de la elaboración del *Quijote.*" In his *De Cervantes y Lope de Vega.* Colección Austral, vol. 120. Madrid: Espasa-Calpe, 1940. Pp. 9–60.

———. *La epopeya castellana a través de la literatura española.* Madrid: Espasa-Calpe, 1959.

———. "Sobre un arcaismo léxico en la poesía tradicional." In his *De primitiva lírica española y antigua épica.* 2nd ed. Colección Austral, vol. 1051. Madrid: Espasa-Calpe, 1951. Pp. 131–33.

Merton, Robert King. *Social Theory and Social Structure.* New York: Free Press, 1967.

Mesnard, Pierre. *L'essor de la philosophie politique au XVIe siècle.* Paris: Ancienne Libraire Furne, Boivin, et Cie, 1936.

Mexía, Pedro. *Silva de varia lección.* 2 vols. Madrid: Sociedad de Bibliófilos Españoles, 1933.

Miranda Villafañe, Francisco. *Discurso de las armas y las letras.* In his *Diálogos de la fantástica filosofía.* Salamanca, 1582.

Montaigne, Michel de. *The Essays of Michel de Montaigne.* Trans. J. Zeitlin. 3 vols. New York: Knopf, 1934.

Montemayor, Jorge de. *Los siete libros de la Diana.* Ed. F. de López Estrada. Clásicos Castellanos, vol. 127. Madrid: Espasa-Calpe, 1954.

More, Saint Thomas. *Utopia.* Cologne, 1629.

———. *Utopia.* Trans. H. V. S. Ogden. New York: Appleton -Century-Crofts, 1949.

Morreale de Castro, Margarita. *Pedro Simón Abril.* Madrid: Consejo Superior de Investigaciones Científicas, *Revista de Filología Española,* anejo 51, 1949.

Morris, William. *News from Nowhere; or, An epoch of rest. Being some chapters from a Utopian romance.* Boston: Roberts Brothers, 1890.

Morton, Arthur Leslie. *The English Utopia.* London: Lawrence and Wishart, 1952.

Mosquera de Figueroa, Cristóbal. *Comentario en breve compendio de disciplina militar.* Madrid: 1596.

———. Preface. *Relación de la Guerra de Cipre y suceso de la batalla naval de Lepanto.* By Fernando de Herrera. Seville, 1572.

Mousnier, Roland. *Les hiérarchies sociales de 1450 a nos jours.* Paris: Presses Universitaires de France, 1969.

Mucchielli, Roger. *Le mythe de la cité idéale.* Paris: Presses Universitaires de France, 1960.

Mumford, Lewis. *The Story of Utopias. Ideal Commonwealths and Social Myths.* London, 1923.

Murúa, Martín de. *Historia del origen y genealogía de los Reyes Incas del Perú.* Ed. P. Bayle. Madrid: Consejo Superior de Investigaciones Científicas, 1946.

Navarra, Pedro de. *Diálogos entre el rústico y el noble.*

———. *Diálogos muy subtiles y notables.* Zaragoza: Juan Millán, 1567.

Neusüss, Arnhelm, ed. *Utopía.* Trans. María Nolla. Barcelona: Barral Editores, 1971.

Nifo, Agostino. *De vera vivendi libertate.* Venice, 1535.

Núñez de Alba, Diego. *Diálogos de la vida del soldado.* Ed. Antonio María Fabié. Madrid, 1890.

Olmedo, Félix G. *El "Amadís" y el "Quijote."* Madrid: Editora Nacional, 1947.

Olmos García, Francisco. "Acotaciones a los episodios de los galeotes en el *Quijote.*" In *Mélanges offerts a Charles Vincent Aubrun.* Ed. Haim Vidal Sephiha. 2 vols. Paris: Editions Hispaniques, 1975. 2:147–58.

———. *Cervantes en su época.* Madrid: Ricardo Aguilera, 1968.

Orozco Díaz, Emilio. *Temas del Barroco.* Granada: Universidad de Granada, 1948.

Ortiz, Luis. *Memorial del contador Luis Ortiz a Felipe II.* In appendix to Fernández Alvarez, Manuel. *Economía, Sociedad y Corona.* Madrid: Ediciones Cultura Hispánica, 1963. Pp. 375–462.

Palencia, Alfonso de. *Tratado de la perfección del triunfo militar.* In *Prosistas castellanos del siglo XV.* Ed. Mario Penna. Biblioteca de Autores Españoles, vol. 116. Madrid: Ediciones Atlas, 1959. Pp. 345–92.

Palmer, Stuart. "High Social Integration As a Source of Deviance." *The British Journal of Sociology* (May, 1973), pp. 93–100.

Pedro IV, King of Aragón. *Tractat de Cavalleria.* In *Tractats de Cavalleria.* Ed. Pere Bohigas. Els Nostres Classics, Collecció A, vol. 57. Barcelona: Barcino, 1947. Pp. 96–154.

Pedro de Portugal, Constable Don. *Sátira de felice e infelice vida.* In *Opúsculos literarios de los siglos XIV al XVI.* Ed. A. Paz y Melia. Madrid: Sociedad de Bibliófilos Españoles, 1892. Pp. 47–101.

Pérez del Barrio, Gabriel. *Secretario y consejero de señores y ministros.* Madrid, 1613.

Pérez de Guzmán, Fernán. *Generaciones y semblanzas.* Ed. J. Domínguez Bordona. Clásicos Castellanos, vol. 61. Madrid: Espasa-Calpe, 1924.

Pérez de Herrera, Cristóbal. *Discurso al Rey Felipe III en razón de muchas cosas tocantes al bien, prosperidad, riqueza y fertilidad destos Reynos.* Madrid, 1610.

Pérez de Montalbán, Juan. *La villana de Pinto.* In vol. 2 of *Novelistas posteriores a Cervantes.* Biblioteca de Autores Españoles, vol. 33. Madrid: Ediciones Atlas, 1950. Pp. 525–37.

Pérez de Oliva, Hernán. *Diálogo de la dignidad del hombre.* In *Obras ecogidas de filósofos.* Ed. A. de Castro. Biblioteca de Autores Españoles, vol. 65. Madrid: Ediciones Atlas, 1953. Pp. 385 –96.

Petrarch, Francesco. *Canzoniere.* Ed. Piero Cudini. 2nd ed. Milan: Garzanti, 1976.

——. *De sui ipsius et multorum ignorantia.* In *Opera quae extant omnia.* Basel, 1554. Pp. 1142–68.

——. *De la vida solitaria.* Spanish trans. Medina del Campo, 1553.

Poema de Fernán González. Ed. Alonso Zamora Vicente. Clásicos Castellanos, 128. Madrid: Espasa-Calpe, 1946.

Polak, Frederick Lodewijk. "Cambio y tarea persistente de la utopía." In *Utopía.* Ed. Arnhelm Neusüss. Trans. María Nolla. Barcelona: Barral Editores, 1971. Pp. 169–89.

Pompery, Edouard de. *Les thélemites de Rabelais et les harmonieux de Fourier.* Paris, 1892.

Pulgar, Hernando de. *Claros varones de Castilla.* Ed. R. B. Tate. Oxford: Clarendon Press, 1971.

——. *Glosas a las Coplas de Mingo Revulgo.* In *Letras.* Ed. J. Domínguez Bordona. Clásicos Castellanos, vol. 99. Madrid: La Lectura, 1929.

Puyol y Alonso, Julio. *Estado social que refleja el "Quijote."* Madrid: Imp. del Asilo de Huérfanos del S. C. de Jesús, 1905.

Quevedo, Francisco de. *Marco Bruto.* In *Obras en prosa.* Ed. L. Astrana Marín. Madrid: Aguilar, 1945. Pp. 687–744.

——. "Noticia, juicio y recomendación de la *Utopía* de Tomás Moro." Prologue to Spanish trans. 2nd ed. Madrid: Aznar, 1790.

Rabelais, François. *Gargantua.* Ed. J. Plattard. Paris, 1946.

Ricken, Ulrich. "Bemerkungen zum thema *Las armas y las letras.*" *Beiträge zur Romanischen Philologie.* Berlin, 1967. Pp. 76–83.

Rivadeneyra, Pedro de. *Historia del cisma de Inglaterra.* In *Obras escogidas del padre Pedro de Rivadeneyra.* Biblioteca de Autores Españoles, vol. 60. Madrid: Ediciones Atlas, 1952. Pp. 177–357.

Rodríguez Marín, Francisco, ed. *El ingenioso hidalgo Don Quijote de la Mancha.* By Miguel de Cervantes y Saavedra. 10 vols. Madrid: Patronato del IV Centenario de Cervantes, Ediciones Atlas, 1947–49.

Rodríguez de Montalvo, Garci. Preface. *Amadis of Gaul.* Trans. Edwin B. Place and Herbert C. Behm. 2 vols. Lexington: University Press of Kentucky, 1974.

Rojas, Cristóbal de. *Teoría y práctica de la fortificación.* Madrid: Luis Sánchez, 1598.

Romera-Navarro, Miguel. "La defensa de la lengua española en el siglo XVI." *Bulletin Hispanique* 31 (1929): 204–55.

Rosales, Luis. *Cervantes y la libertad.* 2nd ed. 2 vols. Madrid: Ediciones Cultura Hispánica, Instituto de Cooperación Iberoamericana, 1985.

──────. *El sentimiento del desengaño en la poesía barroca*. Madrid: Ediciones Cultura Hispánica, 1966.

Rosen, George. *Madness in Society. Chapters in the Historical Sociology of Mental Illness*. Chicago: University of Chicago Press, 1968.

Ruiz, Juan. *Libro de buen amor*. Ed. and trans. Raymond S. Willis. Princeton: Princeton University Press, 1972.

Ruiz de Alarcón, Juan. *The Truth Suspected*. Trans. R. C. Ryan. In *Spanish Drama*. Ed. Angel Flores. New York: Bantam Books, 1962. Pp. 135–89.

Ruiz de Virués, Fray Alonso. "Apología de Erasmo." In appendix to Bonilla y San Martín, Adolfo. *Luis Vives y la filosofía del Renacimiento*. 3 vols. Nueva Biblioteca Filosófica, 32–34. Madrid: Bruno del Amo, 1929. 3:123–28.

Ruyer, Raymond. *L'Utopie et les utopies*. Paris: Presses Universitaires de France, 1950.

Ruyssen, Théodore. *Des origines à la paix de Wesphalie*. Paris: Presses Universitaires de France, 1954. Vol. 1 of *Les sources doctrinales de l'internationalisme*. 3 vols. 1954–61.

Saavedra Fajardo, Diego de. *Idea de un príncipe político y christiano representado en cien empresas*. In *Obras completas*. Ed. González de Palencia. Madrid: Aguilar, 1946. Pp. 143–691.

──────. *Introducciones a la política y razón del Estado del rey don Fernando el Católico*. In *Obras completas*. Ed. González Palencia. Madrid: Aguilar, 1946. Pp. 1224–56.

Sabuco, Miguel. *Coloquio del conocimiento de sí mismo*. In *Obras*. Madrid, 1888. Also in *Obras escogidas de filósofos*. Ed. Adolfo de Castro. Biblioteca de Autores Españoles, vol. 65. Madrid: Ediciones Atlas, 1953. Pp. 332–72

──────. *Coloquio de las cosas que mejoran este mundo y sus repúblicas*. In *Obras*. Madrid, 1888.

──────. *Nueva filosofía de la naturaleza del hombre*. Madrid, 1587. Also in *Obras escogidas de filósofos*. Ed. Adolfo de Castro. Biblioteca de Autores Españoles, vol. 65. Madrid: Ediciones Atlas, 1953. Pp. 332–76. [Re. Miguel Sabuco, see translator's note, chap. 6, n. 47.]

──────. *Obras*. Madrid, 1891.

Sainz Rodríguez, Pedro. "Una posible fuente de *El Criticón*, de Gracián." *Archivo Teológico de Granada*, 1962.

Salas Barbadillo, Alonso Jerónimo de. *El caballero perfecto*. Madrid: Juan de la Cuesta, 1620.

──────. *El caballero puntual*. Madrid, 1614.

Salazar, Diego de. *De re militari*. Alcalá, 1556.

Salazar, Pedro de. *Crónica de Carlos V*. 1548.

Salillas, Rafael. *Un gran inspirador de Cervantes: el doctor Juan Huarte y su "Examen de ingenios."* Madrid: E. Arias, 1905.

Salomón, Noël. *Recherches sur le thème paysan dans la comédie espagnole au temps de Lope de Vega*. Bordeaux: Féret et fils, 1965.

Sánchez Albornoz, Claudio. "Raíces medievales del *Quijote*." In his *Españoles ante la historia*. Buenos Aires: Losada, 1958. Pp. 13–31.

Sánchez de Arévalo, Rodrigo. *Espejo de la vida humana*. Spanish trans. Zaragoza, 1491.

————. *Suma de la Política*. In *Prosistas castellanos del siglo XV*. Ed. Mario Penna. Biblioteca de Autores Españoles, vol. 116. Madrid: Ediciones Atlas, 1959. Pp. 249–309.

Sandoval, Fray Prudencio de. *Historia de la vida y hechos del emperador Carlos V*. 3 vols. Ed. C. Seco Serrano. Biblioteca de Autores Españoles, vols. 80–82. Madrid: Ediciones Atlas, 1955.

San Pedro, Diego de. *Tratado de amores de Arnalte y Lucenda*. Ed. K. Whinnom. Madrid: Castalia, 1973.

Santos, Francisco. *Día y noche de Madrid*. In *Costumbristas españoles*. Ed. E. Correa Calderón. 2 vols. Madrid: Aguilar, 1950–51. 1:248–348.

Savoye-Ferreras, Jacqueline. "El mito del pastor." *Cuadernos Hispano-Americanos*, no. 308 (February, 1976): 30–43.

Seneca, L. Annaeus. *De tranquilitate animi*. Paris: Les Belles Lettres, n.d.

Silva, Juan de. *Don Policisne de Boecia*. Valladolid, 1602.

Simón Abril, Pedro. *Apuntamiento de cómo se deben reformar las doctrinas y la manera de enseñallas*. In *Obras escogidas de filósofos*. Ed. Adolfo de Castro. Biblioteca de Autores Españoles, vol. 65. Madrid: Ediciones Atlas, 1953. Pp. 293–300.

Stéfano, Luciana de. *La sociedad estamental de la baja Edad Media española a la luz de la literatura de la época*. Caracas, 1966.

Suárez Fernández, Luis. *Política internacional de Isabel la Católica*. 5 vols. Valladolid: Instituto "Isabel la Católica" de Historia Eclesiástica, 1965.

Suárez de Figueroa, Cristóbal. *El pasagero*. Ed. F. Rodríguez Marín. Madrid: Biblioteca Renacimiento, 1913.

Tasis y Peralta, Juan de [Conde de Villamediana]. *Poesías de Juan de Tasis, Conde de Villamediana*. Madrid: Editora Nacional, 1944.

Téllez, Fray Gabriel [Tirso de Molina]. *Cigarrales de Toledo*. Ed. V. Said Armesto. Madrid: Renacimiento, 1913.

Thomas, Henry. *Spanish and Portuguese Romances of Chivalry*. Cambridge: The University Press, 1920.

Torquemada, Antonio de. *Los colloquios satíricos, con un colloquio pastoril*. Bilbao, 1584.

————. *Jardín de flores curiosas*. Salamanca, 1570.

Torre, Alfonso de la. *Visión delectable de Filosofía*. In *Curiosidades bibliográficas*. Ed. A. de Castro. Biblioteca de Autores Españoles, vol. 36. Madrid: Ediciones Atlas, 1950. Pp. 338–402.

Tovar, Antonio. "Lo pastoril y lo heroico en Cervantes." In *Homenaje a Miguel de Cervantes en ocasión de su IV centenario*. Buenos Aires: Universidad de Buenos Aires, 1947. Pp. 27–41.

Trevor-Roper, Hugh Redwald. *The European Witch-Craze of the Sixteenth and Seventeenth Centuries and Other Essays*. New York: Harper and Row, 1967.

Valbuena Prat, Angel. "Censo de personajes novelescos y legendarios, históricos y mitológicos, nombres geográficos y de autores citados por Cervantes en sus obras." In *Obras completas*. By Miguel de Cervantes. Ed. A. Valbuena Prat. Madrid: Aguilar, 1967. Pp. 1747–1801.

Valdés, Alfonso de. *Diálogo de las cosas ocurridas en Roma*. Ed. J. F. Montesinos. Clásicos Castellanos, vol. 89. Madrid: La Lectura, 1928.

———. *Diálogo de Mercurio y Carón*. Ed. J. F. Montesinos. Clásicos Castellanos, vol. 96. Madrid: La Lectura, 1929.

Valdés, Francisco de. *Espejo y disciplina militar*. Brussels, 1589.

Valdés, Juan de. *Diálogo de la lengua*. Madrid: Calleja, 1919.

Valera, Diego de. *Espejo de verdadera nobleza*. In *Prosistas castellanos del siglo XV.* Ed. Mario Penna. Biblioteca de Autores Españoles, vol. 116. Madrid: Ediciones Atlas, 1959. Pp. 89–116.

Vázquez, Fray Dionisio de. *Sermones*. Ed. Félix G. Olmedo, S.J. Clásicos Castellanos, vol. 123. Madrid: Espasa-Calpe, 1956.

Vázquez de Menchaca, Fernando. *Controversiarium illustrium*. Valladolid, 1932.

Vega, Félix Lope de. *La Dorotea*. Ed. E. S. Morby. 2nd ed. Berkeley: University of California Press, 1968.

———. *Las fortunas de Diana*. In *Colección escogida de obras no dramáticas de Frey Lope Félix de Vega Carpio*. Ed. C. Rosell. Biblioteca de Autores Españoles, vol. 38. Madrid: Ediciones Atlas, 1950. Pp. 1–13.

———. *Pastores de Belén*. In *Obras escogidas*. Ed. F. L. Sáinz de Robles. 4th ed. 3 vols. Madrid: Aguilar, 1964. 2:1173–1320.

Vélez de Guevara, Luis. *La serrana de la Vera*. Ed. R. Menéndez Pidal and M. Goyri. Teatro Antiguo Español, vol. 1. Madrid: Junta para Ampliación de Estudios, 1916.

Vida, G. *De Reipublicae dignitate*. Cremona, 1556.

Vida Nájera, Fernando. *El concepto y la organización del Estado en las utopías*. Madrid, 1928.

Vilar, Pierre. "El tiempo del *Quijote*." In his *Crecimiento y desarrollo*. Trans. E. Giralt Raventós. Barcelona: Ediciones Ariel, 1964. Pp. 332–46.

Villalón, Cristóbal de. *El Crotalón*. Ed. A. Cortina. Colección Austral, vol. 264. Buenos Aires: Espasa-Calpe, 1942?

Vitoria, Francisco de. "De potestate civili." In his *Relectiones theologicae*. Ed. L. G. A. Getino. 3 vols. Madrid: Publicaciones de la Asociación Francisco de Vitoria, 1933–35. 2:169–210.

Vives, Luis. *De subventione pauperum*. In *Opera omnia*. Ed. Gregorio Mayans. 8 vols. Valencia: Monfort, 1782–90. 4:421–94.

———. *In Allegorias bucolicorum Vergilii*. In *Opera omnia* (q.v. supra). 2:1–71.

———. *In Georgica Publii Virgilii Maronis Prealectio ad Antonium Bergensem*. In *Opera omnia* (q.v. supra). 2:71–82.

———. *Introductio ad sapientiam*. In *Opera omnia* (q.v. supra). 1:1–48.

Vossler, Karl. *Formas literarias en los pueblos románicos*. Spanish trans. Colección Austral, vol. 455. Madrid: Espasa-Calpe, 1944.

———. *La soledad en la poesía española*. Trans. J. M. Sacristán. Madrid: Revista de Occidente, 1941.

Weber, Max. *Economy and Society*. Trans. E. Fischoff et al. 2 vols. Berkeley: University of California Press, 1978.

———. *Protestant Ethic and the Spirit of Capitalism*. Trans. Talcott Parsons. New York: Charles Scribner's Sons, 1958.

Welter, Jean Thiébaut. *L'exemplum dans la littérature religieuse et didactique du Moyen Age*. Paris: E. H. Guitard, 1927.

Yndurain, Francisco. "Relección de *La Galatea.*" In *Homenaje a Cervantes.* Madrid: Cuadernos Insula, 1947. Pp. 105–16.

Zamora Vicente, Alonso. "La Epístola a Mateo Vázquez." In *Homenaje a Cervantes.* Madrid: Cuadernos Insula, 1947. Pp. 189–93.

Zárate, Fray Fernando de. *Primera parte de los Discursos de la paciencia cristiana.* Madrid, 1597.

Index

Absolutism, 49, 175, 192
Acuña, Hernando de, 190, 225 n.29
Adler, George, 34
Adversity, 79–80, 103
Agrarian society, 40, 42–43, 74, 97, 153–55, 203 n.55. *See also* Rural life; Village life
Agriculture, 42, 74, 153, 154–55
Alamos de Barrientos, Baltasar, 53–54
Alava y Viamont, Diego de, 110, 114
Alborg, Juan Luis, 23–24, 168, 187, 200 n.1
Alcalá Yáñez y Ribera, Jerónimo, 22
Alemán, Mateo, 66, 209 n.47
Alexander, 54, 75, 135
Alonso, Dámaso, 224–25 n.10
Alonso de Herrera, Gabriel, 141, 154
America, 32, 90, 132, 179, 186; conquest and colonization, 10, 30–31, 72, 109
Animals, virtues of, 149–50, 173
Appearance, 117–19; alteration by sorcerers and enchanters, 120–24, 126; chivalry judged by, 210 n.1
Aquinas, Thomas. *See* Thomism
Archaism, 52, 96
Argensola, Lupercio Leonardo de, 108–9
Ariosto, Lodovico, 81, 109
Aristotelianism, 173–74, 181
Aristotle, 75, 164
Armor, 93, 109, 110–11, 114
Arms, humanism of, in *Don Quixote,* 19, 92–115
Arms, profession of, 43–44, 92–96, 101, 103

Arms, use of, 43–44, 50, 74, 160, 193; chivalric mentality on, 51–62, 63; connection with inner renewal, 11–12, 100–102; knight's virtues dependent on, 94, 113; moral symbolism, 93, 97, 100; peace through, 162–64, 166; virtue as goal of, 98–100. *See also* Army, of the modern State; Warfare; Weapons
Army, of the modern State, 11, 37, 57–58, 66–67. *See also* Military, modern; Warfare: modern
Artillery, 58, 106–7, 108–11, 213 n.64
Astrologers, belief in, 120, 121
Augustine/Augustinianism, 100, 129, 132, 162, 166, 212 n.37
Avalle-Arce, Juan Bautista, 77, 140, 148–49
Avila, Luis de, 57, 102, 202 n.41

Bacon, Francis, 178
Balbuena, Bernardo de, 133, 136–37, 156, 157, 173
Barahona de Soto, Luis, 42, 133
Barataria, island of. *See* Governor, Sancho Panza's role as
Baroque, the, 23, 119, 139, 176, 178, 192; Aristotelianism in, 181; attitude toward nature and rusticity, 156, 158, 221 n.118; concept of "thine" and "mine," 152; incertitude about reality, 117–18, 122
Bataillon, Marcel, 18, 19, 77, 91, 92, 219 n.64; on Erasmist elements in

Bataillon, Marcel (*cont.*)
  Cervantes, 27–28, 198–99 n.26; on
    pacifism in Spain, 163
Bernáldez, Andrés, 155, 214 n.86
Biographical utopias, 190
Bjornson, Richard, 9, 195 n.4
Blood, belief in differences in, 71, 94, 188
Bodin, Jean, 49–50, 133
Body, human, interest in, 69, 180–81
Bohigas, Pere, 210 n.1
Bonilla y San Martín, Adolfo, 28, 131
Book of the Courtier, The (Castiglione), 98,
  185
Bourgeoisie, 71–72, 73–74, 95, 97
Braudel, Fernand, 8
Bruni, Leonardo, 75
Bucklers, use of, 109–10. *See also* Shields
Burkhardt, Jacob, 27, 119

Caballero perfecto, El (Salas Barbadillo),
  189–90
Caballero puntual, El (Salas Barbadillo),
  114–15
Cadalso, José, 35, 183
Calderón de la Barca, Pedro, 107, 118, 119,
  158, 217 n.29, 221 n.119
Camos, Marco Antonio de, 68, 71, 93, 163
Campanella, Tommaso, 33, 34, 42, 48, 86,
  180. *See also* City of the Sun, The
Campillo, José, 32, 176
Capitalism, 37, 46, 48, 71–72
Carande, Ramón, 7
*Carlos V y el pensamiento político del Renaci-
  miento* (Maravall), 17–18
Carvallo, Luis Alfonso de, 146–47
Castiglione, Baldassare, 76, 98, 167, 185
Castrillo, Alfonso de, 65
Castro, Américo, 27, 139, 148, 206 n.5,
  216 n.9
Castro, León de, 172, 223 n.157
Catholic Church, 25, 29, 82–83, 100–101,
  174, 210 n.1; on natural equality, 72;
  role in ordination of knights, 114; sac-
  raments, 174, 206 n.5
Catholic Sovereigns, time of, 36, 48, 50,
  52, 64–65, 144, 159
Cavaller, Lo (Menaguerra), 93
Caxa de Leruela, Miguel, 176
Cervantes, Miguel de, 79, 89–90, 96–97,
  116–17, 142, 213 n.70; concern with

warfare, 61–64, 66–67, 106, 109–10;
  economic effect of war on, 46; experience with modern military, 104–5;
  Golden Age as theme in, 133, 134–35,
  173–75, 215 n.3; and medieval tradition, 29–30, 48; nonconformism, 62–
  63, 205 n.89; recourse to reality of
  enchantments, 121–22; Spanish patriotism, 159–60, 221 n.122; use of pastoral myth, 146–47; utopianism, 9, 18–
  19, 32–33, 115. *See also* works by name
Cervantes de Salazar, Francisco, 107
Charles V (emperor) (Charles I [king of
  Spain]), 24–25, 28, 31, 81, 149, 159–
  62, 191–92; Avila's praise for, 102; celebration of centenary, 17; challenge to
  Francis I, 57, 165; effect on Spanish society, 36; utopianism connected with,
  147
Chevalier délibéré, Le (Marche), 190
Chivalry, 30, 50, 68–69, 71, 129, 174,
  204 n.81; concept of war, 111, 165–66;
  connection with myth of the Golden
  Age, 134, 135, 176, 216 n.9; contrasted
  with modern military, 51–62, 63; corruption in, 62–66, 80, 210 n.1; as dimension of utopianism, 12–13, 134;
  Don Quixote's attempt to restore age
  of, 92, 124–25, 161; heroism inspired
  by, 197–98 n.20; humanist esteem for
  ideal of, 96; music as important to,
  155; nonconformity with modern
  world, 62–64; origins, 54; pacifism,
  45; reward for, 47; role in social reform, 73–75; transmutation of reality
  as precondition for, 117; value of works
  as principle of, 198–99 n.26; as vehicle
  of personal renewal, 101; wealth as pillar of valor and virtue in, 43–44; world
  of, combined with pastoral world as
  ideal society, 146–47, 156, 219 n.64.
  See also Knight-errantry; Knighthood
Chivalry, literature of, 23–24, 93, 150–51,
  174, 176, 197 n.13; combined with pastoral literature, 146–48, 151; disappearance of, end of 16th century, 23,
  197 n.13; *Don Quixote*'s relationship to,
  13, 18, 22–24, 97, 111, 184; fate of, in
  Don Quixote, 147; idea of the island in,
  186; importance of love, 77–79, 88;

model of personal conduct found in, 74–75; popularity of, 24–25, 188–89; as utopian method for Cervantes, 178–93

Christianity, 43, 75, 82, 135, 145, 161; and desire for restoration of nature, 141, 150, 174; as source of utopian literary formulas, 203 n.55; universality based on politics of, 166–67. *See also* Catholic Church

Cicero, 75, 91

City life, 137, 139–40, 143, 150, 151, 165

City of the Sun, The (Campanella), 33, 38, 52, 153, 155, 203 n.55; on war, 74, 104

Civilization, 136, 137, 144, 153

Class, social, 44, 71–74, 92, 131, 179, 187–88; concept of virtue based on, 103; of knights, 93–94; in modern state, 68. *See also* Estates of society; Social rank

Classical literature, 75–76

Collectivism, 48, 152–53, 177

Colors, in military dress, 111, 213 n.71

Comic theater, 22–23

Commoners, 44–45, 50, 210 n.7

Common sense, use in governing, 169–71

Commonwealth, the, reform of, 86–87, 92, *See also* State, modern

Consumption, 33, 42–43, 45, 154

Cortes of Toledo (1462), 204 n.71

Cortes of Valladolid: 1518, 132, 149; 1542, 61–62, 110; 1555, 197–98 n.20

Counter-Reformation, 31, 70, 73–74, 198–99 n.26, 206–7 n.7

Counterutopia, 33–35, 134, 175, 199 n.36, 224 n.7; Cervantes's attack on pseudo-utopianism as, 10–11, 13, 18, 180, 191, 193

Courage, 92, 97, 107, 120; of the knight, 112–13, 131–32; quixote (cuisse) as symbolizing, 114

Court life, 38, 141, 155–56

Covetousness, 39–40, 64

Crotalón, El, 65–66

Cuisse (Quixote), meaning of, 114, 214 n.86

Death, dance of, 119

De Civitate Dei (Augustine), 132, 166

De Reipublicae dignitat (Vida), 156

Descartes, René, 91, 179

De subventione pauperum (Vives), 37, 68

De sui ipsius et multorum ignorantia (Petrarch), 74

Deviance, 50, 52, 116, 217 n.22; through excess of social integration, 50, 175, 202 n.47

De vita solitaria (Petrarch), 138, 217 n.23

Diálogo de la dignidad del hombre (Pérez de Oliva), 69

Diálogo de la verdadera honra militar (Jiménez de Urrea), 56–57, 59, 81, 166, 209 n.47

Diálogo de Mercurio y Carón (Valdés), 50–51, 162

Diálogo entre el rústico y el noble (Navarra), 86

Diana enamorada (Gil Polo), 156

Díez-Borque, José María, 217 n.30

Díez de Games, Gutierre, 33, 56, 80, 98, 135

Discipline, 51, 54–55, 60

Discreción. See Prudence

Discurso de las armas y las letras (Miranda Villafañe), 219 n.64

Distributive justice, 163–64

Dogs' Colloquy, The (Cervantes), 109–10, 157, 161, 174–75, 187, 222 n.124

Don Quixote (apocryphal/false), 187

Dreams, 84, 118–19, 149, 183

Duels, 51, 56, 93

Ecclesiastics, 48–49, 117

Eclogue. *See* Pastoral literature

Economic privileges, 41–44

Economy, 37–40, 71–72, 90, 95, 96–97, 176; and changes in social life, 73–74; effects of Charles V's policies on, 31; fixed, 33, 42–43, 45; in the Golden Age, 140, 152–55; of primitive peoples, 135–36

Education: as preparation for governing, 169–70; value of travel for, 89–91

Enchantment, 119–22; Don Quixote's belief in power of, 119–20, 121, 123–24, 125–26, 128

Encina, Juan del, 140, 145, 155

Enemy *(Hostes)*, 58–60

England, 177, 192

Enrique IV of Castille, 165
Enríquez de Guzmán, Alonso, 49
Entremeses: of Cervantes, 24, 26, 188; definition, 24
Epístola a Mateo Vázquez (Cervantes), 25, 198 n.22
Equality, principle of, 72–73
Erasmism, 76–77, 91, 143, 173, 226 n.32; influence on Cervantes, 26–28, 30, 79, 198–99 n.26
Erasmus, 27–28, 52, 70, 75, 100, 162; Golden Age as theme in, 132, 149; letters to Francis I and Charles V, 166; on military dress, 213 n.71; simplicity as theme in, 138
Escapism, 31–32, 183; idealism as philosophical brand of, 127
Escapist utopianism, 47, 143; concept of work, 153–54; definitions, 10–11. See also Evasion, utopianism of; Pseudo-utopia
Espinel, Vicente, 142, 187
Estates of society (Ordines), 41, 44–45, 68, 69, 71. See also Class, social; Social rank
Esteem, 81, 103–4
Estella, Diego de, 77, 78
Europe, 71–72, 116; reformism and utopianism, 30–31, 76–78, 193. See also countries by name
Evasion, utopianism of, 47, 63, 104–5, 117, 127, 132, 138; transition to, from utopias of reconstruction, 31–33, 175. See also Escapist utopianism; Pseudo-utopia
Evil, 12, 51, 83, 164–65; in sorcery and enchantments, 120–21, 122
Ex-soldiers, treatment of, 192, 226 n.32

Faith, 11, 69, 206 nn.5, 6
Fame, 73, 82–83, 204 n.81
Fantasies, 24–25, 121, 202 n.47
Febvre, Lucien, 8
Felipe (Philip) II (king of Spain), 60, 90, 160
Felipe III (king of Spain), 25
Felippe, Bartolomé, 44, 47–48, 163, 202 n.41
Fernández, Lucas, 94, 145
Fernández de Velasco, Juan, 140
Ferrer de Valdecebro, Andrés, 40, 167
Feudal society, 46, 54

Fichte, Johann Gottlieb, 127, 148
Filosofía vulgar (Mal Lara), 81, 172
Firearms. See Weapons
Flanders, 90, 95–96
Forner, Juan Pablo, 210 n.7
Fortunas de Diana, Las (Lope de Vega), 217 n.29
Fortune, concept of, 70
Foucault, Michel, 215 n.26
Fourier, François, 34, 153
France, 36, 72, 92, 104, 165, 177; chivalry in, 54, 64–65
Franciscans, 74, 77, 193
Francis I (king of France), 57, 165
Freedom, 136, 139, 153, 156–57, 159
Free will, 11, 70–71, 72, 76, 112–13. See also Will
Freyer, Hans, 140, 185

Galatea, La (Cervantes), 40, 62, 79, 183, 215 n.3, 221 n.109; as example of pastoral genre, 147, 148, 149; political significance of, 161–62; social ambience, 25; written under influence of pseudo-utopianism, 11, 33
García de Castrojeriz, Juan, 43, 98
García del Palacio, Diego, 54
García de Paredes, Diego, 39, 99, 201 n.12
Garcilaso, 81, 133, 136, 140, 145–46
Gayangos, Pascual, 23, 24–25
Gentleness, 76, 102
Germany, 54, 58–59, 95–96, 104
Gil Polo, Gaspar, 138, 155–56
Gil y Carrasco, Enrique, 200 n.44
Glory, 82–83
Goatherds, 156; Don Quixote's speech to, 134, 136–37, 138, 152, 161. See also Shepherds
Golden Age, myth of the, 12, 26, 132–41, 148–56, 158, 167; ability to inspire reformist nonconformity, 176–77; attempted restoration, 157, 173–75; deterioration, 174–75; Don Quixote's mission as restoration of, 83–84, 86, 88, 92, 123, 128–29, 131–32, 209 n.54; fusion of chivalric and pastoral society, 219 n.64; for humanism, 40; as an ideal, 86; importance of music, 155; knights as combatants, 166; Ovid's portrayal, 132, 133, 134; paradigm of nature as principle of, 150–56; peace as

part of, 164; political utopia of, 156–77; portrayed in *Don Quixote,* 134–35, 136–38, 143, 152–53, 184; praise for natural justice of, 52; psychoanalytic interpretation of, 173; superiority of country life, 42, 86, 148–49

González de Cellorigo, Martín, 32, 127, 176, 185

Goodness, natural, 135, 136, 137–38, 150

"Good shepherd," as image, 146, 147, 148, 157

Government, 29, 31, 51–52, 157, 179; criticism of methods of election to, 73, 207 n.18; utopia of, 168–72, 175. *See also* State, modern

Governor, Sancho Panza's role as, 12–13, 41–42, 68, 167–69; fitness for, 52, 168–72

Gracián, Baltasar, 109, 156

Greece, ancient, 54, 145

Guarda cuidadosa, La (Alborg), 200 n.1

Guevara, Antonio de, 33, 65, 76, 109, 166, 183; Cervantes and, 198 n.21; on economic activities, 42, 48; on Golden Age, 133, 136; influence of utopian thought, 17–18, 52; interpretation of pastoral myth, 146, 147, 149; on patterns of consumption, 45, 201 n.31; on reading novels of chivalry, 24–25; reformism, 85–86; on rural life, 84–85, 139, 141, 143, 144, 151, 218–19 n.53

Guillem de Vàroich, 59, 98, 114, 163–64

Gunpowder, 104, 105, 106, 108

Gutiérrez de los Ríos, Gaspar, 40, 74

Guzmán de Alfarache, 117

Habit, 98, 112–13

Hand-to-hand combat, 56

Happiness, 133, 162, 173

Harquebuses, use of, 106, 108, 110–11

Hatzfeld, Helmut, 9, 29, 147, 206–7 n.7, 210 n.1

Hazard, Paul, 29

Health, equation with virtue and nature, 142–43, 144–45, 155, 175

Helmet, Mambrino's, 127–28

Hermas, 145

Heroism, 102, 117, 143, 168, 189, 198–99n.26; in books of chivalry, 23–24, 197–98 n.20; decline of, 106, 188–89; definition, 24; failure and humiliation

as counterpoint to, 79–80; in modern State, 12, 108, 128–29; spirit of, 20, 81

Herrera, Fernando de, 57–58, 89, 107, 110–11, 141, 150; biography of More, 180; on Garcilaso, 136, 140

Hidalgos, 47, 71, 97, 109–10, 175; economic privileges, 41, 44–45; use of personal combat, 56–57. *See also* Nobility (social class)

Historiography, 8–14, 21–22, 182–83

History, 13, 82, 148, 183; *Don Quixote* interpreted from perspective of, 28–30, 34–35, 37; Maravall's approach to, 8–14, 195 n.2; role of Golden Age in philosophy of, 132–33

Holy Brotherhood, 49–50

Holy Roman Empire, 25, 28. *See also* Charles V

Honor, 56–57, 81, 103–4, 188; relationship to being honored, 81–82, 209 nn.47, 50

Honorable, achievement of as title, 80–82, 209 n.50

Horkheimer, Max, 180

Horses, use of, 109–10

Hostes (Enemy), 58–59

Huizinga, Johan, 84, 161, 209 n.55

Humanism, 20–21, 39–40, 91–92, 158, 166, 190, 203 n.55; aspirations, 73–74; Augustinian elements in, 100, 212 n.37; in Cervantes, 198–99 n.26; comparison of arms and letters, 98; desire for peace, 162; doctrine of individual merit, 11; Don Quixote as product of, 96; Golden Age as theme in, 132–33, 173–74; importance of love, 77–79; importance of solitude, 140, 141, 143–45; misunderstanding of the State system, 50–51; opposition to capitalist spirit, 48; origins, 54; in Palacios Rubios's work on knighthood, 111–13; Plato's influence on, 164; on possessions, 43; regard for proverbs, 172; on self-renewal, 99; and the study of letters, 74–76, 91–92; traditional ideals, 37, 52–53, 102; utopianism, 17, 26, 33, 52–53; on valor in battle, 107; values, 90, 140, 141

Humanismo de las armas en "Don Quixote, El (Maravall), 8–9, 18, 30–31

Humanism of arms, in *Don Quixote,* 19, 92–115

Humor, 22–23, 34, 162, 189
Hurtado de Mendoza, Diego, 39, 46, 52, 106

Idealism, 74, 84, 94–95, 183, 210 n.1; philosophical, 127, 148; seen in Don Quixote, 29, 100
Imperial tradition, 190–92
Incas, 133, 136
Indians, American, 149, 152, 156
Individualism/individuality, 50, 69–70, 72–73, 85, 96
Industrialization, 131–32, 175
Inner man. See Self
Inquisition, the, 31, 198–99 n.26, 206 n.5
Interpretation, relationship to author's stated purpose, 21–24
Irony, 18, 24, 25, 111, 180, 189
Isaba, Marcos de, 48, 66, 106, 108, 226 n.32
Islands, as device of utopian literature, 140–41, 185–86
Italianate (Italianist) school, 145–46, 176
Italy, 90, 95–96, 119

Jerome, St., 12, 14, 138, 141
Jiménez de Urrea, Jerónimo, 80–81, 101, 102, 112, 209 n.47; on the chivalric mentality and modern warfare, 51, 56–57, 59, 166; translation of Le chevalier délibéré, 190, 225 n.29
John of the Cross, St., 218 n.41
Juan de los Angeles, 157
Juan de Santa María, 152, 164
Juan Manuel, 41, 54, 64, 149, 169; on knighthood, 40–41, 43, 55, 59
Jung, Carl, 173
Justice, 29, 51–52, 112–13, 135, 137, 188; arms as serving, 163–65; in the Golden Age, 167, 168, 222 n.144; in the modern State, 49–50, 52; as part of Don Quixote's mission, 59, 161; peace through, 166–67, 212 n.37

King(s), 104, 106; knights' fidelity, to, 53, 58–59. See also Monarchy
Kingdoms, conquest by knights, 45–46, 47, 51–52
Knight(s), 38–39, 56–57, 93–94, 97, 150, 167; conquest of kingdoms, 45–46, 47, 51–52; duty to uphold distributive justice, 163–64; economic interests, 42; in the modern State, 49; ordination, 114. See also Knight-errantry; Knighthood
Knight-errantry, 21, 68–69, 73, 83, 129, 181; and displacement from one place to another, 62, 205 n.87; Don Quixote's attempt to restore, 88, 131, 157, 161, 182, 209 n.54; justice as goal, 123, 165; restoration of, 88, 131–32; role of obedience, 53–54; Sancho not qualified for, 168; value of travel in, 89–90; virtues connected with, 99, 103. See also Chivalry; Chivalry, literature of; Knight(s); Knighthood
Knighthood, 54, 62–66, 67, 68, 73, 104; and acquisition of virtue, 103–4, 111–13; attempt to construct spiritually, 78, 80, 104; corruption in, 62–66, 210 n.1; effects of modern weaponry on, 106; enemy in war as private personal enemy, 58–59; as an estate of society, 41; ideal of in Don Quixote, 29, 136–37, 188; as implying universalism, 160; meaning of for Don Quixote, 113–15; money and natural wealth, 40–46; as rural mode of existence, 140–41, 154; Salas Barbadillo's satire on, 114–15, 189–90; squire as rung on ladder to, 169. See also Chivalry; Chivalry, literature of; Knight(s); Knight-errantry
Knowledge, 75–76, 89–91, 121, 169, 171–73, 179. See also Letters

Lady, knight's, 78, 89
Laguna, Andrés, 212 n.51, 222 n.144
Laín Entralgo, Pedro, 222 n.124
Land, as representation of wealth, 38–40
Las Casas, Bartolomé de, 38, 179, 182, 191; utopianism, 10, 17, 186, 193
Law(s), 52, 54, 78–79, 156; in More's Utopia, 171; and natural justice, 168, 222 n.144
Lechuga, Cristóbal, 60, 82
Leisure, 154
León, Luis de, 155–57, 159, 168
León, Pablo de, 184
Lepanto, battle of, 82, 104, 160
Letters, 44, 74–76, 91, 98–99, 162–63, 163. See also Knowledge
Licenciado vidriera, El (Cervantes). See Man of Glass, The

Life, dream of, 118–19
Ligier, Herman, 34
Lissarrague, Salvador, 124
Literature: classical, 75–76; portrayal of insane characters, 116. *See also* Chivalry, literature of; Novel; Pastoral literature
Little Gypsy, The (Cervantes), 38
Londoño, Sancho de, 55, 110
Long-sufferingness, as virtue, 102–3
Lope de Vega, Félix. *See* Vega, Félix Lope de
López Bravo, Mateo, 152
López de Ayala, Pero, 64, 141
López Estrada, Francisco de, 147, 151, 161
López Palacios Rubios, Juan, 111–13, 213 n.80
Love, 21, 77–79, 88–89
Lucena, Juan de, 46, 59, 140–41, 142, 202 n.33
Lull, Ramón, 33, 51–52, 64, 93, 97–98, 211 n.23
Lunatics. *See* Madness
Luque Fajardo, Francisco de, 214 n.85

Machiavelli, Niccolò, 82, 106, 135, 159, 168
Madness, 116, 122–25, 128, 215 nn.22, 26
Magic, belief in, 119–21
Maldonado de Guevara, Francisco, 160–61
Mâle, Emile, 145
Mal Lara, Juan de, 81, 148, 172
Malón de Chaide, Pedro, 78–79, 88
Man, 135; reform of, 71–77, 79, 82, 104, 182, 208 n.37. *See also* Perfectionism; Self
Mannerism, 119, 122
Mannheim, Karl, 32, 184, 199 n.36
Man of Glass, The (El licenciado vidriera) (Cervantes), 67, 111, 128, 197 n.6, 215 n.26
Maravall, José Antonio, 7–15
Marche, Olivier de la, 190
Marcos, Benjamin, 218 n.48
Mariana, Juan de, 75, 156, 172; on the Golden Age, 133, 135, 152, 157, 164, 216 n.11
Market system, rejection of, 153–54
Martin, Alfred W. O. von, 71
Martín Cordero, Juan, 190, 226 n.30
Marx, Karl, 131, 153
Mathematical physics, 225 n.11
Mathematics, 61, 179, 182

Maxims (Proverbs), use in governing, 171–73
Medieval period, 25, 27–28, 51, 54, 158, 198 n.24; in Cervantes's thinking, 29–30, 181; concept of courtly love, 78; in Guevara's thinking, 85–86; heroism of, portrayed in *Don Quixote*, 20; impossibility of reformism in, 84–85, 209 n.55; knighthood, 80, 210 n.1; and the modern State, 158, 159; nature as paradigm, 149; peace as political task, 162; practice of arms, 92, 97; social movements, 73–74; Spanish politics during, 36–37; travel in, 90; view of shepherds, 145
Menaguerra, Ponç de, 93
Menéndez Pelayo, 29, 64, 210 n.1
Menéndez Pidal, Ramón, 19, 24, 69
Merit, 11, 69–73, 82, 103–4, 209 n.47
Merton, Robert, 217 n.22
Mexía, Pedro, 149–50
Microcosmia y gobierno universal del hombre cristiano (Camos), 68
Middle Ages. *See* Medieval period
Military, modern, 63, 66–67, 111, 159, 213 n.71. *See also* Army, of the modern State; Warfare: modern
Military schools, first, 60
Military techniques, new. *See* Warfare: modern
Miranda Villafañe, Francisco, 219 n.64
Moderation, 112–13
Modernity (Modern mentality), 12, 30, 32, 37, 158, 178; approach to discipline, 54–55; humanism's stand against, 143–44. *See also* State, modern
Monarchy, 95–96, 165. *See also* Spanish monarchy
Money, 11, 33, 37–48, 155
Montaigne, Michel de, 52, 92, 107
Montalvo, Garci Rodríguez de, 74
Montemayor, Jorge de, 71, 78, 81, 151, 152, 155–56
Morality, 60, 71, 81–82, 150, 172, 225 n.11; of heroism, 24, 79–80; in knighthood, 39, 89–91; learning as means to, 75–76; as purpose of chivalric literature, 188–89; values in village life, 142–44. *See also* Virtue(s)
Moral literature, use of animals as examples, 149–50

More, Thomas, 75, 86, 175, 179–80, 221 n.122; attitude toward money and wealth, 38, 42, 44, 48; on modern warfare, 109, 213 n.64; utopianism, 33, 34, 63. See also *Utopia*
Morris, William, 86, 131, 165, 177
Morton, Arthur Leslie, 32
Mosquera de Figueroa, Cristóbal, 58, 82, 101, 108, 112
Mucchielli, Roger, 71, 173, 183
Murúa, Martín de, 133, 136, 156, 167
Music, in the Golden Age, 155
Mysticism, 77, 78, 88

Name changes, 113–14, 214 n.85
Natural society, 22, 165, 172
Natural world, 20–21; belief in control of, by occult forces, 119–22, 215 n.19
Nature, 20–21, 27, 43, 149–56, 167; appeal to in government of Barataria, 12–13; equation with virtue and health, 142–43; government in accordance with, 170–75; law of, 149–50; proverbs on, 172–73; restoration of, 173–75; as subject of Renaissance dialogues, 150–51
Naval battles, changing nature of, 58, 104
Navarra, Pedro de, 76, 81, 86, 144, 146, 148; invention of war machines and mines, 108; on wealth, 39
Necessity, rights to goods limited by, 42, 45, 153
Necromancy, belief in, 120–22. See also Enchantment
Neoplatonism, 78, 79
New man, becoming a, 74–75, 77, 79, 82. See also Man; Self
Nietzsche, Friedrich, 126–27
Nobility (character trait), 91, 94–96
Nobility (social class), 47, 70, 72–73, 92, 96–97, 188, 209 n.50; changes in, 11–12; corruption among, 64–66; Don Quixote's traditional sense of, 50; economic privileges, 41, 44; hereditary, 94–95, 104; and military profession, 92–96; not fully identical to knighthood, 104; rebellions against in France, 36; as repayment for military services, 95–96; respect for, based on presupposed virtues, 93–94; shifting to nobility of soul, 94–96; support for reform

movements, 62, 132; troops of as superior to municipal troops, 39; virtues connected with, 103–4. See also Hidalgos
Nonconformism, 62, 97, 175, 184, 192; in Cervantes, 62–63, 187, 198–99 n.26, 205 n.89
Novel, 34, 182; *Don Quixote* as first modern, 13, 24, 182; as vehicle for portraying utopias, 13, 184
Novelas ejemplares (Cervantes), 26, 34, 66–67
Numancia (Cervantes), 159
Núñez de Alba, Diego, 39, 46, 47, 105–6, 226 n.32

Obedience, 49, 53–55
Occult forces, belief in, 119–20. See also Enchantment
Olmos García, Francisco, 205 n.89
Ordination of knights, 104, 114
Ordines. See Estates of society
Original sin, 135
Ortiz, Luis, 21, 31
Ovid, 132, 133, 134

Pacifism, 45, 66, 163, 226 n.32
Painting, portrayal of Golden Age, 133
Palacios Rubios. See López Palacios Rubios, Juan
Palencia, Alfonso de, 55, 61, 64, 90, 157, 184
Palmer, Stuart, 202 n.47
Parr, James A., 9, 13
Parson, Talcott, 202 n.47
Pastoral island, myth of the, 140–41, 185–86
Pastoral literature, 21, 133, 146–48, 151, 174–76, 191; in *Don Quixote*, 184, 191; importance of love, 77–79; *La Galatea* as, 147, 148, 161; on solitude and self-renewal, 139
Pastoral myth, 12, 40, 67, 96, 148, 154; connection with ancient weapons, 111; insularity in, 140–41, 185–86; political-moral interpretation, 146, 161; 16th-century renewal of, 174–75
Pastoral world, 71, 81, 134, 155, 164–65, 191; combined with chivalric world as ideal image of society, 146–47, 156,

219 n.64; utopianisms of, 12–13, 33, 148, 168. *See also* Rural life
Patience, 102–3
Patriotism, of Cervantes, 159–60
Pauline teachings, 74–75, 77, 97–98, 161
Peace, 157, 162–64, 166–67, 212 n.37
Peasants, 98, 141, 144, 176, 186, 191. *See also* Pastoral world; Rural life; Village life
Pedro IV (king of Aragon), 53, 59, 93, 98
Pedro de Portugal (constable don), 102, 143, 208 n.30
Perception, 117–18, 120, 125
Pérez, Antonio, 216 n.7
Pérez de Guzmán, Fernán, 39
Pérez del Barrio, Gabriel, 63, 166–67
Pérez de Montalbán, Juan, 71, 148
Pérez de Oliva, Hernán, 69, 98
Perfectionism, 51, 75–76, 183, 185–86, 188, 225 n.19. *See also* Man; Self
Peru, primitive, 133, 136
Petrarch, 74, 99, 100, 212 n.38; on solitude, 138, 144, 217 n.23
Philip (Felipe) II (king of Spain), 60, 90, 160
Pikes, use of, 110
Plato, 76, 164
Platonism, 181, 185
Poetry, 13, 91–92, 95, 182, 183
Political theory, 12, 134–35, 178
Politics, 36–37, 50–51, 56, 164; application of Golden Age myth to, 134–35, 156–77; significance in *Don Quixote*, 9, 28–29, 86–87, 156–66, 167–71, 173–74
Poor, the, 44, 46, 68, 155
Power, 18, 40, 45–46, 156; of love, 78–79, 89; political, 36, 48–49
Prehumanists, 132
Primitive life, 132–33, 135, 172, 176–77, 191
Privilege, 41–44, 50, 97
Production, means of, 42–43, 74, 153–54
Productivity, 33, 42–43, 45
Profits, in the modern State, 37–39, 48, 106
Property, in Golden Age, 152–53
Proverbs (Maxims), use in governing, 171–73
Prudence (*Discreción*), 90–91, 112–13, 133, 144, 155, 210 n.7

Pseudoutopia, 9, 10–11, 18–19, 32; for Cervantes, 62–64, 123, 199 n.36; utopianism of the Golden Age as, 132; utopia of reconstruction degenerating into, 175. *See also* Escapist utopianism; Evasion, utopianism of
Public affairs, reform of, 85, 86
Pulgar, Hernando de, 62, 144, 205 n.87
Purification, 11–12, 92
Putnam, Samuel, 14

Quevedo, Francisco de, 40, 167, 184, 186
Quixote (Cuisse), meaning of, 114, 214 n.86

Rabelais, François, 34, 52, 119–20, 203 n.55
Realism, 12, 224–25 n.10
Reality, 12, 117–18, 122, 127, 179, 210 n.1; Cervantes's concept of, 180–83; escapist attitude toward, 31–33, 199 n.35; relationship of utopianism to, 178, 180–81, 183–85, 188; transmutation of, 117–30, 148
Reason, 18, 29, 115, 116, 124–25, 149; conflict with will, 128; government by, 167–68; role in acquiring virtue, 112–13; and utopianism, 13, 34, 179, 184
Reconstruction, utopia of, 10; transition to utopia of evasion, 31–32, 175
Reformism, 34, 62, 83–84, 131–32, 154, 199 n.36; advocation of, in utopian works, 180, 184–85; bases for, 74, 75, 103; for Cervantes, 26, 27–28, 62–64, 78, 205 n.89; and Charles V, 31, 198–99 n.26; connection with knighthood, 65–66, 111–13; development in Europe, 76–78, 190; of Don Quixote, 69, 74, 79–81, 84–85, 86–87, 92, 111; of Guevara, 85–86; image of the shepherd in literature of, 146, 148; and myth of the Golden Age, 134–35, 173–75; sense of reality, 181; in time of the Catholic Sovereigns, 144
Reichenbach, Hans, 127
Religion, 75, 88, 123, 129, 158, 170–71. *See also* Catholic Church
Religious orders, name changes in, 113–14
Renaissance, the, 69, 84, 85, 96, 106–7, 190; acceptance of enchantment and sorcery, 119; emphasis on individuality,

Renaissance, the (*cont.*)
70, 72–73; nature as paradigm, 149–
56; neoplatonism and Platonism, 78,
185; pastoral novels in, 148; political
forms in Spain, 36–37; rebirth of the
human person, 73–74; relationship to
medieval traditions, 27–28; Spanish,
23, 30, 132, 139–40; utopianism of,
30–31, 33, 191; value seen in travel,
89–91
Renaissance man, 82, 117
Repetition, role in acquiring virtue, 112–
13
Reputation, relationship to honor, 81–82.
See also Fame
Restoration: of nature, 173–75; "newness"
of reform as, 131–32; pastoral element
in, 147
Restoration, utopianism of, 63, 67, 97,
107–8, 154, 157
Retablo de las maravillas, El (Cervantes),
188
"Return," myth of, 173
Return, utopianism of. *See* Evasion, utopia-
nism of
Ricken, Ulrich, 19
Rinconete y Cortadillo (Cervantes), 187–88
Rivadeneyra, Pedro de, 179–80
Rodríguez Marín, Francisco, 170, 209 n.47
Romancero, 24, 197 n.18
Romans, 54, 132, 203–4 n.62
Rosales, Luis, 79
Rosen, George, 116
Rousseau, Jean Jacques, 132, 133, 141,
151–52, 177, 182
Ruiz de Alarcón, Juan, 137
Ruiz de Virués, Alonso, 173
Rural life, 22, 67, 86, 137, 139–41, 176;
belief in enchantments, 122; connection
with myth of the Golden Age, 133–56;
existence of crime, 164–65; Guevara
on, 85–86; as source of health and vir-
tue, 142–44, 175–76. *See also* Pastoral
world; Village life
Russell, Peter A., 195 n.8
Ruyer, Raymond, 224 n.1

Saavedra Fajardo, Diego de, 109, 152, 157,
178

Sabuco, Miguel, 21, 56, 86, 155, 204 n.71,
218 n.48; on healthfulness of country
life, 143, 144–45, 155
Sabuco de Nantes, Oliva, 218 n.48
Sacraments, Catholic, 174, 206 n.5
Sacrifice, 77, 79–80
Sainz Rodríguez, Pedro, 197 n.13
Salas Barbadillo, Alonso Jerónimo de, 22,
101, 114–15, 143, 189–90
Salazar, Diego de, 20–21, 66
Salomón, Noël, 176
Sánchez Albornoz, Claudio, 198 n.24
Sánchez de Arévalo, Rodrigo, 113–14,
145–46, 150, 153, 200 n.3; on knights,
43, 53, 56, 94, 98
Sancho de Moncada, 170
Sandoval, Prudencio de, 57
Sannazaro, Jacopo, 81, 151
San Pedro, Diego de, 137, 139, 197 n.19
Santos, Francisco, 22, 151–52
Satire, 34, 148, 187–88; *Don Quixote* as,
9–10, 12, 23, 187
Savage, the, 156, 191
Savoye-Ferreras, Jacqueline, 220 n.79
Scholasticism, 158, 181
Science, 71, 92, 158, 179, 181; and belief
in occult powers, 119–20, 122, 215 n.19;
modern war as matter of, 60–61; rela-
tionship to utopianism, 178, 224 n.1
Scientific method, 169, 178
Secularization, 116, 122, 158, 174,
220 n.79
Self, 30, 69, 71, 78, 94, 144; renewal of,
74–75, 102–12, 138–39; transforma-
tion of, 79–80, 89–91, 92, 99, 100–
102. *See also* Man; Perfectionism
Self-government, 179
Self-sufficiency, 33, 42–43, 45, 155
Seneca, 75, 132, 137
Shepherd, The (Hermas), 145
Shepherds, 42, 74, 136–37, 151, 155–57,
186, 191; closeness to nature, 150, 153;
as exemplars of virtue, 144–46, 148–
49; portrayal in *The Dogs' Colloquy*,
174–75. *See also* Goatherds
Shields, 93, 109–10
Silva, Feliciano de, 77, 146
Simón Abril, Pedro, 38, 169–70, 179
Social conscience, 73–74
Social integration, deviance through excess
of, 50, 175, 202 n.47

Social purity, attempts to safeguard seen as deviant behavior, 50, 202 n.47
Social rank, 47, 70, 76, 85. *See also* Class, social; Estates of society
Society, 8, 13, 24, 71, 137, 183; Cervantes's belief in reform of, 63, 189, 205 n.89; classical literature as basis for spiritual perfection of, 75–76; corruption of natural goodness, 135; deviance from norms of, 50, 202 n.47; Golden Age as model of, 131–33, 135, 176–77; humanist ideals for, 51, 203 n.55; individual alienated by, 139; nature as model for, 150; need for reform, 62, 79, 85–86, 92, 96; pastoral and chivalric world as ideal image of, 146–47, 161, 219 n.64; portrayal in *Don Quixote*, 28–29, 60, 117, 192: *See also* Natural society
Society, Spanish, 10, 30–35, 36–37, 92, 188; Cervantes's relationship to, 25–26, 30, 63, 198 n.22, 205 n.89
Socrates, 75, 208 n.30
Solitude, 138–40, 142–45
Solomonic government, 168, 175
Sorcerers, belief in, 119, 120–21
Sovereignty, 50, 67
Spain, 10, 25, 28, 36–40, 122–23, 193; Cervantes's patriotism, 159–60; development of reformism in, 76–78; Nietzsche on, 126–27; utopianism in, 30–33, 179–93. *See also* Society, Spanish
Spanish monarchy, 25, 80, 159–60. *See also monarchs by name*
Spiritualists, 74, 76
Spirituality, 26–28, 30, 76–77, 100
Squires, 97, 169
State, modern, 26, 36–37, 68, 128–29, 158, 166; administration of, 11, 33, 37, 48–49, 52, 61; as arbiter in distributive justice, 164; chivalric-pastoral utopia as opposed to, 18, 33; Don Quixote's rejection of, 11, 158–59; military in, 51–62, 63; misunderstood by humanism, 50–51
Stoicism, 43, 100, 141, 150, 173, 203 n.55
Suárez de Figueroa, Cristóbal, 140, 163, 221 n.118, 223 n.151
Suárez Fernandez, Luis
Swift, Jonathan, 177, 224 n.7

Tacitus, 155, 159

Tasis y Peralta, Juan de, 138
Tasso, Torcuato, 34
Taxation, 41, 65
Téllez, Gabriel (Tirso de Molina), 22, 217 n.29
Thelemites, Rabelaisian, 34, 52, 203 n.55
Thomism, 10, 174
Tirso de Molina (Gabriel Téllez), 22, 217 n.29
Toledo, García de, 57
Torquemada, Antonio de, 47, 133, 144, 151, 173; on art of necromancy, 120–21, 122; interpretation of the pastoral myth, 146, 148–49, 153
Torre, Alfonso de la, 43, 150
Torre, Felipe de la, 146, 148
Trabajo. *See* Travail
Tradition, 26–28, 37, 41, 95; deviance from society's norms based on, 50, 202 n.47
Traditionalists, 54–55, 137, 154
Tranquillity, as a virtue, 102–3
Transformation, power of, 121–22. *See also* Enchantment
Transmutation of reality, 117–30, 148
Tratado de la perfección del triunfo militar (Palencia), 55
Tratado del esfuerzo bélico heroico (Palacios Rubios), 111–13
Tratos de Argel, Los (Cervantes), 215 n.3
Travail (*Trabajo*), 80, 95, 202 n.33
Travel, 89–91, 90
Trent, doctrines of, 69, 70, 114, 206–7 n.7
Trials of Persiles and Sigismunda, The (Cervantes), 72, 79, 159, 162, 187–88, 221 n.109; meaning of *trabajo* in, 80; recourse to reality of enchantments, 121
Truth Suspected, The (Ruiz de Alarcón), 137

Universalism, 160, 166–67
Urban life. *See* City life
Utopia (More), 33, 37, 56, 153, 155, 203 n.55; acceptance of modern warfare, 104; influence of, 179–80; law in, 171; Quevedo on, 184; use of island as device for, 185. *See also* More, Thomas
Utopianism, 32, 65–66, 71, 174, 176, 178–79, 203 n.55; attitude toward primitive values, 144; aversion to concept of "thine" and "mine," 152; of

Utopianism (*cont.*)
Cervantes, 63, 147, 180–93; collectivist system and money, 48; definitions, 10–11; failure in *Don Quixote,* 26, 115; Golden Age as paradigm in, 132–33; of Guevara, 85–86; importance of love in, 77; insularity in, 140–41; limitations on rights to goods, 42; novel as ideal genre for portraying, 13, 178–93; the pastoral and the chivalric as dimensions of, 12–13; political, 134–35, 156–77; relationship to modern science, 178, 224 n.1; in 16th-century Spain, 17–18, 30–35; use of nature as model, 150. *See also* Escapist utopianism; Evasion, utopianism of; Pseudoutopia; Restoration, utopianism of

Valbuena Prat, Angel, 159
Valdés, Alfonso de, 33, 146–47, 159, 162, 183; on creating new men, 77, 238 n.37; *Diálogo de Mercurio y Carón,* 50–51, 162
Valdés, Francisco de, 60
Valdés, Juan de, 25, 172
Valera, Diego de, 42, 64–65, 206 n.6, 211 n.31; on Roman military discipline, 54, 203–4 n.62
Valor, 38, 43–44, 56, 93, 115, 213 n.80; relationship of use of modern weapons to, 106–7, 111
Value(s), 22, 50, 78, 82, 148, 184; equation with works of nature, 151; money as replacement for, 38; in traditional agrarian society, 43
Vázquez, Dionisio, 206 n.5
Vázquez de Menchaca, Fernando, 140
Vega, Félix Lope de, 24, 121, 137, 171, 175–76, 217 n.29
Vélez de Guevara, Luis, 139
Verdadera nobleza (Valera), 211 n.31
Viaje a Turquía, 106, 160, 212 n.51, 222 n.144
Viaje del Parnaso, El (Cervantes), 22, 91, 159
Viana, Pedro Sánchez de, 133, 216 n.7
Vice(s), 92, 101, 135, 144, 184–85, 210 n.1; correction of, as purpose of satire, 187; in the modern military, 105
Vicente, A. Zamora, 198 n.22

Victorial, El (Díez de Games), 33, 56, 80, 135
Vida, G., 156
Vilar, Pierre, 199 n.35
Village life, 109–10, 141–44, 149, 150, 157; economy, 45, 48; Guevara on, 85–86, 143, 144, 218–19 n.53. *See also* Pastoral world; Rural life
Villano del Danubio, El (Guevara), 86
Virtue(s), 70, 72, 83, 89, 94, 128–29; acquired by commoners in warfare, 105–6; acquired in service to absolute monarchs, 95–96; acquisition of nobility through, 71; agriculture's relationship to, 74; arms as serving, 163–64; attributed to animals, 149–50; attributed to the nobility, 96–97; Christian, 97–98, 102–3, 206 n.5; class-based concept of, 103; Don Quixote's concept of, 96, 103–4, 115; in the Golden Age, 167; of the knight, 80–81, 93–94, 97–99, 101–2, 166, 211 n.31; knight as mirror of, 53, 65; models of in chivalric literature, 189; and modern weapons, 105, 106, 111, 112; in primitive people, 135; relationship of erudition to, 75–76; relationship to being honored, 81–82; relationship to social position, 92–94; relationship to wealth, 37–40, 43–44; as resting on wisdom, 91–92; of the Romans, 203–4 n.62; in rural life, 43, 133, 142–44, 154, 175–76; shepherds as exemplars of, 144–46, 147–48; sought through personal courage, 112–13
Vitoria, Francisco de, 150
Vives, Luis, 52, 68, 132, 162, 166; on money and the profit motive, 37, 39; on virtue, 75, 99
Vossler, Karl, 18, 94–95, 137, 139, 140, 145

Warfare, 21, 43–44, 46, 93, 165–66; contrast between modern and chivalric styles, 53–62, 63; modern, 11, 12, 53–62, 63, 104–12; for monetary gain, 38–39, 47–48
Wealth, 38–48, 65
Weapons, 61–62, 106–12; as means to personal fulfillment, 94; use of modern,

106–12; use of old-fashioned, 109–11.
    See also Arms, use of
Weber, Max, 168
Weisheipl, James A., 10
Will, 77, 79–80, 89, 126–30, 148. *See also*
    Free will
Wisdom, 89–91, 145–46, 167, 171–73
Witchcraft, 122
Wolves, 121
Work, utopian concepts of, 153–54

Works, 80, 100–101, 104, 198–99 n.26,
    206 n.6; importance of, compared with
    faith, 69–73, 206 nn.5, 6, 207 n.16; in-
    dividual merit through, 11, 69–73,
    103–4, 206 nn.5, 6

Yndurain, Francisco, 198 n.21

Zárate, Fernando de, 102–3